Crystal River

THREE NOVELLAS

CHARLIE SMITH

LINDEN PRESS ■ SIMON & SCHUSTER

NEW YORK LONDON TORONTO SYDNEY TOKYO SINGAPORE

LINDEN PRESS
Simon & Schuster Building
Rockefeller Center
1230 Avenue of the Americas
New York, New York 10020

DESIGNED BY BARBARA M. BACHMAN

Manufactured in the United States of America

10   9   8   7   6   5   4   3   2   1

Library of Congress Cataloging-in-Publication Data
Smith, Charlie, date
    Crystal river: three novellas/Charlie Smith.
        p.   cm.
        Contents: Storyville—Crystal river—Tinian.   I. Title.
PS3569.M5163C79   1991
813'.54—dc20   91-12086
                                                    CIP

ISBN 0-671-70530-X

"Crystal River," in a slightly different form, first appeared in *The Paris Review* (Summer 1983). A portion of "Tinian" appeared in *Bomb* (Fall 1983). My thanks to the editors. I am grateful to the MacDowell Colony for time and a place to work during the writing of *Tinian* and *Storyville*. Particular thanks to Marian Young, Allen Peacock, and George Plimpton.

The author acknowledges with thanks permission to reprint lines from *The Collected Poems of Wallace Stevens*, by Wallace Stevens, copyright 1936 by Wallace Stevens and renewed 1964 by Holly Stevens. Reprinted by permission of Alfred A. Knopf, Inc.

CONTENTS

Storyville

A MAN TOLD him about a woman who married her own son.

—I can believe it, he said. I can see how that would happen.

—Can you? the man said; not me. It shouldn't be possible. Even in the dark, even if he's grown, even if he's been gone for years, a mother ought to know her own son.

—No, he said. I can see it happening. The world's a confusing place. Maybe she just got confused.

—Confused? The man stared at him. You're drunk, he said, and perverted.

—Perverted? It's *your* story. I didn't tell it.

The man punched him in the face. He couldn't feel the blow, but it knocked him down. He lay on his back. He touched his mouth: there was a numbness under the numbness. He liked the feeling. Somewhere above him, the shape of the raconteur swam.

—Tell it to me again, he said. Tell it again. Maybe I didn't get it the first time.

It was a night when they'd let all the stars out. Yeah, boys, he said, raising his hands to them as if he might pluck a few, it's good to see you. Y'all enjoy yourselves. Why is it, he thought, when I get drunk I talk like a cracker? The town opened before him like an empty suitcase. He wandered down Main Street, turned left at the park, and came to the pier. A single light burned at the end of it. He smelled peaches, sweet syrup. Why was that? he wondered. It is another phenomenon. Another one of life's mysteries—this getting drunk and experiencing figments. Once, in the middle of downtown Tampa, he had smelled the meadow rue that grew in his mother's garden. Once, outside a courtroom in Jacksonville, he had seen his brother, dressed in a red suit, dive through a window. Mostly he accepted the wonder of what he saw and smelled, what he tasted, but his brother diving was so vivid he called home. His brother, since they had argued over who his father's hunting guns belonged to, wouldn't speak to him—a temporary thing—but Martha, his sister-in-law, said he was right there, right out in the yard, building a rabbit hutch for the kids' new bunny, and besides, Buddy didn't own a red suit. It was peaches, all right, peaches from a can, slick with syrup.

Lights were on in the construction catamaran. The boat Fernie Billings was building from a kit and from whatever he could make for himself in Kelly's Machine Shop. He'd seen him bending over the white fizz of a torch, cutting a piece of metal for the boat. Next week, so he heard, they were taking her out for a shakedown cruise. Then it was goodbye Florida, see you when we get back from around the world. It was the kind of thing kids talked about in high school and men talked about in barrooms. I am going to get a sailboat and sail around the world. He'd thought about it himself. But they don't let lawyers sail around the world. Lawyers are like doctors: folks can't get along without them. Unless maybe they are drunken lawyers who show up in court drunk and make a scene. Judge Terrel had thrown him out, as if the court were a barroom. He'd had the bailiff remove him. Which was hilarious, since the bailiff was his cousin. —I'll tell on you, he'd said. If you don't let me go I'll tell Shirley on you. —Shirley doesn't care what you say, Harry, his cousin the bailiff told him; Shirley stopped paying attention to you at least three years ago. He thought: Three years—who'd have thought it could be so long? How do you know when you stop making sense? It isn't like you stop talking the minute you become irrational. Sometimes you talk better. But it was only drunk—he knew this—that he could fool himself. Sober it was different. Ah, whiskey. He stumbled toward the lights.

They had launched the hull a year ago, on a Sunday afternoon when the mullet were schooling in the bay. Old men, boys, women with their skirts tied around their waists, had waded into the shallow water and drawn the mullet up in nets. They dragged them from the Gulf like sacks of silver. They'd rolled the building frame to the water and floated the hull off. Empty, painted blue, it'd bobbed in the dark-brown water like a miracle, as children swam around it, ignoring Fernie's threats. He lit a cigarette and angled toward the boat. In the west, piled on the clear horizon, off beyond the headland that sank itself like a dark body into the bay, gray cumulus lay stranded by night. He loved seeing clouds at night, anything that was different from what it was supposed to be. Like a chicken in the bathtub, or eating a chocolate pie in bed.

There were three of them on the boat, working aft, fiddling with the life raft. Hanging over the rail, he peered down at them. They were glad to see him and they weren't. "It's Harry," Bake Stokes said. "What's up, Harry—the bar burn down?"

"I don't know," Harry said. "Did it?"

"If the bar burned down," Willie Tendal said, "they'd find Harry in the ashes, fused to his beer bottle."

"Actually I don't drink that much beer," Harry said. Carefully, his foot pawing into air, he let himself down onto the boat.

"Come aboard, Harry," Fernie Billings said as he unfolded the end of the orange raft.

"When you taking this boat out?" Harry said.

"We're going out now—on the motor," Bake said.

"Great. It's a night for a boat ride."

"You don't need to go, Harry," Willie said. "We haven't got insurance for you."

"Don't worry about me, boys. I've been traveling by boat all my life."

"Out to sea, ay?" Bake said.

"That's me."

He squatted beside the raft, swaying slightly. "Put out that cigarette," Willie said.

"What for?"

"We're going to gas up the raft. You might start a fire." He held up the gas bottle, fussing with the nozzle.

"That's carbon dioxide," Harry said. "Carbon dioxide's what you use to put *out* fires."

"Toss the cigarette, Harry," Fernie said.

"Yeah," Bake said.

He tossed the cigarette over the side. It hissed on the water. He could still smell the peaches. Maybe this is the onset of the d.t.'s, he thought. Maybe for me they have come gently, smelling of peaches. Aye, Lord of Life, the loneliness stabs right through the drink. Had he spoken out loud? They bent over the raft. Bake set the nozzle, and the rubber boat began to swell. "It's like it's coming alive," Harry said. "It's like you are making a new creation."

"It's just a fucking raft," Fernie said, his limber mouth biting the air.

They took him with them—he remembered the *puttputt* of the motor and remembered lying on his back looking up at the full house of stars, remembered what seemed, in drunkenness, to be his soul lift like a sheet off his body and blow away, drifting higher and higher into the blackness until it, too, became a star, which he lost among the millions of others; but this may have been only a dream, because it was occluded and distorted by the sounds of voices, by argument, by his own voice arguing and then pleading, until, tired of him, a half mile from shore, Bake Stokes took him by the shoulders and shoved him overboard.

The water was warm and thick at first as chocolate sauce. He drifted on his back for a minute, but a slap of wave into his mouth brought him upright, choking. He could see the random lights of the town, the mercury lamps, the glow of the courthouse clock, the lamp burning in Stafford Jones's window because Stafford was a night owl. He'd be at the kitchen table this late—it must be after midnight—feeding sardines to his cat. "Pussy, pussy, you're so sleek," he would say. Harry wanted to go to sleep. No, not sleep; he wanted to walk around the town looking into windows. He wanted to float out to sea. That's the way to travel, Fernie: on your back, boatless, destination unknown. It was such a grand and beautiful night.

He swam a few strokes toward the beach, pulled up, and treaded water again. No need to hurry; the end of the evening would come soon enough. It's not that drunks hate reality, he thought; it's that reality's not enough. First a criminal lawyer who grew bored with the sameness of assaults and robberies, now an overseer of estates, of the heap of chattels some widow woman or old bachelor wanted to pass on to the next unfortunate generation. He had enjoyed getting people off, saving them from prison, but the sameness of their stories, the eyewitness, the alibi from mother or girlfriend, the guilty verdict, the sorrow or anger in the defendant's eyes, the stern judge, were too much for him. Better the old papers, the diaries, the deeds written in the ornate script of dead forefathers, the Spanish land grants, the tangle of family mystery and myth.

Around him the small waves flicked phosphorus. There was someone on the beach. A shape in dark clothes standing next to the gazebo under the cabbage palms. He raised his arm to wave, dropped it. She might not want a hello from the sea. Some talking dolphin, stopped by for a chat. He swam toward shore, head up, the drink whizzing in his brain, feeling himself stagger even in the water, compensating as best he could, thinking: The thing about the ocean is there's no wall to lean against.

"Hello," he cried, rising to his feet. She hadn't moved. The swim, the drink, made him dizzy. He dropped back to his knees, pushed up again. For one second the stars became a smear. "I'm all right," he explained, though she hadn't moved or spoken. "I've just been swimming." He bent over his knees to let the nausea pass. "I have to start working out," he said. "It's the only thing to do. I don't know how you feel about it, but I think it's a little ridiculous to be sentenced to a planet where you have to spend most of your life beating your body half to hell just to get to where it'll survive." He straightened up. She was dressed in dark skirt, dark blouse. An ample scarf was tied around her head. "I mean," he said, "this isn't Jupiter after all. We're already built for the gravity. We ought to be okay without having to exercise. Whew, that was a longer swim than I thought."

"Do you always swim in a suit?"

"Well, not always. Bake Stokes threw me overboard. He said I was a jinx. Though how you can jinx a boat ride around the bay I don't know."

"Are you a jinx?"

"I think of myself as a charm."

The mercury lamp behind her pressed a small corona around her shoulders. She was narrow and tall, and she held herself stiffly in her arms.

"You're my lawyer," she said.

He squinted at her. In a small neat conjury, with a familiar abruptness that pleased him, he recognized her. "Oh. Yeah. You're Laura Dell. I'm working on your father's estate."

"I hope it's not too entangled."

"The entanglement's the fun."

He stepped forward, wiped his palm on his pants, and shook her hand.

"Strange," she said softly, letting his hand go, "to touch someone just out of the water. They're cold and slick, but not like a fish. Even drenched and drowned, you can recognize the humanness."

"I like that. For me, even fed and wearing dry clothes I have a hard time." Under the scarf, which was a scarf—beaded, filmy— that a woman in her fifties might wear, though she was young, hardly in her thirties, younger than he was, her eyes were hooded, her face split by shadows. "Why are you out here so late?"

She turned to go.

"Wait. I was going to walk around the town looking in windows. Don't you want to come?"

"You're a Peeping Tom," she said over her shoulder.

"No, not that, or not what you think. I like to see how people live, their furniture and what they've got on the mantel, how they sit at the kitchen table."

"Loneliness."

"Sure."

"I have to go."

"Can I walk you home?"

"You have to get out of those clothes."

"Oh, no; it's summer."

"See you," she said.

He watched her walk away, solitary up the empty street. As she passed the pool hall, the purple lights spelling out the owner's name went off. The click to dark, or something in her—she seemed to flinch. Her long dark hair draped her shoulders like a fan. She didn't look back—holding herself in her arms—though he wanted her to.

My name is Laura Dell and I have fetched up, as they say, still breathing, in this dead sea town. Seeking quietness and a simple order, I have returned to the place of my birth. Here I know the streets, the stores, the houses canted over flower beds and sandy yards. I can take you by the hand to the edge of town where in a field grown up in sheep sorrel and sand spurs we can look back up the one paved street. There is, first, at the field's near edge, the aluminum factory building, with white-painted roof and windows painted-over white, where wrought-iron garden furniture is manufactured; then there is the Dupree Number Two Fish Shack, where you can order fried red mullet roe, snapper and sea trout fillets, fried oysters, and smoked mullet; then there are the fish shacks, which are narrow single-story houses on stilts, each approached by a cleated gangway, each backed by a narrow dock where the mullet and oyster boats tie up; beyond are the city docks; Blasingame's, a drugstore; the bank; Bell's, the hardware store; a small two-story pink-brick office building; the courthouse, a gold-painted building with a minuscule cupola decorated with painted clocks on two sides; the city hall; then stores, houses, and the cracked gray concrete road bending north along the river. Behind the town, away from the bay and the river, are the neighborhoods that are shabby, the yards sand-blown and small, the houses small and needing paint, the children running about barefooted, in torn clothes. Here and there skiffs have been placed across sawhorses, and nets, nylon now, not cotton, are draped across the spines of the boats. There are gardens featuring spindly-necked cabbages and collards, a few tomato plants, beans risen on string runners like frail windbreaks, the wind-sawing leaves of white corn, and, in early spring, radishes and the delicate ladyfinger pea. Women sit on the porches dipping snuff and spitting it into the yard. The men work at the factory or on boats in the Gulf; they return with their eyes clotted with despair or humor or resignation or clouded over from the danger of their work; they rarely travel and then usually only to the state park fifty miles up the road, to camp in the back of pickup trucks; occasionally they go to Orlando or Tampa, once in a while to one of the beach towns farther south.

In my hometown no explanations are necessary. I am known already; everyone who sees me has a past to refer to, some knowledge that will do. I speak to Mrs. Sanibell in the grocery store, and the discreet and inquisitive sympathy I see in her eyes does not find its way into her mouth. I am a strange one, I weep often, often I cannot sleep at night. I wander the rooms of this dying house telling myself stories from my childhood. Out loud I say, There is a misery in the world, but I know this is not the answer and may not even be true. I perform the small tasks of a housekeeper—cooking, repotting strangled plants, washing and waxing floors, beating rugs with my old tennis racket—and there is some comfort in this, some small and requiescent peace. I seek a stillness now, by which I mean a life I do not explain to others. I wake early, and often it is as if the first spurt of blood in my veins drives my heart quivering out of my chest onto the floor, where, gasping for air, I grope for it, lost, defenseless, terrified. It is only love's exhausted day, I say to myself; this is what comes after, but solace is not in the saying, it is in the simpler rounds of life. I rise, wrap myself in my mother's old yellow kimono, and go out on the back porch, where in the fresh dawnlight I say: *bird, tree, sky, sea.* I come into the world as innocent as a voyager from the stars. I say, *grass;* I say, *leaves;* I say *clouds* and *salt breeze.*

There is one name I do not say.

He had his secretary call, but she couldn't get her on the phone. "I have to go around there," he said. "I have to talk to her about things."

His secretary, who was his dead mother's age, began to complain about her husband. She was a pillar of the church, she lived in the house her husband had bought the year they moved from the country, she collected for the March of Dimes, she was a member of the library board, she made devil's food cakes at Christmastime, which she delivered in hatboxes to her neighbors, she pinched her husband in a vise of relentless demand. A typically evil person, he thought. Unacknowledged, a master magician, she would die and be buried to rounds of praise, and no one would know she was the devil's spawn. "He's sixty-two years old," she said, "and he can't even fix a faucet. Can you believe that? And he's a country man, which I can tell you isn't such a grand thing; you'd think he could fix a leaky faucet."

He tried to imagine her as a girl sitting on a country porch, her hands stinking of tripe, dreaming of a world beyond the corn-fields. He tried to imagine her making love, for the first time or for one of the first times, her loose body heaving against the body of the man who would become her husband, her large hands groping like gloved iron for the red sprout of his penis: all he could see, in sadness, was the hurry, and the miserable inatten-tion, and the disappointment—just one more of life's lies—the pathetic vulgar words like flies in syrup. Sometimes, he thought, there's nothing you can do. You can't raise people up, or be yourself raised up, no matter what. Such thoughts made him gentle with her.

"I have to go," he said.

"When will you be back?"

"I don't know. Did you get copies of the deeds?"

She looked at him as if he had asked to see her underwear. "I haven't had any time," she said. "I'm so worried. I don't know why I stay in this life."

"It's okay. I'll stop by the courthouse."

The day was bright, the sun a white fire. Cicadas ground their instruments. It took him half an hour to find the deeds and get them copied. There was a question about whether or not they were true. There was a story—he'd heard it first as a boy—that her great-great-grandfather had come by the land they owned on the northern end of the county, up by the paper company woods, by stealing it with false deeds from its rightful owners. There were darker stories, of night rides and gunfire, of bodies wound in chains and dropped in sinkholes, of an old man going crazy, discovered weeping in his wedding suit on the front steps of the Methodist church, his mouth filled with straw. He liked the sto-ries.

Come on, day, he said, ease up. The sun was dazzling, so hot it almost erased the town. Out in the bay, the Gulf was a fire. Shrimp boats, white as churches, fastened the horizon to the sky. He loved this block. The big oaks, and under the oaks the shabby queen palms, hardly taller than his head, socked with bright-orange fruit. As a child he had ridden a tricycle up and down the block, trying to sell crayons and bits of his mother's jewelry to the neighbors. The neighbor wives had brought the jewelry back, clucking to themselves, he supposed now, over its meager glamour. Her yard was fenced by unpruned tea olive hedges. The bushes were in full, heady flower. The scent, so sweet it was almost astringent, filled the street. He wondered how high it went, if jays and mockingbirds skidding above the yards flew through it.

There were holes in the grass and a garden gone to seed, rank with garlic and loops of potato vine. The holes were freshly dug, mounds of salt-and-pepper sand beside them. The house was old, high, stoop-shouldered, complete with batten turrets and a steep roof from which dozens of the cypress shingles had come loose. He knew her; she had come back to St. Lukes maybe a year before, another one run down and pummeled by the world, arriving by Trailways or by packet boat or by car—he didn't know—carrying two mismatched suitcases or everything she owned in a sack, wheeling a hoop trunk up the front walk—he didn't know; she arrived wearing jeans or a long skirt with a torn and muddy hem, tennis shorts or a shiny leather suit bristling with light—he didn't know. She had come into his office like someone fleeing rain, shaking her bony self, not wanting, even after he had settled her in the brocade chair and gotten her a cup of tea, to talk about what brought her to a lawyer's office, until in exasperation and bafflement, leaning forward over the scuffed knees of his seersucker suit, he had begun to tell her a story about the time her brother —dead now—had locked him in the attic of her old house with the stacks of magazines and the trunks filled with summer dresses and the collection of military hats her father had gathered from around the world.

"My mother used to go up there and speak fancy stories about her life," she had said.

"Speak? You mean out loud?"

"Yes. She told tales to herself. She thought the mushrooms on the lawn were fairy babies. She thought the moon made a road of silver on the ocean that, if you were good, you could walk up to the stars. She said the sky was a net and that if we lived under the sea, like dolphins, the cities would be made of silk."

"How about you—what do you think?"

"She used to walk about on her elegant ankles, putting on airs in front of her children, slandering this and slandering that—I hated her and wanted her to rot in hell, but that was too bad, because I loved her too." She smiled, a sly, almost wicked smile, which she gathered quickly back into her face. "You can't beat that old love," she said. "It crops up everywhere."

He thought she was mad, and delightful.

She wanted the estate settled finally. She wanted true deeds for the property, all her father's holdings—not much particularly, but murky—straightened out. "Like a piece of new rope," she said.

Her face was bony, almost but not quite narrow, but her lips were full and her eyes, which were an indefinite gray—the kind of eyes that change colors, he thought—had tiny flecks of gold in them. They were intelligent, sad, wry, enslaved.

He told her he would take care of the estate, told her his fee.

"You're cheap," she said.

"Well, this isn't Tampa," he answered.

"Inexpensive," she said. "That's what I mean."

"Cheap's okay."

Then he didn't see her again—he thought about her and then he stopped thinking about her—until the night he walked up out of the Gulf.

He crossed to the garden and picked a potato flower blossom. It was yellow and fragile, as large as his hand. He twirled it between his fingers as he came up the walk, which was cracked and sprouted through with quack grass. This is a day to go sailing, he thought, though he had rarely sailed, a day to head off to the island. Sometimes it seemed that if he looked away from his work for five seconds he might never go back to it. He waked in the mornings coughing, his lips rimmed with whiskey spit—hangoverless, thank God—his body bent and stiff as if rheumatism had descended in the night, the floor littered with the books he'd tried to read after getting in late, some bouquet a client had given him—as primer for yet another late payment—withering on the table, nickels in the bed, a grim prestidigitated fate hovering like a painted ornament before his eyes, and he'd haul himself up hacking, past making promises but not past dreams, and look out the cloudy window at the palms and beyond them at the Gulf unraveling like a wide blue sleeve in the dawnlight, and he'd think: It is still possible—not probable, but possible—for you to make something of your life. Then, the thought of work like a headache, he'd sit on the edge of the bed and laugh.

There was a bird's nest in the mailbox, a withered bay wreath on the door. He pressed the buzzer, which didn't ring, and then knocked. She let him in, whispering the door back. She was dressed in a long white crepe gown—not a wedding dress exactly but maybe the dress of a bridesmaid, if bridesmaids wore white—and had a torn denim jacket thrown over her shoulders. He wanted to tell her a story. He said, "I think people ought to express themselves with their clothes. I think it's the kind of harmless diversion that can keep us from going mad."

"It hasn't worked with me," she said, smiling. "I'm as mad as a horse on fire."

He pictured her, rearing. Her large eyes were nearly blue. There was a faint shyness about her, which dissolved as she led him through the rooms. He had been in the house a hundred times, had seen a hundred houses like it. There might have been a time of revolution here, but it was long gone. Everything was memory, like his brother's house, which was the old family place on Turnabout Street. Red velvet sofa and chairs, dark-legged like the shaved legs of black women, antimacassars, tasseled lamps with stained parchment shades, a small green rug in front of the fireplace, *The Rape of the Sabine Women* over the mantel. She brought him tea in a cracked china cup. He was pleased to find it laced with whiskey. "I thought you'd like it that way," she said.

"I do."

"I didn't expect you. What do you have for me?"

"I've called, but there was no answer."

"No, I guess there wasn't."

"I brought some documents, a few deeds. To clear everything, we'll need some way to substantiate your family as the legal owners of the Whigham property."

"I'll show you what I have."

She took him to the attic and showed him stacks of bundled papers, receipt books, and her great-great-grandmother's diaries. Eating from a bag of potato chips, she stood over him as he knelt in the sallow light, turning pages. There was always a road back, always a means to make what had disappeared long ago come alive again. The lawyering was just a cover: it was this, these cobbled pages, powdery papers, the ritual articles of lives long gone, that fascinated him. The diaries were ledger books bound in black leather. He knew what he was looking for: some record of a sale, the story of a family moving to or coming to own a thousand acres of pinewoods one May day in 1827. "I'm amazed that you have this," he said.

"I have everything. We never let anything go."

"You're like my brother."

"I know your brother. Buddy. He's a doctor."

"Yeah. Buddy." He laughed. "Sometimes I wake up and remember he's got all our parents' furniture, and I want to run over and strangle him."

"You don't care about that, do you?"

"No, I don't really. I don't want to own the stuff; I just want to know what it's about."

He couldn't find the passages he sought, but there were others. "Listen to this," he said. " 'This morning Papa bought me a fist of glass fused from sand that had been struck by lightning. He called it a sky diamond, though it is made from earth. It is white, cloudy, partially clear, round as a piece from a furnace; tiny bubbles like trapped breath float in it. He called me to the summerhouse and gave it to me, unwrapping it from a piece of dark-blue velvet. As I looked at it, like a glass toad in my lap, I felt his fingers begin to stroke my hair. The touch was light, but I sensed the force behind it. He felt me tremble and stopped. "You are a beautiful child," he said, "and for you there will be many presents." And then he began to stroke me again.' "

He glanced up at her. She looked as if she had stopped breathing. "It breaks off there," he said. He closed the ledger, marking the place with his finger. "Do you know about these books?"

"Yes. But I've never read them."

"Where was she when she wrote this? Was she here, in this county?" He could see her, this girl, or see a yard that she might have sat in: the frank red mallow flowers, the sea stumbling beyond the live oaks.

"Probably in Georgia," she said, "the sea islands. It was probably before my family came down here; or maybe only part had come."

"They loaded everything in wagons and traveled on dirt roads that were like tunnels through the trees, that seemed to head off into an emptiness that would never end."

"I don't think it was quite that romantic."

Her hands were long, the fingers knobby and strong: feminine hands that had been put to work. He said, "Where did you come from?"

"I'm from St. Lukes, Florida."

"I mean where did you live before you came back here?"

"Everywhere. All over."

"I didn't think you'd be coy."

"I'm not. But I have lost my health."

"You mean you had a hard time."

"I don't want to claim anything special for myself."

He stood up. The book was heavy in his hands, like something soaked. A high window let down a grainy cloistral light onto the red-painted floor. "Can I take this with me?" he said.

"No . . ."

One morning when I was six, the dolphins came up the river. My father took me to see them. It was a clear day in early spring, I remember, the mallow flowers were blooming again along the roads and the reeds along the riverbank were topped with silver tassels. He held my hand as we walked up the street in the direction of the old Spanish fort. There were others heading that way, small children running ahead of their mothers, a few men who had left work to see this strange sight. We turned off the road and crossed a grassy field and came to the riverbank. The river was not wide—a boy could throw a rock across it—and it was filled with dolphins. The water boiled with their leaps and surges; they jumped high, whole sleek shining gray bodies rising out of the black water. They ran in closed, abruptly dispersing ranks, shooting upriver, veering off like airplanes or those fireworks that soar up on a single stem of light and break into blossom. I was entranced and terrified. I began to cry, so that my father, misunderstanding, started to lead me away. I protested, but he grabbed me up and held me in his arms, thinking I needed to be soothed. I didn't say—maybe I couldn't say—that I didn't want to go home. I wanted to run into that churning water; I wanted to leap and swim after them; I wanted them to carry me away.

So he returned, afternoons and sometimes evenings. She would brew him a cup of the fierce dark tea that she laced with whiskey, and he would carry it up the three flights of stairs that smelled of cedar and wintergreen to the attic and with her sitting in an old porch rocker beside him he would read the diaries. His brother Buddy, the general practitioner, said, It's this world we have to live in; like it or not, this is our place; you have to accept that. Staying put, he said, that's heroism. Who says, he said, that I care anything about heroism? —You're a drunk, and that's all drunks care about: their fantasy life, where they're kings of all they survey. —No, he said, it's not like that, not like that exactly —not a king. A boy maybe, but not a king. —You're a lawyer, his brother, who was after all his twin, said. You were born here; settle in. —Okay, he said, wanting, as always, to please him, I will. But instead he took three days off and went out on one of the shrimp boats. He took a trip, drunk in the wheelhouse of a fore-and-aft shrimper, to Biloxi and back. He saw snatches: blue like blue bolts of cloth whipped up into the sky, a key ring made from a coin stamped with the head of a Caesar, the red ruffle of a woman's underskirt, Jefferson Davis's butternut overcoat, a live oak as large as a gymnasium, the sun balancing on the rim of the world like a man in red tights. In his mind a story was being told, an old, endless story of many parts, an ancient tale of journeying. Lying in the narrow bunk, he heard someone speaking the words of the story to him, and with the voice accompanying him, he traveled to far strange places; he saw mountains ringing the lake city of Tehuantepec, saw oceans of grass riding the high plains, saw a long silver train curve like a snake out of black fortresses of the northern woods. Always there was urgency, always there was someone ahead he must not lose sight of, always there was the smell of alyssum and hyssop, a wind rubbing its back against poplar leaves, his father whispering in a low voice, or a woman speaking, or a bird fleeing in high passage, calling as it fled over the face of the world. Arnie Williams, the captain, like Bake Stokes, wanted to throw him overboard, and there was a moment, before the mate, his high school friend David Bodine, talked him out of it, when ("For certain this time, Harry") he was going to put him ashore, in Pass Christian—"Let the useless son of a bitch get his own self back"—but by the time they made the long sweep past the piney woods of Hail and Farewell Point, he was on his feet, holding himself up by the long upsweep of net above the iced mounds of shrimp in the hold, calling country taunts across the water at the men scouring boats along the docks.

She would rock in the old chair as he read out loud from the diaries. The woman's—the girl's—script was delicate, spidery as something written with a diamond point, and looped and roved on the unlined pages like crazed bird flight. Her name was Eureena Dell, and in the days of which she wrote she was a girl of fourteen living in her father's house. "Last night," she wrote, "a traveling orchestra conductor visited us. He played and sang songs from Germany and Scotland. The German songs were dark and miserable. They always seemed to be trying to find something in the dark, but it was the kind of dark I think my father finds when he's been drinking and he stumbles around under the big trees in back of the house calling out the names of people who died long ago. They frightened me, those songs. I was afraid to lift my eyes to see my father looking at me. When he sang the songs from Scotland—highland ballads, stories of lost love in a mountain country—as sad as they were, I felt, for one small moment, an intense rush of happiness, as if I were lying in a high meadow under the stars. I looked at my father then, at his face that was not rapt but clouded with thought, and I remembered the sour smell under his jaw, and the way in his nervousness, which I know, he scratched the insides of his wrists, and I felt then as if the darkness had entered me, like an irresistible enemy, and for a moment I could not breathe. . . ."

He said, "My brother doesn't think I should be seeing you."

"You're not seeing me."

"Yes, that's right, isn't it."

"You're searching for answers to legal questions," she said archly.

You're making a fool of yourself, his brother told him. *The word is going around.*

—It's nothing new, Harry had told him, feeling the easy simplicity of truth in him.

—That Dell girl is too much for you.

—Who isn't?

—She is strange, and I think something has been broken in her. Martha says she needs to be in an institution. Nervous breakdown.

—We're all nervous, we're all breaking down.

His brother had once wanted to do research, he had wanted to be a surgeon, but he settled for general practice, the love and trust and respect of his townspeople. He had immaculate, featureless hands; they looked, Harry thought, as if he polished them with smooth soft stones at night. His sandy hair, brushed back from a high glistening forehead, seemed something shaped and pressed in a fine shop somewhere and flown in under glass to be fitted to his narrow skull. They were twins, but not identical; Harry had his mother's hair—coffee-colored, rank with curls—and her faded blue eyes, stained skin. —I am not any better than she is, he told his brother, and I know anyway there is no way to explain the fascination. The word, *fascination,* hung in the air between them as his brother looked at him without fondness or understanding, and he thought: Have I betrayed her already? Have I exposed too much? Quickly he said then, I don't want to explain myself to you. I don't have to.

His brother had smiled sharply, mildly triumphant. For two years, their fourth and fifth years on earth, Buddy had called him *baby*—what does *baby* want for breakfast; how is *baby* this morning; does *baby* need the potty—until Harry, proving his brother's case, was reduced to tears, until he ran to their mother, crying for her to make Buddy stop. His mother had told him to ignore his brother—how could he do that?—to agree with him, to smile and laugh, brush it off. He had tried this, but his brother was able to outlast him; eventually, inevitably, Buddy would wear him down—*Baby, baby, baby,* he would shout, relentless as the anopheles, until Harry folded up into tears. His only recourse was endurance—not the excellence of resistance or the self-enhancement of retaliation, but simply lasting; eventually his brother moved on to other interests, and Harry found himself still breathing.

His brother had looked at him with light-colored triumphant eyes. —Drop it, Harry, he said. You've got enough problems without some fruitcake girl screwing your head around. It's silly to have a grown man hanging out at night and all hours of the day in some crazy woman's attic. People talk.

Harry had looked across the street where in the Hillmans' front yard several dying oleanders held on to their late flowers, flowers ragged and lank as old bouquets; he looked past the oleanders at the dark corridors of grass that ran between the Hillman house and the houses next door, leading nowhere except into places he could not see, dark or woods—woods. He didn't answer. —Well, his brother had said finally, it's just one more thing you won't face up to—like your drinking and like your practice. It's just one more thing.

—Sw-ing low, sweet cha-ri-ah-aht, coming for to car-ry me ho-o-ome.

—Harry, Harry, his brother said, almost fondly, at least indulgently. They were about to touch each other, furtively, out of necessity, like bandits crouched together by a dark road: reassurance. His brother turned away, his hand rose slightly, brushed against the torn pocket of Harry's khaki trousers. Harry's hand fell to meet the smooth marble fingers.

She leaned forward in the rocker; her ginger hair fell over her face. "I remember your brother," she said. "A prissy boy in blue pants with bright-yellow piping. He was very smart and fastidious. You could see his old man's face in his young one."

"It's one of those hewn and polished faces, like something you see in a wall niche in Italy."

"We can, of course, since he's not here, destroy him entirely."

"Let's don't and say we did."

"All right."

The ledger lay open in his lap. The girl's life, the life of Eureena Dell, this woman's great-great-grandmother, a life lived in the coastal grasses under the huge live oaks, in a house built of tabby stone, with a mad father, rose before him. "I have woven my hair into two long braids and wound them around my head. I look old, old and tired, someone who is not a friend to man or woman. All night they rang the church bells. A ship has gone down. I went to the window to see. Off the island it burned, the masts and spars on fire. The sparks leapt into the sky. This morning it is only a black body awash. . . ."

She wore jeans and a sleeveless white shirt. Her arms were freckled. He wanted to stroke her fingers, he wanted to put them in his mouth. He said, "When I was a child I used to go with my father on road trips. He was a history teacher and an assistant coach on the football team. But you know that, don't you?"

"Yes."

"He coached for twenty years, but he never got to see the Sea Devils play, because he was the scout; he was the one sent to watch the next week's team. I was grown before I thought how strange that was. He would drive each week to a different town, one of the other small towns in the Orange Belt Conference, and I can remember them all, all the names: Spanishtown and Wilton and McCree and Osceola and Port St. James and Rawlitt and all the others. We would come into town about sunset on Friday and head for whatever restaurant my father considered best and have supper. He liked barbecue shacks and the fish houses where he could get good soft-shelled crabs. He always had a place, always had a route he traveled."

She leaned back in the rocker, her almost blue eyes following him, her mouth moving slightly as if she were repeating the words after him. A patch of light lay on her knees like a puppy.

He said, "Wilton had palm trees lining the main street; Osceola had a water tower on the courthouse square, painted bright yellow; Port St. James stank of pulpwood, and there were dirt alleys behind the downtown buildings that the children played in. My father would point these things out to me; he would say, in Rawlitt, 'That smell is tobacco from the cigar factories—doesn't it smell like something made out of gold?' He would show me the bullet holes, black as flies, up on the wall of the courthouse in Spanishtown, where a detachment of English soldiers shot at the high sheriff as he stood in his window shaking his fist at them. What he made me see was that each town was different and that each thought of itself as the center of the world. In a way it was a terrible revelation, as obvious as maybe it was. He knew that I thought St. Lukes was the only place, and he wanted me to see that everybody thought of their town as the only place."

Maybe it was the journal that made him speak of what he never forgot. He wanted a drink, he wanted to drink all night at the Chicken Bar and then go out back and throw himself in the river. Not to drown, but to float, like a patch of hyacinth, out to the Gulf. My whole life so far, he thought, has been a party. That's what Buddy hates. He hates to see a man having fun. Ah, Jesus.

From the small wood behind the house a barn owl pushed its call into the afternoon air, the *whoo-oo, whoo-oo* small and ingenious and as finely fashioned as smoke rings. An owl calling in daylight. You can let anything you want be a signal for you. Everything makes a human sound if you listen long enough. He said, "Around here people stay. The Gulf sustains them. The fishing fades and revives and fades, but it never disappears. The fish come back; there are always at least partially enough. In the mountains where we used to go for the summer the old guys who farm the hillsides don't plan to stay. It's simple. The land dies, and they just call the dog, put out the fire, and move on."

"You read that somewhere."

"No. But I heard it. It may not be the truth anymore." As it wasn't true that there were enough fish to go around. The cycles, the diminishing mullet runs, weeded the less sturdy out, starved them out, forced them to the cigar factories in Tampa, north to the auto plants in Atlanta. What was sad, he guessed, was that it was the ones who had already made their peace—at least lived in accommodation—with the natural world who were forced out. It was the natural world giving out on them that got them in the end.

She said, pressing her shoulders against the cane chair back so that her breasts rose, "That book, that diary, is just a story. It's not true anymore except as a story. It's like the story you tell about your father."

"I know. It's come to that, hasn't it?"

"What's important is what's alive now—do you believe that?"

"I wish I did. They say it's good for your health to think that way."

"Are you just a dumb cracker?"

"Part of the time."

"I've been changed. I'm more now. Though what I've learned I could have learned here."

"What have you learned?"

"That we are born dead."

"Say my name."

"Olivia Dell."

"That's not my name."

"It's the name . . ."

"What?"

"I don't know."

"Yes you do."

"Don't pounce at me."

"I can't, I wouldn't—my foot's asleep."

She let out a soft spill of laughter, raising her head as she did so. There was a long thin scar running from under her ear diagonally downward to the well of her throat. He thought: Jesus, I am alive on this planet, I am here, life just keeps turning up new wonders. You are born on the seashore and you stand there for fifty years on the weedy beach and life washes up all manner of glittering articles.

With bent knuckles he touched her knee. She didn't shy, though she didn't look at him either. He opened his hand, cupped the kneecap. You can be dumb as hell, he thought, but still you know. I think it's wonderful how intelligence is not really necessary in this life. He leaned forward, over the scrawled pages of another life, and for a moment he could smell the musty paper, the scent of age and dissolution that was the scent of dried timothy, or a scent like quicklime when the savor's gone out of it, and it was as if for a second he could see her, this Eureena Dell, dressed to die, sitting in a high room looking out over treetops at the wild and useless ocean where maybe the rain, if it was a rainy day, swept its indecipherable figures across the surface, or where sunlight, if it was sunny, blinked like a million yellow eyes, and for one second, before Laura's hand, falling as if something in her had not decided but given up, caught his fingers and drew them to her narrow breast, he looked, he was seeing, through the pale eyes of a fourteen-year-old girl, looking not at the rough form of a dark father, but at his own father, who had been dead now ten years, as he stood at the back porch sink washing the dust of football practice from his arms and turned to him with the solemn face of a man who believes he has not done with his life what he ought and said, Son, life's not a dream. You know that, don't you?

His skin is as smooth as my own. He breathes whiskey into the bedroom air as I touch him lightly here and there: forehead, the eroded point of his chin, left nipple, the triangular patch of hair above his groin. His skin smells of apples and whiskey, faintly of salt. I press my lips into his inner thigh, where the skin is soft, barely jelled, hardly formed. I touch him with my tongue, move into the soft bush of hair, sup there, carefully, easily, like a small animal drinking from a forest pool. I seek the solvent of his presence, of the physical body riding high as a ship above my own. I pull him on top of me; we do not speak; I hear his breath coming harder, shorter, like a man who knows he is dying and is afraid. I lift my hips into him, meet him, fall, meet him; we are knocking at the doors—his body believes there is a mystery to be revealed, but I am sliding away into the dream, already sliding away into the dream of myself alone in a field of flowers; it is the same field I saw as I came down from the mountains in the Mexican Sierra, a field of yellow poppies stretching to the horizon over which the wind moves, over which the unifying, selective, omniscient hand of the wind moves, touching all, bringing far to near, asking the same questions, giving the same answers to every living thing. . . .

He let her dress him in the old clothes she found in the attic trunks. The clothes didn't matter—the striped vests, the stiff trousers, the collarless shirts stained yellow under the arms didn't matter—nothing that she made him do mattered. He would do anything. They read from the diaries in the big sagged bed, fanning each other with painted fans, rising to their knees to orate the most fearful passages, leaning their backs against the black headboard, which was carved in scenes of battle and rest, of soldiers assaulting a fortress and of bodies or sleeping soldiers lying around a palm-fringed oasis pool. The words of the young girl, Eureena Dell, the dead grandmother—was she grandmother?— detonated softly in the air around them. They saw her, they conjured her into life between them, they spoke of her as a living person, they talked to her, they took her to bed with them and let her ride their backs and their sweated thighs, they raised her small stiff breasts to their mouths and sucked the delicate nipples, they licked the slight salt from her pubis. "I take long walks," Eureena said, "I walk at night down the lane to the bower where my mother planted roses. In the dark the floribunda blossoms shine like giant white lamps of warning. Each part of the world, each article, seems to me a warning now and an almost casual beckoning, a small voice calling me farther. The lane is dark, but the road is darker. It curves through the trees to the marsh and retreats again into the trees. I follow it as far as I dare—which is not really very far; I am only a young girl—and always, at my back, I hear dark wings beating. I sense shapes moving that are not the familiar shapes of my life but beings that have no love for me. I feel the pain in me, the fear; it is as if something in my body clutches and holds me back. Each evening I walk only a little farther before I turn back, exhausted. . . ."

Laura led him to the bathroom and washed him in the tub as if he were a child. "I like this," he said, "this is just great. It is, I believe, the life I was born for—what do you think?"

She said, "Your skin is like a dolphin's"—turning him under her coarse and gentle hands, touching him with a lustless solicitude, her fingers probing the openings of his body. She skimmed back the skin of his penis and pressed open the narrow slit in the head, she sank first one, then two fingers into his rectum, turning them, pressing deeply inward, so that without hearing himself he moaned and felt something in his being softly explode and begin to flow. She dried him with rough towels that made his skin shine and she led him by the hand to the bed, where from what seemed to him a poised moment of hesitation, like the moment before you throw yourself off a cliff, she would assault him with her body, ferociously, tearing at the flesh she had just spent an hour cleansing, pummeling him, driving her body against his as if he were a locked door she must break through. There was an odor to her that was unlike anything he had smelled before, sour and fragrant both, an odor that seemed to drift out of one of the deep wells of the body, as if in the dark she opened herself, not figuratively but actually, exposing to the humid night and to him the opulent minnery of organs and blood. When she came she said nothing, she was silent, but her face flushed and under her eyes rose two welts of blood-filled skin like red blisters about to burst. He was the one who cried out—lost in the ride, that was what he wanted, the lostness, the tossing away of his conscious mind—yelling his animal voice into her bruised face, his body trembling like the body of a man being whipped.

Drifting back, letting his arms go slowly, he said, "Sometimes I think my eyeballs will burst."

She had no tenderness, only surrender. She drew herself away to look at him. "I want to see your face undisguised," she said.

"I don't think I'm ever disguised very well. I think it's us guys who can't disguise ourselves who have to stay home—where they were born, I mean. The locals don't mind your quirks, they don't

really care if there's piss in your pants or if you have to knock off
a piece with the field hands every once in a while."

"Is that what you do?"

"Nah, not me. I can't get them field hands to pay me any
attention."

"Let me fix food for you."

"What kind of food?"

"Anything you like. What do you love most? What did you
love as a child?"

"Creamed sweet corn."

"Fine. I'll fix you that."

He rolled onto his side, rolled back. She was a bulwark in the
bed, some breakwater holding waves off. He said, "Here's my
birthmark, here's my broken foot, here's my terror, here's my
dream."

"Everything."

"Yes. That's what it's about, isn't it?"

"But what does it come to?"

"I don't know—domesticity?"

"Yes. I would like that. I don't like things with meaning."

"Well, my brother says there couldn't be many things with less
meaning than this."

"We're safe, then."

Safe, yes. At night they walked around the town. Dressed in
archaic clothes, they took long walks on the path that ran along
the beach. They stopped for ice cream dressed in ancient finery.
She carried a ruffled parasol and ate with her fingers in public.
One night he saw his brother sitting across the fish house from
them. His brother's lips were compressed into a thin disapproving
line, and he looked to Harry as if he wished with his whole being
that he could order him out of public. Harry waved to him.

They rarely went out during the day. Harry went to the office,
where he tended to estates and wills, to the mostly aged who were
his clients, the old women whom he loved because they would sit
in the back office talking of their lives, the old men ready to
confess. He knew the story about Rachel Wells, who as a baby,
was found in a leather satchel on the front steps and raised by the
family who found her. He knew the story about the bitter man

David Stone, who charmed his wife into the piney woods and tied her to a tree and left her there to starve. He knew that old Mr. Harvey Dace, who walked about town in linen suits, who was on the bank board and on the police board of review, was bankrupt, that the big house and the fields north of town would go not to his relatives but to the federal government to pay off his tenant farm loans. He knew that Mrs. Evelyn Washman had not made love to her husband for forty years and did not regret it. He knew that the Williams estate had been left by old man Bennie Williams eternally undivided, a vexation to his heirs so profound that Bennie junior at the reading of the will had lunged out of the house screaming, straight into a heart attack that slammed him dead into the yucca bushes beside the front steps. He knew that Mrs. Daylene Postapervis was leaving her money not to the First Baptist Church, as promised, the deacons having already planned and named and held a special service for the Sunday school they figured to build, but to her illegitimate daughter, whom no one else he knew had ever heard about, since in her eighteenth year, pregnant by an itinerant trumpet player, she had been shipped off by her father, long dead now, to a home in Boston, where she delivered the child and handed it over immediately, without ever seeing the girl's face, to those who would take care of it, and hadn't done so.

But now these stories grew faint in his mind. He listened absentmindedly to the old gentlemen and ladies who revealed their lives to him. Since he had met her, since she had taken him into her house and arms, since he had begun to read the story of his life in her flesh, and since he had begun to read in the black-leather-bound ledgers the story of Eureena Dell, doomed child, ghost who walked, he had not paid attention. Fernie Billings finished his boat and took her on a cruise, intending, he said at the party in which he and his crewmen were dressed in identical aloha shirts and got drunker than they had planned to on a pineapple rum punch made by the schoolteacher he had promised to marry but would never, to sail the red boat all the way around the world, from Florida to Florida. It was two weeks later that they heard that the boat had been lost in a storm off the Grand Gull Banks west of the Keys, lost with all her crew.

They attended the funeral together—there were four bronze caskets, weighted, so the funeral director Willard Davis told him, with articles precious to the departed—standing apart in the warm late-summer rain, his arm hooked in hers, mist beading the dense black veil she wore. It was walking back, in the rain that polished and freshened the town, that seemed to him the first rain of fall, of the coming winter, nodding like an old married couple at the weekday housewives and shopkeepers, at Lonnie Burke digging holes for the fence surrounding the courthouse, at Mrs. Liberty Trelles, his secretary, who since he was often absent took more and more time away from the office and was this afternoon hurrying to meet her husband, who was to drive her to the farmers market, where she would embarrass him arguing over the price of speckled butter beans, at the fishermen and the fish house operators, at Reddie Spurt, who ran the oyster bar and who serviced in her spare time the duck hunters and country men who came there for a night away from home—it was on the way home, as they passed under the mulberry tree belonging to Mrs. Tendreese Constantine, which he had climbed into when he was eight and fallen from, knocking the breath out of himself so that for two minutes he thought he had died there on the packed sand sidewalk and that the stars he saw were angels, that he said, "My father—who is presumed dead—actually only disappeared."

She wasn't listening. "Disappeared?"

"Yes. He went away and never came back. It was very strange."

She laughed her skidding, tinsely laugh. "Tell me."

He said, "As my father grew older, he spent more and more time alone. He bought a cabin cruiser and drove it out into the Gulf. He would come home from school, change clothes, and take the boat out. He retired from teaching and coaching, and his trips became longer. He would be gone for days, occasionally for a week or more. He wouldn't say where he went, or what he did when he got there. My mother, who felt very secure as long as nothing changed, became alarmed."

"And you?"

"I was scared to death, but I didn't say a thing."

"What happened?"

"The trips continued. At home he was more silent than ever.

He would sit in his big chair in the living room, reading. He didn't hear when he was spoken to; he didn't answer. He became just a big silent goof who went out alone on a boat. It was embarrassing. I mean he wouldn't even around town speak when he was spoken to. My mother had to carry on conversations for him. We suspected that he talked to her when they were alone at night, but if he did, she didn't mention it, and around us, he would hardly say a word. He became a ghost," he said, letting his hand drift to her bare arm, running his fingers over the fine silver hairs. "One day he put out and he didn't come back. The coast guard searched, but they found nothing—no wreckage, no sign at all. There had been a storm between St. Lukes and Pensacola, and the officer who brought us the news that the search had been called off speculated that he must have been caught in it. My mother pushed the man out of the house, slammed the door in his face, and came apart."

"What did she do?"

"She yelled at us to go find him."

"Did you?"

"No. We were busy, we couldn't go, so she went herself."

"She went looking for him?"

"Yes. We didn't try to talk her out of it—we felt bad enough as it was—but we did try to shepherd her away from doing anything terrible. We hung around her a lot, and we took her places, and we tried to pay attention to her, which as typical sons we hadn't done much of, but she was different from us, she had another kind of mind, and she gave us the slip."

"Gave you the slip?"

"Not the slip really, but she began traveling, on her own."

"Stop," she said. "Sit down here."

"Okay."

They had reached the W.O.W. park, a block from her house, a narrow, shady aggregation of concrete picnic tables under unenthusiastic cabbage palms by a brief weedy beach. They sat down on a bench near the water. The sea was gray and flat, blue-gray farther out. Mockingbirds and gulls walked together on the grass. The rain had stopped.

She took his hand, spread it flat on her thigh. Her light fingers stroked his. "When you do something like that," he said, looking at her corroded knuckles, "I think I might be on my way to heaven after all."

"That's just an illusion."

"I know. But why not illusion? It seems to me a perfectly good way to live on a planet like this."

"What did your mother do?"

"She began to venture around to the little coastal towns, looking for traces of our father. By the time he disappeared he had been staying away for weeks at a time. She went down the coast as far as the Everglades; she traveled north to Pensacola and Biloxi, once all the way to New Orleans. Nobody had seen him, nobody had ever heard of him. She moved inland to the farming towns, but the answer was always the same: Horace Bates, a tall stooped man with nervous hands, had never been seen there. In Chilicote she met the mayor, who began to court her. The mayor, who was a gentle man, a lawyer and a cattle rancher, would drive a hundred miles to visit her. He began to accompany her on her search trips. Eventually he persuaded her to marry him. She moved to Chilicote, where they lived in a big yellow house at the edge of a cypress pond. But she wouldn't stop searching."

"Even after they were married?"

"No. The trips became more infrequent. She would go long periods almost content, but sooner or later she would get into the car and go out one more time to look for Papa. Mr. Horace Bates, she called him, as if he were an important person she was supposed to meet. She carried a photograph that she showed to people. In the picture he is sitting in a lawn chair in the backyard. He's wearing a Hawaiian shirt and white shorts, an outfit I never saw him wear in life. He's peeling an apple with a pocketknife. Someone has just called to him; there's a look of surprise and pique on his face, and guilt maybe, like someone caught in the middle of a mean thought. I could barely recognize him myself, from the picture. Mother would call us from one place or another; her voice would be spooky and low on the phone; 'I've missed him again,' she would say, as if the trail might be only hours cold instead of years. She was found dead in her car, of a heart attack, the coroner told us, sitting straight upright behind the wheel in an orange grove just north of Kissimmee. She had the photograph in her hand."

He looked out to sea. Sometimes the light—sun or moon—made a road on the water that as a child he thought he could walk away on. But he could never figure where it might lead, that narrow silver track. What would he find on the next shore? The picture he carried of his father was not the one contained by the photograph, nor was it a picture of romance, some vision of his father hawk-eyed in the cockpit of his cruiser riding the main; it was simply—the vision that appeared cresting waves of drink, despite drink—of his father sweaty and frightened, a small man reduced by years and loneliness, poling his heavy boat up one of the coastal bayous, one of the wrenched black-water streams of that country where the sun was rebuffed by the overbearing branches of alder and ash and willow, where the fat cottonmouths lay their curves like smiles on the water, where leeches hung suspended, weightless as dust, just beneath the surface, where the bottom, if you could reach it, was strewn with roots and congealed rotted leaves and, underneath, the mud was slick and deep and black. Rolled up from the bogs of sleep he saw this, deep in the center of his eye, had seen it many times, this vision or dream, or memory, of his father straining to the limits of his body against the long pushpole, moving the boat an inch, two inches, felt with him the boat suck backward, like a loved one receding in time; he saw always first the picture in its wholeness, from the middle distance: the bow greasy with swamp muck, the overarching branches of willows and water maples, the stream black and curving away behind; and then, moving closer, he saw his father isolated, first the figure, shabby and nearly defeated in his worn clothes, the collar of his blue shirt ropy, tan trousers torn, barefooted; and then the face with its gray singe of beard, the vertical lines in the cheeks like gouges in driftwood, the cords of the neck standing, dark brows massed, thin lips thinned down to a white cut. But it was the eyes that threw him back reeling. The eyes small and round and the gray of clouds just filling with rain, eyes that were filled now, in his vision, in his close-coming view, with terror, with the simple ghastly evidence of the soul's defeat, sudden and brutal and final. He did not know why it should be so, why that terror should be in his father's eyes. It was a vision, a dream that came to him in the night. Came to him all these years later, followed him like a sick dog to the Gulf's edge, where he stood against the dock railing, talking to the water. It followed him across his bedroom and into the kitchen where his mother, dead too, had prepared the meals of his childhood; followed him to the office, where it perched on bookcases and in the dust behind the closet door. It was terror he saw, his father unmanned by it. It was the moment when what holds us to life is overrun. It was the moment when his father knew he had lost the world.

But then—where was he now? in her bedroom, smelling of chalk and rosewater and rotted sex?—but then he dreamed at night of the girl, of Eureena Dell. Her life was like an odor lifting off the gnarled pages, her life was not a dream but a story, it was intermingled now with the stories told to him in the back office downtown, with the story he lived with this woman whom some nights he discovered in restlessness lost in the rooms of her own house, discovered crouched under the front windows, her face pressed to the streaked pane, whispering to herself harsh words of resolution and torment—accusations, denials, confessions. He would attempt to draw her into his arms, and it was like lifting the newly dead, the drowned—her body helpless and disjointed, refusing the world. It was in the story of his father, of his mother, who had wandered through the seaside towns carrying her solitary hope that she might find him living in one of them, unnoticed perhaps, tired, sick perhaps, but maybe still welcoming. Eureena said, "He bought me a pony when I wanted a horse. I am afraid always that I will do something terrible. I hate him for this. I was only a girl, only a child in an organdy dress. My world was sunlight on the marshes and the smells of negro cooking and the dreams of a girl. How can you forgive whom you love most?"

For years I rode the transcontinental buses. Ocean liners of the earth, they carried me under sails of diesel smoke across the great seas of America. The states became colors. Utah was ocher, Arizona was blond, Vermont was blue-green, like a piece of lapis stone in the grass. I remember, as if it happened, riding day after day, leaning my face against the wide tinted window watching the fence posts of Kansas or Iowa ticking by, the patches of old snow white as dead eyes in the flat fields of eastern Colorado, the fir trees in Wyoming marching under the wind toward Canada.

They arrested me because I couldn't keep myself from embracing people. After I lost the child, I wanted to give my love to everyone. Indiscriminately. In a restaurant I would get up from the counter stool and embrace a passing waitress. I had to feel her life beating against mine. There were men one after another, like unbuttoning a dress in the dark. So many buttons, my fingers tired and nimble. They arrested me somewhere, in Belle Fourche, South Dakota; or Cobs Bay, Oregon; or Falls Church, Virginia. Two men in uniforms the color of dried grass, with eyes the color of dried grass, took my arms and led me to a car. They put me alone in the back seat, where I rode for miles looking at fields of corn and wheat. As I looked out at the fields, over which arched a sky that was filled with clouds as large as continents, I felt myself fill with laughter at the size of it all, at the landscape that though tamed and chained was larger still than anything anybody had been able to put in it. Somewhere my baby could be lost there, somewhere my child could be lying on a blue blanket in a field, looking up at the same blue sky. Anything was possible in a landscape like that. One of the deputies turned around in his seat and told me to be quiet, but the other deputy shushed *him.* I stuck my fingers through the wire grille and for an instant, before he jerked his head away, touched his hair, which was dark brown and as soft as a child's. "I love you," I said. "I will love you forever and ever."

But you came back.

Yes.

I think: Louvered blinds on the sun porch the color of cane syrup; the long crack in the linoleum on the kitchen counter, which my mother told me looked exactly like the Mississippi River; the yellow-and-brown torn straw rug in the playroom; the small round holes cut by my father just below the roof peak for the martins; the small sweet white-fleshed nuts I shake like half-wings out of the pine cones. I think: bird, tree, sky, sea. I say, I believe what you once believed: I must live in the center of the world.

Then he looks at me with his round faded blue eyes, which are full of something that is like love but is not, something that is certainly devotion, that after all is like freedom, that may actually be freedom, but I am falling again, I am falling into the hole in the garden into the gray coralline earth I am falling away not even raising my hand making no gesture at all I am falling into Delphi I am falling into Denver I am falling into Mexico I am falling into wheat I am falling into wet blue flowers, I am falling, chinaberry, falling . . .

Her sleep was so silent that rearing up in the shallow darkness to look at her he imagined her dead, her breathing so faint that it was barely breathing at all, her chest still, her hands half clenched against her ribs. Even in sleep she was ungainly, an awkward dreamer. But maybe she didn't dream; there was a stillness in her that was deep and impenetrable, an absence. She had said a name, but she wouldn't say it again. She listened to him read from the ledgers with an unvarying attention. —Do you think sometimes this is your story? he asked her. —Yes, of course, how could I not? —I've always thought, he said, that the world was constructed—whether by God or nothing—so clearly as a home for us that sometimes it seems amazing to me that any of us could get lost in it. He said, Do you know that you can eat any plant in North America that isn't bitter or milky? And you can eat anything that swims in fresh water. Anything, even the snails and the little blind fishes that swim in caves. The ocean is different, but maybe we've just been out of that water too long. I don't think it's the world's fault if we get mixed up. —But we do get mixed up, she said. —Yes; and it's terrible, isn't it? —Yes. Some days I forget how to put on my clothes, she said. I sit on the side of the bed and wonder what is that brown laced thing on the floor, what is that bright patch hanging from the post? And then I go to the window and it's no different: there's blue and various green, all solid—I'm sure of it—but without definition or any connec-

tion to my life. —What do you do? —I go into the bathroom
and run cold water over my hands, and then I go into the kitchen
and chop onions. —What's terrible about it, he said, what
frightens us so badly, is that I think we know, in our guts, that
we never have to be mixed up. I mean it's sometimes strange and
often amazing and it is like a haywire circus in the way it keeps
throwing up wild combinations, but we are not lost in it, we are
not on the wrong planet. —Do you believe that? —When I'm
drunk I do. —What about now? —Your skin is a sacrament;
that's enough for the moment. —No, she said, it's not. —Oh?
Then tell me what's better. —Searching. —Searching? —Yes. —
All right, then we'll search.

I I

HIS BROTHER wouldn't sell him the boat. "I'll pay you twice
what it's worth," Harry said. "I'm already offering you twice what
it's worth, maybe three times," but his brother, stern and obdur-
ate in his white summer clothes, would not give in.

"I'm not going to sell you a good boat so you can run off on
some craziness," he said, and spit into the grass. They stood on
the glossy back lawn of his brother's house.

"It's not a good boat," Harry said.

"That doesn't matter. I'm not going to sell it to you."

"Then I'll take it."

"You do and I'll have the coast guard on your ass so fast you'll
wish you never heard the word *boat*."

"It's too late. Not only have I heard the word; I've been on one.
Let me have the boat, Buddy." He thought: Someday I am going
to have a brother who is generous and kind, a brother who explains
the world to me and guides me gently into it. Perhaps not in this
lifetime, though. The wind blew hard off the Gulf, steady and
nearly as palpable as a river, whipping the yellow flames of the
lanterns Martha had hung in the Chinese elms. One week ago
Laura had sat up in bed and said, Get a boat, and we'll go find
your father. He had answered that finding his father was not one

of his main considerations. Oh, no? she said. It's what you talk about. He said, I talk about a lot of things. I talk about fishing for speckled trout and seining for mullet, and I talk about Mrs. Harty's estate and I talk about Eureena Dell and I talk about my brother, but I don't say much about my father.

—Time, she said, that's what we are running out of.

—I feel as if I'm outside time. That's why I like it here. Did you notice that nothing has changed in this house?

—Yes, I've noticed.

—Well?

It was true. From the mantel hung the powder horn her great-grandfather had carried into the Battle of Natural Bridge, the time the Yankees had tried to thread the swamps to surprise the home guards. It still had powder in it, hard and glossy as a lump of coal. Some of the chairs had cowhide bottoms nailed on by slaves. In the attic were not only diaries but every scrap of clothing anyone in the family had ever worn. And out in the garage were hay bales like melted lumps of brown sugar. In the old garden, where you could still find garlic and a few strawberry plants, the potato vines and Cherokee rose reared snaky and full of thorns as high as his knees, only here and there the shallow holes she had long since stopped digging.

Let's get going, she said.

Content to be led, even to the edge of this cliff and over, so long as she went with him, he acquiesced. When his brother wouldn't sell him his boat—a small blue-painted wooden cabin cruiser with a ninety-horse Chrysler inboard, very like the boat his father had disappeared in—he decided to take it. Buddy didn't believe he would actually steal the boat. He gave his secretary six months' severance pay and closed the law office. He took seven thousand dollars out of his money market account. He latched the shutters against hurricane and locked the front door of his house. You can become what you want to become, he said to the house, and to the street, and to the town of St. Lukes, Florida. He felt his heart lift as he walked the three blocks to Laura's.

Her street was lined with the same stubby green palms that grew along Main Street, the bright-orange fruit which as a school-boy he had tried each spring unsuccessfully to eat. The trunks had thick triangular spines like the fins of sharks. He plucked a handful of fruit and held it to his nose as he walked. It was tangy and sweet-smelling, the size of the marbles called jawbreakers, just as inviting as it had been when he was ten years old. He licked one of the smooth balls, split it with his fingernail, and pressed his tongue against the red pulp. The sharp alkaline taste made him gag and spit. His father had told him once that life was too short to learn everything by experience. Sometimes, he thought now, even experience is not enough. He threw the fruit into the street.

He looked down the street, which had been a part of his life always. He had played the child's game of chase-and-kill in the yards of these houses. He had sat in the loquat tree in Mrs. Archibald's backyard, stuffing himself like the cedar waxwings on the sweet fruit. He had wormed out tunnels in the stand of bamboo in the Williams's yard, tunnels that led to small rooms hollowed out among the thick stalks, rooms where the abbreviated light hung like gold clouds over his head. The yards could be defined by the fruits that grew in them. There were fig trees in the Bakers' backyard, which each summer Mrs. Baker picked the fruit from for preserves. In the Taylors' were persimmons, orange and nearly as large as grapefruit. The Powells' had kumquats and oranges, the Cohens' yellow plums. Old Mr. Vargas, who lived alone in a house that teetered over cypress pilings, had scuppernongs, vines that had broken free from their moorings and climbed like kudzu into the oaks. Mrs. Shakey had sweet apples. The Lindseys' had spindly half-leafed trees that filled each summer with hard yellow speckled pears. He thought: I could eat my way across St. Lukes. Under such bounty no one would starve. For years he had a child's access, no yard closed to him. Then we grow up and become responsible, then we are not allowed to crawl around under the bushes. He did not miss his childhood mostly, remembered it as a time of soaring highs and plummeting lows that wrenched him breathless, and so was glad to receive his passport of education and age into the more ordered world of adults. But something in him, he thought as he turned up Laura's walk, must be reaching back. This could be argued as a mission of retrieval. What exactly am I doing? I am about to get in a stolen boat with a crazy woman to go search for my father? Who has been dead for fourteen years? Disappeared. Disappeared for years. Oh, Father, riding on the sea.

Two leather suitcases stood on the porch. In one were the clothes he had brought over for her to pack. She was in the kitchen, drinking a glass of water. —Do you want anything? she said. He told her no, he didn't want anything. The late-afternoon light lay across her thin shoulders like a golden shawl. She had never seemed so beautiful, equine and sturdy, her bones hard as cypress rails. —This is what you want to do? he said. —Yes, she said, this is what I want to do. —I'm scared, he said.

—It's natural, she said. You're a homebody, and now here you go out into the world.

—I never thought I would leave St. Lukes, Florida.

—I never thought I would come back.

They did not leave immediately. She wanted to wait until dark. One more time they made their way to the bedroom that smelled of rosewater and mildew and chalk. They lay down on the broad bed fully clothed. He took her in his arms. Sometimes he wanted to press himself right through her body, enter her wholly, live inside the prison of her flesh, like a monk in a desert cell. So it was now, his head buried in the rich fall of her hair.

—For once in my life, he said, I wish it'd be true that I could actually die without the company of a particular human being.

—It's already that way.

—You think I'd die without you?

—Maybe.

—Well, then you'd better not leave me.

He had drunk two water glasses of whiskey already. Stopped by the Chicken Bar to say goodbye. The country wizards had laughed. Why, he thought, even when I am at my most purposeful, do I seem silly? His face was not handsome; it was slightly lopsided, more so when he was drunk. You see it all the time, he thought: the afflicted who haven't adjusted well. But then we're all adjusting—right? He had torn pages from the ledger, and sitting on a green stool under the upturned trough of fluorescent lights, he read from them.

"There is no one to tell my secret to. It has made me lonely, lame with doubt, a person apart. But I am tired of crying. Father won't let me ride the pony without him. She's a piebald gray, a wicked thing with a hard mouth. Father's afraid I will, on my own, ride away and not come back. But I would not ride away, not yet. At night I listen to the wind pushing itself through the sweet apple tree below my window. The wind comes and goes; it makes a life all of its own in the world. This morning I waked early, sick to my stomach. I vomited into the chamber pot. In my dreams there are fierce characters, black shapes that rise out of the ground like men in dark capes to shout at me. I think of the life I've lost, of the secrets I now carry, and I mourn. I hate my mourning, I search with my hands to find a way to cleared ground. I dream of the west. . . ."

Reddie Spurt pushed her freckled face close to his to ask him why he was crying.

—You don't generally do that, she said, that's why I ask.

—I know, he said, I don't.

—Maybe you miss Fernie and all those boys.

—Maybe.

—You know, if you didn't have one ear higher than the other you'd be cute.

He laughed. —Jesus, Reddie.

—No, I mean it. You ought to scoot your hair out and cover 'em up.

—Well, thanks, I'll try it.

It was that kind of world. The haze in the bar was like mist on the sea. In winter the hunters would clump in in their heavy boots stinking of blood and the woods. Later tonight a fight would break out, a couple of the wizards pushed past their limit, flailing to break a passage where a man might rest in peace. So one day you say yes, so one day you pack a bag, steal your brother's boat, and head out to sea.

He said—I hope you know what you are doing.

—No you don't. You don't care about that.

—Good, he said. I'm glad to hear I don't. I was beginning to get worried.

Her hair smelled like the fur of an animal, as her body smelled of fruity obscure odors, scents of the sea and of the woods, and of a life without other people in it.

. . .

But I do know, I do know. The fetus rising in its fish-thrash, rolling in the darkness, falling in the darkness. At four months I felt her move for the first time, felt the sudden, expected though unimaginable prod of soft bone against flesh, felt her, quick and startling, as one waked into an empty house, and I knew for the first time that my body was wholly a mystery to me, this secular, fleshly habitation, this passageway.

The sea opens before us. It is light, then deep green, then indigo. The long swells run west, heading for Texas. We have swung out beyond the farthest buoys, whose bells clang like huge distant doors banged by wind. The sky is light, as if there is not enough darkness this evening to go around; small clouds pile on each other's shoulders like children climbed to see a sight. The wind is fitful and small, leaping along the wave crests.

So the great plains were not wide enough; what is left is this gulf of waters, this sea. He says we will travel outboard for twenty miles until we reach the islands, then turn toward shore to run through the lagoons and into the Intracoastal Waterway. The sea will give us distance, but the Waterway, he says, will give us safety. No one will miss us before morning. No one will come after us, he says.

I lie on the foredeck on my stomach, feeling the boat rise and fall under me. It lifts me on the swells, and for a moment I hang at the peak, suspended, my body weightless. The moment is too brief for me to love it, that suspended instant when I am cut loose from this world, but that is what it is, that risen, hung status, a moment between earth and space, life and death. It is as if for that split second I have been wiped out of existence. But I do exist, regardless of this momentary worldly illusion. Perhaps there are points we pass through, moments or even places, hamlets or road crossings, fields, where we can pass out of this world. Perhaps, if instead of continuing on we turned off, veered right or left, we would pass through and beyond into another world entirely. Perhaps my baby with her bright brown eyes spied such a turning and flung herself through it. So I follow, so I seek these risen moments, so I lie on my stomach on the damp deck of this stubby boat, my chin resting on the gunwales, looking down into the flowing sea. I am on the lookout above this dark and foaming sea that passes under and out of sight. They will not have to wake me when my child's face, bright as phosphorus, appears from beneath the dark waters. I will be here, I will be awake, I will be watching.

Through the upward-louvered windshield, Harry Bates looked at her lying on the deck. She was flattened out on her belly; like fellahin praying, he thought. She had disappeared from him the minute they stepped on the boat. She asked the direction like a passenger and seemed content when he told her they would head west through the Refuge passes into the open sea beyond Bright Head. It had been no trouble to steal the boat. Buddy kept it gassed up, and though he also kept it padlocked, it was moored at the far end of the city docks and Harry had a key. Buddy hadn't believed he would take it, but Harry knew he would send the coast guard after him anyway. His brother was a serious man, who did what he said he would do. They were spiritually linked—that was the way Harry put it—because of the brother blood that ran between them, but Buddy, as he had told him many times, took guff from no one. There was no need to try to explain, though Harry figured he had been explaining himself all his life.

Now I have become a pilgrim, he thought. Now I am on my journey.

They ran west at three-quarters throttle through light seas. The moon laid its silver coat on the water. He had run full throttle up the calm waters of the bay, throttling down when they met the wilder seas on the freeboard. He planned to run west past Gull Island, then dip in through the pass to the Waterway. On this part of the Gulf the Waterway was only the string of bays that ran between the islands and the mainland. The bays were calm and wide and, he figured, safe, especially at night. There were too many shrimp boats out for the coast guard to find them. For the first couple of days they would stand in on the river mouths, motor upstream on the Suwanee or the Steinhatchee, and lay by under the trees until dark. By the time they got to Port St. Joe they would be free of any net the coast guard might have thrown, free to run in daylight.

He didn't know if she had any sort of plan. Maybe she had insight and would tell him what they were really up to. The search, he figured, was just a game they played, nothing more than the flag they could run under. He took a banana from the satchel at his feet, peeled and ate it. Everything tasted better on the sea. He had come out here all his life, first with his father, then with his brother and with kids from high school, then alone. He had never understood his father's silence. It was impenetrable, effortless, and redundant, like the silence of the pinewoods or the ocean. Dark as the grave, he thought, and gripped the brass wheel tighter. The gauges glowed green in the dark: fuel, speed, engine-oil pressure, gear-oil pressure, water temp, voltmeter, tach—all steady. The cabin, floored with rubber mats, smelling of borax, was immaculate; his brother could perform an operation in here if he wanted to. Belowdecks was a small kitchen and a pump sink, a fold-down plywood table, and, under the foredeck, four bunks, two on either side. In the bow was the head, also pump flush. They had a picnic basket of food, two sleeping bags, a couple of suitcases of clothes. In a plastic waterproof pouch he had passport and cash and the black ledger containing the final written testament of Eureena Parker.

I am one strange lawyer, he thought, and leaned his face down to press his lips onto the sour brass of the wheel rim. The land off starboard, half a dozen miles away, lay in a darkness deeper than the night. On this part of the coast, free of tourist trade, the towns were spindly and slight, collections of stilt houses and fish shacks, an occasional factory or oil dump, nothing much. They perched at the river mouths like herons. There was a hundred miles of wilderness before you came to the coast of the tourists' dreams. Here pine gave way to cabbage palms, to palmetto scrub, to marsh, to calm salt indivisible sea. Dark as dreamless sleep, the land lay under the body of night, and they rode on, skimming the light sea, outbound, cut free.

They ran for six hours before the first gray seepage of dawn appeared in the eastern sky. He watched now for the tower that marked the channel into the Deer River at St. Nicholas. The river mouth was nothing more than an opening in the low fret of marshes. The town lay three miles upstream on the last—or first as it was for them now—high ground.

He thought as he slowed and veered toward the rusted channel buoys that it was true life could step off into dream and keep going. Routines, the complacent habits we strung ourselves on, could fall away in a moment, be transformed in a breath's time into another life wholly. His brother, in a moment of disgust one night after being called to sew up a couple of knife fighters down at the Chicken Bar, had said the South was still the only place where a man would ruin his whole life in one night. Perhaps that was true, but perhaps the South was not the only place; perhaps it was a major feature of life in the world, which we worked so hard to protect ourselves from knowledge of. Perhaps it was the whole deal. Adam and Eve ushered stinging from the garden, the voice booming over them, its refusal of them sucking out happiness and hope: Go away, betrayers; get out of my sight. And then naked-ness wouldn't do, then lounging in the branches of the oaks was not enough, walking in the flowery woods was not enough, no more peeing in the creek. We got a new deal going, brother, and you gonna have to change your ways.

He laughed out loud thinking of the look on Buddy's face when he discovered his boat and brother gone. Stumblebum Attorney Takes to High Seas. Madness Feared. That wasn't all that was mad. Eureena, darling, I was too late to rescue you.

Holding the wheel with one hand, he bent down and got out the ledger. In the green dashboard light its looped figures looked like the tracings of sound itself, some pattern of rise and fall, a pen following blindly the hints and scuffles of indecipherable noise, some distant language or intercepted radio beam from space. A pantomime, he thought. I don't even have to read it. Like my own life, which you could stand quite a ways from and still understand.

"I have written letters [she wrote], but there is no one to send them to. My aunts are distant, I am afraid that such circumstances as I find myself in would not be believed in the parlors of Rich-mond and Baltimore. And I would have to say to them words I cannot say to myself. From my window I watch the wind moving

like a giant snake through the grass. The apples are sweetening in
the tree. Old Livery says that on the outer farms the bears come in
fall to eat the fruit from the apple trees. 'They climb jes like
human beings,' he says, ' 'cept they make a worse mess.' I don't
think it is possible for an animal to make a worse mess than we
do. Father is angry all the time. I see the disgust in his eyes when
he looks at me. I am dizzy with the sweep of feeling in myself:
disgust, pity, rage like a fire in the trees, moments when I am so
filled with love that I want to throw myself at his feet and beg
him to do anything he likes with me. It is not my fault, but what
matter is that? I was a child, but I am no longer. I have been
tricked into another life. It is as if out on a walk I stopped in a
shadowy place and there, as I reached to pluck a flower, I realized
myself changed, become another, one I do not know or understand. I believe that in some measure we must all feel this as the
tug of life's demands begins to pull us into its arms, and maybe it
is this knowledge that, in the midst of a horror that wakes me in
the night like a hammer beating on the headboard of the bed,
strands me here nonetheless in wondering passivity, able only to
write in these ledgers my small, circumspect reports, my few
signals that cannot mean what they say, or if they do, cannot
rouse, cannot give alarm. . . ."

He looked at Laura through the open window. *She* had no
diaries that he knew of. Some secret, though, that she wouldn't
tell him. He didn't mind her craziness; he had a high threshold
for that. And secrets, as far as he was concerned, were fine. He'd
listened in the late afternoons, the office window open so that he
could smell the ambient sea, to the old women and men of the
town, the secret confessors, as they told him the worked-over
stories of their lives. He had his own, ones they knew or thought
they knew, stories they passed on among themselves, as one more
trinket, handicraft of local manufacture, and so accepted him into
the confraternity of loss and selfish grief, but of this one, this
Laura Dell, large of frame and wary, tall and ungainly as a half-
grown child, whom he came on in the kitchen long after lights
out, sitting in the dark, sipping tea, he didn't know. She sat
outside the circle, in the half-light, sometimes in no light at all.
We're all out there, he thought, winging our songs into the void,

but sometimes, and mostly, even for the drunks, there is a sense of someone else, of others, like men skipping rocks on a pond, there beside us in the murk; we might not speak, we might even feel befouled or embarrassed by their presence, but they are there, and we know it. But occasionally, once in a while and much less often than you would think, there is one who, by madness or loss, or some combination of congenial mysteries, is truly detached, without connection, who approaches the threshold from which she launches her individual story into the universe entirely alone, from emptiness to emptiness.

She wore jeans and a shirt the color of crushed grapes. Her dark hair was knotted low on her neck. She hadn't raised herself all night, lay like a penitent, her arms stretched out grasping the gunwales, her head stuck out over the prow. She lived some dream too, something back there in her past that had displaced her. As he watched she reached behind and scratched in the small of her back; the bottoms of her bare feet were yellow. He would do anything in the world for her. There wasn't anything she could ask of him that he wouldn't do. Stealing a boat—Jesus, that was nothing; he would steal a fleet.

He throttled down three quarters, and they came slowly up the channel. In the gray dawnlight the black marsh mud gleamed. The mud was pocked with crab holes. As the boat's slight wake brushed shore, the crabs, white and armored with single long yellow pincers, scurried away from it like roaches. Idling up, they passed the boat warehouse and a derelict shrimper, boards stripped from its wheelhouse, a lantern on a staff dangling above it, half sunk at the edge of the channel. Two women in gray country dresses jigged lines from the tabby wall set against the low bluff that raised the town out of the sea.

He took the whiskey bottle out of the satchel, uncapped it, and took a long pull. Even in my vices I walk the retrograde. Just the drink; that was always enough. She makes me rosy and content, he thought, I just swing along. He blew across the mouth of the bottle. Foghorn. *Whoo, whoo.* And Eureena Dell, who were you to all this? Another scattered shard revealed by the absent turn of a spade. No way to reach back through time to give you anything. He could see his mother sitting in the gazebo in the backyard.

Through the lattice her white skirts shone. Maybe the search for his father was only her way of dealing with a restlessness that had been there always. But what was it his father went to find? Why does someone in the midst of his life one day lock the door and leave? His father didn't say. And Harry, already headlong in retreat, had been scared to ask.

They passed the town, a collection of white and pastel buildings with tin roofs, and a single two-story red-brick structure that Harry remembered was the courthouse. They had not played football against St. Nicholas; it was a town he had only occasionally passed through. There seemed to have been a festival going on. Strips of colored crepe hung over the main street; wind had torn them loose and blown them into the sycamores along the river. In the still morning they hung from the peeled branches like pieces of an abandoned design.

He stayed on the far side of the channel, running in close to the reeds; no sense in giving anyone in this small burg a fix on who might be passing upriver. Beyond the town, which petered out into a few summer cabins with screened back porches hanging over the water and then, beyond a closed store with HC Sinclair pumps still standing like used-up sentinels in front of it, to pinewoods, they left the signs of habitation behind. This coast, back from the palms and grasses of the shore, was all pines, woods that ran west and north for miles, owned by paper companies. Most of the rivers were spring rise, coughed up out of the limestone bed. He eased the throttle on down. The engine was a murmur. A doe, accompanied by two spotted fawns, looked up from the river edge where she drank, raised her white flag, and crashed away through myrtle bushes. The woods were dark, soaked with night. A red-tailed hawk, lifted from behind the wall of trees, rose on energetic wings and slipped downstream on a draft, following, like a gull, the line of the river. The sky, mirrored on the tarry surface, lightened.

Seven miles up, beyond a sandy headland backed by willows, they came to a cut where a small local spring came through high limestone banks and joined the river. Large holly trees prospered on the banks and along a short ridge formed by the rocky uplift. The opening to the spring was narrow, but wide enough for the boat. He called to her then, for the first time that night, to help him fend away from the banks as he eased them up the clear runoff stream. The slow prop kicked up gouts of yellow sand. Then he shut the motor off and they drifted into the clear circular pool. The spring was maybe fifty feet across, an upright white-walled tunnel sunk like a collapsible funnel into the earth. Gallberry scrub grew up the steep banks; on the rim were more hollies and three or four live oaks, their muscular branches hoisted out over the water. New sun lay in patches, sunk shafts into the pool.

The boat eased and bumped against the bank. Laura jumped ashore with the painter, which she tied to an alder branch. He said, "Now life will start; now we are safe." She looked back at him, smiling broadly, and then she waved, a big scooping wave as if the air between them was tangible and dense and she was trying to tear out a clean passage between them.

They dragged two of the foam mattresses from the cabin, laid them on the floor of the wheelhouse, and slept. In the ease of his weariness he felt his body turn toward hers, sensed in the drowsiness before oblivion his arms slide around her, heard for the briefest of moments as he drew her close the slow and steady beat of her heart. It seemed to come from the air around them.

Dream, yes, and now the new world, in which anything can be made. I don't know whether I am asleep or awake. I hear the keening of june bugs, a bug beating against glass—natural sounds —but there are voices too. I lost my way once. In New Orleans they locked me up for a prostitute. I bought a short wet-look vinyl skirt and stood in front of a pawnshop on St. Charles, talking to the hookers there. I had questions for them, these women who had walked through life and out the other side. Two or three of them had children at home, like anchors to hold them steady, I guess. They were bold, these women; pioneers I thought of them as, scouts and forward observers, for this is a world where men are stronger and they will use their strength against you. I once pointed out to my husband that women live in a world where half the adults in it, just by right of sex, have physical power over them. You don't know what it's like, I told him, to walk around in a world where at any moment force can be used against you. He laughed and told me men have their troubles too, and I didn't deny it and wouldn't, but I wanted to make him understand— men think of their power in relation to other men, as women do among their own sex—that for women it is possible to lose our hope in this refugee life, to become one of those bundled hurrying figures blown along at the edge of darkening weather; we can begin to flinch and draw apart. I think I must have lain with men in those weeks I lived in New Orleans. I remember the heavy sump smell of bodies, weight pressing on me. I remember stepping out onto my second-floor porch and looking across the backyards, where boats rested on sawhorses and women in light dresses sat on back steps shelling beans. The sea smell and the wind would strike me hard, as if I had emerged from a cave. I think there was a man in the room then, sitting on the bed as he pulled on a pair of dirty white socks. When the police came in their van I went gladly, stooping under the low ceiling with women who laughed and jostled. We sat side by side under the dim interior light, our clothes our eyes our lips gaudy with color, bright as jewels; we were bright and raucous as tropical birds.

So I open my hand on the body of the man next to me. There is heft here and strong arms. My mother said, Be careful who you give to, because there are things you can't take back. She lived her life under the press of that belief, squeezed from restraint to miserliness. She poured love like hot syrup on the natural world, on staked fruit trees and half an acre of strawberry plants, on stray animals and birds. Mother, love will out, it will crawl under the wires to go partying in the night. What this man, this Harry man, doesn't know is that I would give myself to whoever asked. My child is astray. I see her ghostly, swimming, in sunlit water. I must take everything into me now, I must entertain the leaves and the sand and the yellow mugs hung from the kitchen wall. I must say yes, I must wave away what differences you think there are between you and me, World. I will remember everything, yes, everything—all but one act, all but one moment: let that moment, that act, corrode and blacken, let it mire itself and merge with darkness.

· · ·

Harry, Harry, he thought, where are you now? What have you gone and done? He looked up into bright blue day, at the woman sleeping beside him. A catbird meowed from the oak trees. The boat was still, free of tides. He sat up, his body creaking, and thought: Oh my God, I have ruined my life. And then he wanted to run, race for the exit. How do I get out of here? Jesus almighty God. He uncapped the whiskey bottle and took a long pull. Ah, the drunkard's alchemy: acid that turns to ease. What now, day?

He kissed her awake, bird kisses, pecking into the hidden parts of her body. Here, let me drink from you, sup the soft unblemished skin of your inner thigh, let me skim my face into the long fine straight hairs of your groin, let me lick the taste of your salt body. She groaned and arched against him, her wide bony hips rising to his mouth. The triangle of hair was wide and dense, darker than the hair on her head. When they made love the wetness ran from her body like a tapped spring; it splashed their skin hot as candle wax.

He pressed his face hard against her, into her, tongue straining to touch as deeply as possible, reach far back. She cried out and took his head in her hands, drove him deeper, held him against her as his chin, the frame of his face, banged against the pelvic mantle. "Oh, oh," she cried, and gasped, and then the sounds she made became inarticulate, short barks of breath, came faster than the quickest pulse, until they merged into a single cry, a shout, scattering birds.

Then he lay back and she took him in her mouth. He felt her large teeth just scrape the skin of his glans, the pull of her sucking, the heat of her. She sucked for a long time without bringing him to orgasm. Once, for a moment, a bright light seemed to snap across his eyes, but the moment faded. He drew away. She looked up the length of his body, found his eyes. "You are still scared," she said, and smiled, Yes, he was, frightened now by trees, the new blustering world. "You're not alone anymore," she said. "I know," he answered. "I know."

They ate oranges and cold ham from the basket she had packed. He drank whiskey and thought about the journey. They sat with their feet dangling off the bow, listening to the birds take up the morning. It was early; the sun lingered in the holly, pulled itself up through the evergreen live oak leaves. She said, "We can live without purpose now."

He thought about it—without purpose. "Maybe they will come after us," he said.

"No," she answered, "they won't."

"My brother is a stiff man when it comes to his possessions."

"I think in his mind you will have vanished from the earth."

"Like my father."

"No. He's here."

He looked around, as if she meant these woods. "I'm not really looking for him," he said. "He's gone."

"No. He's here. You just haven't seen him yet."

He looked at her then, at her long hair falling across her shoulders, catching light, he looked at her face, which was long and bony, not a pretty face at all but ravishing to him, dear, and he thought she must be trying to find something lost, she must be trailing some kind of mystery. He couldn't figure what it was; didn't really want to know.

He stood up. "We have to go if we want to get around the elbow."

"What is that?"

"This stretch where the coast bends in. We want to make Port St. Joe by tonight."

"If we go too fast, won't we run out of coast?"

"That would be hard to do. Theoretically we could keep going all the way around South America and back up. We could go all the way to Alaska. That's probably twenty thousand miles."

"Theoretically," she said slowly. "What about actually?"

"Actually they'll probably catch us before we get to St. Marks."

She drew her legs up and wrapped her arms around her knees. "You'll find out," she said, "that nobody's looking."

But the point was moot, because he couldn't start the boat. He'd left the ignition on all night, and the battery was dead. "What a dumb thing to do," he said.

"It doesn't matter," she said. "This is fine."

She had changed into a long blue silk dress with a scalloped front and ruffles along the hem. She looked as if she were going to a funeral ball. "Why don't you dress up?" she said.

He said, "I forgot to bring my old-time clothes."

"I packed them for you."

And so she had. In the bag he found a collarless shirt, striped like a barber's cloth, and houndstooth trousers with suspender buttons and wide bottoms, and a double-breasted waistcoat. He put them on and strutted around the deck through patches of sunlight as she made small appreciative noises. She whirled a circle in her ruffled skirt so the hem flew and the material made a sound like birds fluttering among leaves. "We are quite a pair," he said, grinning, and he thought: Life is just a play-pretty, let the good times roll. He drank the whiskey down and they danced on the foredeck, holding each other at a stately distance, looking into each other's eyes as if everything of importance—past and future —swam in there: though as he twirled her on the teak deck he thought—odd, it seemed to him—of his mother, of the time when walking in the woods behind the town he came on her unsuspecting, caught sight of her ahead of him as she wandered among a stand of young pines, embracing one tree after another. He had shied then, stumbled silently away, horrified at what he had seen and at the chance of her seeing him, as if, under this precise and rigorous instruction, he had learned, to his dismay, that there was some knowledge he should not have, that would harm him. He was grown then, more than a boy; he knew to avert his eyes from such a sight. Two years before he would have run across the strawy woods floor and embraced his mother, pulled her away to giddy questions; but that afternoon, trailed behind her, he could not. He could only run away and try not to remember what he saw: her eyes wild and her face streaked with tears and from her painted mouth sounds emerging like the brokenhearted cries of animals, indecipherable beyond the instantaneous knowledge of some unappeasable grief. Had his father already vanished by then? He thought not. He was off on the roads, traveling toward another football game.

Looking at the woman, he thought that it was her gray eyes that called up these memories in him, as if, in the entrapment of her gaze, he was free to think of what was painful and frightening without unease. He laughed out loud and threw his head back, whirling her around him boldly enough to clear the dance floor; she held him in strong arms as he caught a glimpse of small birds flickering through the leaves of overarching oaks and of the blue sky behind waving like a grand flag.

Let it go on forever nonstop, he thought, but then a crow cawed close by and his concentration broke and he pulled away from her to look into her eyes that were the color of smooth granite and he said, "Why have we come out here, and what will we do?"

She slapped him lightly across the cheek, whirled out of his arms, and danced away to the rail, where she stopped and leaned back as if she might go over backward into the spring. Her breathing was shallow and fast, and she fanned herself with her palm. "We're out here looking for your father," she said.

"But he disappeared fourteen years ago, and my mother has already looked everywhere. I believe he went down in the Gulf."

"No," she said, "he's alive somewhere. I can feel it. I have that kind of sense."

He sat down on the flat cover that housed the engine and looked at her. "You're the strangest woman I have ever known," he said.

"I don't doubt that," she said, and laughed.

He stared at her, and it was as if his whole life seemed to rise out of her, as if in her, turning slowly around to look over the side, he could see his father, lean and tall, stoop to clean coral mud off his hunting boots, and his mother, her face red and streaked with sweat, come out of the laundry room carrying a white pile of fresh sheets. He thought he wanted someone in his life who knew every story he had to tell. He said, "Is it possible that you and I have gone crazy at the same time?"

"What does it matter?" she answered, opening the stiff bodice of her gown. "We're not within range of anyone's judgment. Even our own."

"That's a relief."

He watched as she removed her clothes, dropping each antique piece on the deck in front of her. As she bent to slide the long frilled bloomers down her legs, he thought that the shallow curve of her back, trenched by the long keel of bone, was the most beautiful sight he had ever seen, thought: I am a king in my own lifetime to have such a one beside me. He crossed the deck to her through the yellow coins thrown down by the sunlight, but she held him away, would not let him take her in his arms. "Now I am going to wash this world off me," she said, and touched his cheek. "Let me be for a little while."

He stepped back, with disappointment showing on his face, and watched her as she climbed onto the railing and dived into the spring. She broke the water cleanly and descended. He moved closer to watch her. She stroked downward through water that was as clear as crystal, uncluttered by any living thing, that rippled and surged with her passage. The deep white cone held her; she fell away from him, her long legs scissoring strongly. Then, ten, fifteen feet down, she stopped and turned, looked up through the tons of water at him. He could see her clearly; she hung in the water motionless like some ancient creature trapped in ice, looking back at him. He wondered if she could see him leaning out over the side. He waved and smiled and she waved back, her long arms moving slowly. Then fear shot through him, slivers thin as angel's hair, and he realized how easily she could disappear, how she could one moment simply turn away from him and vanish.

He retreated to the cabin, drank a last swig of the warm whiskey, and stripped off the old clothes. They creaked in his hands as he folded them and laid them back in the open suitcase. She called to him as he was undressing, but he continued, pulling on his old khakis and his blue lawyer's broadcloth shirt. He could hear her paddling around. He went to the stern, lifted the engine cover, unfastened the battery, and pulled it out.

"Why don't you bring back some groceries too," she called as he made his way forward. She swam on her back, her whole body laid on the surface, shining as if lacquered. She wiggled her toes at him. "And make sure you get plenty to drink, boyo." She laughed and sank away, turning as she fell, spinning into the depths.

He climbed carefully over the side, stood in the cold water and dragged the battery off the bow, climbed the steep clay bank and made his way through the hollies and the gallberry bushes to a small clearing. There were piles of trash in the clearing, some of it half burned, scattered cans and beer cartons, a single brogan,

dusty with fire ashes and missing its laces. He kicked the shoe as
he passed. A road led out of the clearing through straight rows of
tall pines.

After walking a mile he came to a highway. He waited for
fifteen minutes before a man in a pickup came by and gave him a
ride to town. The man, fat as a boar and dressed in overalls from
which all but the last blue had faded, was carrying a load of
manure for his neighbor's garden. Harry told him everything. He
couldn't stop himself and didn't want to. "That's a curious thing
to do," the man said, and dashed sweat from his forehead as if it
were acid. "I believe," the man said, "somewhere before it started
I would have given up on a project like that."

"I didn't know I was going till I went," Harry told him. The
day was fair, coming up blue and sturdy above the endless ranks
of planted pines. As they drove, Harry watched the trees, trying
to get the line of the planting, the straight rows flashing by, but
he kept losing it. He imagined the orderly rows of pines, emblems
of the power of commerce and civilization, like far-flung scouts,
even now subduing the wilderness, bent to service, imagined them
running for miles into the sandy outback, leaping rivers and
swamps, endless trained woods.

He left the battery at the Gulf station, went to a bar on the
river, where he had a breakfast of smoked mullet and then got
drunk. He was three hours in the bar, and he asked everyone who
came in if he had seen a man named Horace Bates, a tall man with
a stoop who once taught American history and coached football
teams. No one had seen the man or heard of him. He didn't say
the man was his father, though he told them his name. He wasn't
afraid anymore that he might be caught. Through the open windows of the bar, he smelled the rusty, indefinite odor of the river
marshes, strong and full of the kind of life he knew. He had sat
in buildings like this all his life, peeling frame structures perched
on the edges of rivers. Bleached oyster shells like loose pavement
dumped along the bank, a view of unshaven men in baseball caps,
a pool table under fluorescent light, a woman with chemical hair
behind the bar. He had lost nothing, he figured, by going away,
but no one could tell him anything about his father. He leaned
over the counter, slick with beer and oyster juice, and said to the

woman, who was black-haired and who at the moment he spoke stood with her back to him, looking into the long mirror as she harshly rubbed lotion into her freckled face, "From now on I'm not going to hide anything."

She turned, the ends of her fingers gleaming with slickness, and said, "That is a great relief to all of us. You want another, buster?"

He took a cab back out to the boat. The driver wore a purple suit that was shiny at the knees and elbows and a straw snap-brim hat from which the glaze peeled like dead skin. Harry, drunk and rolling in happiness in the back seat, thought the man was his father. "Are you sure you're not him?" he asked, laughing. He hung over the front seat and watched the world pour down the highway at them: pines and palmetto scrub and the long ditches like ribbons made of dark water. "I think you must be him," Harry said, "and you just won't tell me."

"I don't know what you're talking about, pardner," the cabbie said, and pushed the hat up on his forehead.

"Sure you do," Harry said. "My father was tall and lean as a cypress rail, and I know that driving a cab in a river town would suit him fine. You must be him."

"Maybe you shouldn't drink so early in the day," the man said, and began to whistle a tune Harry had known all his life. It was "The Water Is Wide," a song his father had sung to Harry and Buddy when they were children. It would always give him a secret empty feeling when his father sang it, this song of lost love, a feeling that was so deep, so full of trembling and sorrow, that he could not even share it with his brother. Now as he heard the tune, melancholy and slow, coming from the cabbie, it brought back, like a door thrown open on the heart's secrets, a sadness that fell through him like a wing-shot quail. He began to cry; he fell back on the seat and held himself in his arms and cried, and it seemed to him that all the griefs of the world were in the cab with him, all the losses, every miserable living thing that was doomed and had to go on living anyway, every leaf and tree, every hibiscus flower, every silver sea bass swimming up the tidal river, even the sugarberry trees turning themselves into yellow flames on the old earthen battlements of the Spanish fort, even the crazy woman in

St. Lukes—one of his clients—who stopped muttering for a moment to look into Tallent's shopwindow at the red silk dress hanging there, even the man sitting alone in a basement in Santa Monica turning a coronet in his hands, every boy, even the one he once was, whose father in the backyard on a warm fall evening cried *Harry!* as he dropped the worn football one more time: "Catch it in your hands, son, not against your body," every man —every father, every son. And the woman was there too, this Laura, gangly and askew, formal even in her pleasures, breached and broken—as he was—by life's latest miserable turning, reaching now into the darkness of the mysterious alien world for one more piece of sweet bread, one more embrace, and he thought: The reason I must find my father, the reason I must find out what his end was, is so I can have my own end.

But what of this other, this Eureena Dell, whose pages written one hundred fifty years before he had torn out and stuffed in his back pocket, that he pulled out now, uncreased, and laid flat on his knee. He was ready—that was clear—to trade his old life for another, but now it seemed that just as the new line opened, a line that though maybe ridiculous and leading to destruction was, *at least,* a line, this frail story appeared to hamstring him. It's not about you, Harry, he said to himself, it's not your story. But it *was* his story; this was the thing about good stories, about the oldsters creaking out their fanciful demented tales in his back office, where on summer days he could smell the grapey perfume of kudzu flowers: it was his story they told. Something human that made him human. Just as it was not so strange to toddle off with Laura Dell, lonely as she was. It isn't loneliness that makes us less than human. It's abandonment. Laura's not fleeing, she's searching. If you're still looking you're okay. Any high school guidance counselor could tell you that. But this other, this fair Eureena, trapped in a bedroom of a house on Wassibaw Island, where in phrases that were more Elizabethan than American, or even Southern, she wrote down a tale so dark, so irredeemable, that it made his skin crawl: for this girl what light was there? She wrote, "Sometimes I sit up all night waiting, for someone, for something, for anything." You couldn't say to her, Well, get up, girl, and go away—flee. There were times when flight wasn't possible. And how could she fight one so strong, one whom she loved? She said, "I make pinwheels from colored paper that I paint with inks that once belonged to my mother, and I set them out on sticks in the garden. From my window they look like bright birds, or like the shining eyes of angels. The wind comes and goes —I hear their soft, pleading voices in the night."

He sank back into the lumpy seat, which smelled of sugary perfume and vomit. The cabbie's head was shaped like a light bulb, a few twists of black hair curling up off his thin neck. In a minute Harry would notice a black wing—crow or death, figment —flying toward him down the long corridor of pines, and drunk, he would raise his hand to greet it in foolish welcome. But the wing would pass on, so quickly that he would turn in his seat trying to catch a glimpse of it out the back window: nothing, dream, alcoholic hallucination, like the smell of peaches the night he came up out of the Gulf and found Laura. There was only the sky piled with pure white cumulus, and the same pines, receding now, the rows speeding into the distance, unbroken and permanent. He wanted another life.

So even gathered into the shelter of arms I remain alone. My father once gambled away his whole paycheck on a boat race. He bet Horace Bates of St. Lukes, Florida, two hundred and thirty-five dollars that Slidell Wilkins's Kingfisher outboard could beat Franny Tilton's inboard. The course was to Cross Island and back, a distance of twelve miles. Franny won by two miles. I watched him do it, standing beside my father as his grin faded. I said, Daddy, I thought Baptists weren't supposed to gamble. He looked at me as if I had slapped him. Sometimes, he said, I have to do something that makes me feel like I am alive, no matter what it costs. . . . So I venture into the world again. A crazy woman combing sea, woods, and town for her lost baby. My husband, who forced me into the car and away that morning, told me we would come back for her, but we didn't. He wouldn't let me go back; he wouldn't let me go in there and see. There was steam in the bathroom, silence. He said we were going to Oregon, with a nonchalance in his voice as if Oregon was only next door instead of twenty-five hundred miles from Louisiana. But the nonchalance disappeared as he drove, and when he got out of the car forty-six hours later for the first time, except when he pulled over to pee, he went straight into the motel room, locked the door, and with the pistol my father gave him to defend me from the bad men of the world, he blew the side of his handsome head against the bathroom wall.

THEY TRAVELED along the Panhandle, stopping at the water towns to ask for information. He did not drink, and in the first days after pouring the last bottle out a childish gaiety overtook him, a feeling of exuberance trimmed with promise. Clouds seemed to have passed out of his life. The condition was only temporary, but while it lasted he began to see their journey as a kind of elaborate confection, useless and possibly harmful, but sweet and fine-wrought just the same; what she suggested he performed, and what he performed he performed with delight. At first they asked only passersby, drinkers coming out of bars, filling station attendants, but soon Harry grew bolder; he visited the chambers of commerce, school board offices, the county court-house. In New Constantine, he had lunch with the chief of police, a florid man who raised chickens in sheds behind his house, who told him that many men passed through the town, a fishing village half tumbled down the low shell banks at the mouth of the Straight River. —You would be surprised, the chief said, how many wandering solitary people there are, men and women. In the middle of your family you think everybody else comes from a family too, or that the ones who don't are crazy or derelict on some city street, but that's not at all true. The world is full of wanderers and crackpot solitaires, all those folks who got cut loose somehow, either on their own or because somebody else cut them loose, and we have our share passing through this little town. We get called regularly out to one of the motels on the highway to roust some joker who has spent the week drinking himself most of the way to kingdom come and now can't pay his bill, but it's the other ones, the ones who ain't crazy or half drunk, the guy trying on hats all by himself down at Cohen's Fishing Supplies or the fellow dressed up in a suit who orders the special dinner at Chacey's and then tips the waitress ten dollars, that give you hints about the strangeness of the world. Just last week there was a lady I came on out here at the county park sitting in her car about dawnlight, crying. She was so caught up in her crying that she didn't even want to crank down her window to talk to me, and Lord, I hardly liked to disturb her, but I'm the police, so what do you do? She said she was traveling—traveling—not from any place in particular or *to* any place in particular, just traveling. She had Missouri plates on her car—it wasn't stolen—and she wore a wedding band, but it was on her right hand. Maybe she was freshly widowed, I don't know, or maybe she was looking for something, but she wasn't drunk and she didn't appear crazy and there she was off in a cracker corner of Florida all by herself, crying like a lost child at six thirty-two in the morning.

—What did you do? Harry wanted to know. The man was a familiar, another who liked the stories.

—Well, I'm bad to be optimistic—it's a drawback sometimes for a policeman—and people, after all, do have their private lives. I pointed out to her that down on the beach this time of day you could often see dolphins running, which she might like to take a look at, and over here at Willinoe they were about to start up on the seafood festival, which might not be much but really was sometimes fun, especially at the oyster-eating contest when those young boys got to trying to outeat each other. I just tried, I guess, to interest her a little in what was going on in the world around her. Sometimes that helps. She didn't care for distractions, though —I guess she already had plenty—so I let her go. The truth is you see a lot of folks like that in this world—though I haven't seen any sign of this Horace Bates you're looking for—and there's not often much you can do to divert 'em from their misery or their fixation or whatever it is. You just try to shepherd 'em along a little, so they don't hurt theirself or anybody else, and pass 'em on. So I passed her on.

But no, Harry Bates thought, I'm not one of those who could pass them on. I would have gotten in the car with her. Become an explorer, a wayward traveler; he saw himself as always that way. I come from a family of adventurers, he thought. I am of the line of pioneers who rumbled in their grass-sailing wagons across the plains, the Daniel Boones who slipped alone into Kentucky. I would have gone with her, I would have talked her into taking me along.

He mentioned this to Laura, and she laughed. —You were just sitting there, eh, waiting for a lady with a journey in mind.

—I believe it was something like that. A trigger.

—You've become, so you think, a priest of your own destiny.

—Well, I decided to come along. It's cost me.

—Maybe you had no choice. Maybe it was just the next thing.

—I do believe it was that, but I think the difference—the difference, I mean, between how I used to live and how I live now —is that I recognized it.

—You think that's the top. Recognition.

—I don't know. But it seemed to me something different, and better, than anything that's happened to me before.

They lay on the two mattresses in the wheelhouse. The windows were cranked open, and the night was so full of itself that it seemed any minute the stars might break loose from their mooring and drift into the cabin. Phosphorus blinked on the small wave crests. From the town—Links, Florida—they could hear faint cries from a bar down the road and hear the wind chinking softly in the seaside pines. He sat up, grasped her ankle. It was smooth and cool; his thumb fit into the hollow behind the knob of bone. —Maybe that's important, he said, recognition. What do you think?

—No, she said, that's not enough. Her mouth twisted—he could see it in the dimness—with a harshness that had begun to appear regularly. —Knowing's not enough. You have to go get. You have to go get and bring back.

—Alive?

—What?

—I'm just teasing.

—Don't tease me. She pushed his hand off her. —It's flesh and blood, she said, it's real. You have to take it in your hands again and hold it to you. You have to feel its breath on you, you have to know she's breathing.

—Who's she?

—Someone who's not a fantasy.

—Like Eureena Dell.

—We can't find her.

—Maybe not my father either.

—Oh, he's out there. He's too close to be gone.

But it wasn't of his father he thought, it was of the island girl. Heavy with the incubus child, she didn't speak of the child, only of her heaviness, and that only occasionally; she spoke more often of the amethyst light that lay above the pines at evening time, of water standing in the well bucket ("thick as syrup"), of a tree of sails, sails like white washing hanging in a tree that she saw one moonlit night from her window, a ghost ship passing, sinking below the horizon until the mainmast pennant was faint as a bird and then gone. "I am very careful now," she said. "I walk carefully, slowly, as one grown old, as one who has seen the follies of a life and nearly outlived them and now knows something of the sadness of living and of its strange wayward joys. I can sit all morning with a skein of bright yarn in my hands, turning it in my hands so that the clumsy spun texture of it receives and lets go color. I am at home, I am pleased, with the feel and shape of it, though I do not use it to make anything. Rittie, the maid, can't keep herself from pushing life onward, no matter where it comes from; she coaxes me to make something pretty and useful: 'Little boots,' she says, 'or one ob dem caps like de chile sailorsmen wear,' but I won't be tricked. I want nothing from this yarn beyond its unadorned presence. I ask nothing of it that it doesn't already give me. For a moment, at rest in my grandmother's rocker in my room, the hank of yellow yarn in my hands, I feel a peace stealing into my body. It is faint and easily frightened and will not stay. It is more delicate, and I love it more than anything in this world. . . ."

The feeling, some moment of peace. What *was* it his father had gone to find, and what was this bony beautiful woman after?

—You are a gallant man, she would say, but you are so-o-o frightened. Poor little boy. My baby.

He would look at her then as the lights of another town leaned toward them, the small nick and splash of waves returning exhausted from the sea making slight noise against the hull, and he would remember how his talented brother had called him baby— *baby, baby, baby*—and how the word had burned in his mind, tormenting and subduing him. Now it didn't matter; the word from a woman, from this woman, was sweet, beguiling. He would get up and lean out the open window and look at the town spread out along a riverbank or at the bay, whichever bay it was, sprawled like a dark body festooned with lights, and he would think of the days that had passed from him, lost now in the declensions of memory, and of the days to come, the new countries that would open to them, the new worlds and the mysteries.

In Baytown they followed the river inland until it became as clear as tap water, until passing beneath the hull they could see the long rusty grass bent all one way by the current, the mullet streaking in flashing silver schools downstream, and, once, the black body of an alligator, like a piece of darkness torn loose, gondolier tail sweeping as it surged through the clear underfirmament. In Apalachicola they spent the night in a tall wooden hotel painted the purple color of a king's robes. In the bar a leathery shrimp fisherman told them stories of lying in the jungle on Bataan as Japanese soldiers charged over his body. Like roaches, he said, they were like roaches; the hardest thing I ever had to do in my life was keep from screaming. They picked oysters off the beds inside the bay at St. Georges, and he taught her, with poles they bought at Woolworth's in Destin, to fish for speckled trout and perch.

Their bodies tanned and her dark hair absorbed streaks of sunlight so that in the morning as she leaned off the bow to draw in her line her whole head shone gold. Traveling, they went naked, pulling into the small forested river coves at night, where they roasted the fresh fish on wire grilles over a fire of willow and yaupon. On clear nights away from towns they slept out under the stars, letting the breeze and the small citronella pots they bought in Port St. Joe keep off the mosquitoes. As in St. Lukes, he would

wake in the night to find her sitting upright on the tattered
blankets, staring with fixed concentration into the dark: dark here
of tall pinewoods or glassy moon-threaded bay. She would not
speak to him then, would not answer his abrupt anxious questions
(as the next day she would not admit the incident), would only,
finally, rouse from her absorption and see him, her eyes looking at
him as if from a great and impenetrable distance, and smile, and
her hand would flutter up like the dizzy wing of a bird and touch
him, here and there, here and there, cheek, shoulder, lips, the
aching center of his body, and she would turn to him, fold her
long awkward body against his, and he would take her in his arms
and hold her hard, feeling once again, as consequence perhaps, as
necessity surely, the desire to crush her body through skin and
muscle into the beating center of him, to merge with her so
completely that there was no longer any division between them
and they were one being.

They traveled along the brief neon coasts of Alabama and Mississippi, veering northward up the wide murky bay at Mobile,
stopped outside Biloxi to walk the bayfront grounds of Jefferson
Davis's last mansion. In Gulfport, they spent a day walking the
docks, talking to shrimpers, sitting in the fall sun on the high
prows of shrimp boats as captains told them no, they had never
seen anyone who might be his father. Walking back to the boat,
where the marina owner's son pumped gas into the two flat red
tanks in the stern well, he said, We don't even know if we're
going in the right direction. For all we know, if he's still living,
Papa may have gone south. He's probably down in Miami with
his feet up on the rail of his condominium balcony, entertaining
Cuban ladies.

She wouldn't agree; she *knew*, she said, where he had gone; they
were going in the right direction. —If you know so much, he
said, why then don't we just go directly to him and save ourselves
all this traveling? —Don't you like it? she asked. And he had to
admit that he did; the days were long and easy, running through
the wide Panhandle bays, chugging up the black-water rivers,
sitting on the old wooden docks, which were often all that was
left of the past in the resort towns, watching scuffed old men fish

for flounder. —I never thought before about taking off, he told her. I figured no matter what happened I was just going to have to hunker down in St. Lukes, Florida, and take it.

Now you know you can get away, she told him, now you know how easy it is. You just have to have something to find.

They take the hearts of monkeys and put them into dying babies. I read about it in the newspaper. Soon they will use dogs, trout, even plants. They will discover, as I have, that we are interchangeable. Like cards shuffled, a new hand drawn forth from the same pictures, over and over. It is solace to me, this thought. My daughter can be created from what exists on this planet. She is available, still there, a lightning bug circulating among the willows, a piece of French toast sizzling in a pan, a cup of water, a cry. Ah, from my flesh you could make another child, but I must have this same, this same child. Come, Harry, speak to me, tell me a story so frank, so helpless, that from it my child steps forth. I lie in your arms, I lie in your hallucinatory world waiting for you to tell me a story, waiting for you to conjure my baby into the light. Tell me another story. Carry me down this shaded water trail to the place where she left me. Say her name. Make her live.

He asked about his father everywhere they went, but the questions were only provocative of other stories; he had no thought that they might find him. At first it was only something to do, a way to explain the adventure they were on; she asked it of him, proposed it and pushed him on with it, and he was willing to comply. He came to enjoy it. And he began to think that perhaps his mother had not really been looking for his father either.

"I think she just liked traveling and meeting new people," he said one night as they sat under a canopy he had rigged over the afterdeck. It was raining lightly and steadily. They couldn't hear the rain hitting the canopy, which was striped orange and white —a parachute he had bought from an army-navy store—but water dripped from the edges of the cloth. The boat was anchored in shallow water below the city docks in New Orleans. In the river two tugs formed up a line of barges. "I don't think she had any intention of finding Papa," he said. "She just liked getting in the car and riding out to see people."

Laura smiled as if she had known this all along. Her coarse brown hair was pulled back in a ponytail. She wore lime pedal pushers and a pink blouse patterned with small white flying birds, sea gulls. He thought she looked like a housewife from the fifties. "Then aren't you glad you couldn't stop her?" she said.

"I never realized."

He got up, carefully lifted the sagging cloth, and let the water run out over the gunwales. "Maybe it was mission work," he said.

"What is that?"

"She was planning to go to China as a missionary when my father met her. He talked her out of it. Or gave her something better."

He had never been able to picture his mother, who was tall and blond, with the body of a distance runner, who would not during his childhood attend church even on feast days and holy days, being a missionary to anyone. Maybe he had gotten the story wrong. "My father always told me she was set to be a missionary. She was going to Canton, I think. A lay worker; the next thing to being a nun."

His father told him once that the day he met his mother he had gone down to the Ford dealer and bought the first car he ever owned. Until that day, he said, taxis and foot travel would do, but not after meeting his mother. "I wanted to ride in a big car," his father told him. "I wanted to drive up to her house in a shiny new automobile." Harry understood that feeling. For Laura he wanted to show progress in the search for his father; he wanted to change his life for her—if not *for* her, then while he was in her company. Goodbye St. Lukes, he thought, goodbye lawyering, goodbye family and friends. Now there was only Laura, and the girl Eureena, and their larky quest.

The river was a sullen brown, and bits of debris floated on the surface. The previous day, when he rose at dawn, he had seen a dead cow floating past, its white belly swollen. At night they wandered around the Quarter, looking into shops and stopping in bars for a soft drink. He felt the urge to drink something stronger, but for the time being he let it go. There was a bar that played Bach's concerto for oboe and violin on the jukebox. It had a courtyard in back where lemon trees flowered beside a low stone fountain. The waiter told them the courtyard and fountain were all that remained from the house of a Creole princess who had been murdered by her lover. A tourist story, but he was pleased to hear it told. They liked to sit near the lemon trees, listening to the water splash the stones. They would stay there for hours, leaning into their chairs without talking, letting the sweet orange drinks go warm on the table before them, like soldiers exhausted from battle, or like family members worn out from quarreling, or only, maybe, in the sweetness of rest. The common inhabited world seemed a strange place, the conversations, the obligations untranslatable, the actions obscure. He watched a woman at a nearby table fanning herself, and the white hand gripping the lacquered tines, the crust of thin bracelets shaking on her veined wrist, for a moment, took on an orphic significance, as if, beyond her and because of her, there might begin to appear from the shadows of the bar mixed colored figures moving in a small trans-figuring dance. He knew Laura delighted in those who lived apart, in the street musicians and the tap dancers, in the prostitutes lounging on balconies in Rousseau Street, in the man in a red nightshirt they caught a glimpse of through a gate grille, weeping as he chased a small gray cat across a courtyard strewn with pieces of blue and yellow confetti. The nights, their long silences, the dense perfumed air, would put him in a stupor, so that, like one drunk, he would not, some nights, know how he got home. Off Jackson Square was a bakery where they would stop for coffee and sweet rolls. The smell of baking, the floury handprint on the dark-blue counter, the soft yellow lights falling into the street, the sound of the breeze shifting its weight in the acacia trees, made them happy. Or they made him happy. Even on the quiet nights he could see on her face the lines of her distraction, which he wanted to erase.

He slung himself into the lawn chair beside hers, articles they had shopped for together in a store in Biloxi. He touched her unshaven calf, ran his hand to her ankle. He said, "If you went for a missionary I would go too. I'd convert those heathens like there was no tomorrow."

She smiled and looked away across the river, toward the far shore a mile distant, where the low shapes of warehouses hunkered. "I'm afraid," she said.

"Of what?"

"Of what's waiting for me."

"It's nothing but open water and new towns. The bayous are lovely, like derelict parks."

She shifted in her chair, pulled her leg away from his touch. A small trembling slipped across her thin lips. "No," she said. "That's your prospect, not mine."

"We're together; it's for both of us."

"I shouldn't have made this up."

"I think it was the perfect thing to do."

"You like everything."

"Everything with you in it."

"A man about to be executed by his neighbors . . ."

"What is that?"

"I don't know—a thought. It just came to me."

"You mean me?"

"Why not? Isn't that your story?"

"I don't think they cared enough to execute me."

"When I met you you'd just been thrown off a boat."

"When you met me I was sitting behind a mahogany desk in a law office."

"About to be executed?"

"No. Not yet. Though I guess that's what it felt like."

She drew her legs up, hugged her knees. The drift of mist under the streetlights, the cries from the late streets that slipped away from the docks like empty-handed thieves, the faint smell of burning rubber, seemed not part of a new life but only a harangue on the old. She licked her kneecap, said, "Read me from the book."

He took the ledger from the satchel, opened it, and reinserted the pages he had torn out. "There's not much left," he said.

"She's the mother of her father's child." There was a small note of wonder in her voice.

"Yes."

"Read me that."

"She never says it."

"What does she say?"

"Now she's talking about the birth pain."

"Good."

This: "Such a clever, conniving pain. It's as if all my life and history are gathered in this moment. It is pain and a summary of pain. There is no defense against it, and the oddness and shame of this most common experience, this bringing forth of new life into the world, which is the one act that should most closely join us to God himself, is an experience that when it takes place we defy and resist with every fiber in our being, body and soul. I have never wanted anything to stop so much—not my father's hands, not the morning after, when I woke in his big bed and saw on the lawn the gathering of winter robins, come like an army of rude scavengers onto our lawns, not the day when I knew there would be no home for me in this world. This was greater, more terrifying, this did not so much take me by the hand or speak to me as hurl me headlong into the animal mud. I screamed until my throat tore, screams that if they were heard would have torn the eardrums of a god. I was only a beast after all, grunting out my get on the ground. A creature of slime and blood and groans. I begged Rittie to kill me, to strangle me, to place—it appeared to me this way —her small hands around my neck and crush the life out of my throat. I didn't care for life or myself, or the bonny murderous world; only that the pain stop. The shuttered room was so dark. The lamp beside the bed smoked and bubbled in its chimney. I could smell the whale oil in the wick, a swampish, colicky smell —or so it seemed to me—and then I could smell my body, the rich, grassy odors that were no different from the birth odors of a cow or a horse. I sank, falling through the subterranean rooms without the means to save myself, falling until a moment came when I could feel the muscles in my limbs again, and I began to swim, like a puppy tossed into a pond, wildly for the surface. And then down again, paralyzed, sinking. It is a pummeling I think

now that makes it possible for us to accept this monstrous creation that the midwife places at last in our arms. If by the time
she was born I had one ounce of resistance left I would have
dashed the cheesy bantling against the wall. But there was
nothing left of me. I would have loved a stone if that was all I
bore."

They sat in the random city silence. Mosquitoes whined. Beyond them, in the darkness, the river hauled its ancient tarnished
body to the sea. On the far shore the scattered lights looked like
sucked candies. She spoke, but the sounds cracked in her throat.
She said, "What happens next? What comes after?"

"They take the baby away from her, her father does. Then the
diary stops."

"Yes," she said, "it stops."

"Have you read it?"

She didn't answer. She placed her palms on her face and with
her fingers pressed hard against her forehead. The pressure left red
marks. She pushed herself up harshly from the chair, tipping it.
"Come on," she said. "We have to go."

"We have to leave?"

"No, you idiot. We have to go. Come on."

Without looking at him again, she pulled a shawl around her
shoulders and left the boat, walking fast. He put the lantern out
and followed her.

It calls me now, a voice rising. My husband would not let me go
back into the house to see her. I let him take me away when I
should have fought with all my strength to stay. But not seeing
her, I don't know. Yes, I do know. On my hands, my body; all
my flesh is strange to me; I want to become a skeleton, air. Corpus
Christi. The body of Christ. The body of my child. Olivia. Can it
be? The truth will not come to me. It hovers in the air above me,
this damselfly of truth. Her eyes were brown as honey. She had
two stars in the center of her right palm, a small gray birthmark
like a flake of ash above the left ankle. Her hair was gold, her
forehead was high and clear, her mouth long and full. She had

broad shoulders like me and that boniness that runs in the Dell family. She said my name, Hora, Hora, like "time" in Spanish. I have waited through my madness to do this, to return to the place where I lost her, but now I am afraid to go. We lived in a board-and-batten cottage on Sand Street. There was a large oleander by the front door. My husband let her eat the flowers, which are poison. It was not the first time I had run away; it was not the first time being a mother and a wife became too much for me. I would wander the streets of the barrio; I would go into bars where I was the only woman and drink and play the jukebox. All the Mexican songs were sad and sentimental, mourning loss. Oh, my sweetheart, they cried, why have you abandoned me? Oh, my child, my body. Grief is a dark heavy hand, pressing me down, pressing me to the floor. I must rise up and seek my child. It is the only thing that can save me. I must find her where she lives in the trees of New Orleans. She swims in the shallow coves; she lets the gray sand run through her fingers. This grief will kill me else. What now besides finding could save me? This man I let like a stray dog into my house? His lovely stories? No poet ever saved anyone. I went out to the garden and dug her grave, but I had nothing to put in it. I could dig forever and never find her or fill the hole. What does she live on now—on air? On light? On the salt of the sea? I ran away. I let my husband lead me to the car and take me to Oregon. That shallow frightened man, that escape artist. He blew his brain blood onto the walls of a motel bathroom. There, too, outside the door, the sea ran and fetched. I washed my hands in salt water. The blood made a scarf around my hands, a scarf that drifted away, lost itself in the sea. I bang on the gates of the city: Let me in! Let me in! But when the aged porter draws the creaking bolt, I shrink away, terrified, smirking and bowing, unable to enter. Oh, darling, darling, darling, I would tear the flesh off my bones to remake yours. Here, take my hands, my arms, my breasts, my bones—take all you need of me as you did in those sweet days when you rocked beneath my heart. Let me make you again, here on the earth, out in air, in the field where I stood while the meadowlarks sang their silly songs. What is my body for, what is all this love for, if not to give you life, if

not to raise you up sleek and smiling from the dark well of the
world?

On foot, by taxi, then on foot again, they crossed the city. The
bells of streetcars rang, the rocking lighted carriages lumbered
down the center of the streets. A man in vague clothes, pushing a
cart, called out to them to buy his tamales. A bucket of crab shells
clattered into a trash can. The great old trees, oaks hung with
moss, more formal than houses, seemed sibyls of another world,
holding fast to some aged philosophy that had nothing to do with
the workings of human beings. They came to streets of small
wooden houses, of small stores on the corners with screen doors
that banged as people went in and out. An old horse trough was
tipped on its side and leaned against the wall of a house. Cabbage
palms, their tops torn out, stood like empty light posts at the
edge of the street. There were gaps in the pavement that sand and
spurrey weeds sprouted through. The air smelled peppery and
sour, and even this late it was still hot, like laundry steam on
their faces.

At a closed gas station where flattened oil cans had been nailed
over the doors and the windows had been boarded with plywood,
they turned down a narrow street that had been paved once in
bricks but now was covered with a gritty scurry of sand, as if a
dune had sneaked into town and collapsed there. The lime radi-
ance of a few streetlights revealed the cockeyed unpainted houses
with their sagging porches, where even in dimness he could see
the night-flowering vines hanging like remnants from the eaves
and hear the soft waft of conversations as men and women rocked
in the darkness. It was late, but there were still children out; a
couple of small boys ran ahead of them, and on a broken raft of
sidewalk a lone girl skipped one-legged through the figures of a
complicated hopscotch. Winded, he slowed and spoke to her,
thinking of his life at home after dark, when he walked the streets
of the sea town peering into shopwindows, weighing like an obscure trader the heaps of merchandise. Ahead, a boy in pale shirttails shouted a warning at someone dashing across a vacant lot. "I

think," Harry said, as if they had been in conversation all along
—instead of hurrying through streets silently like a couple under
the banner of a demented drive that must break or die—"I think
I've been a kind of child all my life; one of those little boys who
didn't want the supper bell to call them home. I think what I'm
lonely for isn't something out in the world at all but just something that used to be in me, or something I used to do, like one
of the games these kids play."

There was an urgency in him, but it was not the urgency of
their errand; it was something else entirely, a desire for explanation and then rest.

"I almost don't know where it is," she said. "Can you imagine
that?"

"What? What are we looking for?"

"Don't you know?"

"How would I know?"

"Haven't you paid any attention at all?"

"Ugh. They used to say that to me when I was a kid."

"No wonder you never got out of that little burg."

As she walked she brushed her arms rapidly, as if she were
skeeting off bugs. Her long skirt of varicolored Indian cotton
rippled against her legs. She wore one of her old straw hats, musty
from the trunk, tied by a red ribbon around her throat and thrown
down her back.

She started to cross the street and stopped.

"What is it?"

She cocked her head, looking at a white wooden housefront
across the street. She said, "Is that balcony red?"

He looked at the long section of iron grillwork extending off
the second-floor porch. There was a face, a god's or lion's head, in
the center of it. "It might be."

She ran her hand over her face. "What has come over me? Why
is this so difficult?"

"What are you trying to do?"

She whirled on him. "Would you just shut up? Would you just
either shut up or haul your sorry carcass on down the road?"

"No," he said. "What's going on?"

She struck him, her wrist catching him in the neck, her painted fingernails just nicking his cheek. He staggered back in surprise. "What in the hell are you doing?"

She swung to face him. "You're just a rider," she cried. "You haven't got what it takes to participate."

"What are you talking about? I'm the one who lit out with his brother's boat."

"Ha!"

"Ha? Laura, what's the matter with you?" He couldn't believe she would turn on him. It was as if a cold hand had reached into his guts and was fumbling around in there.

She stepped toward him, her arm raised as if, awkwardly, she were about to throw something at him. He moved backward, but then he stopped. He didn't really mind if she hit him.

She swung and he caught her wrist. She twisted, sinking on her knees, as if he was hurting her. He let her go, but as he did so she came up with her other hand, rising, fist closed, and caught him in the shoulder. Then she struck at him fiercely, her head thrown back, the bottoms of her fists and her arms hacking against his chest. This is okay, he thought; let her get through this. Then one of the blows caught him just below the ear, and for a second, on his feet, he went out. It was brief, he didn't even stagger, but then, without realizing he had been gone, he returned from a distance, as if from another room. Like a man waking from ether he stared into her face, which was, for a second, unrecognizable. He saw the hewn mask of her anger, the blotches in her cheeks, the dark diagonal eyebrows that seemed to stab into the clenched space between her eyes. He raised his hand to fend her off, but then he let the hand fall. A couple of children leaned against a car, watching them.

"All right," he said. "All right."

The blows thumped against him and subsided. She dropped her arms and stood before him breathing hard. Her hair strung over her face. He thought: Well, now we'll be quiet; now everything will calm down. He could feel the blows on his body still, like bruises, and thought of Eureena, of her body ripped by the child. Her father had taken the child away, and then the diary stopped. People vanish. Love dies.

"Do you feel any better?" he said.

She didn't answer, only turned away toward the house across the street. A light burned behind green curtains in a downstairs room. There were a few blossoming oleanders in the yard. Their white flowers looked like small absences in the dark leaves. He said, "I don't know where my father went. If I ever find out, it won't be anything I do. It isn't like being an orphan, where you can trace the mystery to its source. There's no agency to contact. He disappeared."

It was as if he recognized something. She took a step toward the house. He touched her arm. "You try to tell yourself that because the mystery can't be solved it must not be that important. But it is important. Sometimes it is almost everything. But still you can't solve it."

She looked at him. Her eyes, hooded and shadowed by the streetlight, were dark. There was no color in them at all, though there was a brightness like fever. A tiny bead of spittle was trapped in the corner of her mouth. "Who are you?" she said. "What are you doing?"

She ran toward the house. Startled, he followed behind her, up the narrow walk poorly paved in oyster shells. She skirted the side and disappeared, heading for the back. There were tangles of wire and old appliances in the narrow alleyway between the house and a small weathering building next door. He stumbled, caught himself against the clapboard wall. Paint flaked under his fingers. He heard a screen door slam, and then he heard a woman—not Laura —scream. The backyard was paved in brick. The bricks were slimy, purple under a naked porch light. A baby carriage, its top furled, was pushed against the door. He thrust it aside and entered the house, entered a kitchen that was filled with the smells of baking and boiled milk. A child, a girl of six or seven, sat on her knees at a card table in the center of the room. She was just rising to look toward an open doorway beside the stove. There was a white scum of milk on her upper lip. He didn't speak to her, but as he rushed past he patted her on the head. Her hair was blond and tightly kinked; it felt like wool under his hand. A sound of scuffling, cries, came from the other room. He called her name, thinking as he called of the other names, of Eureena, of his father, of his mother struck into silence in an orange grove in south Florida. The doorway led into a short hall, the bare boards of which—clapboard like the outside of the house—were painted lime green. The sounds came from a room at the end. Hoarse breathing now, without cries. He reached the doorway. Inside, two women fought. Laura and a young blond woman, barely out of her teens, grappled in each other's arms. On the bed, laid on a square of yellow satin cloth, was a naked baby. Its hair was black and shiny; it raised its arms, crying. The women struggled, grasping each other around the shoulders. There were red scratches on the blond woman's face. She grunted, shoving her weight against Laura, who was trying to turn her, or was trying to turn away from her, toward the baby on the bed.

"Here now," he cried, beside himself. "Stop this."

There was a wild tension in his body, and a stiff bent strangeness as if his bones were made of stamped tin.

They careened against him; for an instant he held them both in his arms, for an instant he could feel the heat of the blond woman's body, her slender bony shoulders, her sharp elbow, which nestled briefly in the cup of his palm like a joint groping its socket. He shoved them, trying to create a space between them; he thrust his arm against Laura's back, reaching to turn her. Her shoulder flinched—to shake him off—and the blond woman, for a second almost released, pushed her with both hands, so that her legs crossed. Her arm flew up, like a wing, she punched with the other hand at the blond woman and fell hard, her shoulder smashing into the baby's face. He heard the crunch of it. And he heard the blond woman's scream, which was the scream of pure loss and torment, and in his mind the lights seemed to fade against the green walls.

He pulled her up then, dragging her to her feet as she flailed, as she cried out the name she had first spoken in her bedroom in St. Lukes, but there was no real strength in her, none that could prevent him as the young woman fell to her knees beside the bed and scooped the baby into her arms, nothing in that frail house that could stop him from dragging her out, through hallway and kitchen, past the small girl standing now in her chair crying, nothing beyond the back door, where the empty carriage teetered like something about to take flight on the edge of the porch, nothing in the yard, no tangle of corroded fence wire, no broken washing machine with one torn sock still caught in its roller, no dogbane-perfumed oleander bushes, no street of New Orleans easy-living folk just rustling into life, no tree-humped shaded avenues, no tourist neon, no floribunda rose like a banner swagged down the face of a rich man's house, no cry of street peddler or dancing silver-toed feet, nothing in that city on the ancient river of rivers, nothing in that swampy lit world that could bar his way —nothing.

He had no words for her, no strength to propose an alternative. The lights glittered on the water. Before long it would be winter; the worn grass would fade to blond, the river would darken, robins worn by long flight would appear in the sandy yards. On a Sunday afternoon he would go over to his brother's house and help him plant the boxwood he had selected to fill the gap below the porch. With Martha in the back seat, they would drive up the coast to Wilderness Beach, where when they were children their father had taken them goose hunting. They would look for the spot where their father had erected the blinds out of reed and palm fronds, but they wouldn't find it. Once, the bay was filled with life, and even now you might see an eagle perched in the bare branches of a ruined cypress, or an osprey crossing in long carol of flight the yellow marshes, or hear the faint crash of deer moving in the thicket, but more often this world of coastal marsh and woods was empty. It held a hesitant air of contingency yet, as though what had abandoned it might still, if you pushed only a little farther into the complicated woods, be sighted, but the woods were deep and thick with briers, and no one would search there. They would walk a ways down the faded beach, they might take off their shoes and wade a few steps into the clear, faintly rustling surf, and for a time, briefly, they would stand there, side by side, forgetting grievances for a moment, or forgetting to pursue them, looking out toward the grassy islands, and if it seemed they were, almost, watching for something, it was as if, almost, they were allowing something to look for them too, even though in a moment they would turn back to the shore where Martha chatted amiably with a couple driven up from Tampa for the day, almost absent to what ruled them as men and brothers, two who, like the rest of us, might not in this long life come near resolution or the completion of the understanding that saints and heroes claim to know, but who nonetheless breathed on, two aging brothers, joined as always in the frail but enduring simulacrum, human love.

It took four hours to reach the open Gulf. He didn't question her, and later he was happy with himself for this. There was a point, he thought, beyond thinking and understanding, and it pleased him to believe that they had reached it. From the carnival of the city that spilled in a traffic of barges and tugs into the river, they passed slowly through the marshlands of the delta, riding the edge of the channel, which was marked by lighted buoys and by the derelict remains of abandoned vessels, traveling toward the deeper dark beyond the wide spilled skirts of the exhausted river into the salty unmeasured haven of the Gulf. When at last they had sailed beyond the final marker lights and the sea opened before them under its net of white-faced stars, he tied the wheel and joined her on the bow. Her skirts drawn around her knees, she stared forward toward the horizon, where the black continent of ocean joined the black continent of sky. The red bow light faintly flooded and drained her face. They didn't talk. After a while she said, "Let's ride in the water," and he, understanding, said all right. As her clothes dropped about her feet, he was struck again in sweet fascination by the beauty of her lanky bone-ruled body, by the awkwardness and by the delicacy of the spirit that stirred the shabby form of her. It was as if—he had realized it the first time he touched her, or even before, when she sank into the chair across the office desk from him—something infinitely fragile peeped and clucked from amid the messy declarations of her flesh, and it was this—with her determination, and her helpless refusal to bend, her stupid madness—that made him love her. She was as hapless as he was.

He followed her down, hand over hand down the bow line into the warm gorge of the sea. The boat churned steadily, slowly onward. They rode, fully immersed, on either side of the bow, their bodies flagging behind, dragged through the warmth and darkness like trolled human bait. "Are you all right?" he said. "Yes," she answered. "I'm fine." The sky was wild with stars. When she reached around the bow, through the light purl of froth for his hand, he was grateful. The long night bent them onward through the easy southern sea. She held his hand in hers. It seemed hours before she let go.

Crystal

River

WAS ON the back porch washing greens when Harold drove around the side of the house with a stolen canoe on top of the truck and a bushel of oysters in back.

"I thought you were down fishing on the flats," I said as he came up the steps with the oysters in a sack over his shoulder. "Your mama said you'd be down there all week."

"That's right," he said. "I was planning to."

He dropped the sack and pulled half a dozen oyster knives out of his pocket. "Throw that stuff out," he said, looking at the greens. "We need to put these babies in the sink."

"Just a minute," I said.

I lifted the sopping greens in a mass and mashed them into a pot. "Let me put them on the stove."

"Just put them in the fridge," he said. "We'll need the pot."

I went into the kitchen, found a couple of ham hocks in the refrigerator, and put them with the greens to simmer. When I came back Harold was dumping oysters into the sink.

"Where'd you get the cuties?" I asked.

"Panacea. And they are just delicious."

"Did you try one?"

"Of course. You got horseradish?"

"Sure."

I went inside and got it out of the fridge.

"We got to clean these things off first," he said when I set horseradish, Tabasco, ketchup, saltines, bowls, and forks on the plank beside the sink. "You remember those oysters we got in Savannah?"

"The muddy ones?"

"Yeah. We had to wash them all afternoon."

"They were good."

"Ugm."

He had poured most of the bushel into the sink. I mixed sauce in a bowl, selected the shortest of the knives, and began to open.

"You want one?" I said.

"You crazy?" He speared the biggest one with a fork, dipped it in sauce, and ate it without a cracker.

"Christ," he said. "Nobody but you can eat your sauce."

"I like it hot."

"You sure do." Gold sand stuck to his wrists and to the backs of his hands.

"How come you came back from the flats?" I said.

"Teddy got sick." Teddy was his brother, a pill addict and drunkard with a penchant for rifling the medicine cabinets of any house he happened to be in and swallowing whatever he found that might carry a charge. "He was mixing wine and phenobarbs —I had to carry him in this morning to get him pumped out."

"Jesus. Is he okay?"

"Yeah, he's fine, fine as Teddy gets. But it knocked us off the flats. On the way back I stopped for this bushel, and I figured that since I was already primed for a trip I'd come over and see if you wanted to go down Crystal River. You want to?"

"It might be a nice idea. Where'd you get the canoe?" It had FORT BENNING REC. DEPT. stenciled on the bow. There were a couple of deep dents in the aluminum near the center.

"It's one I relocated from the army," he said.

"Didn't they miss it?"

"I told them I lost it on the Toccoa. The water was too high, and when we went under it got away from us and we couldn't catch it."

"Sounds like a rough trip."

"Terrible."

He went out to the truck and came back with a bag of ice that he dumped over the cleaned oysters in the sink. "There," he said, tossing the bag on the floor and picking up a knife. "I'm ready to go. Come here, you sweet succulents."

"Hold on a second," I said.

I went in the house and got the vodka out of the freezer.

"Now you're talking," he said as I set the bottle on the shelf behind the sink.

We stood at the sink shucking oysters and sipping vodka, looking out through the screen at the warm March sunshine leaning into the garden. The cocker pup from next door came up the steps and scratched at the door, and I let him in. He curled up under the sink and went to sleep.

We ate through the end of the afternoon into the evening.

At five the Amtrak train roared by down beyond the garden fence on its way to Miami. From the porch we could see passengers eating supper in the dining car.

Later we drove up to the store for milk and came back and made a stew. We ate the stew, with a side dish of greens, at my worktable in the dining room, then went back out on the porch and finished the rest of the oysters. They were delicious to the end, cold and salty, full of sea water.

"It's like eating the ocean," Harold said as he banged a last, hard-to-open shell on the lip of the sink. "That's what I told Lola."

"She like oysters?"

"Not much. I had to turn them into poetry to get her to try the first one."

"Ugm. Frieda was like that."

"Wouldn't eat them?"

"Not at first. Then she couldn't do without them. The last time I saw her we went down to Apalachicola and she outate me by half. Finished sixty-three and eight bottles of Blue Ribbon."

"I guess she got the hang of it. You going to see each other anymore?"

"No. The divorce'll be final in two weeks, and I don't expect we'll have much to talk about after that. Everything's been settled."

But then I could see her that minute. Leaning over the hoe to pluck a flower from a potato vine. Awkward city girl, I yell, and she swings around to agree with sighs of exasperation. It's so, isn't it; I don't know what to do, she would say, and I would get up from the steps, cross the garden, and take her in my arms, saying,

No, I take it back; forget the garden. And I would drop to the
ground and kiss her knees as she threaded the flower into my hair.

"I'll miss her," Harold said.

"Well, you ought to go see her."

"I probably will."

"Give her my love."

"You betcha."

We finished the oysters and dumped the shells into the sack.
Harold took the sack out to the garbage. I carried the vodka into
the living room, lighted the lantern, and when Harold came back,
we had a final drink sitting in the wicker chairs in front of the
empty fireplace.

"It's getting colder," Harold said. "It'll be cold tomorrow."

"You think we'll be all right on the river?"

"I don't see why not. You've got your duck bag, don't you?"

"Yes. What about you?"

"I just got a piece of cotton, but I can wrap up in a poncho."

We finished the drinks, I blew the lantern out, and we went
into the bedroom and got into my bed.

I woke during the night with Harold's hand in my groin.

"I can't sleep," he said.

"All right."

I turned around, slid down under the quilt, and, as I had done
so many times since our childhood, took him in my mouth. He
smelled just like a woman. I sucked him until he was ready to
come, then pulled away and let him catch it in his hand.

"Have you got a towel?" he said when he finished.

"In the bathroom."

He got up and got it.

"I was horny," he said when he had crawled across me and slid
back under the covers.

"Ugm."

"You want to come?"

"I don't think I can."

"Don't you feel bad?"

"I don't feel much of anything."

We hadn't turned on the lights. I kissed him on the lips, rolled
away and went to sleep.

11

I LAY IN bed in the first gray light thinking: I am a man here, I inhabit this life. I heard Harold rummaging in the kitchen. The morning train came through, bound for Chicago, rattling the windowpanes. I reached over my head and touched vibrating glass. This hooks me into that run too, I thought. I'm plucked onto the line too.

"I think we ought to make this the rule, Harold," I called.

He stuck his head in the door. He had on my old felt hunting hat.

"Make what?" he said.

"Your getting up early to take care of things."

"Jack, my boy," he said, pulling the hat down fore and aft, "I was just getting my turn out of the way. Don't you have any pots?"

"They're under the sink."

I got up, pulled shirt, pants, and sweater out of a pile on the dresser, and put them on.

He was throwing cans of food into a cardboard box on the dining room table when I came out.

"Got to get some Viennas," he said. "Can't go into the wilderness without Vienna sausage."

"And saltines," I said. "Jesus, it's cold." I opened the refrigerator and looked in. "Did we drink all the vodka?"

"Don't start that. We got to stay sober until noon at least."

"Okay." I took the pot of greens out. Liquid broke the gray rind of pork grease as I set it on the table.

"You want coffee?" I said.

"I wouldn't mind it."

I fired the percolator and went into the bathroom. Through the window I could see frost in the garden. Broccoli and peas bent over by cold. No Frieda there. Here, only Harold and I, in the oldest of partnerships, still rubbing up the life between us. I collected my kit. When I flushed the toilet I could hear water running onto the ground below the house.

We drank coffee and ate cold greens from the pot. Harold didn't mention last night, and I didn't bring it up either; we had long since stopped talking about those things. But when I got up to go into the bedroom for my gear I bent in passing and kissed him, lightly, on the crown of his head. He looked up from his bowl of greens with amused eyes. "Run one out and run another one in," he said. "That's how it works."

"Yeah, boy," I said.

In the bedroom I stuffed clothes into a plastic bag and got my tent and sleeping bag from the closet.

Harold carried the box of food to the truck and put it in the back.

"Anything else?" he said.

"Snackers."

"We can stop at the store."

Behind us the sun was climbing into pines as we pulled out on the road. Davis Kreps, my across-the-street neighbor, pulled himself in his wheelchair one-handed along his front porch toward the day's first warm spot. I waved to him across Harold's lap. His good hand came up, and he shouted something I couldn't catch.

"Davis is drunk already," Harold said, throwing a wave.

"He's never undrunk," I said.

We passed the House That Never Spoke, Willis Faver's old family place he had let fall back into a ruin of weeds and bamboo after his mother died, and pulled up under a tasseling yellow pine in front of the store.

"Have you ever been in Willis's mama's place?" I asked.

"No."

"He didn't even take the curtains down after she died. Everything's still there. There's a pump organ in the living room and hand-painted pictures on the walls."

"Hand-painted, huh?"

"And out in the shed bamboo's grown up between the bumper and the fender of his mama's old Buick."

"I'd like to have that."

"Me too." The gassed-up memory.

We pushed through the door, into the store.

Fruit—oranges, apples, tangelos—was piled in bins along the wall, bright as lights. Old potatoes in wire-footed racks, eyes sprouting. Frosty glassed-in drinks. An old redheaded woman, Mrs. Harley Cantrell, was eating cheese and crackers off a newspaper behind the counter.

We want snackers: olives, green and black; pork rinds; canned boiled peanuts; kosher pickles; hot sausages—could we have half a pound of rat cheese, please?

"I got pickled eggs in the truck," Harold said.

"Mrs. Cantrell," I said, "you ever pickle eggs?"

"I wouldn't have them in the house," Mrs. Cantrell said, smiling. "Where you boys off to?"

"Crystal River."

"That down in Florida?" she said, not too enthusiastically.

"Yes'm."

She pushed a wisp of hair out of her eyes with the back of her wrist, stacked a cracker with cheese, and stuffed it into her mouth.

"I never ate a pickled egg in my life," she said through the mouthful. "That's drinking trash."

"Kept in a jar in the Ponderosa Sugarhouse," Harold said, "right between the pigs' feet and the parched peanuts."

"That I couldn't say. This be all?" she said to the pile on the counter.

"Believe so," I said. We each paid half, pulling bills from front pockets.

"You got enough money?" I said on the way out.

"For what?"

"Beer. Goodies."

"Sure."

Blossoms floated in the branches of a dogwood near the street. Two small boys, shirts flapping, pedaled full speed toward town.

"We can get beer at the line," I said. "Save cash."

"You betcha."

We slipped south through town out into a country of low pastures and thick horizon-hampering woods. Live oaks and cypress hung over black-water ponds. Cabbage palms dying around a red house. A black man peering from an outhouse door.

Ferns sprung green in fire-blackened woods. They're like blueberries in fired fields up north. Come out of nowhere.

"Harold, have you ever eaten a dog?" I said.

Harold plucked his crotch and said that no, he never had, but he had certainly wanted to.

"It's white meat," I said. "Sweeter than pork."

"I'd like to eat Mama's Chihuahua," he said. "You eat a lot of it?"

"Only on my travels."

At the top of a rise we passed a sign that said: FLORIDA STATE LINE. Across the road from a barn yellow with moss. Silver crocus faded among rusted farm implements.

"The very first bar, Harold," I said.

"I got my eyes open."

We flashed down oak-canopied roads, the canoe an aluminum awning shading our eyes.

A blue-shingled store at the edge of a persimmon orchard rose into view.

"Here it is," I said.

Harold pulled up in a flurry of gravel. We broke from the truck, tucking in shirttails and striding. What a cold, clear morning, a few clouds like spuds above the trees. Persimmon leaves unfolding big as oranges.

"A case of Blue Ribbon and a furburger," Harold said to the unshaven man in overalls behind the counter.

"And a what?" the man said.

"Nothing," Harold said. "I thought it was a fly."

The man looked at him and stepped into the back and returned with the case. We paid and I lugged it to the truck.

"Where'd you say the pickled eggs were?"

"In a box in the back."

I pulled the gallon jar out and set it on the seat between us. The beer went on the floor under my feet. I ripped the cardboard open, plucked out two, opened them, and handed one to Harold.

"Here you go," I said.

He pulled out on the highway and accelerated to sixty before he took a sip.

"Good as springtime," he said.

"Fine with me."

I let my arm out into the air, making signals at empty fields.

III

THE RIVER boiled out of a spring just south of a shade tobacco town on the Panhandle. It ran forty miles, clear as tap water, through the woods to the Gulf at St. Lukes. You could sit in a boat in the river and watch blunt silver mullet race upstream over grass and white sandbeds. The sand looked firm until you stepped out on it. Then you sank halfway to your knees into an underlayer of coffee-colored mud. In high-water season the river flooded the woods so that unless you swung hammocks between the trees there were few places to camp. Pickerel grew in the still water near the banks, and hyacinths floated in clumps in the stream.

We pulled up in grass behind the high diving board and got out. Harold jumped out of the truck, ran up the diving ladder, and looked down into the water.

"These are the ears of the earth," he said. He hopped one-legged to the end of the board and emptied his beer into the spring. "A little poison, dear," he said, "to help you sleep." He unzipped his pants and pissed into the water, leaning back to make a high arc. The urine splashed and made a froth on the water.

"Did I tell you I once pissed off the flying bridge of a cargo ship?" I said.

"No. did you hit anybody?"

"Just a crate of chickens."

"This piss," Harold said, zipping up, "will mingle with waters that flow untrammeled to the sea. My body is now part of the stream, I am the stream, I am a dream of water running."

"From a tap all night."

"Every time I flushed your fucking toilet," he said, "water ran out on the ground. You must have a lush little cesspool under the house." He climbed down and came over to the truck. I was untying the canoe.

"My mushroom garden," I said.

"I'd like to keep Lola there," he said. "Squatted, naked."

"We could have her duckwalk around the backyard in the nude, eating radishes."

He squatted and quacked. " 'Harold, can I get up now?' 'No, Lola. Keep walking.' " He duckwalked to the back of the truck. " 'But, darling,' " he squealed, holding on to the tailgate. " 'My knees hurt.' Did you ever get Frieda to duckwalk?"

"Yes, I did, duck and crab. I made her do it in panty hose, wearing a wig. She loved everything I made her do." Where was she—blond and speaking Italian? "Harold," I said, "do you think there is a timeless quality to rural life?"

"Yeah. Timeless and shitless."

We lifted the canoe off the truck, flipped it, and carried it to the water. Minnows darted away from the bank as we slid it in. We loaded our supplies and covered them with a poncho.

"Did you bring paddles?" I said.

"I reckon I must have." He lifted the canvas tarp in the truckbed. "Here they are."

Harold was heavier, but because I was more experienced, I took the stern. He got in, and I shoved the bow around into the river. I stepped in and pushed us off, the toe of my boot catching in the water. When we were out in the stream I shipped the paddle and let the canoe drift. Harold hunched forward in the bow, his collar up around his ears. The sky was clouding over.

"Imagine that you are De Soto," he said without turning around. "This is what you would have seen." He swung his arm toward cattails and grasses that grew against the far bank. Behind them leafless hardwoods and evergreens tangled with pines.

"De Soto was going the other way."

"I'm sure he had to turn around somewhere."

I uncovered the case and took out two beers. "Here you go," I said, and when he turned around tossed one to him. I held us steady in the current. The river was shallow. We passed over rusty grasses flowing our way. Up ahead a mullet jumped like a spit seed, landed on its side, and disappeared. I turned the cold bottle in my hands and leaned forward into a sip.

I could conjure Frieda spinning into sunlight on this cold day. Weeping at a hotel desk in the Yucatán. Do you want to ride in a carriage? No, no, no. Thick hair on her forearms, her nipples still pink at thirty. Frieda, are you throwing snowballs outside Denver? Are you traveling by train through the mountains? My stomach turned to think of her. We must be careful today not to splash each other. The sky is almost completely clouded over. High, heavy, light-deceiving clouds.

"What we need is wine," I said.

"Wine?" He turned around.

"Yeah. With beer you have to stop, because it's awkward to paddle with a bottle, but with wine we could just pause for a sip and go on."

"Maybe we can get some."

"There're no stores on this river."

"That's right."

I set the beer between my feet and began to paddle.

I V

W E H I T Goose Pasture in the afternoon. You round a reedy bend and there it is: a grassy peninsula backed by pines. Two nylon camp tents perched on the bank above the river. A girl stood in front of one of them with her arms stretched above her head. She was naked.

"Jesus Christ," Harold said under his breath. "It's my mother's penis." We shipped the paddles and drifted down toward her. She was tall, with black hair to her waist. When she saw us she didn't move.

Don't scare, I thought. Stay where you are. I could take in small breasts and her black pubic hair. We slid up to the bank.

She looked down at us, kicked her leg above her head, whirled, and disappeared into the tent.

"*What?*" Harold said.

She reappeared, still naked, carrying a .410 shotgun. It looked like a BB gun, but it wasn't. She pointed it at us.

"Get out," she said.

I felt my face drain, and I thought I was going to faint. Was this going to be some kind of robbery? I put my hands on the thwart in front of me and leaned forward, looking up at her.

"*What?*" Harold said, this time to the girl.

"Get out," she said. Harold stepped onto the bank. I crawled over the cargo and followed him.

"Is this Tangiers?" Harold said. "We were supposed to be in Tangiers by dark."

"Shut up," the girl said. She had gray streaks in her hair, but she looked to be about twenty. She directed us with the gun into the tent.

The floor was covered with a blue shag carpet and was piled with down sleeping bags in several colors. A heater burned in one corner. Light filtered through green fabric. There were no poles, and the ceiling was high enough for the girl to stand upright.

Harold held his hands out. "I can read palms," he said.

"Shut up," the girl said. "Take your clothes off."

Everything focused on my belt buckle. It was large and brass and it came loose and there was my pubic hair, not covered by underwear. I dropped my pants.

I raised my eyes to her belly. Her pubic hair grew onto her thighs; a faint line of it rose to her navel. I straightened up, unbuttoned my shirt, and let it fall to the floor. Harold was naked beside me. His body was white as a chicken's.

"Lie down," the girl said. We lay on our backs on the sleeping bags. They were soft, soft. She leaned the gun against the side of the tent and knelt between us. She kissed first Harold's penis, then mine. His hands fluttered up as she kissed him; he half rose and fell back. His penis wavered and rose. "Some dummy," he said weakly.

She stroked him while she sucked me until I was hard.

She sat up. "You first," she said to Harold. She straddled him and slipped him into her.

"You stand over him," she said to me. She fucked him, with a short tight motion that made her breasts jiggle, while she sucked me. I reached between us and took a nipple between my fingers. It was thick and red as roses. Harold came, but I didn't.

"Ah," she said. "Ah." She flushed across her collarbones.

She let me go, got off him, and pushed me down. Harold lay with his eyes closed, one hand tracing small circles in the hair on his chest.

"You do me," she said to me.

I got on and we went at it. Her legs locked around my waist.

What I imagined was Frieda fucking her lover. She ran her hands down his sides and took him in her mouth. He stuck a finger in her asshole. Thinking of her seemed more dangerous than what I was doing. It made my stomach churn. Frieda spread her ass and let him look.

I came right through both of them, through both of them into the girl. I pressed my palms flat on her temples and rode through, a moan escaping with the fluid. I let my body go loose against her.

"You aren't with me exactly, are you?" was the first thing she said. Where was everybody else? "I like the pattern your hair makes," she said.

"Thank you." I smoothed her hair off her forehead, uncoupled, and slid off her. Harold moved up against her other side.

"Do you do this a lot?" he said.

"When I want to."

"Where're the other people?"

"There's no one else."

I pushed up onto my knees and got my shirt. The gun leaned against the wall at the front of the tent, but I didn't reach for it. Harold lay on his side against her, stroking her stomach. Old *ejaculatio praecox* Harold. She watched me dress.

"You don't wear underwear?" she said.

"Not for years."

"Where are you going?" She had wonderfully delicate hands, long-fingered, the nails bitten back.

"Right now?" Palm moist, soft around me.

"In the canoe."

"To the end of the river."

"The river goes underground in the swamp."

"There's a canal."

"I'll go with you."

"Naked?"

"I have clothes."

I looked at Harold. He was sitting up, pulling on his pants.

"We can ride you with us," he said. "You know how to paddle?"

"Sure."

Harold dressed, and we went outside and waited for her. Thin snow had begun to fall.

"My, my," Harold said. "Look at this." He waved his hand at flurrying flakes.

"This is a strange thing," he said. Then he laughed. "It's better than fishing on the flats."

We turned as she came out of the tent. She wore jeans and a green down parka, and she carried the gun.

"You're not going to start that again?" Harold said quickly.

"Maybe we'll need it," she said.

"Why don't you get one of the bags," I said.

"Okay." She went back into the tent and came out with one of the sleeping bags wadded under her arm.

We climbed down the bank and got into the canoe. The girl got in the middle, making space for herself between boxes. She laid the gun across her legs. The snow danced in a light wind.

I looked back at the tents. No vehicles, no one around any-where.

"Did you put out the heater?" I asked.

"It's not mine—I didn't bother with it," she said.

V

WE PULLED up under a high bank. Roots stuck out of raw black earth. Harold jumped ashore and pulled us around. The girl stepped out, and I followed.

We climbed the bank to a grassy field. A board cabin with a screened-in front porch lay back against oak woods.

"Looks all right to me," Harold said. He returned to the boat. The girl and I approached the cabin. Pear and apple trees had been set out in the front yard. They were just head-high. Flower husks and dead tomato vines crawled the ground below the porch. The girl tried the porch door.

"Locked," she said.

"That doesn't matter." Her name was Alene. The door was held by a finger hook. Taped to the screen was a hand-lettered sign that read: NO FIREARMS OR FOOD INSIDE. I jerked the door open. High-backed rocking chairs were turned around and leaned against the front of the house, their rockers sticking out like old legs kneeled praying. The house door was bolted from the inside.

"Why don't you try a window?" she said.

"I don't want to break something that'll let the cold in." I kicked the door until it broke open. Raw wood snaggled off the lock. Alene brushed past me into the house.

"Anybody home?" she called.

The room we entered was dark, sparsely furnished. The curled edge of a straw mat on the floor caught light from the door. I found a kerosene lamp on a table under one of the front windows, lighted it, and we walked through the rooms. The bedrooms were pine-paneled, small and depressing, like a damp shirt on a cold day, with their iron bedsteads and their striped mattresses. The kerosene in the lamps on the tables was dark and clotted. In back was a kitchen with a wood stove and a hand pump and behind it a screened porch with a plank counter along the back side. We reentered the living room as Harold pushed through the front door carrying the ax and one of the food boxes. He balanced a beer on top of the box.

"It's good to be home," he said. "Did you tell them we'd be staying for supper?"

"Supper and breakfast. They said come on in."

He set the box and the ax on the floor.

"You folks going to help any?" he said.

"We've been touring the place."

"I'm not touring," Alene said. "I just wanted to see if the bastards left anything I could use. What a shabby hole."

"Now, you'll get used to it," I said.

"Don't play with me." She picked up the ax and went out on the porch.

"Takes your mind off your worries, doesn't she?" Harold said. We followed her out.

"You could gather a little firewood if you wanted to," Harold said to her. "We'll get the rest of the stuff up." She didn't say anything. She stood against the screen, looking out. The river curved through snow flurries around a bend into the trees. The way her spine curved, deeply like a hook, as she pressed her belly against the screen, made me want to run my hand up her back. She looked at the river, saying nothing.

"Or whatever you want to do," Harold said. We left the house and returned to the canoe.

We unloaded the boxes and pulled the canoe up onto the bank. Our feet sank in mud as we worked.

Coming up the bank, we could hear sounds of wood splintering coming from the cabin.

"Looked to *me* like it needed a little trimming," Harold said.

She was hacking up the rockers.

"Bang them to pieces," Harold said. We went into the living room and set the boxes down. Harold pulled two beers out and handed one to me.

"You might save one of them, Alene," he called. "I'll need to sit down after a while."

"There're chairs in there," she said. I stood in the door watching her. She used the ax awkwardly, not closing the distance between her hands as she brought it down. She broke the rockers up, though. After a while she let up and stood back, panting a little. I moved in and gathered up the pieces that lay around her, carried them in to the fireplace, doused them with kerosene from the lamp, and lighted a fire.

The fire snapped the chill in the place. I pulled an armchair that was covered with green, rose-flowered cloth up to the fire and sat down to think about where I wanted to sleep. A light wind whisked snow against the windowpanes. We should have gotten Alene to bring the other down bags. They had been deep and soft. It was bad to just go off and leave them. It didn't look, though, as if we were going to be able to get her to do anything she didn't want to. Out on the porch, she was still chopping. The floor vibrated faintly with the blows.

Harold pulled a gas stove from a box and began to pump it up. On camping trips he always brought plenty of country goodies to eat, but he didn't like to pioneer. I stretched my legs out and sipped the beer, looking into the fire.

"You got sweet potatoes, Harold?" I said.

"Of course."

"What else we going to have?"

"Stew. Artichoke hearts."

"Wonderful. This is a night for artichokes." My mind was dancing around, Frieda somewhere in a sheepskin, walking in the snow.

"Here, get me some water," he said, holding out a pot. I took the pot, went out to the kitchen, and cranked the pump handle. Somebody had sown a garden out back, but it was gone now, dog fennel wands nodding among broken corn stalks. Dark was coming on, and the snow blew into trees. Either the well was dry or the pump needed priming. I came back through the house.

"I'll get some water from the river," I said.

"Okay."

On the porch, Alene was gathering up the split chairs.

"I'm going for water," I said.

"Wait," she said. She ran into the house. I heard the wood clatter against the hearth. She came back out.

"I'll go with you," she said.

We walked through descending night to the river. The snow fell so lightly that I couldn't feel it. Flakes caught on our clothes, hung for a moment, then winked out, like little lights, into the cloth.

Three big cedars grew at the edge of the bank. Their riverside roots were exposed, and I grasped them to help myself down the steep cut, feeling in my palms the softness of the finest roots, which hung like whiskers from the larger stock. Alene came down the trail that we had carried the supplies up.

I made my way carefully across the mushy ground, over leaves and broken, river-worn branches, to the water, knelt, and filled the pot. I felt her behind me, and then she touched my hair. I looked out at the river, which flowed smoothly, the color of coffee, undisturbed by the falling snow. She placed her hands on my shoulders and leaned against me. My knee sank deeper in the mud.

"You guys in the army?" she said.

"Harold used to be."

"Where'd you get the canoe?" She indicated with her foot the government stencil.

"Harold relocated it."

"He did what?"

"He took it."

"They won't come after you?"

"Not down here."

Something, a sadness, seemed to gust out of her thin body. I took her hand that stroked my cheek and kissed it in the palm.

"Are you married?" she said.

"Divorcing."

I looked up. Her gray eyes touched mine.

"How come?" she said.

"I didn't love my wife." I felt, as I spoke, something in me subside and fall away. I had a moment of intense exhilaration. But then, behind it, came something else. As Frieda fell suddenly away, fell away, in the vision I had of her, from the window of her new house, where she leaned over the kitchen sink to water ferns, I saw something else rise, another shape, larger, darker, deeper in my life: it was that that held me, that shape that had stood gazing at me all along, inevitable and changeless, and in a moment the exhilaration was gone and I felt a panic that nearly threw me sprawling into the river. I emptied the pot to direct her from tears that had come into my eyes, but she saw.

"Are you okay?" she said.

"No. I'm not." I refilled the pot. Particles hung suspended in the drawn-up water.

"Well, you'd better straighten up," she said. "I like you."

"Then I guess I'd better pull myself together."

"You're damn right." She ruffled my hair, leaned down, and kissed me on the back of the neck. "That sure is dirty water," she said.

"It's just tannin—acid from cypress roots. It's not dirty, and it keeps the water sweet."

"Maybe you know. Let's get out of this stupid snow."

"All right."

We climbed the bank and returned to the cabin, holding hands as we walked.

VI

THE BEARS have moved farther south, deeper into woods— what bears there are—and no panthers cry at night. The ivory- billed woodpecker has not been spotted for a generation, and bald eagles, which once nested in the tops of the tallest cypresses, are not seen anymore, as, for that matter, are the old tall trees. But in the morning, when I came out at first light, there were raccoon tracks in the snow on the front steps, and when I walked to the riverbank I saw, as I shook snow from cedar branches, a flock of ring-necked ducks rise from the water. The ducks flew off south beyond trees under a clear sky. I descended the bank and washed my face in the river. I scooped a handful of snow off the canoe gunwale. It tasted of metal. A snow rug lay in the bottom of the boat. I brushed my teeth in the river water and returned to the cabin.

Harold and Alene were asleep. Harold lay on his back in front of the fireplace, his arms out of the bag, a look of displeasure on his face. I knelt and kissed his open mouth. The saliva rind on his lips tasted of beer. He didn't wake. I looked around, and Alene was sitting up with the bag pulled around her shoulders, looking at me.

"Are you a queer?" she said.

I held my finger to my lips. "No," I whispered, "but Harold and I are close."

"Close to being queers?"

"He's an awfully fine boy."

"I see." Her eyes sparkled. The way the unzipped halves of the bag hung down her naked chest, like an unbuttoned shirt, excited me. I stood up and stepped over the stove and empty beer case to her. I reached down and touched her gray-streaked hair, and she pressed her face against my leg.

"Take your clothes off and get in here," she said.

"All right." She lay back.

The zipper stopped just below a crescent of pubic hair. I un- dressed, peeled the bag back, and got in with her.

Her mouth was hot and sleepy, and my lips moved from it

across her high cheekbones, over her nose, which had a depression in one side of it like an old wound, down her face, past chin and unlined neck to her breasts. The inverted nipples unfolded, one after the other, as I kissed them. I kissed back and forth between them, bringing them up, keeping them hard, as a flush spread across her chest. I kicked my feet in the bottom of the bag, seeking space.

"In high school they called me sunny side up," she said as I licked a nipple. I raised my head.

"Everybody did?"

"Certain ones. Do you think they look like fried eggs?"

"No; they look like hills in Italy."

"Old and green?"

"Covered with olives."

"And a blue sky and sailboats in the harbor?"

"And boys in striped shirts running down the beach."

"You *are* a queer."

"Must be." The bag was too tight for me to get my face down to her groin. My fingers fluttered through hair, and I slipped one inside. "Oh," she said, "oh." She took me in her hand and stroked me upward against her body. I wanted to caress her, to hold out against completion until she was soaked with feeling, until we were drowned, but when she touched me the rhythm broke. I rolled onto her, fumbling for connection, and we came together, my backside freezing in the cold morning air.

The bag was too small. When we finished I pulled my sack over us.

"Where did you go to high school?" I said.

"Different places. What were you doing outside?"

"Brushing my teeth." I told her about the ducks. "There was a whole flock of them," I said, "sleeping on the water. The moment I came up, before I could even get a good look at them, they broke into the air, panicking."

She yawned. "You should have shot one. I wouldn't mind a duck for breakfast."

"You wouldn't want to clean it."

"I'd love to eat it."

I pulled my leg loose, slipped down the bag, and punched Harold with my foot.

"Harold, wake up and start the fire."

He opened his eyes and looked down his chest at me.

"You crazy?" he said. "I was lying here waiting to hear the sound of rocker boards crackling, and all I'm hearing is whump, whump, whump. I'll take a little coffee with cream and a slab of hot corn bread, please."

"A *little* coffee? Here it comes." I threw the bag off and jumped on him. "I always wanted to get you trussed." I tried to hold him, but his arms were free and it was me, quickly, who got held.

"You want to smell something good?" He laughed and pulled my head down into his armpit.

"Jesus, Harold." I squirmed loose and sat up. He threw his arms back over his head and laughed. The hair in his armpits was redder than the hair on his head. The cold hit me, and I snaked off him, scrambled up, and got into my clothes. Alene lay on her side watching us, the bag pulled up to her chin, venturing nothing.

With a stick I scraped a place in last night's ashes, piled wood, doused it with kerosene, and lighted a fire. I squatted on my heels and held my palms out to the flames. The heat danced on my skin. Alene got up and stood beside me. She warmed herself, making little half turns in front of the fire. Light bustled on her thighs. She bent over and with her fingers combed out her hair. A faint, unpleasant odor rose from it.

"You'll catch it on fire," I said.

"Save me the trouble of combing it," she answered, but she moved back a step.

"Where'd the gray come from?"

"Early strain."

"I was wondering," Harold said as he pulled on his pants, "where did those tents at Goose Pasture come from?"

"From somebody," she said, twisting her hair into a bun. "You got a pin?"

"No," I said.

"Shit." She let the hair fall loose down her back.

"Well, at least that explains it," Harold said. "Did you get any water when you went down?" he said to me.

"No. I'll go get some now."

I got the coffeepot from the box and went out.

When I returned, as I reached for the house door, I heard inside the sounds of their lovemaking. I retreated down the porch, cleared the top step of snow, and sat down. The air was still, the day too cold for birds. I felt completely abandoned, as if when, the night before, I had declared myself free of Frieda (if that was what I had done) I had done so only after another hand seemed offered me, and now that hand, it turned out, wasn't there. Maybe that is what I had done. Maybe I dreamed Alene as the sweet field I could lay myself down in. "Like that, like that," I heard her say from inside, where they rolled. Like that. I dipped my fingers in the cold coffee water, pressed them to my eyelids, and rubbed, again, the sleep from my eyes.

VII

I WAS IN the stern, imagining that the ache in my knees was cancer climbing my bones, we were rounding a bend past a sand-bar backed by budding black willows, Harold had just reached behind for one of the last beers, when she raised the gun and fired into a low-hanging myrtle across the river.

"Jesus!" Harold jumped. "Is it Indians?" Then we both saw what she'd hit; a hornet's nest the size of a basketball. She'd shredded the bottom of it.

"Great God almighty," Harold said. Hornets, black-bodied and big as thumbnails, tumbled from the nest. They didn't fly—it must have been too cold; they spilled like beans into the water. Then a few got their wings and flew sluggishly around the shattered nest. They would have been angry, I guess, if they could.

"They look like dwarfs," Alene said, cracking the breech and tossing the empty shell into the water. "Fly, little buggers," she called to them.

"No, you don't want that," Harold said.

She took another shell from the pocket of her parka and re-loaded.

"You want to try?" she said to Harold.

"Nah—okay." He set his beer between his feet and took the gun. He smoothed his hair back with one hand, sighted along the barrel, and fired. His shot cut the nest loose, and it fell into the water among the tangle of branches.

"Now we'll have them with us to the Gulf," I said. "Let me try."

Harold handed the gun to Alene, who reloaded it and passed it to me. Hornets floated on the water, humming.

I fired. The shot cut the top out, and the nest sagged, deflated, taking water. White crawling hornet pupae murmured in the mess. Shreds of gray nest paper floated among the bodies. I handed the gun to Alene.

"God's wrath on the hornet world," Harold said.

"Shit—mine," Alene said, reloading. She fired again, and the nest went under. "Where's another one?" she said. "Let's find another one." Her eyes danced with glee.

"They'll show up," I said. "Why don't you keep your eye out for some meat."

"Ah, smothered squirrel," Harold said. He looked back at the floating hornet bodies.

"Dog meat," I said. "A fat pup, white with black spots."

"Not again."

"Yes, again—dog meat."

"Dogs?" Alene said. "I try to hit every one I see in the road."

"Of course you do, darling," Harold said.

"Dogs, guineas, and children," I said. "I haven't run over a child in nearly a month."

"You remember that one I got up near Thompson?" Harold said.

"That one on the shoulder? Yeah, I didn't think you'd ever get back on the road. What was he doing?"

"I don't know—digging something. Jesus, did he squeal."

"What?" Alene said. "A kid—a nigger?"

"No," Harold said. "A white boy, about ten years old. It was great. His head busted just like a watermelon. Juice everywhere.

We had to stop at a filling station to wash it off the front of the car."

"Did you kill him?"

I trailed my fingers in the water—eee, hornets—and wiped them on my pants. "He wasn't walking when we left."

"I think I'll run over Lola when we get home," Harold said.

"You couldn't hit Lola—she's a dodger."

"Who's Lola?' Alene said.

"That's Harold's young woman," I told her. "Lola's a grounds-keeper up at Southwest State."

"The insane asylum?"

"That's right. You should have brought her, Harold. We could have rolled her in meal and fried her."

"Wouldn't she be sweet? The last time I talked to her she said she'd decided to take flying lessons. She wants to be a crop duster."

"Buzz your house on Wednesdays."

"Trip her with telephone wires."

"Poor Lola."

Alene swung the gun in an arc, sighting into treetops.

"Watch for movement," Harold said. "Anything moves, blast away."

We pulled around the bend into a long reach of open water.

"Those hornets," Harold said. "I once dropped a hornet's nest into the boat."

"You did?"

"Yeah. Red Baker and I were doing the Chiporee. I don't know how it happened, but we passed under a nest and Red managed to hit it with his paddle and knock it into the canoe."

"Did you get stung?"

"No. We hit the water at the same time the nest hit the boat."

"How'd you get it out?"

"I reached in with my paddle and flipped it into the water. We stayed submerged until we got out of sight—Jesus, I never moved so fast. I thought we were going to be stung to death."

Sun had burned the snow off; trees dripped water, and the ground along the banks was damp and mushy-looking. We paddled around bends where budding willows dragged lank branches in the dark water. The sky was clear, the air thin, sunny and cold.

I swung myself through the rhythm of paddling, my hands chafing, a knot untying in my shoulders, and I thought again of the way paddling a canoe slips you into the heart of things. The first day out is hard—your back aches and your hands hurt—but during the second, aches begin to dissolve and you ease into the flow of the river, and after a while the steady rhythm of paddling, the three-mile-an-hour journey past a landscape that changes as slowly as your heart beats, around bend after bend, each the same in its willows and moss-backed logs, into reaches long as lakes, is the rhythm of a deeper movement that we slip into, easy as breathing, as we travel, which replaces whatever madness we have come out of and carries us out of time.

That is how I had explained the lure of river travel. Explained it as I lay on living room rugs drinking tequila, my friends on sofas slipping into mescaline dreams. You become a part of the river, I would say, current and cargo. But that seemed to me now an awful fantasy. Here was the world, today, half frozen and natural as a goat, concussed hornets floating in a steam. Frieda was there still, green-eyed and frightened of bugs, and I stopped paddling for a moment, thinking of her naked body and of the eyes of her lover looking. I liked him looking. She pulled her knees up, in my mind, her legs fell open, she touched the scar inside her thigh, her hand drifted to her sex, and she spread the lips of it with her fingers. She brought the fingers to her mouth and tasted of herself. I didn't mind—I wanted to dream it. I wanted her legs loose for another in my mind. I wanted them loose in fact. As they were in fact. I wanted to hold the vision of her, locked in her new lover's arms, tease it out slowly into my mind, even if it hurt, even as it hurt. I had loved her too little, then too much, and I couldn't find a path between the two. Blocking whatever path there was stood whatever shape I had seen last night. Beyond her supple, Annie Oakley body stood that other dark form, which I could not embrace.

I reached forward and stroked Alene's hair.

"Don't get it wet," she said.

The river lay flat as a highway, empty and sparkling in the sunlight.

"What is that?" Harold said.

"What?"

"That sound?"

I listened. "It's the Crystal River shoal."

We rounded the bend between high, palmetto-covered banks, and there was the shoal, thrown across the river like a petticoat. I had forgotten it. It was a narrow place where the river lost depth and fell a couple of feet down a limestone ledge. The water, suddenly cinched and dropped, bucked into plumes of spray. Past a front line of heaving waves, the river foamed for a hundred yards toward still water as it widened out and calmed before it bent past the headland of bare oaks.

"You want to stop and take a look?" Harold said.

"Yeah, let's do."

We swung over and climbed the bank through the palmettos. Harold ran ahead, kicking his legs high through wet fronds. "What snakes there are, stay still," he cried. He reached the highest point and, leaning out over the water that had pushed a white edge of foam against the bank, made gestures with his hands.

"Last year in Colombia," he hollered in an English accent, "we ran rivers like this by the dozen." He turned to me as I came up to him, shouted as if I were somewhere else and the river louder. "Do you hear me, Jack? By the dozen. Little river, turn to gin."

"Gin," I yelled. "Martini rapids. Vodka collision."

Harold reached down, scooped up sand and bits of plant matter, and flung them at the water. "Be calmed, waters," he yelled. "Hornet Harold commands you. I believe we can take it, Jack."

"We have to chance it," I said. "There's no other way. This is an adversary relationship. Mercy, God's good grace, will get us through."

Alene came up. She had a palmetto frond tied around her hair for a headband.

"Cousin Alene," Harold said, "does the situation smell sweet to you? Do you believe Jesus will carry us through?"

"What jerkoff wouldn't," she said.

I put my arms around both of them. I wanted us all to jump in the water. A fine mist wet our faces. Let's do this every day. Let's not ever do anything else.

"Let's go, then," Harold said. He ran down the bank yipping as Alene and I followed.

We tucked the poncho around the boxes and shoved off. Alene sat on the center thwart.

The river flowed sluggishly toward a central chute, beyond which reared a six-foot fan of spray; the river, stumbling, had kicked up its own water. We made for that.

"Harold," I called over the noise of water, "stand up."

"What for?"

"In case there's a view."

We all got up. Alene stood on boxes, higher than either of us. Standing, I ruddered us into the center of the channel. The river seemed hardly to move; leaves floating beside the canoe turned lazily in the clear brown current. The bow leaned out over the fall —so slowly—tipped forward, we caught, surged forward the length of the canoe into the high brown wave, Harold striking with his paddle as if the wave were a bear, and as he fell, I felt the bow scrape bottom, and then I was in the air too, grabbing for Alene—wanting her, separately from this, curiously, completely —missing, remembering to hold on to my paddle as I went under, gasping, breath knocked nearly out of me, freezing, fighting up until I surfaced ten yards downstream in waist-deep water, the swamped canoe sagging beside me, empty beer bottles and the gas can floating away out of reach downstream.

We dragged the canoe to shore and tipped it out in the shallows. Everything was soaked except my clothes, which were still dry in their plastic bag. Harold built a fire, and we hung the sleeping bags in the trees. We stood around the fire naked, shaking with excitement and the cold.

Alene stood with her back to us, the gun cradled against her hip. Goose bumps pimpled her buttocks. Harold squatted and cupped his genitals. "What a ride," he said. "What a ride."

"We went straight under," I said.

He laughed. "We didn't make it past the first wave. It was wonderful—it just caught us." He stroked penis and testicles gently upward, looking down at himself. "Unclench, boys," he said.

Alene laid the gun down and went to the canoe. She began to push it back into the water.

"What are you doing, honey?" Harold said.

"I want to run it again," she said.

"Let's do," Harold said to me.

So, naked, blue-lipped, chattering, we ran the shoal again.

On the second run Alene took the bow, I sat in the middle, and Harold took the stern. Emptied of cargo, we popped through like a cork. After the fourth run we were too cold to try another. My face felt frozen; I could hardly move my mouth. We pulled the boat ashore and got into dry clothes. The only thing Harold could wear of mine was a sweater. The bags were nearly dry, and we spread them out on top of the reloaded cargo. Harold scattered the fire, and we pushed off. The sky was clear, the sun white as the moon in the south. Harold began to sing. We passed the bend and put the shoal behind us.

VIII

THE SUN was going down like a peach into the river and we were still paddling when we heard laughter coming from a cedar grove above a grassy meadow on the right bank. Two red-white-and-blue-striped canoes were pulled up in the yellow grass. We beached in mud and climbed the slope to the cedars. In a needle-floored clearing, two couples looked up from a fire on which ribs lay roasting on a grill.

"Hey," one of the men—tall, with a belly—said as we came through trees into the open space. He was drinking something from a white plastic cup.

"All of you stand up," Alene said, raising the gun. A plump woman in padded duck-hunting pants jerked half a step forward, her toe kicking coals so that the grate tipped and nearly fell. She looked at the tall man, and they both rose.

"What do you want?" the other man—gray chin beard and glasses—said in a hard voice. He moved closer to a woman whose hand had frozen among salad greens on a camp table. The tall man stretched his hand over the fire toward the plump woman, changed his mind, and came around and stood beside her.

"What is it?" he said.

"Just get steady and put your hands out in front of you," Harold said. "I've always wanted to talk this way," he added. He held an open pocket knife loosely in his right hand.

"Stay calm," I said to the four of them. I pointed at a cooler under the camp table. "What's in there?" I asked.

"Some beer," the tall man said.

"Jesus, oh, Jesus, fucking robbers," the plump woman said. She looked up into the cedars.

"Shut up," Alene said.

"You got any freckle-face potato chips?" Harold asked.

"What?" the tall man said.

"Or any calico, any red calico?"

"Jesus—what?" He took a step back.

"Stay still," I said, then crossed the clearing and got the cooler. I could smell the woman's sweat as I bent down, bitter, like the smell of roaches. I had an impulse to stroke her leg—her thighs were slender in jeans—but I touched only the cooler, picked it up, and carried it back to the other side of the fire. Harold speared a sheaf of ribs off the fire with his knife.

"What else have you got that we might need?" he asked over a mouthful. He offered me a hunk of meat, but I didn't want to take it right then.

"Nothing, man," the bearded man said. His army fatigue pants were held up by a white leather belt. A marine assault knife hung from the belt. "We haven't got any money," he said.

"We don't want money," I said. "We're doing this for love."

"We're doing this to make an impression," Harold said. "We don't want to go down into history only as simple, Christian folk."

"You won't," the tall man said. He scratched under his arm. "Listen, you assholes—"

"Shut up," Alene screamed. She raised the gun to her shoulder and aimed directly at his face. "We don't want to hear your side of it."

"Don't!" the woman at the table cried. The tall man blanched. His hands opened and closed—curdled, curdled is the word that came into my mind, but curled is what his fingers did. The woman had screamed the single word "Don't," but she hadn't moved.

A small breeze slipped vaguely among the cedar branches. Alene lowered the gun.

"Why are you here?" I asked the four of them. "Do you do this often?"

"Nearly every weekend," the tall man said.

"We usually bring retarded children on the outing with us," the woman by the fire said.

"More fucking therapeutic campers," Harold said. "The goddamned woods are being overrun by the afflicted—Jesus. Assholes!" he screamed. "Are you people Americans?"

"We're from Tallahassee," the tall man said. "John and I teach at the university."

"Retardation?"

"Education."

"Well, let this be a lesson to you," I said. "The woods aren't safe."

"*Donnez-moi un cerveza,*" Harold said. I handed him one. "We don't want to do anything to humiliate you," he said, "but we want you to keep the special children at home. Behind fences. To whom, by the way, am I addressing my remarks?"

The four of them said nothing.

"Well, all right, you're petrified. It's understandable. Let's see," he said, pointing with the beer can. "You'll be Split Silk Capone, you'll be Peewee White, and you ladies are their mistresses, Patootie and Miss Marvin."

"Oh, stop it," the plump woman cried. She began to weep. "What do they want?" she said.

"Now, now," Harold said, "now, now." He flicked the knife as if there was water on it. "When my brother was little," he continued, "and we had to take him to get a shot, he would scream at the doctor, 'Wait, I want to tell you something,' every time the doc would try to get the needle in. The doctor would hold up and ask him what he wanted to say, but he never wanted to say anything; he just wanted the business to stop." He swigged the beer. "You see, we understand."

"Anything else, Arnold?" he said to me.

"I'm fine," I said.

"Enough, Matilda?"

"Let's go," Alene said.

"Cover the rear," Harold said to her.

We returned down the slope, carrying the cooler between us.

"The woods full of the afflicted," Harold said. "It's crazy."

"Keep your asses frozen," I heard Alene say, still in the clearing.

We walked downhill through soggy grass. Daffodils flowered, singly and in clumps, along the edges of the meadow. We loaded the cooler into the canoe, got in, and waited for Alene. She came running down the slope.

"Wait a minute," she said. She fired from the waist into the bottom of one of the canoes, reloaded, and fired into the bottom of the other one.

"You never stop thinking, do you, Alene?" Harold said.

"Come on," she said, and jumped in.

We pushed off. The flimsy winter sun was straggling in the river as we paddled into the current.

IX

I JUST would rather not get up. Where I am is fine with me. It's winter, and I'm in the woods tucked in my down bag in this little orange tent.

I watched flames dance against the wall. Alene lay with me, her bag pulled on top of us. She lay on me, and her long light weight felt fine. I don't even want supper. I kissed her nipple, rosy as a burn. I held it in my mouth until it hardened. It's like a little scallop, fluttering open. I touched her low down, and she squealed.

"Your hands are cold," she said, pushing me away.

"They'll warm up in a minute." I rubbed them rapidly on my thighs. "There, is that better?"

"No-o," she said.

"What?"

"You're just warming your leg."

I rubbed my hand again, hard, on my thigh.

"How's that?"

"That's fine. Touch me there. I like it when you touch my leg there. Your hands are so soft."

"Comes with the territory," I said, and chuckled. I wasn't hungry, I wasn't thirsty, I wasn't anything but content. No, I'd like another beer.

"Harold," I called, "toss me a cartridge."

I watched his shadow rise, disappear, and then his head came through the flap.

"Here you go, Commander," he said. "You want one, Snake eyes?" he asked Alene.

"No."

He squatted in the opening.

"What you doing?" I asked. "Come in out of the cold."

He crawled in, pulled a bag around his shoulders, and knelt in front of us. "I'm listening to the jeeps," he said.

We had been hearing them for an hour or more, hearing the straining whine of engines far off, coming through rough country. We reckoned they were jeeps, four-wheel-drive something.

"You're dreaming again, Harold," I said.

"I keep listening to them."

There was nowhere for us to go but back on the river. We were camped in the middle of an old raised road that was cut now by the river where a bridge used to cross. Creosoted pilings, bound by steel hoops, leaned in the water; two live oaks, fully leaved, hung over the stream on either side of the road drop-off. The road itself was grown up in myrtle and alder bushes. From the crown we could look across the tops of young planted pines on both sides of the river to horizons of old woods, wavering bluely in the distance.

"We've got no trouble, Harold," I said, and pulled Alene close. I lay on my side; I raised the beer and took a swallow through the corner of my mouth. We could hear the engines working way back in the woods.

"They're miles away," I said. Alene kissed my chest. Her lips were soft. I held her head against me. I wanted to pull her into my body. It was all right, no matter who was coming.

Harold crawled in close. "This is the last time," he said, "that I ever go camping in the winter."

"How come?" With our bags around us we formed a tent within the tent.

"It's too cold—you can't wash the smoke off you."

"Don't stand so close to the fire."

"Ah, Jack—I'm doing the cooking."

"It *would* be nice to take a dip."

"Yeah. In the summer we could just jump right out of the boat into the water. You remember that school of minnows we jumped into on the Ochlocknee?"

"I remember. We caught them in our hands."

"Pebbles on the bottom shining like mirrors. There were mussels in the water—you remember?"

"We were scared to eat them."

"Have you guys known each other all your lives?" Alene said. Her legs moved against mine.

"Just about." She drew my hand to her and took a sip of my beer.

"Sounds like it," she said. "You're just a couple of crackers."

"Harold's worried about the jeeps," I said. "He thinks they're coming to get us. Maybe they're tanks, Harold."

"I don't know," he said seriously.

"Who gives a shit?" Alene said.

Harold pulled the bag up and leaned forward until his head was between ours. In the darkness he had made, he hummed like an engine.

"NNNNNN, NNNNNN," he went, changing gears.

"You'll never get out, Harold," I said. "You can't take a Ferrari into the swamp."

"Ah, Jesus," he said, and rolled onto his back. "If it were summer and I were naked."

"You can get naked," Alene said. "Do. I want to see your peter."

"Okay." He stripped, crawled between us, and pulled the bag over the top.

"Let me see," Alene said, crouching.

"It's too cold for flashing," Harold said.

"Let me look." Harold turned on his back so she could get to him. She bent close. Her hair swung against his groin. "Your prick's the same color as your skin," she said.

"That's not unusual—it's my prick."

"Jack's is dark—how come it's so dark, Jack?"

"Yeah, Jack," Harold said. "Where'd the purple come from?"

"Too much polo, I guess." I touched myself. "I used to worry about it; now I like it."

"Polo?" Alene asked.

"No—a purple dick."

Parts of our bodies kept slipping out into the cold. Alene kissed my penis, then Harold's. I stroked the hairs all one way on her arm. She raised her head, listening. With my index finger I traced her profile from her hairline to her chin.

"Quit," she said. "I'm trying to hear." She laughed and fell back. "They're coming to get us," she said.

We were silent.

"I thought the river went underground," Alene said.

"That's some other river," Harold said. "Somewhere else."

I wanted, suddenly, to get out of there. Out of the tent.

"What's there to eat?" I asked.

"Beans and tomatoes," Harold said. "The pot's on the stove."

"You want anything—Alene?"

"No."

I dressed and went out. The sky was crowded with stars. I descended the bank and washed my face in the river. The water stung my cheeks and hands. Chips of light floated in the river.

It was too cold to be out, but I didn't want to be in the tent. I stood up and breathed deeply. I felt the cold way down in my chest.

I returned to the fire and spooned a plateful of beans. I could hear them fucking. Fabric, flesh flapping. What could I do about it? She didn't mind which of us she had. Frieda was a thousand miles away. Wearing one of my old sweaters, shaking frost from her hair. There were birds in the live oak by the river. I heard them when I passed under it. I squatted, then sat down in front of the fire.

The sound of the laboring vehicles rose and fell. There seemed to be at least two. I couldn't tell if they were getting any closer—they seemed to be straining in one spot, far back. Maybe they are coming for us. I finished the beans and tossed the paper plate into the fire. The edges browned and caught, a brown stain appeared in the center, the whole plate caught, crumpling. Another beer. Green expensive cooler; Red Label, a brand I never drink. No need for a cooler in this weather. How to keep them from freezing was the worry. The beer was cold and bitter. It made my fingers ache to hold it. I wished I had gloves. I had worried about paddling in cold weather, about my hands numbing from dipping in the water, but it was no trouble. I didn't wet them, and the action of paddling kept them warm enough.

I dragged the cooler over and sat down on it. I couldn't stop thinking of Frieda. We had been separated a year, and now, within, at most, two weeks, the divorce decree would appear in my mailbox. I had to let her go. Every day, since I had started the stumbling divorce machinery more than six months before, I had been telling myself that I had to let her go. Last night, once again, I thought I had, but here she was, still rising like the moon, in my mind. Go on, Frieda, dear, go on. Her hair was blond, finer than Alene's. She stood, in my mind, in front of the picture window in her cottage at the beach—here, fifty miles from here, in Florida—and kicked her foot higher than her head. It was the one thing she remembered from her college dance class ten years ago. It was a wonderful girlish maneuver—she would do it anywhere: in the grocery store, waiting in line for a movie—and it had been, I thought, the first move I had seen Alene make: one high kick before she whirled into the tent and came out with a gun.

Someone grunted in the tent, and I heard the sound of damp flesh slapping damp flesh. I got quickly up and went to the riverbank. The bound pilings leaned in the current like old drunk men in overcoats. A tangle of bushes obscured the road on the other bank. The tops of young pines were silvery.

"Goodbye, goodbye," I called. My voice flew, echoless, into the night. "Goodbye." If she were here I could throw her in the water. Hypothermia, not divorce, would keep her under. "Goodbye," I yelled, and again "Goodbye."

"What are you hollering?" Harold called from the tent. I turned and saw his head sticking out of the flap. His hair was wild salad. "Be quiet," he said. "You'll let them know where we are."

He crawled out and stood up, fully dressed. He cracked a beer and came over. We looked down the river.

"After these pines, it's marshes all the way to the coast," he said. "Who were you saying goodbye to?"

"To Frieda." I held myself in my arms.

"I figured. Is it bothering you?"

"The divorce?"

"Yeah."

"I guess so. I'm trying to let it go."

"You ought to." He took a mouthful of beer and spit a stream of foam into the water. He followed that with a piss.

"Ugm," he said as he arced it. "The simple pleasures."

"You're making a feature of that," I said.

"I like to put myself into the things I do." He zipped up and sat down. I sat down beside him.

"Is there any chance you'll go back with Frieda?" he asked.

"No," I said quickly. The thought scared me. "I can't let myself think about it. She's gone."

"You were together a long time."

"Half our lives."

"It makes me sad," he said. I looked at him. His face was turned away, eyes looking downstream. An ache spread through my chest, into my shoulders.

"I'm sorry," I said.

"It's natural. You ought to take a trip."

"I'm on a trip."

"Why don't you do what I did when I quit smoking?"

"What's that?"

"I took my last pack of Luckies out to the garden, dug a hole, and buried them, right between the peas and the tomatoes. I said a little funeral service over them. I told them I loved them but they were dead and goodbye."

"I don't think Frieda would go for that," I said.

"Maybe a photograph. Too bad you didn't marry Lola. I'd help you bury her."

"I'll help *you*."

"First thing when we get back."

"If we do."

He looked at the ground and shook his head. His hair fell forward over his face. He pushed it back.

"I wonder if they're—whatever they are—coming this way."

"I don't know. It sounds like they're stuck."

The faraway sound rose, grinding, as if trees were down in front of wheels. We were silent.

"This has certainly turned into something, hasn't it?" he said after a while.

"I'm kind of liking it—it splits the distance."

"What do you mean?"

"We're off here in the boondocks away from our real lives, and we're cutting up in this wild way that we never could at home— at least I thought we never could, then I started thinking this is just the way it was when we were kids, running around free, sneaking through the bushes raising cain. It takes me back."

"Mebbe so," he said.

"You remember when we used to hide out in trees and jump on each other? We're getting to do it again."

" 'Cept we're grown—and it's not each other."

"Adventure has just come along—we do it. Do you mind Alene?"

He chuckled. "I'm enjoying her."

"If that's what it is."

"Something."

He got up and went down to the river, where he held his beer can under the water until it filled, then threw it out into the stream.

"I'm going to bed," he said when he had climbed back up the bank.

"I'll be along shortly."

He put his hand on my shoulder. "I'm sorry, Jack," he said.

I pressed my cheek against his wrist. The hairs were scratchy against my face.

"It'll be all right," I said. He returned to the tent.

"What you been doing?" I heard Alene ask through a yawn.

"Talking to Jack," he said.

I put the beer down beside me and scratched my thighs with both hands. I wished I itched all over. If it were summer I would throw myself in the water. Where did this restraint come from? I would like to float on my back, in this stream, to the Gulf. Lie on my back listening to the wind in the marshes. Well, well, oh, well. I got up, went down to the river, and rinsed my face. There was no way to get around the cold. Except by crawling into my warm down bag, where I have been momentarily content. The engines kicked, far off. I waited until no sounds came from the tent. Then I went in too.

When Harold, fumbling in the dark, woke me, I thought he was getting up to pee. But he sat on his bag, pulling on his shoes.

"What are you doing?" I said.

"You hear those fucking jeeps?"

In the woods they were still at it.

"What are you going to do?"

"I'm going outside. I can't stand it."

"Would you guys shut up," Alene said sleepily but in full command.

"Okay," Harold said. He finished lacing his boots, picked up the gun, and went out.

I heard him throw wood on the fire. There was a silence, then a loud whomp and a gust of light that lit up the tent. "Jesus," I heard him say.

"Warmed up, Harold?" I said.

"Damn." Tossed a little gas on the fire.

I chuckled and pulled the bag around my ears. I could hear the engines through the down. Then I thought: Well, they can see our signal now. I heard a scrabbling, then a shirring, leafy sound and twittering as birds left their roost. I poked my head out.

"What the shit are you doing?" I asked.

"I'm getting up here." His voice came from among branches.

"In the tree?"

"Yes, dammit."

"You going to ambush them?"

"I'm going to get up here."

"Holler if you spot them." He was silent a moment, then he said, "I forgot about the fucking birds. Christ, it's cold."

I drew my knees up and held myself in the bag. Alene had swum up to admonish; now she was snoring lightly again. The engines whined away in the woods. You lie in your camp and wait to be found. It could be anything coming. Robbers or cops. What could be driving this way at midnight? A squeal rose and fell away. Rose and fell again. Like guineas in the bushes, spooked by a dog. The sound came on. Oh, Jesus God, help.

I got up, pulled on clothes and shoes, and went out. I crossed the clearing and looked up in the tree. I couldn't see him up there.

"Harold," I whispered, "where are you?" I was shaking from excitement.

"Help, murder, police," he whispered back.

"I'm coming up," I said.

I grasped the lowest branch, swung myself up, and climbed to his perch. He was straddling a limb, holding with one hand to the trunk, about halfway up.

"What are we going to do up here?" I asked when I had settled beside him. I swung my legs in the dark.

"I had to get out of the tent," he said. He had the gun propped against the trunk.

We listened to the motors. They seemed to be getting closer; maybe they were, but it was taking a long time.

"Now the birds are stuck in the cold," I said. Blackbirds, I guess they were.

"I forgot they were up here. They almost made me fall—I thought the tree was exploding. Did you like that gas?"

"Ugm."

I thought of the birds huddled on a mudbank, lost in the bushes. Frightening birds seemed a worse error than robbing campers, if error it was.

The vehicles came on. My heart sped up, I could feel it hitting heavily in my chest. Leaves rustled in a light wind, as if the birds were still in the tree. I could see over bushes that the road petered out in the planted pines. If they were coming, they would have to come some other way, else crush trees. Maybe they were driving bulldozers. Maybe there was another road we couldn't see.

"We're as bad off here as in the tent," I said.

"No, we're not." Leaves blocked much of our view. Harold swung back and forth, peering out.

"Don't you remember," I said, "when we played army when we were kids? The guys up in trees always got trapped."

"I just want to see what's coming," he said.

"Well, I'm going down."

"Suit yourself."

I climbed down, threw another stick on the fire in passing, and crawled into the tent. Alene woke as I came in.

"What are you crazy people doing?" she asked. She spoke through her hair without raising her head.

"We were in the tree."

"What? What tree?"

"The one by the river. Harold's still there. Let me in."

"No. I want to sleep. Why is he in the tree?"

"The jeeps; outlaw buggers after us."

"We're the outlaws."

"We sure are." I got into my bag without taking off clothes or shoes. She turned her face away.

"Go to sleep," she said.

"I don't know if I can." I lay on my back, heart pounding. Cold came through the bag, through the top and bottom.

"Don't lose yourself, boy," she said.

I lay there listening. The engines had hooked to my heartbeat. They must be coming for us. In the night, in this wilderness. I turned over, pulled the bag over my head, and pushed myself up on my forearms. In the cave I made, I couldn't see, but I could hear. Nothing to think about now: they were coming.

I heard a scrabbling in the tree, then feet running across the clearing, and Harold appeared at the flap.

"I see lights," he said. "Let's get out of here."

"Okay." I jumped right up.

"Come on, Alene," Harold said, shaking her. "Somebody's coming."

"Oh shit," she said, but she got up and began pulling on her clothes.

Harold collected the supplies while Alene and I wadded up the bags and jerked the tent down. We carried everything to the canoe and threw it in. Alene and Harold got in. I paused on the bank. Harold sat in the bow, blowing into his cupped hands.

"Come on," he said.

"Just a minute." I scrambled back up the bank to the clearing and scattered the fire. I stomped the coals into smoke. I could smell the rubber soles of my shoes as I beat the flames down. Vehicles coming through the pines. Oh, Christ Jesus. I ran to the boat.

"Okay, okay," I cried. I pushed off with the paddle. We glided out into the river. A new moon was up in the west. It held the old moon in its arms. We pulled steadily away from camp, from stalkers drawing closer. Along the banks the reeds were topped with silver. It was a fine, clear night, deep in the heart of winter. This was no time to be on a river. We left the sound of engines behind the third bend, but we paddled steadily on into darkness.

"Diminished. I'm diminished," Harold cried.

"Not you, Harold—it's me. Goddamn, paddle," I said.

We could follow the course easily past banks darker than the river. Stars shone in the water. I paddled carefully; without entering the rhythm, I tried to make each plunge of the paddle into the water as soundless as possible.

Pines gave way to grass; tidal mud stank on the banks. The breeze died. We paddled steadily, as the river, bunched against the sea mouth, twisted on itself.

"Yip, yip," Harold cried; he held his empty beer can under until it filled, then tossed it ahead of us into darkness. It splashed heavily. "Mullet, jump," he cried. "Lost, lost."

"And by the wind grieved," I said, "O mullet, come back again. Alene, hand me a beer."

She threw one back. I cracked it and paddled holding it. The moon had slipped below the horizon. I wanted out of this boat, and I placed my hands on the gunwales and rocked it to let them know. Harold lurched and nearly fell in.

"Watch it," he said. I looked back at the thin froth of bubbles trailing. No sounds from the rear but our own wake gurgling.

"Harold, you're not diminished," I called forward. "You're just unsatisfied."

"I am reduced," he replied, "below the level of essentials."

"You people are fools," Alene said. The collar of her parka was turned up around her ears. It pushed her hair up in a dome around her head.

"That's not true," I said. "Harold's upset because we ran out on this cold river."

"Without even snow to obscure us—I can say that. I can tell what I've done."

"What is it, Harold?"

"I've outlawed us," he said.

"You saw lights."

"Maybe it was Saint Elmo's fire."

"Swamp gas."

"Farts in the duckweed, quack, quack." He reached behind him into the cooler and drew out another beer.

Tense and angry in the cold, we were little huddling, paddling centers of warmth out here in Florida. We wanted to take chances: Harold had run as much because of plain energy as because of marauders. We wanted to frisk, to festoon the journey with splashes—I did, at least—but it was cold, the water stung like bees, this was a flimsy boat, it was night, and we had to be careful. Alene spit into the water out of a scowl. Harold took his song softly up. It was "Foggy, Foggy Dew," a tune both of us had known since childhood. I joined him, remembering my father singing it when I was little and the fright it gave me to think that

the woman of whom he sang—who was clearly not my mother—
was the woman he loved.

"You sing like frogs," Alene said.

"But we sing, sugar," Harold answered. "We sing."

He hummed and took it up again. A beautiful woman whom
he lost in the foggy, foggy dew.

The tide ran against us. We had to keep paddling or lose
ground. My neck ached. When Alene began to curse, I shipped
my paddle, knelt forward and embraced her. "I am *freezing*," she
said.

"Do you want to paddle?"

"No."

"Then there's nothing we can do."

"Let's stop." She held herself tightly under my arms.

"We're near the end of the river—we can stop there. There's
nothing along here but mud and grass." Hungry crabs staring out
of holes.

"Fuck," she said.

"Why don't you have a beer."

"I don't like beer."

"Okay." I got back on my seat.

We rounded a nearly 180-degree bend. Sticks with strips of
cloth tied to the tops marked the channel. I tucked my head and
paddled.

The sky lightened in the east. The day came up fair. The river
broadened as we approached St. Lukes, and a breeze came up,
walking the water toward us. Gulls rose from pilings in front of
an abandoned marina and wheeled above us, crying. An old barge
lay half out of the water on the bank, thin waves lapping at the
pilothouse. Flour dust floated in patches on the water. A freighter
loaded at the mill, its lights faintly gleaming. We passed the city
docks. A man in jeans and a blue work shirt swept trash down the
public boat ramp. He didn't look up. We slipped past the point
where the old Spanish fort slept under live oaks and cedars hung
with moss, and headed west along the shore into the refuge. Grass
alternated with stretches of gray, seaweed-strewn sand. Grassy
islands floated in Oyster Bay, tiny as yards. We reached a beach
in the deepest bend of marshy cove, pulled in, and came ashore.

Grass grew back from the beach to a sand road and a stand of cedars. A sign on a post in shallow water said: ST. LUKES NATIONAL WILDLIFE REFUGE NO CAMPING NO FIRES. We spread the poncho on the grass in front of a bank of yaupons, threw the bags down, crawled in, and went to sleep under a fair, empty, frozen sky.

X

I WOKE out of a dream to the sound of geese honking, my heart throbbing like a sting. Harold and Alene were asleep. I got up and walked down to the water. A flock of Canada geese swam out near the point, jostling and talking among themselves. The bay was in a flat calm. Shaggy-headed islands hung low on the horizon far out. One or two had stands of pine rising out of the grass.

In the dream I had been a kind of houseboy for Frieda in a house that I was unfamiliar with. I ran errands and cleaned, I guess. She would smile at me on her way out in the morning. We had been lovers, but we were no longer. I never saw the man she was with now. She teased me, laughing, as she whirled by in a blue dress; I could hear them talking above the sound of a television in the next room. In the morning I would find their empty glasses and rumpled sheets. Even in the dream I felt a pressure to act but could not. Then, for a brief period, the scene shifted and I was walking alone down a sandy road under a canopy of huge live oaks. I was completely at peace. Everything was solved. Later I was at Frieda's again, but I remembered the peace that had filled me on the road, and I strained in sleep for the rest of the night, half awake always, it seemed, to find my way back there.

I touched my wrist and found the racing pulse. It wasn't going to tell me anything. I knelt and dipped my fingers into the cold water, but I didn't touch myself—better sleep in the eyes than salt. The bay was empty but for the geese, not even oystermen out.

"Good morning," someone said behind me. I turned around. It

was an old woman in a long housedress, a gray cardigan sweater, and sneakers. She watched me from the road.

"Hello," I said. She crossed the grass, glancing at Harold and Alene, and came up to me.

"Camping?" she asked.

"Yes'm." Her white hair was tied back in a scarf. She was eating a grapefruit half with a spoon.

We looked out at the geese, without saying anything. She spit a seed into the sand. I was glad to see somebody.

"You live here?" I asked.

"For fifty years," she said. She swung her arm toward a green roof among pines. "I live up yonder," she said. "I used to live with my brother, but he died five years ago. Now I'm the only one here."

She spat another seed. "It's a forsaken place," she said.

That was the first time I had heard someone use a word like that in real life. She said it simply, as a fact. There was no emotion in her face or in her voice. I felt a pain in my chest, suddenly, like a heart attack. I filled with something, and I wanted to sit down. Things were simpler than I had thought. You just lived quietly and there life was, honking in the bay. In my dream I had walked on the road happy as a ghost. She looked at me.

"You feel all right?" she asked.

"I don't know," I said.

"Well, it'd be terrible if you did—you got a white face."

"I been out of the light," I said.

"Hadn't we all." She looked out at the bay. "When I was a girl, this bay was full of geese. We used to scoop feathers off the water for pillows. You could fill a mattress in a morning." The geese bobbed in the water, honking.

"I wish I had one," I said. "Let me sit down here." I sat down on the sand. Cold came through my pants. I felt as though things were getting solved whether I wanted them to or not. Frieda was lost to me, no matter what I did. I had wanted to hold her even if I had to imagine her naked in her lank-haired lover's arms. I didn't care, didn't care. But there was something else, something else besides watching through a crack in a hall door as my wife fucked another man. Things could be released. I was going to break if I didn't let go my hold. And here this woman walks up in sneakers, her freckled hands now holding her sweater around her, a man's sweater with buttons carved from antlers . . . perhaps her brother's sweater. If the place was forsaken, she seemed all right. I couldn't say. Perhaps the sweater was her brother's. But what could this sadness be if it wasn't for Frieda?

"Why, you know it snowed here evening before last," she said abruptly. "It was the first snow I've seen in ten years."

"It caught us on the river," I said.

"Which river?"

"Crystal."

"I don't care much for the woods in these kinds of days," she said.

"It didn't do us much good either."

She turned and looked at Harold and Alene, who lay close against each other, in separate bags, asleep.

"That looks like a hard way to do it," she said.

"Well, we're not orphans. We're out here for fun." Did she mean fucking?

"I believe indoors is where I'd look for it. But then," she said, "the woods is wide, and you can find God's beauty in there."

"It goes both ways."

"I reckon." She squeezed grapefruit juice into her mouth. "If y'all want something hot to eat you can come up here to the house —I'm going to be eating lunch directly."

"We'd like that."

"By myself I get out of the habit of cooking, what with just one person. But y'all are welcome to come. I've got some soup."

"We will, then."

She turned to go, then stopped. "I'm out here walking for my doctor," she said. "He says it helps my blood, and I have to do it three times a day." She swung her arm as if she might throw the grapefruit husk, but then she let her hand fall, still holding it. "I don't mind the walking," she said. "I think I could look out at this bay all day long. I've learned that now." She started away.

"You and your friends come up to the house if you want," she said, half turning back.

"All right. We'll be there when I can get them up."

"Goodbye, then."

"See you later."

She walked away up the road, bending forward slightly, as if she had walked for a long time with a cane that was no longer there.

I looked out. The geese were too far away to be scared by us. Unless Alene took a notion to bag one for brunch. But a .410 wasn't going to kill from here, not with quail shot in the load.

I ran a few steps down the beach and slowed to a walk. Thin waves, like the remnants of our own light wake, slipped noiselessly up the sand and fell back. Small blue crabs hunkered in the clear water near shore; they scurried away as I passed. The sky was high and white, the sun shone weakly through. There was nothing on the point but grass giving up to water. I turned around and came back.

"Oh, children," I called when I reached the camp. "Time to rise."

Harold looked up.

"Doggie bag," he said. "You, Jack, bring my doggie and my doggie bag. Are the cops out there?"

"In three Mercedes outboards," I said, kneeling on my bag. "They're armed with twelve-gauge pumps, and they say this time they're not fooling."

"Tell them I'll be with them shortly." He yawned. "Is that geese honking?"

"Sure is."

"My Lord, look at them." The geese had drifted out toward the center of the bay; they were still far out.

"I used to come down here hunting with my daddy and the preacher when I was little," he said. "Must have been down here half a dozen times without ever firing a gun."

"Firing one now wouldn't set the table."

He sat up. "Look at them—just talking to themselves. Was somebody here?"

"Yeah. An old woman; she lives up there. She said this was a forsaken place."

"Forsaken by whom?"

"The county commissioners, I guess. She asked us up to lunch."

"I'm for that."

"Well, let's go." I shook my shoulders. I was nervous. I wanted to keep moving, and I didn't like the way Harold was sucking his teeth. I wanted to run across the land. I got up and walked down to the water.

Harold had told me a story once of a friend of his in Vietnam who had fallen out of a helicopter. They had been in a field getting picked up, his friend had climbed aboard, the helicopter had taken off, but about fifty feet above the ground it made a sudden lurch and his friend fell out the open door. He landed on his back in the field ("I could have caught him," Harold had said) and immediately tried to get up.

"We had to hold him down," Harold had said. "He kept saying over and over, 'I got to go, I got to go.' His eyes were wild—no, not wild, just focused on something else. He rolled back and forth in our arms.

"It was strange," he said. "He was broken up inside, and he thought he could run away from it—from his body."

I kicked a clot of seaweed into the water. It seemed, at that moment, all I wanted to do too—run my ass down the road. I went over to the canoe and got a pickled egg out of the jar. I wondered what the freezing point of vinegar was. Silver fingerling fish played around the stern of the canoe. For yards out I could see the bottom, the sand ridged like muscles.

"You down there martyrizing?" Harold called. "You decided to remain aloof?"

I turned around. "I've decided you don't know how to pickle eggs," I said.

"What?" He came up, pulling my sweater over his head. He spoke through wool. "You say that to the culinary wizard of the country?" His rusty head popped through. "Here, let me have a bite." I gave him the egg.

"They haven't been in long enough," he said, chewing. "I just set them up last week."

"And more pepper," I said. "They need more hot pepper."

"That's your affliction," he said. "Which reminds me—I was

thinking about oysters last night. We ought to stop at Pony's on the way back and get some."

"And some smoked mullet."

"Oh, yes—but I heard they don't have it anymore. The town passed an ordinance against burning inside the city limits, so they can't run the smoker."

"Eejits."

Alene had risen and was bent over, tying her bag. What a fine ass in jeans. She had on one of my sweaters, too. She came down to us, carrying the bag.

"Which way now?" she said. She threw the bag in the canoe.

"Up there." I pointed at the green roof.

"What for?" She pushed her hair back with both hands.

"An old lady asked us up to lunch."

"Is that who you were talking to?"

"It certainly was." I touched her breast through the sweater. Soft nipple sleeping.

"Are those geese?" she asked. She shaded her eyes with her hand, though the sky was not bright.

"Yes," I said.

"Why don't you shoot one?"

"Alene—we can't shoot everything. That woman who was just here told me that when she was a girl they used to gather down off the water and make pillows out of it."

"Isn't that something." She reached into the canoe and pulled out the gun. "Let me see if I can hit one."

"Ah agh," I said. "Don't you do that." I grabbed the gun by the barrel and held it pointed away down the beach.

"Quit it," she cried, trying to jerk loose.

I pulled the gun up, it fired into the sky, and I took it away from her. She reached for it, then dropped her hands.

"You shitpiss," she said. Her eyes were cold and murderous. She was willing to shoot me. Something changed in me when I saw that look. I knew how it was for her, how it was going to be.

"There's no reason to kill those birds," I said. "Just cut the shit out."

"You don't do that," she said. "You don't do that." She turned her face away and looked out at the bay. Her eyes could have blasted the whole flock. I felt terrible, and relieved. I had broken the back of my little romance. Then I nearly reeled away, as the shadow I had called up on the river seemed to move toward me out of the corner of my eye. I touched Alene's rigid shoulder. She snapped my hand away.

"Don't touch me, shit," she said.

"Alene . . . damn, don't."

"You all don't hurt yourselves," Harold said quietly. "Let's go up and get lunch."

He started up the road. We stayed where we were. He stopped.

"Alene," he said, "come on. Aren't you hungry?"

She turned, without looking at me, and followed him, without speaking. I let them get ahead, then followed too, feeling that I had torn another chance loose and lost it, feeling my penis rise as I watched her ass move in her jeans—not shadows—and I walked along that way, behind them, Harold's hand resting casually on Alene's shoulder, me trailing, touching myself through cloth as I walked.

The house was screened in across the front and around one side. A galvanized pipe ran off the roof into a wooden water tank. Lank, freeze-burned azaleas grew in the dirt yard. Harold held the porch door open for Alene and waited on the top step for me. I came up, adjusting my crotch. He looked at me and smiled but said nothing.

The porch was bare except for a twine seine net folded in a pile next to the front door and a swing hung by chains from a rafter at one end. Alene bent to look through curtained front windows.

"Who is this?" she asked. "It looks like a funeral parlor."

I knocked on the front door. I heard footsteps, and the old woman pulled the curtain back and looked out through the glass panel. She opened the door.

"Come on in the house," she said. She turned her back and was already heading down a dark, carpeted hallway when we got through the door. "Come on to the kitchen," she said. I caught up with her as she banged through a screen door and onto another porch, which ran along the back ell of the house.

"I just leave that front," she said. "I can't afford to heat it, and

I don't even turn on the lights." In the backyard a few chickens scratched at dirt. A barbed-wire fence separated the yard from an open lot that was backed by a fallen-in barn and a shed. A gourd martin house hung from the top of a pole between the barn and the shed.

"We can eat in the kitchen," she said. Her sneakers squeaked on the bare boards.

She led us into a high-ceilinged kitchen that was bright with light. Geraniums flowered in cans in the windows. We sat down at a table that was covered with a flowered plastic cloth. She crossed the room to a pot steaming on the stove.

"You mind helping me, honey?" she said to Alene as she lifted the pot off the stove.

"No, thank you," Alene said.

"I'll get it," Harold said quickly, and took the pot. "Where do you want it?"

"Just put it right over here on the table—wait a minute." She folded a towel and placed it under the pot. I rose.

"I'll get the bowls," I said. Alene stared at the door.

"They're in the cabinet," the old woman said.

I picked four bowls and saucers out of mixed crockery and set them on the table. The woman laid spoons on the cloth.

"Y'all want bread?" she said.

"You betcha," Harold said.

She took a half loaf from the refrigerator. "Milk?"

"Fine," I said. She set the bread and a quart of milk on the table. "There." She sat down and tucked her head in a quick, wordless grace. She looked up. "Y'all eat," she said.

The soup was vegetable. I blew into a spoonful and tasted it. It was just what I needed. Whole tomatoes flaccid as the hornet's nest. Oh, oh. I took another spoonful, closed my eyes, and ate.

"I'm Miss Alma Brannen," the old woman said. "I'm glad to have you here."

"I'm Jack Dupree," I said. "This is Harold Johnson."

Alene said nothing. She leaned close to her bowl, spooning in soup.

"Who are you, darling?" Miss Brannen asked.

"I'm the one that got shamelessly hauled down here," she said.

"You did? Why is that?"

"Kidnapped," Alene said.

"This is Alene," Harold said. "This cold's got us tired out." Alene gave him a hard look. She took a slice of bread, ripped it in half, and dunked it in her soup.

"I'm not too tired," she said.

"Lord, I am," Harold said. "I felt the cold all night long."

"If you hadn't got scared and run." Alene laughed. "Crackers," she said.

"Well, I'm an old cracker woman myself," Miss Brannen said. "Florida cracker. I been down here crackering on this bay all my life."

"I don't see how you stand it," Alene said. "I know I couldn't."

"Be thankful you don't have to, then," Miss Brannen said, and laughed through perfect false teeth.

"Don't you worry," Alene said.

I felt like slugging the little maniac. Christ, Alene. The cuffs of her parka were dirty, but the wrist that slipped out as she raised the spoon was clean and white. She held her hair out of her soup and didn't look at anybody. And I wanted to touch her. I wanted to sit on sunny back steps with the scent of her hair in my nostrils as she leaned against me and think about my dream. How peaceful I had felt walking on that road. But though the trees I could see through the window opposite were green—cabbage palms and pines—it was winter, and the sky above branches was that high whooping white, whiter than pearl, that appears in winter only, and what would the dream mean to Alene, and to Frieda tossing in sheets next door? I picked a butter bean off the side of my bowl. This was enough—I was thankful, thankful enough to be in this warm kitchen, eating soup. And maybe I didn't need to press my face into Alene's gray-stained hair at all. Wrenching the gun away from her had done me good. The little explosion of action had popped me out of myself. Frieda's grip—someone's—had for a moment weakened.

I looked at Alene as she thrust her fierce face toward her bowl. For a second I saw the thing in her face, her look—brows bunched —the thing that was as different from me and what I knew as I

was different from geese cruising in the bay; it was a lie, this easy
kitchen relaxation, this warm soup—there was no dream, there
was no shadow, there was simply this woman here, simply fine
dark hairs on a clean wrist, simply her, now, I wanted, and I
reached across the table and with one finger touched a wisp of hair
in front of her ear.

"Whatever you do is all right," I said. "I'm sorry about before
—I don't expect anything of you."

She flicked my hand away. "I don't worry about that," she said.

Miss Brannen rose. "Let me get you some more soup," she said.

"I wouldn't mind a bit," Harold said, getting up too.

"I'm fine," I said.

Instead of answering, Alene got up, placed her spoon next to
her bowl, and walked out onto the porch. I watched her wash her
hands in the sink, dry them on a towel, then stand looking into
the yard. She raised her arms and pressed her open palms against
the screen. It was a gesture a man might make, and the way she
cocked her knee forward, keeping her weight on the other leg,
was a man's attitude too. I had never seen a woman do that.

At the stove, Miss Brannen filled the bowl Harold held.

"I don't usually make this much soup—or make soup at all,"
she said, "but I've been collecting leftovers for a week, and this
morning I decided to go ahead."

"It's delicious," Harold said. "Just a little more."

"Wouldn't you like some more—Jack?" she asked me.

"No, thank you. What day is today?"

"Sunday," she said.

I couldn't keep my eyes off Alene. She stood stiffly, looking
out, her palms flat against the screen. As I watched, she thrust
her hair back smoothly with one hand and turned. Her face was
calm, though her eyes didn't seem to be seeing us.

"A car just drove into the yard," she said, and turned back to
the screen.

"It's probably Jimmy Peters," Miss Brannen said, crossing to
the door.

"Who is that?" Harold asked.

"The ranger." She paused with her hand on the latch. "He'll

probably tell you not to camp here," she said. "They're right touchy about it; and Jimmy is one of the touchiest." She went out.

"Oh, fuck," Harold said, looking at me. "The bastard is looking for us."

He jumped up and ran to the back window and came back to the table. "We'd better get out of here," he said.

"You think so?" My heart pounded, but not for fear of capture only.

"Come on," he said, going out the door.

For a moment I couldn't move. My shoulders were heavy as cement, though a sharp pain had shot suddenly through them. Four bowls on plastic cloth, three empty, one full; four spoons. Geraniums in the window. Sweet potato roots crawling in a jar. All right. All right. I pushed myself up with both hands. Another slice of bread, for the energy that was in it. Thank you, Miss B., but we've got to run.

Harold ran down the back steps ahead of Alene. I followed with the slice of white bread in my mouth.

"We can cut through the woods," Harold said.

We ducked under the fence and ran through the lot, scattering chickens. Behind us in the house someone yelled, but no matter, we dashed between barn and shed (my hand slapping the martin house pole for luck), into woods.

The ground was covered with leaves and pine straw. The woods, dark and gummy in summer, rattlesnake and chigger woods, were stiff and odorless. A branch lashed my face. I caught up with Alene and ran beside her. Ahead, Harold fought as he ran, forcing branches back, but Alene ran as if she were the leader of an easy race: upright, head back, hardly bothering with snaps of undergrowth.

We broke out into the marsh and ran through the tough, waist-high grass toward the canoe. Fiddler crabs slipped into holes, quick as roaches. The geese still floated in the bay. Such a high reach of sky I wanted suddenly to tear through. Alene! Alene! I touched her parka, my fingers slid down its nylon skin, but we could not stop for caresses. There ahead the canoe, left dry by tide; it sat, flat as a shoe, in sand.

We reached the beach as the ranger was getting out of his government pickup.

"Hey," he said, "wait a minute," and crossed the grass, holding his gun in its holster.

We walked to the canoe and stopped beside it. Harold touched the bow, brushed off nothing, and straightened up.

The ranger came up to us. He was tall and wore a cap.

"I want to speak to you," he said.

"Okay," Harold said. "I got a minute."

"I don't," Alene said. "I'm going."

"Be quiet, Alene," Harold said. It was the first time he had spoken harshly to her. He reached for her, but she pulled her arm away.

"No, thank you," she said.

"Come up here to the truck," the ranger said. He unsnapped his gun and ran his hand along the butt. The pain in my shoulders had moved into my chest. Wait, wait just a minute—we're all right.

"I'm not going with *you*," Alene said to the ranger. He started to speak as she whirled on us. "And I'm not going with *you*," she said. She began to drag the canoe by the stern into the water.

"You wait right there," the ranger said. He took a step forward.

"No," Alene said. She waded into the water, pulling the canoe. We didn't move.

"I can't let you go," the ranger said, and grabbed the canoe by the bow.

"You can't do anything about it, squirt," Alene said. She got in the canoe. It rocked, barely afloat, in the shallow water.

"Stop it right there," the ranger cried.

"Shit." She laughed and reached for the gun that lay across the boxes in front of her. The ranger reached for his gun too, but he wasn't as fast as Alene. From the waist she had the .410 leveled at him before his pistol was halfway out of the holster. "You dummy," she said.

The ranger's face went white. For a second I thought she was going to shoot him. But she didn't. She didn't back down on it, though; she just had other plans.

She made him ease his gun out and throw it into the bay. Then, she made Harold tie up the ranger with a cargo rope. She didn't bother with us.

"What now?" Harold said, trying to joke. He was smiling hard.

"I don't care what happens to you," she said. She crossed the grass and got in the truck.

"Easy come, easy go," Harold said.

I touched my face; there were tears. I had an impulse to follow her, to go where she was going, to see one more time how she banged past whatever was trying to stop her, to learn whatever lesson I hadn't learned from Frieda, but I stayed where I was.

She leaned out the window. "You'll just have to learn to live with it, sport," she said, I guess to me. Then she wrenched the truck into gear and gunned it out of there.

Nobody ever saw her again, nobody I ever heard about. They found the truck a week later on a street in Mobile. Alene was wanted before she pulled the gun on the ranger, and we had a lot of talking to do, but in the end, after a nonjury trial in Tallahassee, we got off with a couple years probation.

She said I'd have to learn to live with it, whatever it was. That is what I am doing.

Tinian

I am not ready for repentance;
Nor to match regrets . . .
— HART CRANE, *"Legend"*

I

E W A S twelve twice and later he was nineteen twice. Two birthdays tracked over and lived again, like the life of the Infanta Morata who, so his uncle said, was able to restart herself over and over—old or young—wherever she chose. For him the mystery of turning twelve twice was only a repetition: fleeing a hurricane from one time zone to the next—Florida to Alabama—: sleeping in the back seat he had flown backwards a moment—an almost unnoticed occasion. But nineteen two times was different. Not repetition only, but circumstance, a new life, a second life breaking into being around him. He had crossed the International Date Line on his way from the States to the Mariana Islands, chasing his brother who would vanish into white light and eternity, like the Infanta herself.

He had followed his mother to Tinian, where she had gone to save his brother, who had disappeared on a phony search for the last Japanese soldier. There were Japanese who, thirty years after the war, still hid out in the jungles of the Pacific islands. Native people saw them slipping along the edges of the banana fields, scrambling up a coral ridge. His brother, who had studied the Japanese language for eight years by correspondence and in college, who was a scholar of the poetry of Bashō and Marichiko, who was a poet himself, who practiced a desultory Zen, decided, after Helen left him, decided in his brokenheartedness, which had driven him mad and taken away his hope, after reading in an East-West journal about the handful of Japanese soldiers still marooned in the Pacific jungles unaware that the war was over, that he would go and find them, lead them out. "It's the final piece," he told

1 4 7

them, "the final piece of the puzzle. Which aches to be completed."

They sat out on the back porch, his brother Effie, his mother, and him, watching the summer evening lay itself down in the stubbled hayfields. The yellow-banded disarrayed fields made Paul think of the sea marshes. As the fading sun drew light from the farm, he said, quoting Sidney Lanier, " 'Who knows what swimmeth below when the tide comes in / Along the length and the breadth of the marvelous marshes of Glen.' "

His mother said, "Why don't you go find the Vietnam POWs? They're more current." She was dressed all in white and wore a white nurse's cap, one of the winged caps from a convent nursing school, though she had no such profession nor had she been in a convent. Her white-stockinged feet were propped on the middle rung of a plant ladder, and she balanced on her chest a tall glass of sugarcane juice. His brother lay on his back on the glider, one foot rocking him slightly, looking down his chest at the fields that Paul knew he did not see. He raised his hand and stared at the back of it, veins or nails, Paul couldn't tell which. It was a feminine gesture, the hand straight out, fingers extended, and curiously arrogant. "Because," he said slowly, speaking to his fingertips, "I don't speak Vietnamese."

"What kind of language are you going to speak," his mother said, "to a crazed soldier who has hidden under leaves in a jungle for thirty years? You think you know words he'll understand?"

Effie pressed his forehead with the backs of both hands. "I know suffering," he said. "It's a common language."

"Poo—all you know is a wife left you. I told you when you met her she was going to do that. Some creatures can't sit still."

"Mama, I met her when I was six; and you told me no such thing."

Paul was amazed that his mother took his brother seriously. As far as he was concerned, talk of ferreting out the lost Japanese was craziness. He pushed out of his chair and crossed the porch to the kitchen door. The smell of boiling mustard greens wafted from the stove, sharp and pungent. "I think you are out of your minds," he said. "Both of you."

They raised their heads, mother and brother, and looked at him

out of identical pairs of amber eyes. Eyes with the hardness and
the dull gleam of chunks of turpentine resin. Like two sets of
grained stone undissolved on the bottom of a stream. He could see
that they didn't understand what he was talking about. Anything
that came into their heads, no matter how bauchy or unusual, was
all right with them, all right just by the mere fact that it *had*
entered their heads. Like the time she had him throw a chocolate
cream pie in her face because she had seen it done in a movie. To
experience it. Like the time his brother built a monkey bridge
across Little Foster Creek, built it from one pine bluff to another
without a path leading anywhere on either side. As if there was no
journey, just a bridge.

"Would you check the greens, dear?" his mother said. "I think
I hear them boiling over."

"You check the goddamn greens," Paul said. He crossed the
porch, slammed out through the screen door, and started across
the backyard toward the barn.

"We'll be eating in an hour," his mother called, her voice lazy
and blurred, as if she were about to fall asleep. "We'll look for
you then."

He walked through the Dog Pasture, kicking flower heads and
singing some light old song to himself. His brother, even in the
middle of his misery, was capable of thinking up an adventure.
Effie had been a shrimper and a logger, a semipro baseball player,
a translator in New York; he had ferried Mercedes-Benz automobiles to Mexico for rich *caballeros;* he had published a version of
the suppressed poems of Baudelaire. On a trip to see his mother
the year before, he had rediscovered Helen Jenkins, who had been
his sweetheart in the third grade, and within a month had married
her. Helen ran her family's thousand-acre cotton and tobacco farm
down on the south end of the county. It was a working farm, a
money-maker, rich with the hematitic dust thrown up by tractors
and harvesters, an enterprise that her father, old Wheeler Jenkins,
had taught her to sweat and toil over. Unlike the Hogan farm,
sprawling up out of the Chicopee River sloughs like a weary old
alligator, gone mostly to ruin and hayfields, the few stringy beef

cattle all that was left of the show herd his mother's father had built up in the late forties. His mother liked the raggedness of the land now, the shaggy fields coming up in gallberry scrub and yellow pine. The only reason she grew hay was that she liked the way it looked in the fields, the way the sun shone on it. "I can learn from that," she told them. "I can sit on the porch and watch the high world have its way with those fields and learn the secrets of life." She never said what the secrets of life were, but nobody's attempts to get her to renew her allotments for tobacco and peanuts were to any avail. She wasn't interested, she said, in banging on a piece of ground to make it cough up silver. Just a touch here and there, she said, that's all it needs. And a touch was all she gave it. In a good year she might clear twenty thousand dollars from her hay and cattle. That and the money their father left her, invested in tax-free municipal bonds and bridge and highway projects, kept her satisfied. The income was, in truth, quite substantial. And she took her investments seriously, visiting the sites of municipal improvements in Memphis and Tampa, walking along the banks of Tennessee Valley projects to check the hang of a bridge or the gimbal and curve of a highway. "If you're going to do it you have to pay attention to it," she'd say, which would make Paul furious because all he had to do was look out the bedroom window to see how she had let what was given first and foremost—stewardship of this four thousand acres of ground— crumble and rust and fray before their eyes.

Not that his father had done much better. Historian, belletrist, biographer of Jefferson Davis, he had viewed the land as his personal link to the glorious time when giants walked the earth. The soul had withered in modern man, as far as his father was concerned, and if he could not resuscitate it, he could at least vivify it in memory, tell the story of the time in which men spoke in private like orators. It had not been enough, freshening the memory: eight years earlier, when Paul was ten, his father—in the privy of the rachitic old barn his great-grandfather had built, the cap piece of the Dog Pasture—fed up with trying to win for himself a place to stand in the worn-away world, had levered himself into heaven with a single shot from his twelve-gauge double-barreled duck gun.

He was buried in Deep Bottom Cemetery, the family ground, which was not a bottom at all but a cedar-covered hill on the east side of the farm, where all Paul's dead kin were buried.

His mother said the grave did not hold him. She spoke, she said, to his father in the night. He came to her dressed in an ice cream suit, which was unlike, she said, anything he ever wore in his life, and talked to her. He stood in the boxwoods outside her bedroom window and talked to her about his troubles. "He hasn't changed a bit," she told them. "*His* struggle is still the overriding concern of his life. He hasn't once asked me how I am doing. As long as I am breathing he figures I am fine, just like he did before he became a shade. It infuriates me. Sometimes I try to break in on him—he hated to be interrupted—but he doesn't, dead, seem to notice. He just keeps rattling on, all wrapped up in the death of the questering spirit in Western man. Jesus Criminy."

The sky was a great bold clear blue. The kind of blue that made him think it must not stop until it hit the Arctic. And the fields beyond the pasture, cut now to stubble, the raked lines curving like a diagram of waves of light toward the line of pines that marked the first fall of land toward the river, shone in the sunlight bright as a palomino's coat. There was a sweet smell in the air: some flower he didn't know the name of. He was eighteen years old, blond, with the same green eyes that had shone from his father's face. His uncle, Maurice, sculptor of religious statues, had said, Paul overhearing him from the second-floor landing after the funeral, that a suicide father aimed the gun at his son. "That trigger says: You cannot make it," he had heard his uncle say, and then his mother had screamed at him to shut up, yelled him into silence. Which son, he thought—me? Along the western edge of the pasture the chokecherries were piled over with fox grapes. Each year the grapes made and each year the birds ate them before anybody thought or took the trouble to climb up and pick them. They left only their smell, the sweet-sour perfume of rotting juice. Three-pointed leaves, the grapes speckled gold, drinking sunlight, and the birds knowing when to come, when to light. Do I know enough to save myself? Can I learn enough? His mother paid no attention to saving anything. Easy come, easy go, she said, come around again someday. But some things never returned, as his father knew. Not in this lifetime. A hundred miles north, near Irwinville, in Georgia, Jefferson Davis had been captured by a squad of Yankee cavalry. They had surprised him as he sat drinking coffee at a campfire in the pinewoods. The Yankees said he had been dressed as a woman, though Davis swore for the rest of his life that he had only thrown his wife's shawl over his shoulders against the cold. The claim left a taint on his honor, a taint that he never quite lived down. Always the accusation. The Confederacy dead and its leader running away in a dress. Some things are lost forever. Some mistakes never get undone.

He squatted in the clover, put his face down into it, and sighted over the purple flowers at the barn. His father's brains had been blown against the east wall. Agh. Agh. Effie thought he could track Helen down, entice her back. Which, Paul supposed, made his uncle's life a lie, his sculpture garden containing the World's Smallest Operational Cathedral, built to the glory of the Encyclopedic Christ, who would someday return. At the Recitations, his uncle, who sometimes attended, would quote scripture. He thought Jesus would smooth out their troubles. But it was with him as it was with all the Hogans: the private and the public life were unconnected; in some important way, too wide a gap had been left. Christ will come again, his uncle said (publicly), he will throw open the doors of heaven and men of goodwill will find a place at the feet of God. But some losses in this life (he said privately) could not be remedied, no matter who was God, no matter what he did. His uncle's concession to wisdom, or maybe it was to age, was to throw the doors wider; as he grew older he found, in his conception, more and more room for the failed and the miserable, for the lost. On a Sunday afternoon when they walked among the concrete pantheons and porticoes, the birdbaths and the fish pools glittering with embedded glass and aluminum disks, the plaster panels smoothed into the pebble walls, upon which were painted in baudy colors scripture verses that, his uncle had confided to him, would, if you read them in order, force you to your knees—walking side by side down a path paved with ballast stones that had weighted the bellies of ships carrying West Indian rum into Pensacola, his uncle, striking his long bony fingers through his glistening red hair, had said he hoped eventually to find a place in heaven for all the doomed ones, all the killers and savages.

"Even Hitler," he had said, "that pomaded murderer. And Stalin, and the woman in St. Petersburg that I read about last week who boiled her baby and served it to her family for supper." Uncle Maurice got his news from the tabloids, because, he said, that was where the cutting edge of our hopes and fears was honed. "Spaceships, million-dollar scores, women with no hair, children born with hands growing out of their bellies—that's where we live, that's where our thoughts reach. It's like stretching up to get the cookie jar high on the top shelf and discovering the spider."

Paul had shuddered as he walked, remembering the snakeskin his mother found in the attic the week after his father died. "What's most extreme in us," his uncle had said, swinging the four iron he used as a staff, "is what we have to look at, what we have to find a place for. If there's anything we can't let in the door —anything at all—then nothing gets in; we're all squatting on the steps, shivering." Paul had raised his eyes to the grotto ahead, the tiny church built out of pebbles and cement. It had a roof made of broken Coke glass embedded in pink stucco. Which led his mother to believe, she said, that the angels must be fairy commandos. It was large enough for a preacher and a congregation of four, if nobody moved a lot. His brother and Helen had been married there; the rest of them—mother, aunts, uncles, and cousins, his brother's old girlfriend from New York, a couple of his baseball buddies, a monk from Colorado who looked like a Hollywood jet pilot—had stood around outside under the new glistening spring leaves of the sweet gum and tulip poplars, listening to the old connective words wafting by like smoke, or prayers.

Paul reckoned all people needed a romance to keep them going. Everybody in his family did, except possibly his mother, who claimed to love the world the way it was. In the fall he would go back to Old Dominion College for his sophomore year; then what, he didn't know. Life would go on; he would have to come up with something. His mother would probably talk Effie out of running off to the South Pacific. There probably weren't any Japanese left in those islands anyway. What would it be like living thirty years alone in the woods with a dream? Just a dream, nothing to work it out on? His father told him it hadn't been God who died; it had been the soul. We've lived, he said, for a hundred years on pride and fear, and it's taken its toll. Perhaps Uncle Maurice, with his net of religious sculpture, could draw the afflicted up.

Say yes, his uncle said. That'll get you through.

His brother could sing before he could talk. He had been a weak child with wobbly heron legs, a child of coughs and night fevers, colicky tears. His mother had carried him from doctor to doctor through the old flatiron building downtown, and she often told Paul the story of how he would sing on their way up and down the iron stairs. "He would trill and coo, bob along like a bobolink, cluck like a mockingbird. I wanted to set him in a cage by the window just to listen to him sing."

It was a gift that vanished by the time he was of school age. That was years before Paul was born, but Paul could picture his mother carrying her swaddled trilling child through the streets of the county seat, uplifted by sweet remarkable song as she worried herself to death over whether her wan baby would die before she could get him cured.

Effie was in fact, even with all his ailments and afflictions about to carry him off, a singularly happy child. Paul's mother had told him that too. The singing was from joy. When he was a tiny baby, she had brought him into bed with her husband, stuffing him between them, causing his father to complain that they would crush the child. His mother never worried about that. "I would raise myself up and stare at him," she would say. "He was so pale, as pale as a potato in the dark, but he would lie there sleeping with the sweetest, happiest smile on his face."

She never got over the smile. The way she looked at his brother, the way her face lifted as he came into a room, the look of expectation in her eyes, made Paul think that she continued to hope, even as his brother's life tailed away into misery's cockeyed effort, that the old original smile would bloom on his lips again and she be sweetened.

The best time they ever had as brothers was the day of Paul's sixteenth birthday. It was one of the worst times too, but not because of Effie. That was the day they got drunk and wound up naked riding cows down the county highway. It was the day, too, that he saw his second dead person. The first, of course, was his father, whose cold lips he had kissed in the flower-heaped living room of their old farmhouse. His father had worn a turban of dark-blue cloth to cover his missing forehead and brain pan. He looked like a sleeping maharaja. The second dead person was a woman.

He had come down the narrow kitchen stairs on the morning of his birthday to find Effie, who was supposed, he said, to be at a lecture in New York, standing at the sink drinking vodka from a china flask. His face was as red as fired iron, and he hung over the sink as if it were the rail of a wallowing ship. Paul got out cereal and milk and began to eat at the table that his grandfather had hewn out of a virgin slash pine. His brother, back to him, lifted his arm and peered under it, as if it were a branch and he was a curious monkey. "How about a little sweetener?" he said.

"Mmm-mmm," Paul said.

"Does that mean yes?"

"In a minute. What's up?"

"Birthday celebration. Sweeney brought this elixir back from Russia last year, and I've been saving it for your birthday, or some such event. But I made the mistake of taking a sample." Sweeney was what he called his best friend, James, a name he had stolen from T. S. Eliot. He raised the bottle and let the clear fluid wet his lips. "You won't believe how good it is," he said.

"I'll believe it." Paul drank the last milk from the bowl, got up and washed his dishes, and took the bottle from Effie. It was white, flat and round like a cavalry canteen, and it had painted on one side a colored scene of a sleigh running through snowy woods. The bottle was ice cold.

"It tastes like snow and fire at the same time," he said after a small sip.

"Like a great blue sky over the steppes."

"Tolstoy."

"André."

"Lying on the battlefield at Borodino. Was it André?"

"I can't remember. Maybe it was Pierre." His brother took the bottle and tipped a meager sip. "No wonder they think they are going to rule us,"he said. "I would too, if I could make stuff like this. You remember the time we drank the white liquor?"

"Sure." That was only six years before, when on a breezy afternoon in midsummer they had thumbed to the beach and been picked up by a liquor runner in a black silk suit. The guy drove a '55 Chevrolet with the seats torn out of the back. Between Quincy and the beach he had pulled a Coke bottle from under the seat, unstoppered it, and given them a drink of the strongest liquid either of them had ever had in his mouth.

"I thought it would kill me," Effie said. "I thought I was willing to die to have it quit burning. What did he call it?"

"The devil's piss."

"It sure was that."

Effie had once painted the long white east wall in what he said was the style of Willem de Kooning. Yellows and whites, pinks and fire-engine reds had collided and ricocheted off each other like brutal bumper cars. Their mother had complained ("I don't want to be beat up first thing in the morning," she'd sniffed), and when he went back to New York she'd had the yardmen paint it over in flat white enamel that left the ghost of color underneath. It shone there now under the lime-white paint, riotous and faded like a circus seen through heavy fog.

Paul grasped his brother's hand that held the bottle, raised it, and took a long pull. The liquor was like melted silver. He turned around, and the room, which a minute before had been hung with morning shadow, brightened, the sun sprawled across the pine-board floor. "Wow," Paul said softly. "Wow." He felt as if he would like to do this, stand at the enameled sink with his brother, both their faces red as coals, laughing and exchanging swallows of Russia, forever.

"See," Effie said, as if he caught exactly what was on Paul's mind. "It was worth waiting for."

Their mother came in wearing her red kimono and tying her hair back with a black silk ribbon. She was barefoot.

"The loves of my life," she said. She crossed the room and kissed Paul on the cheek. She pulled back, her fine smooth-skinned face uptilted, and looked down her long nose at the bottle, "Ephraim," she said, "you're drinking in the morning."

"Queen Mary Voss Hogan, you've got to try this."

"I want peaches," she said. "Elbertas. I was lying up in my bed dreaming of peaches."

"I hope you get them, Mama," Paul said, feeling the liquor like soft strings being plucked.

"You shouldn't put the child through this," she said to Effie, a few gold flecks of affection glinting in her eyes.

Effie said, " 'Into this Dark beyond all light we play to come and, unseeing and unknowing, to see and to know Him that is beyond seeing and beyond knowing precisely by not seeing, by not knowing.' "

"Which makes me think of your father," she said, "whom I have been up talking to all night. That sounds like a Recitation." The Recitations were evening services, held on the side porch in summer, in the living room in winter. As ordained by their father, each family member was required to read a passage of stirring literature to the group. They went on once a week for years, until their father died.

"Dionysus," Effie said. "From the time of heroes. I think it was *pray*, though, not *play*."

"You want to hear me do 'This Living Hand'?" Paul said. Keats and a few cartwheels ought to brighten this party considerably.

"No, no," Effie said. "Too morose. What we need here is sweetness and light. Especially light."

Queen Mary opened the refrigerator door and began to rummage for peaches. "I know I had some," she said to the milk and eggs. "I bought them at the farmers market."

"It's too early for good peaches, Queenie," Effie said, and swatted her on the backside.

"You dickens!"

" 'This living hand,' " Paul said, holding his palm up, open-fingered, " 'now warm and capable of earnest grasping . . .' "

"You've been bad all your life, Effie Hogan."

"Bad to love my mama."

" '. . . would, if it were cold and in the icy silence of the tomb . . .' "

"Here it's this boy's birthday, and you're plying him with wine."

"What better time?" It was a stage play they acted out.

" '. . . so haunt thy days and chill thy dreaming nights, that thou wouldst wish thine own heart dry . . .' " He thought it was the brightest day he had ever seen. A blue jay hopped from branch to branch in the blossoming althaea by the old well, each hop a little kick in his heart. " '. . . of blood and thou be . . .' "

"Where're his presents? You're the mother—supposed to get the presents."

"I tend to business."

" '. . . conscience calmed.' " He lifted his face, which this morning had arrived through years shining to what seemed the first day of his manhood, held his hand out, palm toward them: mother and older brother standing in their strutted attitudes like two sides of a mirror. " 'See, here it is. I hold it towards you.' " Then he realized he had been hearing a siren coming their way. He cocked his ear, lazily interested, wondering at it. It came from town, grew louder, stopping his mother and brother's drama; they were still for a second, like rabbit dogs on the faint edge of a new trail.

"It's the cops, Mama," Effie said. "They've caught up with you at last."

"Shhh . . ." His mother bent her head to listen. Looking at her face, which was the face of a ravishing peasant woman, Paul thought it was as if the siren, which coming up the long hill under the sweet gums he could see was attached to an ambulance, a white-painted Cadillac sleek as a trout, *was* coming for her—in her eyes a look of wild expectation, welcome, and fright at the same time, as if, he thought, leaning over the sink past his brother's half-anesthetized body, under everything she said and did, lurking like an invisible stranger, was this waiting, this eye open for messages. Maybe it was why she heard their father in the night.

Effie, coming out of a dream, pushed away from the sink, shoved Paul with the bottle, and said, "Let's follow it. You want to come, Queenie?"

His mother seemed to shake herself loose from a stiff grip. "I've seen it already," she said.

"Okay, sport, let's go," Effie said, and ran out of the house.

Paul followed him out to Effie's truck, which was pulled up under the horseshoe oak, a two-hundred-year-old red oak that their father, when he was a young man, had hammered two horseshoes into the trunk of. All that was left of the iron shoes was two semicircles of metal, rounded rusted brackets sticking out, under the lowest limb. They got in, and Effie started the vehicle and roared out onto the highway.

The ambulance was out of sight, but they caught it as they came around the first bend. Down in the branch pond the cows stood knee-deep in the black water; egrets perched on their backs, strutted around in the muddy shallows. The ambulance turned down New Spring Road, siren blasting, red bubble on top turning.

They followed the white car to the Willow farm, where it turned in the drive and came to a halt in a flurry of gravel next to the screened side porch. Peter Willow, the old man, stood in the yard waving at them, as if they were far away, the way a man on a tractor out in a big field would wave at a plane inching across the sky. When the first attendant got out of the ambulance, Mr. Willow rushed up to him and threw his arms around him. The man, a boy really, dressed in a white coat and bright-green pants, shook the old man off and strode toward the back porch. Effie had pulled up under a flowering chinaberry tree and cut the motor; he opened the door, but he didn't get out of the truck. Paul started to, but his brother said, "Wait a minute; sit still."

They could see a pair of legs in cherry-red pedal pushers sticking out of the open screen door, lying across the steps. Effie said, " 'Quiet form upon the dust, / I cannot look and yet I must.' " Paul shuddered, experiencing a chill, as if, as his mother put it, the devil was walking across his grave. The purple chinaberry flowers smelled sweet as grape soda, and from the chicken yard beyond the blossoming tea olive bushes came the musty sulfurous scent of bird shit and the sound of the hens, clucking and rustling the dirt. His brother stared out the door at the scene, at the attendant bending over the prostrate form in the doorway, at old Mr. Willow hanging back, kneading his hands at the edge of wild new experience, at the other attendant, who sat alone in the ambulance cab, calling in a report over the radio.

"I discover that all I'm doing is hanging around waiting for the sudden veer," Effie said. "The lost gate in the fence row that leads into the world. It's my only interest." Paul felt the way he had since he was a twelve-year-old at camp and he called home, asked about his fox terrier, Baroni, and was told the dog had been run over by a tractor-trailer truck: from then on he never asked about the ones he loved, fearful that the news would be bad. He didn't want to find this out either, that Mrs. Willow, a skinny woman with hair she dyed yellow as lemons into her sixties, who at church on Sundays confused their names, called Paul Effie, asked him what life was like way up in New York City, had met with her doom. Her hands were so twisted by arthritis that they looked as if she had just withdrawn them from a crimp vise. When she touched him the place she touched smelled of witch hazel.

Effie got out of the truck. "You stay here," he said to Paul firmly, as if addressing a child. He strode across the newly cut lawn, up the concrete walk to the steps, and leaned over the attendant's shoulder. He looked a long moment at the form on the boards, spoke to the attendant, patted him on the back, and went on into the house. Queen Mary *looked* this morning as if she had been talking to their father in the night. Always when their father visited her she came downstairs worn but with her eyes glittering, like a morning-after reveler, body exhausted but spirit propped and shining on a spangled scaffolding of merriment. "That old linen-suited incubus must have given you quite a ride," Effie would say. And their mother would smile her secret smile.

I'll go see, Paul thought, but he didn't move. He didn't want any change, especially didn't want it on his birthday—why had his damn brother done this? He wanted only a golden moment stretching out forever. His father, the historian, had said we must look at history the way the mystic looks at his own soul, we must treat it as our own body being laid open for us; it all comes down, he said, to self-honesty. And for that, he always added, sighing at the moral failure of modern man, we need faith. All Paul wanted was a blackberry pie with a sugar crust. That would do for his sixteenth birthday. He didn't want to see anything that needed an ambulance.

He got out, saying to himself, *I don't want to know.* He was barefoot, and the dew, still on the grass at nine, wet his feet. Old Mr. Willow, who his uncle said was the best truck farmer in the county, czar of cabbages and bell peppers, and the meanest man, had retreated farther away. He stood under a sycamore, pressing one hand against the stripped white trunk as if secretly trying to push the tree over. A brindle cat slunk around his feet, mewing, but he didn't notice.

The attendant in the ambulance glanced at Paul as he passed and went back to talking on his radio. *Hello, John Bivens,* Paul said silently, recognizing him from grade school days, when he had peered through the fence at the high school boys. Along the walk Mrs. Willow had planted sweet alyssum; the tiny white clustered blooms bore footprints; already, Paul thought, her life has been treaded out. Confederate jasmine bloomed in a trellis against the screen porch. There was a sudden flash of blue, and a stooping jay disappeared into the mass of jasmine leaves, bursting out a second later with a tiny gray bird chick in its claws. "Hey!" Paul called. "Hey!" But the jay was gone over the electrical wires above the chicken house. Some bird had built its nest in the jasmine and now lost one of its biddies. It hurt his heart. As he came up to the steps, which were speckled with purple smears of bird shit, the jay swooped again, slamming into the mass of bushy foliage like a fastball. The bush shook, Paul heard a small weak cry, and the jay, cock's head raked back, yellow claws clutching two furry smidges, burst from the leaves and soared off into the sky. "Christ in heaven!" Paul cried. The first assault hadn't prepared him at all. He hadn't expected it to happen again. The attendant had not looked up. His body obscured the body that lay, Paul could see, in a green print blouse beneath him, but he was not administering to it. He was writing on a clipboard. Mrs. Willow's feet, clad in pink furry mules, stuck out the door. The veins in her ankles were blue and bulged.

"What happened?" Paul asked, thinking: God, I wish I'd killed that blue jay. I didn't think he'd hit again.

"Suicide," the attendant said without looking up. What stirred then in Paul was a desire: to see, to make this part of his life's record. He would have climbed over the man's broad back, but the man moved aside, looking up at him with rheumy brown eyes, then pointed down at a .410 shotgun lying against the bottom of a chest freezer against the wall. Paul stepped into the house without looking at the woman, who sprawled on her back, and picked up the gun. He broke the breech and plucked out the single bright-green shell, which was as thin as a crayon. The barrel was cold, and the breech smelled faintly of sour powder. Then he looked at the face at his feet. Her left cheek, freckled, was swollen, ballooned out as with a sudden highbush case of the mumps. Her eyes were closed, but her mouth was open and full of blood. Her unmoored dentures seemed to float in the blood, askew like a nasty joke. Her lips, yellow as beef fat, were drawn back from burst and ragged gums. Her candy hair, unfastened, swirled around her head as would the hair of a drowned swimmer. Her chin tilted up as if lifting for one last breath. His brother was back in the house; he could hear him walking from room to room. *This is what Russia tastes like,* Effie had said, swigging down the vodka. The liquor was cold as ice. Siberia. And my father six years ago, thrown backward against the wall of the old privy, sprawled across the shit holes, the smell of the ancient limed excrement masking the smell of gunpowder and blood. *Our entry is a bloody one,* his father had said, meaning birth. So, too, sometimes our exit. Spill of blood like crushed mulberries, like the swirling pelagic crimson in one of his brother's amateur paintings. What are we doing here? His body felt as if it were silting up, grains of fear and disgust sifting into the spaces between joints, into the crevices and interstices of his flesh. He could hardly move.

The attendant cursed, tore a sheet out of the clipboard, crumpled it, and began to write again. "I hate this shit," he said. "It's so useless." Did he mean death, or did he mean the paperwork? Strange job to be in if death bothered him. Paul heard they got used to it, heard it was no more than dressing a chicken. He looked back at the corpse, and then he could not take his eyes away. He felt as if he could stare on into eternity at such stillness. She wore an expression of arrogant disgust, a disgust and refusal so profound that the red well of her mouth did not destroy it. What could she hate so profoundly that she would wear its emblem into death? It was as if she had never breathed at all, as if she had never lived, as if she had been found here, rigid as a fossil, something permanently attached to this spruce-colored floor. Her green shirt was stamped with colored farm vegetables: tomatoes, pumpkins, tasseling ears of corn. Her unharnessed breasts sagged against the sides of the blouse, making her narrow chest seem wider. Except for the blush streaking her left cheek, her face was white, whiter than any face he had seen. The blood drained to the bottom of the body. He had read that. The buttocks, the ears, the heels, turned purple, the color of ripe plums. I don't want to look, but I must. He would like to take her home, this still object, lay her across the mantel for viewing and safekeeping. As in his brother's meditation, ritual of Zen, stare into the dead face until peace came. The dead shall be raised incorruptible. Uncle Maurice believed that. Better let them lie incorruptible. Like the harp bones of a fossil crustacean pressed into a chalky plate of limestone, shine on into eternity, still here, mute but necessary, like a milepost in the desert. Whew, he thought, it's too much for me. He wanted to go, didn't like death lying around at his feet. His brother was back in the house; he heard drawers opening, furniture moving.

"Effie, what are you doing?"

He heard a toilet flush, and then his brother came to the kitchen door. On his head was a straw hat heaped with artificial fruit: grapes and cherries, a long bright-yellow wax banana.

Paul said, "What are you doing?"

"Getting the feel."

The attendant looked up. "Ah, you guys. Fucking civilians. Get out of here."

"In a minute, bub," Effie said. He stepped out onto the porch, dropped to his knees, leaned over Mrs. Willow, and kissed her, once, lightly on the lips. He had to open his mouth wide to do it. He came up with his lips rimmed with blood, which he licked off with a purple-stained tongue. "There," he said. "There. Stretch her out and send her on." The attendant, who had watched his brother with disgust, shoved Effie so hard that he fell back against a pile of laundry next to the kitchen door. Paul saw then that his

brother was drunk. He made no move to resist the attendant, nor
did he retaliate. He got calmly to his feet, straightened his lady's
hat, and walked out into the yard.

Paul followed him, glad to get into the air. The other attendant, John Bivens, a short man with hair that showed the comb
marks, sauntered up the walk carrying a white bag. "Nothing we
can do but wait for the sheriff," he said, and winked. His brother
had walked off to the fence that separated the farmyard from the
cotton field. The cotton was full of yellow and white blooms. Paul
walked over to his brother.

"Where's Mr. Willow?" he said.

Effie nodded toward the field, then pointed. Mr. Willow was
running through the cotton. He broke stalks down in his passage;
the yellow and white flowers trembled and waved behind him.

"I've seen that before," Effie said. "Jack Burke's car wreck,
where he sat there in the smashed Buick trying to get the engine
to turn over. He didn't even notice his legs had been smashed.
The mind is sometimes a slow soldier, bub."

"Should we go get him?"

"Nah. Then we'd have to comfort him. We'd wind up spending
the day with him, talking him through it. He'll come back anyway when he wears himself out."

But Paul was sorry not to chase after Mr. Willow. The old
man's white hair flopped around his head like a loose cap as he
ran. Paul had not yet found his destiny as savior of the Hogans,
but the inclination stirred in him. He felt as if there were chains
around him, light but permanent, felt vaguely without understanding that he must break them, that he would rather be a help.

"I think we ought to go after him," he said.

"Don't let me stop you, sport," Effie said, tugging down the
straw hat fore and aft. He looked out at the old man running,
stumbling through the robust cotton, and his eyes narrowed.
" 'All changed,' " he said. " 'A terrible beauty is born.' "

Effie had always said he hated the study of history. He had once
told their father that he preferred gossip to history, but he was the
one always who looked for the perspective of time in events, the
meaning against the backdrop of what came before and what
would come after. Old Mr. Willow might run, but what was

chasing him could run faster. Paul felt a huge swelling in him, like a balloon filling with water. "God, I'm sorry for her," he said as the pressure inside him became tears. He leaned his head against the creosoted post and cried. His brother stood beside him looking out at the field, then he placed his hand on the back of Paul's head and stroked his hair. "Some birthday, huh," he said, and let his arm slide around Paul's neck and draw him close against his strong chest. Paul thought: I never want to get loose, I want arms wrapped around me forever. His brother said, "I want to go live on an island. I want to live in a place where there's a thousand miles of ocean in every direction. I want to believe nothing can get me." He was silent a moment, then he said, "That's what's so sweet about drinking."

"What?" Paul said when his brother didn't continue.

"It makes the crowd fall back."

I I

AND THE crowd fell back far. It fell back nine thousand miles, if by crowd Effie had meant everyone he knew from raising and birth. He flew to the Pacific, to Tinian Island, a green scoop of land in the green chain of islands that dangled like a string of spit beneath Okinawa. Latitude fifteen, sunk deep in the tropics, home of trade winds and typhoons, war relics, coconut and plumeria, white coral dust, tin houses, old men wearing Japanese soldier shorts, children running into the simple surf crying like birds. The whole time his brother was packing, Paul thought maybe this could be one of the best times too. Effie said he was going off to hunt the lost Japanese, but Paul figured he was trying to find Helen. She had joined a farm exchange to Micronesia, been posted to the Marianas, stationed on Tinian as an expert in vegetable gardening, princess of the green pepper and the tomato, empress of sweet corn, doyenne of okra and the lima bean.

She, like his brother, was an escape artist, as it turned out. Effie had known her all his life. In the fifth grade he had asked her to marry him, and she had laughed and turned him down. "She told

me she'd rather be cross-eyed," Effie told him later. When he
came back to town the year before, he had asked her again, and
this time she said yes. When he asked her why, after all these
years and after such a firm refusal, she said being cross-eyed wasn't
as fine as she'd thought. She played the saxophone and kept bird
feeders all over the yard. She could drive a cotton picker and a
corn harvester, and until he was killed she had her father's foreman
construct every year two duck blinds up at Lake Io, near the
Georgia line, which she used alone in the deep cold of winter, she
and her black Labrador, Constance, roosting in her pirogue among
the bulrushes, taking out her limit of ringnecks and mallards as
they jetted down the flyway from Canada. Her straight fine hair
was thick as fall grass and the color of persimmons, and it reached
to her waist, though she wore it almost always in a bun, bound at
the back of her head and pinned by a heavy worked-silver clasp
wrought in the shape of a running deer. Her eyes were wide apart
and the blue of minerals, a striking almost pale blue full of glints
and depths but with a curious opaqueness at the bottom, like a
shimmering sediment, that was impenetrable. She was tall and
lean; her hands were large and slender, the nails trimmed short
and chipped, the palms work roughened, wrinkled like an old
man's, the lines of augury chiseled deeply in, as if—if there was
any truth to palmistry—her future was a locked and sure thing
barreling down on her like a juggernaut. Her breasts were large
and hung unpinned in her shirt; Paul dreamed of them at night,
dreamed them as soft gourds hanging over his face that he could
not quite reach his lips up to suck. He had seen the flash of her
nakedness more than once: at Drowned Pond down on the south
end of her property near the swamp, where the three of them
would go swimming late on a summer afternoon. He had seen her
strip khaki shorts and jeans, the frail panties trimmed with lace
like the lace edging of the altar cloth at church, her slender arms,
sun-chapped, rising over her head to pull the shirt off. Her shoulders were broad and bony; there was a fierce rigidity in them, an
extra boniness almost, the blades broad and thin, sharp-edged; her
hips were bony too, scooped out above her belly, her pelvis vivid,
so that he seemed to see an extra dimension in the shadow of her
skeleton shining through, which made a pain catch in his gut.

Her pubic hair was a sheaf, dense and straight, darker than the hair on her head, a mask of hair. He could picture her anytime he wanted to as she skipped through the camellia bushes down the hill to the pond, a cloud of gnats unfurled over her head, dissolving like a cloud of dream or memory as she dived into the dark water. He remembered how the quick, evening-lengthened shadows of birds rushed over the pond, scarring and erasing the surface, and the smell of the muddy banks like the smell of worms and tangy grass, remembered how he would wait, gone nearly breathless, for her head to break through, water-flattened and gleaming like the head of a newborn child, how his stomach would clutch as he waited. He would look at his indifferent brother lounging against the dock rail, a tea glass of red wine held so loosely in his fingers that it seemed it might drop, munching a stalk of sourweed in such a way that the pink-tasseled tip of it twitched against his forehead, his amber passionless eyes soaked with dreaminess, or with that thing in him that was always teetering on the edge of despair; and he would watch the brown bubbles and wave rings sink back into the surface and would picture her long white body swimming silently under the water, the long legs scissoring in a rhythm as stately and effortless as the canter of a fine horse, her long arms pulling the silty water against her, body skimming the bottom, where the snapping turtles and the catfish lived, her eyes wide open, blue as blue stones, beaming into the darkness—he imagined—penetrating murk and water dust, the breath streaming from her lips in bubbles fine as stitches in petitpoint; and then the surge, the gather and thrust, every muscle charged, as she rose in the arc of her passage, the water filling with light until it was the color of stirred honey—and she broke free, rinsed and blowing, her sharp laugh scuttling across the surface toward them, his brother looking up languid as a junkie, raising a single white long-fingered hand in slow acknowledging wave.

She visited him when he was sick, and she danced the Charleston with his mother on the screen porch, laughing as his mother drew her skirts up her fine thighs, frenzied in the fringed and sequined garments she had bought at a roadside secondhand store outside Tampa.

One night in the year of their marriage, the year in which she and Effie lived in a cottage canted on stilts out over the river, where they could hear the bass jumping at night under their bedroom floor, he waked on his summer pallet on the porch to find her sitting beside him, fanning his face. He came awake suddenly but in full possession of himself, his eyes snapping open into the soft breeze she tugged over him. She sat cross-legged on the floor, waving one of the paddle fans that were handed out at church. He lay very still, saying nothing, looking at her as she looked at him with her blue eyes that in the half-light of the screen-muddled stars were black. He could smell the scent of jasmine flowers and hear crickets. On the back steps the dog Jack moaned in his sleep. She wore a nightgown that was not white but in the meek light looked faded: blue or green, pink perhaps. It was pulled up into her lap so that her thighs were exposed. Her hand, large as a man's, the knuckles horny and obtruded like a man's, moved on her thigh, the right, and he saw for the first time in his life that she had a scar there, a patch of muddy skin, shiny as candle wax, the size of a face. His lips moved in amazement and fright, but he didn't speak; he watched as her fingers slowly traced the outline of the scar, the chipped nail of her forefinger rounding the edge of it, drawing it seemed figures in its center, brushing the flesh. He looked at her face and saw she was smiling, a smile he had not seen before, full of lies and shame, fixed on her face, her large teeth glowing ghostly. He turned on the pallet, felt the blood surge in his shoulder as his weight left it; he reached slowly from under the sheet and touched her knee, let his fingers creep the twelve inches to the edge of the scar. The rim was raised slightly, a thin lip of flesh. Inside the circle of mutilation the skin was stirred, like an agitated liquid suddenly frozen. The scar flesh was cooler than the flesh of her leg. He opened his hand on the scar; he wanted to press his face into it. She said, "I had cancer."

"When?"

"When I was a child. My father said I was going to die. He said I was going to heaven."

"Were you afraid?"

"I was scared to death, but I didn't know it. I invented another world. It was a place where all the trees were Christmas trees, filled with lights and snowflakes, and there was always a birthday party going on. Little girls in white and blue dresses were every-where. They had red ribbons in their hair, and they were all friends of mine. We would sit in a circle on a big lawn and tell stories about wonderful birthday cakes and about riding horses through the fields and about cities where the buildings were made out of silver. I would lie in the glider, dreaming about it all, making it up in my mind, talking to the little girls, asking one of them to let me have her ribbon. I was happy."

Her words, as always, came in a rush; she spoke with a stiff abrupt intonation, quickly, as one would strike the hard flakes of resiny wood from a lighter knot. And the words, as always, seemed to overbear her, or threaten to, as if they had been packed too tightly in her throat, as if all those days riding a tractor, leading a cloud of dust across a cotton field, had only catalyzed something in her, something she had to spew out. He said, "I dream things all the time."

"I know you do. I like you for it."

"What happened to the cancer?"

"They burned it off. It had eaten into my skin; it looked like fried bacon, all bubbled up and greasy. They took a machine and burned it off."

"Are you all right now?"

"I'm fine, though scarred."

Her hand moved to cover his. His breath caught, he thought he would begin gasping, but then he forgot his breath as she gently tugged his hand toward her sex. He watched his hand move as if it were unattached to him, watched the fingers flex, then watched them meet the silken hair, did not resist as she turned his hand, gently, as a fortune-teller would, and slid it under her, cupping her. She pressed all his fingers hard against her. He felt the crease, slickened, the pliable flesh, the emptiness of her that he clutched and filled. "Your brother told me to do this," she said. "He has convinced me."

"Why?"

"He wants to destroy my mind."

"He loves you."

"Your brother doesn't love anything. He can't."

"I've never touched anybody before. A girl, I mean."

"Do you like it?"

"I think it'll drive me crazy."

She doubled forward, straightened up. "Oh," she said. "It feels like a fire in my stomach."

She started to pull his hand back. "Did I hurt you?" he asked.

Her laugh snapped out. "No, no, you couldn't hurt me."

He smelled the odor of her, dense and sour, like rotten plums. He pressed his fingers upward, felt a graininess, a place that opened. "Move your fingers more," she said.

Behind her head the leaves of ti plants and scheffleras seemed a jungle, and the night beyond had built a mottled and indecipherable landscape. He heard wind walking through the oak trees and the creak of a barn shutter. He thought of his father sprawled across the flesh-shined seats of the privy, heard his voice which was high-pitched for such a large man and held fast—even in deepest drunkenness—to the precise intonations he had mastered during three years at Oxford on his Rhodes, heard him say syllables that sounded like his name but weren't, heard him say *Suicide is the refusal of beauty. We will kill ourselves because we can't stand the beauty of this world.* The voice was as clear as it had ever been in his life, but it wasn't outside him—it was, he thought then, as Helen arched her back on the pommel of his fingers, only a memory of speech, something he had said at Recitation, when, looking over his cup of oolong, there would appear in his face a design of sadness, like something woven there or impressed on his flesh, and his eyes, moist as cane syrup, would stick to them like syrup, as if they were all—mother, brother, youngest son—the last pulling anchors holding him to the earth; which Paul supposed, they in fact were.

He raised his free hand and touched her breast. It was heavy and as alive as anything he had touched in his life. His fingers sank into the flesh, pressed into it as into a heap of powder; he felt the nipple hard in the center of his palm like a nail that could drive through his hand. She moaned and pressed his hand harder against her breast, her fingers kneading herself through his own fingers, and he knew he would do anything she asked him to do, would pay with his life for this, for more of it, for all of it he could get.

Then, as she drew him away from roiled sheets onto the cool plank floor—coming naked off the pallet, his body so white to him in the starlight it seemed phosphorescent—as she drew with one violent hand the silken garment over her head so that he saw, as if in the pierce of a spotlight, breasts swollen and low-hanging, nipples distended, curve of rib cage, smooth pouched belly, gate of hair dark as a cupful of pond water, he saw on the waist-high shelf against the screen wall the rows of glass jars containing embalmed sea creatures—a shredding octopus, varieties of fish, a green sea snake, starfish yellow as dill flowers; saw the rising ladders of tropical plants: the banana, the fern, the dwarf mock orange; saw in the yard the patches of grass among the scuffed bare places, dark as pools; saw the canted decaying barn where his father had died, up the near side of which in day slick moss shone yellow as gold—saw all this as in the vividness of first recognition, or as a man in deep thirst drinks the first cold swallows of ice water, and he turned his head and saw, standing in the window behind him, his brother, his brother dressed in a white robe that was pulled tightly around him so that his slender body looked shrunken, thin as the horse-riding skeletons in the stories his father read him as a child: his fine thin lips were wet from the clear liquid he sipped from a clear glass held negligently with just the tips of his fingers, his hair was slicked back and damp as if he had just emerged from water, and his face seemed polished, the high thick cheekbones holding faint points of light like punctures, the dark spot of indentation on his narrow chin like an opening leading into darkness—Paul saw all this as she pulled him on top of her, as she fumbled for connection, for the coupling of them, her fingers burning like magnesium fire on his penis, drawing him into the grained slickness of her, as he felt himself falling, not into but upon, not upon but with, saw the tall figure in white robe, and the face that was the white of one who had never seen the sun, and the long arrogant fingers raising the heavy glass: but it was the eyes, burning with a stabbing amber fire, yellow as the eyes of a swamp panther, that would haunt him from then on—as one of all the things that haunted him—the eyes that were filled with a cold and murderous merriment, eyes that he rode under, giddy and terrified, that he reared under as the first hot lashings of his sperm ejected from his groin into the weeping and moaning body of the brokenhearted woman who lay beneath him.

Snake eyes, he said to himself later, and he would shudder thinking of his brother watching, of the stillness that was in him like some kind of living statue, some being that could draw his whole substance into the cold concentration of eyes. Helen was not his friend after that night. She remained cordial, she spoke to him, would even occasionally bring him jars of the fiery pickled cucumbers and okra she put up in the summer; she would ask him about his job—he worked on one of the haying crews—she would ask him when she helped his mother cook supper to get her a spoon, the butter from the fridge, but she no longer teased him, she no longer told him the stories of her life on the south end farm, she no longer let herself be alone with him. There was a look in her eyes of one trapped behind unbreachable fences, there was anger that flared suddenly and randomly, there was a sudden tiredness that would come over her as she sat on the porch listening to his brother draw melancholy tunes from his father's fiddle; and the deep green shadows of the tropical plants seemed to move in her face, like the floating shadows of predatory birds, and in the middle of the dusky silence of the long summer evenings when from far across the fields they could smell the river swamp, feral and singular like the smell of a great beast, and the swallows flickered and wheeled above the old barn, and the last filaments of sunlight turned the sagging cattle wire enclosing the pasture into strings of silver, she would speak out suddenly, abrupt harsh words of accusation and regret, her voice flaring, rising, and falling off: *Why are you doing . . . I don't know any . . . I've got to go . . . Oh, Effie*—this last spoken to his brother's body—into his face, his eyes, as none of the other imprecations were: she spoke into the space next to him, as to a shadow body, and the white scarf she carried with her always—wore roped around her neck as she drove the John Deere down the cotton rows—twisted in her hands until it looked as if she wore white silk handcuffs, and a shudder would pass through her and she would bite her lip, holding something back that was too strong to hold back.

His mother suggested tonic; she concocted a drink of barley and sassafras, shook in a drop of iodine and something even bitterer than iodine that she wouldn't tell, and she made Helen drink it from one of the blue china cups that had come in Queen Mary's wedding trousseau.

When he drove out to their river house—a low long white house with a roof green as holly leaves and fronted by squat columns that reminded him of the harem eunuchs in a childhood book, the back half flung out over the river on stilts—he would often not find her. His brother, lying in the porch swing in his rumpled white clothes, reading to himself out loud from a book of poems that when Paul listened seemed simply florid language, not sense, would stretch his arms down the length of his long legs, scratch his ankles, and tell him he didn't know where she was, maybe she was in the backyard, maybe she was walking in the woods. "I don't keep up with her, sport," he would say. "Like beauty, she has her own routines." Paul wanted to ask him what he had done to Helen, and by implication what he had thus done to him, but he was afraid to. He sensed disaster in any answer his brother might give him. It was easier to get a pitcher from the kitchen and water the floribunda roses in the bed below the front porch, make a cup of tea, leaf through his brother's books stacked in piles on the living room floor. But he did not have to do much or ask anything before his brother would begin to speak. The house smelled of wintergreen, of the sour ashes still heaped in the fireplace from last winter, and of something else, something more sour and piercing than ashes: a vaguely sexual smell, the smell of rotted jism, of the sulfur of unwashed underclothes. On the shined plank floor the bamboo blinds let down a faded yellow light. His brother, stretching in the swing, would finger the green-and-white comforter laid over the back—as if, even in dead summer, he might suddenly be taken by cold—and begin to talk in the high sweet-toned voice that made Paul remember the stories of him singing as a child; he would say, *She told me yesterday that her hem caught in those roses and when she bent down to unlatch it she thought the smell of them would smother her;* he said, *She told me that always in the back of her eye she can see a dogwood flowering;* she said she goes to church simply to be in a quiet place where her mind can run free without

her having to protect herself. As his brother spoke his smile would
lick like a small flame at the corners of his long lips and his hands
would pluck and caress the soft cloth over his crotch. He wore his
hair pulled severely back always now, tied in a tuft at the back of
his head with a twist of copper wire. He looked to Paul like
pictures of John Paul Jones, or one of the buccaneers who roved
the Gulf in the days of piracy. As he talked, Paul would look out
into the yard, where beyond the thick shadows under the pol-
larded oaks the road glittered like salt. On the other side the
cotton fields began, the Jenkins's pride, seas of lime-green maple-
shaped leaves on plants as high as his waist, curving in rows that
occupied vision for half a mile until they splashed up against the
tall pinewoods. The woods his brother spoke of were the woods
behind them and alongside them, the tangled river coverage of ash
and tupelo and cypress, water maple, willow. These were the
woods Helen wandered off in, following the trails that had been
cut there by Seminoles and Creeks, the one-track roads of the
ancient times. In the old days tobacco had been hauled down the
river to Apalachicola, where it was loaded on schooners for the
trip north. There were burial mounds in the woods, heaps of earth
the size of sunk boxcars, from which one could dig, if he was
persistent, pottery shards and an array of flint and shell tools, and
bones, the gray soot-streaked skeletons of a race two hundred years
vanished, ancestors of the fleet-footed ghost people of the swamp
who had fled southward before Andrew Jackson's army, leaving
huts and drying racks, the council houses made of cypress logs,
and even, so the soldiers told, still-smoking fires with pots of
acorn mush steaming in the ashes, but no presence at all, not even
footprints on the empty trails. As a boy he had accompanied an
expedition organized by his father to dig into the mounds. The
workers had dug with hand picks and garden spades, sifting the
black clay-streaked earth through wire screens. They found broken
pots and blue-clay bowls, shell implements and small rotted
leather bags of stones, all the stones round and as small as wrens'
eggs and, when polished, green and glossy as ivy leaves. They had
found these articles of domesticity and ritual, the shell hoes, the
scraps of ceramic jewelry, but what Paul remembered most dis-
tinctly was the moment when two of the men, rocking between

them the cradle of the small boxed screen, had sifted out the tiny gray jawbone and loose teeth of an Indian child. The small wishbone of the mandible that lay in the sagging wire mesh among the thin, serrated teeth—the first teeth of maturity, like Paul's that his father gently pried his bottom lip away from to look at— brought to him, like the piercing memory of his first nightmare, the explicit and stunning awareness of his own death. He could not say—to himself or anyone else—what he felt; there was no brain knowledge at that moment when, his father peering over his shoulder, he had looked into the clotted box and seen the raw and blackened V of bone and the tiny delicate teeth; there was a clutching in his gut, and something powerful and desperate in him clawed for flight. He fell back against his father's hard knees, gasping, twisting against the grip of his father's hands, flailing so wildly that he broke away and ran blindly into the woods, tripping and sprawling into catbrier, which his father untangled and lifted him out of. His father's laughter died in his face and his green eyes went grave when he saw the look on Paul's face; he took him in his arms and held him and apologized. Terrified, Paul had sobbed against his father's chest; and though he was shamed and humiliated, he could not stop until his father carried him out of the swamp and back to the trucks.

It made him sad to remember this now, and it still embarrassed him, his childish fright, and he wished he could return to that time and place with a bolder attitude. His father had been kind, telling him of the time when he was a boy and a carnival dwarf had frightened him and made him run to his mother. Paul hadn't liked hearing that story at all; it made him think less of his father and made him wish he were stronger, and for a moment he had wanted to run away, to leap out of the truck and run down the road, where the sun glittered in the sand, turn a corner into a new world, perhaps one with blue sea and big white boats, and men coiling rope over their shoulders, and sails filling with an outbound wind, some green dream on a far horizon he was boldly flying for.

· · ·

I won't be young forever, he said to himself one afternoon as he
crossed the sunlit yard past the apple trees, in which unpruned
suckers stood up on the branches like witches' wands, and entered
the woods. Arrived in his mother's dog-nosed pickup, he had
found his brother reading in the swing; Effie told him Helen was
in the woods; gone to pick jack-in-the-pulpits, he said. "She likes
the meat-eating flowers," his brother added, spitting a laugh that
was so cold and controlled that Paul decided to go look for her.
Under the tall pines the ground was covered with ginger straw
and the air was cooler. He had not gone ten feet into the woods
before he smelled the stink of dead animal. It was faint and almost
delicate in his nose, faraway. He moved toward the smell through
gallberry and myrtle bushes. In a clearing a water maple sported a
single bright-red branch low in the crown. That summer he had
seen other trees gone half red for no reason he could figure. Along
the roads, at the edge of peanut fields, oaks, maples, and sumac
bushes held up swaths of color, flagrant patches—sometimes half
the tree—turned stunning red months before fall. Perhaps the
county chain gang had sprayed defoliant, but that still wouldn't
explain how trees far from any road had gone suddenly scarlet. He
had mentioned it to his mother, who looked at him with the usual
mischievousness in her eyes—as if she were behind it all—and
told him there were mysteries in the woods no one could understand. He walked over to the tree and plucked a red leaf from the
drooping branch. It was just a leaf, vermilion streaked with green.
He sniffed it, but it didn't smell different from any other leaf.
The dead-animal stink was stronger now, drifting like smoke from
off farther in the woods. Here the land rose slightly, curving away
from the river like the lip of a shallow bowl. In spring the river
crept among the trees, transforming the world into a forested
pond. Later there would be patches of water far back in the woods,
mementos left by the receding tide, in which tadpoles and the fry
of bream and bass swam. In midsummer you could come on one
of these dried ponds and find the black baking bottom covered
with the silver putrefying bodies of small fish. But the smell now
was something more than fish.

He moved toward the stink obliquely, through scattered
bushes. The slant western light fell from behind him, streaking

pine trunks, the frothy tops of gallberry, and the matted straw-strewn floor. "Night, sleep, death and the stars," was what Walt Whitman said the soul sought to reflect on in repose. Effie had read that years ago at a Recitation, grinning luridly. For the last few years the woods had seemed larger every time Paul went into them. He thought it was supposed to be the other way around: places of the past diminishing as one grew older, becoming finally the toy constructions one might place along the tracks of a model train. But these woods were larger, denser, more impenetrable. A ground bird—thrasher or thrush—flew from pine to pine ahead of him, keeping just far enough away for him not to be able—if he had had a gun—to shoot it. The smell grew stronger, fetid stink of rotting meat. He called Helen's name, but softly, not wanting to alarm her, wanting to come on her silently. He imag-ined himself stepping into a clearing and discovering her, an Indian princess tending a small fire. She would look up at him, and the flush of delight and love would spread across her face, and she would get slowly up and run toward him: he would take her into his arms and then—and then he didn't know. She was his brother's wife, to whom his brother had apparently already caused great grief. Her body rolled hugely in his sleep, came to him in dreams. Her flesh in dreams was broad as a bed, sweet as fresh bread. It amazed him that there was so much of her. Sometimes he woke flailing, smothered.

The ground descended toward the river, and he went that way. Nearer the river the pines gave way to swamp hardwoods: sugar-berry, pignut hickory, tulip poplar, which gave intermingling way in their turn to the true swamp trees: tupelo, willow, black birch, pond cypress, and sweet bay. There were puddles of water under the cypresses; the twisted roots of willows were exposed. In the branches of a young tupelo the sunlight turned the leaves into globes of yellow that trembled in the slight breeze. The ground was thickly paved with leaves, a crust of them, fallen last year and the years before.

He came to the boggy ground of the river skirt. Beyond mud, a thin sheet of coffee-colored water spread away, knobbled with cypress knees. A high-heaped bank of myrtles rose between him and the river; beyond them cypresses interrupted the sky. He was near the source of the stink, which was raw and aggressive, piercing like a flame run along skin, the air so dense with rank odor that it might have made a sound. Then he thought he saw a flicker of white disappearing among the cypress trunks on the other side of the water. "Helen," he called, but his voice was a croak. She had come to the back porch the previous week to get water for the haying crew, and the yellow twigs in her hair, the hay dust powdering her forearms, the yellow streak of dust curving across her forehead, made her seem one of the druid queens his father had told him stories of when he was a child. His father had said there were words that could evoke the legend world, the world where trees had souls and rocks spoke and beautiful girls sang like birds. Believing, he had gone forth into the woods, where he yelled out words and phrases, called out *antidisestablishmentarianism*—which was the biggest word he knew—yelled *octoroon, revelation, invertebrate,* each time shielding his eyes from the glare of what would rise brilliant before him. Though nothing appeared, for years he believed he might find the word that would prick the spirit of the hidden world and make it sashay forth, flouncing and grinning.

Off to the right, across the pool, the ground rose slightly and the bushes were less dense; he stepped into the water and headed that way. As he came to the bank—which with its fret of myrtle bushes was higher than his head—he heard thrashing and the buzzing of flies. The light, sinking from the treetops, had the quality of sunlight under water: it carried tones of gray and vermilion, hints of blue dissolved from the sky. A long streak lay on the water surface, as gray as a foxtail. He pulled himself up by bushholds, saying under his breath *carapace, antediluvian, man, woman,* placed his feet carefully in loops of rootstock protruding from the black earth, and heaved through into a small clearing.

What he came on took his breath away. In the center of the clearing, which was smaller than a tenant yard and strewn with the splintered branches of a lightning-stripped sweet bay, was a dead cow, huge and swollen and black and split at the gut, mouth a ripped cavity, neck and withers gouged and laid bare to the bone; half a dozen alligators, as black as anthracite, lunged and tore at the carcass. He had never seen such a sight. The alligators, all but one, were fully grown, gray-jowled, yellow-bellied, their eyes glittering with reptilian yellow sparkles, their four-clawed feet propelling them in short, mouth-open charges at the blistered and pussy and turgid corpse. The gators had rolled the cow; tan and gold leaves clung to its matted hair. The head was intact but just barely, the eyes glaucous welts, dripping as from monstrous sleep down the face.

Stunned, rooted, electrical in the gut, he saw all this in an instant, saw, too, the wheel and dart of a kingfisher—blue scrap—disappearing among the ferny tops of cypresses, and beneath its flight what had startled it: white flicker fleeing beyond blackberry bushes. He was briefly in the clear paralysis of time: the alligators hadn't noticed him standing amid myrtle bushes he had hacked through, but one of them, a large bull with bulging jowls and racking tooth brown as tobacco stain, turned, as if on a swivel, from wrenching a great gout of thigh flesh and lunged at him. He screamed loudly, screamed for his life, fell backward and rolled down the low embankment into the water, rolled until he found his feet as the gator thrashed through the scrub brush furiously, lurching and hissing like the royal voice of snakes, and came after him. It was only the tangle of bushes that saved him. He raced through the water, for an instant his feet sticking—oh, dream, dream—and leapt onto the trunk of a bowed cypress, climbed ten feet up, and hung there as the gator came on in its jerked springing gait after him. Hunter of heat and movement, that gator could follow his sliddering run across the pool, but he could not follow him into the tree.

The bull drew up at the flared base, climbed over the outthrust strut of root, ticking its muzzle against the shredded bark, but it could not figure where he was, didn't raise its head to find him. The muzzle opened to show the dead-white core, and then the jaw snapped shut with a rush of air. The tail thrashed once, clearing a wave, and the gator turned and waddled slowly back toward the bushes. It moved with a sinuous horrible grace.

Paul clung to the trunk, his mind shooting, as one holds to the marooned mast of a foundered ship. For an instant the living thing inside him had tried to leap for the sky. Every cell screamed for flight, but he forced himself to stay in the tree. The alligators were thirty feet away beyond the myrtle bushes. Sun brought a gleam to the dusty ovulate leaves. He heard the heavy gator tails thrashing, whacking against others' thick hides, against bushes. An alligator, he remembered, would tear off a gout of meat, swallow it, return to its wallow, and vomit up the meat, which had been converted by its belly juices in the interim into a stinking gelatin. He didn't know how the cow came to be there; maybe it had wandered off or even been dumped, the woods havens now for wastrels and sporting characters, failed stockmen. Then something flickered beyond the bushes, and he cried out: "Hey! Hey!" trying to get it to wait. Don't you see I am in trouble here? The bent branches of a crooked willow trembled, he saw the sprig of white disappearing, but then the swamp fell silent; nothing moved or gave itself up. Druid poets had been able to turn people into trees, or birds. Mean-natured, fractious, and arrogant from all the intense labor of memorizing the complex myth-making formulas of their poetry, they had been quick to slap the unappreciative back into more primitive forms; even kings were not exempt; more than one had found his mocking word offense enough to get him turned into an oak tree or a beech. He leaned away from the trunk, as if stretching out two feet closer to whatever fled past the bushes could help him see better. The next morning they would be haying in the Garden of Eden pasture near the river. Helen would be there, driving the baler, her white scarf wound around her head under a wide-brimmed straw hat. He hadn't known about the scar. Even when he saw her naked at the pond he hadn't noticed it. It was as if she had just produced it, whipped it up especially for him. His uncle said that one day there would be a place for everyone in God's kingdom. No one of us can be saved, he said, until we all are. He had not thought of his brother as one of the lost, but the look in Helen's eyes as she leaned toward him with her gown updrawn told him this was so. And his brother's eyes, the cold amber of them, penetrating him, passing through his body like cold knives. He was not frightened but fascinated.

He stayed in the tree for half an hour, afraid the gator might come back. The cypress curved like a rainbow, and he hoisted himself up and sat on the hump, trying to see through the screen of bushes. The alligators apparently meant to stay with the carcass all day. Once the bushes surged, and he could see the end of a swinging tail as one of the gators pushed a smaller one back, but none came his way again. He had loved the woods always, but only to wander in. His brother didn't love them at all. If Paul tried to tell him how beautiful the light was as it swept like a sail over the bulrush prairies, flared in the ferny tops of cypresses, his brother would laugh. It's a canvas with no edges, he would say; we can't have that. The only farmwork his brother had ever done was to cut firebreaks along the river woods, plowing twenty-foot-wide tracks through the broomgrass to stall out fires. Paul suspected it was not fire but the woods themselves his brother wanted to keep back.

Then he thought of Helen, the white flicker of her running away. He still wanted to find her. Carefully, afraid of falling, of anything that might bring an alligator back, he eased down the tree, digging in his heels. He thought how solemnity could turn to ludicrousness: this silly moment when an alligator had him treed. Willing his body into silence, he slipped down the trunk, the bark of which was shredded as if it had been clawed. In the still water of the pool he could see the reflection of the sky and clouds firm as spuds. The myrtle bushes trembled and surged, small glossy leaves tossing as in wind, but nothing came through. The alligators hissed and romped behind their curtain of green, pummeling the dead. In his brother's last painting, watery, wavery lines thrust out of cobalt, like arms reaching from a mire. They're like corpses, his brother had said, speaking of his paintings—corpses in that you can stare at them all day and they're not going to jump out on you. At this moment he was in a suspension of time, his life hooked to the brainless lives of reptiles. Who could jump out at him. They could turn and kill me, he thought; seconds from now I could be a torn body.

His feet touched the water and he slid carefully in, not making sound. He felt for the bottom, found it a foot down, and settled his weight. Each flutter of bushes stopped his heart. Alligators pursue relentlessly, but with them, out of sight is out of mind. Something inside him chattered and screamed, sang for flight, but he made himself walk carefully backward, eyes locked on the trembling bushes, toward the rise of solid ground. It was as if moments were endless, as if movement took hours. A water strider darted before him, its thready legs hardly denting the surface. Virginia creeper hung down in loose strands from the branches of a tupelo. A thrush sang and stopped, sang again and stopped, as if fingers pinched its throat. His back ached. Moving in a crouch, he groped behind him for tree trunks, sliding slowly so as not to stumble over the cypress knees. Once he knocked against a loop of root and nearly fell, but he caught himself on a willow branch and pulled himself upright. Finally he was at the bank. Tadpoles lined the land edge, their heads just touching the line where water and ground joined; they looked as if they were waiting for the moment when they became frogs, didn't want to waste a second longer in the water than they had to. He backed up the bank, sure now that the alligators would spring from greenery after him. O Lord, Lord.

He would not let himself feel relief. The light fell on him, as it fell on the scattered leaves and on the mud and on chunks of gray limestone poking like the bones of a skull out of the black ground. It fell obliquely through the trees, groping for the dark waters. He backed away until the myrtle bushes began to disappear behind a tracery of tree trunks, then with a yell he turned and fled, sprinting through the dense woods.

He leapt as he ran, a sound issuing from his mouth like the whining of a beaten dog, his feet—it seemed—hardly touching the ground. He was sure now they would spring after him, myth-ical beasts charging across the shallow pool. He prayed out loud—he guessed it was praying—whining and yipping, trying not to touch earth, trying to take wing. Vines, catbrier, gallberry whipped at him, caught at his clothes, but he ran on, leaping over tussocks of fern and rotting logs. And as he ran, he began to forget the alligators, forget or lose them in the running itself, the clean strong sweep of his body over ground, the dodging of branches, the spring of the grass in the clearing he passed through whipping back against his stride; he was flying, running for joy, for speed, for his body flowing, and he thought: I would like to do this forever, run on and on, see the world this way, live this way, at this fine speed, my body working so well and harmoniously, a jackrabbit man, excellent in action. He leapt, flinging his stride out like a dancer, coming down on his toes, on the balls of his feet, rising again before the heel could hit, his arms swinging in rhythm, hands slightly open, slicing air: he ran on into his momentary freedom, full of himself now, and at the same time free, aware—it seemed to him—of everything, of the shag of fox grape high in a hickory tree, of the lightning-splintered bole of an oak, the dried runnels the last rain had cut in the pine straw, the flicker and flash of a jaybird crying out as it streaked through the leaves of a sweet gum.

He broke out of woods into the yard, which was brilliant with sunshine and empty of human presence, and it seemed to him as he slowed to a walk that the house, leaning out on its stilts over the river, was an odd and foreign invention and so the green canoe on sawhorses and the unpainted shed that was his brother's office and even the pink nets Helen had strung in the chinaberries for bird feeders. The river was sleek and dark as a bear's summer coat, and above it floated a single osprey, glints of white and silver in its wings. He stumbled and fell to his knees and for a moment the sky seemed to wheel above him, as if it were flipping suddenly over, about to slam into the earth. His guts wrenched violently, and he vomited.

He came to, still on his knees, with his throat burning, and it was as if he had arrived from a far place, come back as from a dream from another world. His brother, he supposed still on the porch, could not see him, for the bamboo screen hung above one end. Maybe he had heard him, but to Paul the noise he must have made seemed part of the dream world he had fled from, impossible to hear in light of day. Then he saw his sister-in-law, in a white dress that was blotched with what he first took to be red paint but realized—against his will—was blood, creeping along the ground in front of the porch. Boxwoods and the floribunda roses hid her, almost hid the knife that she gripped in her right hand. Her hands and arms were speckled with blood, which dripped from cuts on her forearms and on the backs of her hands. He started to call out to her, but something told him not to. He got slowly up, watching her, amazed to see her, fascinated. She crept carefully along the hedge, stopping at the edge of the bushes, and drew her legs up so she was crouching. He stepped back and began to walk along the edge of the yard to get a better view. Helen did not notice him; she raised the fingers of her free hand and scratched her cheek, leaving a line of blood. Paul could see his brother on the swing; he held the book up to his face. Effie licked his thumb and slowly turned a page. As he did this, Helen sprang up, sprinted up the steps, and leapt at him. Paul cried out, a cry of waking—*Jesus, stop!*—and ran toward the porch. Helen stumbled as she rushed up the steps, but she didn't fall; the dress swirled around her; the blue ribbon that held her hair tied back was smeared with blood, as if after she had been cut she had thought to tidy her hair. His brother lowered the book as she came, but he did not attempt to rise. A thin smile darted across his lips, compressing them: a smile that was arrogant and hostile and unconcerned, a smile, Paul thought, coming up the walk, that was as mean as anything he had seen in his life. Helen raised the knife as she ran; all at once her body seemed to fall—she did not so much spring as collapse—like someone thrown down from a height, her arm coming down overhand, the blade dull in the shadows under the eaves, plunging at the center of his brother's chest. His brother caught the knife with the book—the blade stabbing through the spine—twisting it away violently, breaking her grasp, and flung it across the porch. Helen fell on her side against him, collapsing, coming down on top of him blood and all—it spattered his white clothes, his face—into his arms, which grasped and held her tight as if she were only his child bringing to him her hurt.

Paul stood on the top step, looking at them. The sweet perfume of the roses was intense in his nostrils, and the smell of blood, and the metallic smell of his vomit, a streak of which shone green on his wrist. He sat down on the steps and looked at them. They did not stir. His brother, holding Helen's head buried in his shoulder, said, " 'At Shiloh they came out of the woods at us. There were so many of them you couldn't miss. We could have been blind men firing and still brought them down. Their bullets cut the peach flowers out of the trees. When it was over we lay there covered in blossoms.' " Helen struggled against him, but he held her. "You're going to have to stop this, girl," Effie said. "This is the last time." He touched his finger to her arm—there were cuts, slices: she must have cut herself—brought it to his mouth, and sucked the blood off. "Once," he said to Paul, "before we were married, once when she was in her period, she cut a hole in my chest with a scalpel and mingled our blood; we combined the blood and drank it."

"What are you going to do?" Paul said. He meant to say, *What are you doing to her?* but the words changed in his mouth. He thought of his uncle polishing the aluminum disks in the wall of his chapel. All we can ask for is that God's will be done, his uncle said. Whatever that is, we'll love it. "Helen?" Paul said. "Helen?" but his sister-in-law didn't answer.

"There's nothing I can do," his brother said. "What you're looking at here can't be fixed. It's a conundrum."

"I have to go," Paul said.

"Yes," his brother said, "you do."

Paul started to go, then he turned back. "What is going to become of you?" he said. He meant both of them; either.

"Someone will get away," his brother said, as he stroked his wife's hair. "We just don't know who."

On his way up the long drive, Paul stopped the pickup and looked back. The white house was small under the huge crowns of the live oaks, a dwindled thing, mirage or replica. When people spoke of the world, they meant only the place they walked around in, the people they knew. That was what the world was, nothing more.

I T W A S a scramble, but they were all gone. Helen contacted friends in the state agriculture department, who signed her on with the aid and research team going out to the islands; she got a passport—which, since the territories were part of the American protectorate, wasn't technically necessary—packed everything she needed in a trunk, and flew out with it a week later. Effie, who never seemed disturbed by anything that happened on earth, became disturbed; he wandered about the garden, took long rides

into the swamp, called from the river house and had long conversations with their mother, in which he argued and raged about
Helen's desertion. His mother, who claimed steadily that she
didn't want to hear any mealy mouth, listened and argued back.
In two weeks Effie was gone, slipped out on a Sunday morning
from the old farmhouse, with the bags nobody had seen him pack,
to the taxi that took him to the airport in Tallahassee. There was
a note on the kitchen table that said he was on his way to discover
the lost Japanese in the jungles of the islands and for them not to
expect him back soon. Paul read the note sitting at the picnic
table on the porch. He could see Effie's footprints in the dew
shining on the front lawn. By the time his mother came downstairs the sun had swept up the tracks and the only sign left of his
brother was the washed cereal bowl in the drying rack by the sink.
His mother had cursed and after brief rage in which she screamed
at the mockingbirds nesting in the pittosporum at the end of the
porch had gone on to her form of therapy: the huge pot of vegetable soup that took her two days to make. Paul, by then so
charged with disgust and fascination that he could hardly think
about his brother without veering into rage, had thought: She'll
get over it. I expect it'll take about a month, but she'll wear her
way into something else and we'll go on, but he didn't believe the
thought.

And so it was summer yet—August—when the first spattering
of brown appeared in the leaves of the tulip poplars along the
swamp margins and sometimes in the earliest light, even in north
Florida, you could sense, like a forgotten memory, the fey hint of
fall slipping in under the sweet breeze, and he was left alone on
the farm, where the hay crews his mother had conscripted appeared early, men a few years older than himself, country boys,
some of whom could write nothing more than laboriously ached-
out versions of their own names—the letters staggering, wildly
looped proofs of identity—who wore their hair long under baseball caps and bright scarves, who chewed Bull of the Woods or
Brown's Mule tobacco and washed down sack lunches with Cokes
they bought at the crossroads store, who waved at him in late
afternoon as they passed in a caravan of trucks stacked house high
with fresh blond bales, one maybe perched on top, lying on his

back staring at the sky. He would go out and walk in the cut field among the torn cornflowers and blue-eyed grass; he would lie down in the prickly Bahia and think about how he was alone in the world and what that meant. The week before, his mother had come downstairs carrying two blue suitcases and wearing her lady-bug hat. She kissed him as he sat in his underwear at the kitchen table eating the grits he'd fried, stopping only long enough to scoop a drink of water from the tap and say, Well, I'll see you sometime, darling; don't forget to water the flowers. When he asked her where she was going she said, *To the islands,* the way she would have said "To the store." He didn't bother to protest; he even helped her carry the bags to her car and stood in the driveway as she roared out of the yard under the painted pecan trees. From her coming into the room to her disappearing hadn't been long enough for him to get the taste of grits out of his mouth. He lingered by the false banana bush watching the dust from her car climb slowly into the pecans. The dust looked like the original substance that the tents of the gypsy moths, sagging among the loaded branches, were made from.

Now, he thought, I can be whoever I want. Whatever stranger rides up to this house, I can tell him anything. Who are you? the stranger might ask, and I can say, I am the son of kings. Then, lying in the grass, a sprig of sorrel in his mouth, he felt homesick. Which is very odd, he thought, because I'm already home. The smell of the hay was spicy and rich, a sunny smell like the smell of sand dunes. The sky was high-tiered and blue. I guess she expects me to close the place up and go back to school. From where he was the house already looked closed, empty as a weekday church. The yard was littered with althaea blooms, blown off the bushes by the previous night's rain. The big branches of the water oaks in back of the house were propped up with poles. He had always liked the way at certain times of the day in certain light the trees and houses—the building of his familiarity—looked abandoned, and he liked it now, the white frame house still as sculpture, the big sycamore in front, with the V cut out of the top to let the electric wires through, quiet as paint. The blue tin roof gleamed as if from fresh rain. "Hello," he said. "Where are you?" trying to prime his father's voice into life. Hey, Papa, where

are you in your white suit? But nothing came back but the *see you,
see you* of a meadowlark.

It was a long journey—sixteen hours by plane and another twelve
by ship—and though crossing the international date line he got
to backtrack over his birthday and be born again, he was tired
soon, worn into a fatigue that was like bereavement or depression,
so that when in the early-morning light over the gray sea he saw
the island rising like a dark-green wedding cake, saw the white-
combed line of the reef and behind it the high rusted wall of the
breakwater, and the beach off to the right backed by low shaggy
trees, and then the tin roofs of houses shining in the sunset and
behind them the road—paved, to his surprise—rising from
among palms toward the plateau, he saw nothing more than this
incidental arrangement, pictured nothing, not even his mother or
brother, wondered about the hotel—if they had one—hoped for a
clean quiet bed.

Out at the rail, where the breeze was cool and sweet with the
odors of vegetation, where chickens were tied by one leg to stan-
chions and an old man shouldered three pared banana trunks and
spit a stream of blood-red juice over the side, he thought—not
quite anonymous among large women in flowered dresses and men
in embroidered Filipino shirts—about how he was loose in the
world, cut free of everything, absent for a moment to the family
awaiting him, and it seemed to him that it was possible to become
a permanent stranger, a traveler who never lighted long enough
to become known, and this thought, which he kept to himself
though already he had spent a day sharing the company of Jacabo,
who was his own age and on his way home after four years at the
territorial high school in Truk—where men fight with machetes
and brass knuckles made out of shark teeth, Jacabo told him—
this thought seemed a great revelation, especially to one who had
never lived anywhere—if one year at college in Virginia wasn't
counted—but in the country of his birth, accomplice to its ways
and hopes: sturdy as a cypress, they told him, dependable, a boy
it was always a pleasure to see. The dock was crowded with people
—vivid in the crepuscular light flaring and fading in the west

away down the flattened wing of the island—and their portable possessions: a few small Japanese trucks, decrepit jeeps, here and there a cow held on a rope by a child, chickens in crates, a pig squealing in the arms of a girl in a pale-blue dress. Marianas now, these islands were once called Ladrones, which meant thieves, Jacabo told him, a name given to them by Magellan's sailors, who stopped here in 1521 on their way to rendezvous with destiny in the Philippines. We still live up to that reputation, Jacabo said, though it is not so much the stealing now as the gambling. If you like gambling this is the place to come. It didn't look like a hot spot: no neon, no fancy dresses, no sporting characters he could see. Just ordinary people, poor and a little fractious now with the boat warping in, women converting a slight unease into reprimands for their children, men barking orders, a couple of spiral-tailed dogs scampering about. Behind the dock rose a wall of lime-green bushes. Roads at either end cut up toward the village, which even so close he could see was nothing more than a scattered gathering—just visible among the bushes—of small tin and plywood houses. The land rose in a series of inclinations to a high plateau, green all the way. In the rearground was the pink spire of a church, and near it he could see the tall mast of a radio antenna.

Jacabo came up beside him, and they leaned against the rail together as the small ship passed the reef and made its wide swing in against the dock. "In the war there were battleships and aircraft carriers here," Jacabo said. The dock looked big enough. Battered now, crumbling accordion steel, pilings wrenched out and leaning over the green milky water, it could have accommodated half a dozen big ships. Except for an old LST up at one end, the dock was empty. "That's my nahn," Jacabo said, pointing at a small gray-haired woman in a dark-blue dress. She stood beside a tall thin man in wide-legged shorts.

"Your nahn?" Paul said.

"My mother. And my tahn—my father." He stood on his toes and waved in a great scooping motion, as if his parents were far away.

"I don't see anybody I know," Paul said.

"It's early. Maybe they are still working," Jacabo said, and laughed. He had a thin face under a rock-and-roll pompadour, a hooked nose in a face the rich gold of polished pine, and neat small teeth that he bared often in a slow sweet grin. "My heart is so full," he said, pressing his hand against his chest. "I don't know how I will stop to die from love."

Paul had told him what he was doing here: following mother and brother to look after them. He said he had a mission, though he didn't know what he meant by that. His friend had told him of the Taotaomona, the First People, ancestors who lived like diaphanous drill sergeants in the shadows under large trees, faring forth in the night to reward or punish the villagers. "They are very serious," Jacabo said, "though sometimes, for no reason anybody can understand, we hear them laughing." Paul thought he might attach his purpose to some such cosmology, and wanted to, but it was his mother who spoke to spirits in the night, not he. Jacabo had offered him a room in his house, but Paul told him he would go to the hotel; he hoped to see his mother or brother on the dock and go with them.

But they were nowhere about. He was noticed but not spoken to by any in the crowd that milled about, greeting relatives and unloading supplies. The ship came twice a week from Guam—on its passage to the district center at Saipan—bringing rice and coffee, beer and other necessities, as well as relatives and friends, and gamblers, from the big island. Grasping his arm, Jacabo took Paul to met his parents—as well as his eight brothers and sisters —but his friend was swept quickly up in the crush of reunion and Paul moved away, looking for a taxi to take him to the hotel. The sky, unclouded except in the west, where stacks of cumulus boiled off the sunset, was a dark rich blue above the island, already punctured with stars, and the air smelled of wood fires, like the back streets of his hometown in winter, and cooking oil. Long runners of beach pea snaked out from the heaped bushes, and the pavement was cracked and spotted with holes, the dock empty of commerce, except for stacks of rusted warehouse reefers with their doors swung open near the roads. Without the ship it would have been an abandoned place, he thought, shouldering his bag. The pale eroded moon hung in the eastern sky. A diffidence came over him, and more, the dense fatigue that had settled on him halfway across the Pacific seemed to press deeper in; he felt so tired he wanted to lie down on the dock and sleep there. He knew that for a while he would be unable to ask for direction or help—there were no taxis, no commercial vehicles at all—and it was as if a new invisibility began to seep over him: the whirl of the crowd, the purposeful energetic activity as pallets stacked with sacks of rice swung out from cranes on the foredeck, the slight trucks lined up to take on their loads of supplies, the group of men standing around the back of a station wagon eating fish they ripped with knives and dipped into a black iridescent sauce, the children in torn clothes crying gaily in birdlike voices, seemed to pass before him as activities taking place in another zone, one that he peered into not from a distance but without presence, or any presence beyond observation itself; he saw but he wasn't there. The night before, from the narrow bow where he and Jacabo rode, lying on their stomachs to feel the lift and plunge of the ship, he had seen the Southern Cross for the first time in his life: four icy stars hanging low above the horizon, artifacts of another, indecipherable world. There were no birds in the air, not even gulls, and though a small breeze blew steadily, thin as a whisper, the air seemed still—untouched was the word that came to him as he edged away from the scene toward the road that disappeared through an opening in the tall ferny bushes. I'll just walk up this way, he thought, and see. Maybe the hotel was near.

He was halfway through the village when the priest stopped to pick him up. The houses, small and plain, as if provisional, garlanded with blossoming hibiscus and meager trailers of bougainvillea and passion vine, were set apart in small grassy yards separated by clumps of the same ferny bushes that prospered by the docks; each had its narrow outhouse, and thick stands of banana grew near the back doors; there were few palms. The priest —who Paul knew was a priest by his belted white cassock, the hood of which was thrown back off rich black hair—pulled his truck up beside him and threw open the door. "Come, come," he said, gesturing with a small narrow hand.

Paul got gratefully in. "I'm looking for the hotel," he said in explanation.

The priest slapped his thighs, ran his palms down them, and

leaned forward over the steering wheel. He cast a sideways glance at Paul. "I knew you were a visitor," he said. "I take it on myself to greet all those who visit here."

Paul told him he was looking for his mother and brother.

"I know them," the priest—Father Marco—said. His lips narrowed to a thin line as he spoke.

"Do you know where they are?" Paul asked.

"Your mother is in Guam, where she goes to work for the family she supports. I thought she would be on the ship." The priest looked searchingly at Paul. "She is a good woman, though I cannot approve of how she makes a living. It is not proper, but still she is kind to all she meets, which is something." He shook his head. "Your brother is different." He looked again at Paul, placing his finger beside his eye and pulling it into a slit. "He is in danger. There are some here who would harm him."

Paul felt a trickle of dread, icy and thin. "And Helen Jenkins —is she here?"

"Yes. Out at the farm station. She comes to speak to me. I am sorry for her."

The priest had started off again; they rolled slowly uphill past houses that to Paul looked starved and strangled, like tenant shacks in Florida. In some of the yards were round concrete cisterns, and here and there poking out of the tangled growth concrete ruins, facades, broken walls, reared like remnants of an ancient civilization. Some of the houses were roofed in green army canvas. "Are there any Japanese?" Paul said.

"The tourists come. They collect bones in the jungle and pray over them. There is an altar across the road from my church."

"What about soldiers? Are there any soldiers?"

The priest laughed. The sound was short and bony, like a cat coughing. "You mean Ichi. He lives on Pig Island. There."

He pointed with his thumb toward the back window. Paul saw a low gray island several miles out. Above it hung a narrow band of clouds.

"My brother," he said, "is on a mission to find the lost Japanese."

"Hmm," the priest said. "He is finding something else, I think."

Paul wanted to know what threatened his brother, but he was afraid to ask. No message had come to tell him that he was supposed to save his brother, but that was what he had decided to do. When he told his uncle this, Maurice had looked at him with grave eyes and hugged his neck. "You follow the directions that come to you," his uncle said. "Let that still voice lead the discussion." Paul had thought that maybe they were all simply crazy, off in the country too long: the repetitiveness and isolation of country life had simply gotten to them. "There's a place for everybody," his uncle said. "It's not our job to make them come inside the circle as it is—it's our job to push the circle out farther to gather them in."

"Are you telling me something is wrong with my brother?" Paul had said.

"You'd be a fool not to know it," his uncle said.

So he was a fool. Because to Paul Effie was simply his brother. Blood, blood—whatever it was: Effie his old-time heart's desire. I don't just want to be like him, he had once said; I want to *be* him.

"What?" the priest said.

"Oh," Paul said. "Did I fall asleep?"

"You said something."

"I was thinking about my brother."

The bushes fell back, and they came to a large open field. Off to the right under blossoming flame trees was the church, pink stucco with white trim. On the far side of the field was a long low building with a catwalk porch running the length of it: the school, Paul decided. On the other side of the church, beyond a row of young coconut palms, Paul could see a couple of concrete houses and a small complex of tin buildings. The antenna he had seen from the boat reared over one of the buildings. Behind the structures the land continued to rise in abrupt tiers of white brush-crowded rock. Paul had read what he could about the island. He knew Tinian was where they staged the invasion of Japan. The planes carrying the atomic bombs to Hiroshima and Nagasaki had taken off from airfields at the north end of the island. In 1944 the air base here was the largest in the world. Now there were only this spare village and the rocky green landscape; the crumbling docks, a road paved with asphalt and gravel.

They passed a small cairn of piled bones. Plastic flowers were woven among the bones, laid in bunches across the top. Just like country graveyards in Florida, Paul thought. "Why is my brother in trouble?" he said.

"He scares people." The priest crossed himself and slightly lowered his head as they passed in front of the church. His fingers were delicate, the forefinger crooked as if it had been broken and set improperly; it veered off at an angle from the others.

"I am not like other men," the priest said as Paul sat in an easy chair, sipping Scotch. The priest was in Paul's room, a large room floored with rice mats, which looked out on a stone courtyard in the middle of which was a large round cistern covered over with green scum. There were shell holes in the stone, and on the other side of the court the wall had been blasted away. The jagged hole gaped blackly. The priest paced the room, his long white soutane belling behind him, rope cincture swinging. "What other men can't do I can do," he said, looking out the window. A few black birds skittered through the darkness. They made a cawing noise like crows, but their tails were forked. "When I was in Virginia," the priest said, "they told me I could not do everything, but I never listen. I know my strength: when I go, it takes five to follow." Paul wondered how long it would take Effie to find him. That was his plan: sit tight and let Effie come get him. You are here to do *what?* the priest had said when he told him he was here to look after his brother. I don't think your brother wants anybody to look after him. You should go home, the priest said, tapping his chin with the tips of his narrow fingers.

"Do you want some doughnuts," the father said. He held an open tin toward Paul. "Breadfruit doughnuts. They keep me fed here; the women bring me food that is very good."

Paul sipped the Scotch and declined the doughnuts.

"You see," Father Marco said, "you would rather drink whiskey than eat sweet doughnuts. I drink a little Scotch or wine because it is good for the health, but I would never overindulge. If I did I would be able to stop."

"If my drinking bothers you, why did you offer me a drink?"

"No, no, I want you to enjoy." He continued to pace the room, his long hair flowing back from his sharp Chamorro face. "They told me it would take ten years to complete my work here, but I will finish in two. Maybe I will finish in one."

Paul got up and went to the sink for another Scotch. There was ice, not divided into cubes, melting in a tray. The bottle the priest had unwrapped from tissue paper was half full. He poured a large Scotch and cracked two chunks of ice against the edge of the sink. "Do you want one?"

"Just a small one, thank you." He took it with his long fingers and sipped it carefully as he walked up and down. Paul could smell some sweet flower, like sweet bay, though that wasn't it.

"I intend to perk this village up," the priest said. "I have come here to make life move. Already I know everyone; the church is full at Mass."

"What about my brother—do you know him?"

"He is dark, very dark. I know him well. You must stay away from him."

"I can't."

"Then you are in very bad trouble."

What could he mean? Paul knew what he meant—he meant the same thing Helen meant: something twisted and dangerous, unstoppable. Where was his lightly singing mother?

"No, I never get tired," the priest said, as if Paul had asked him a question. "I am used to working all the time. I can do what it takes five normal men to do."

He drank his Scotch straight without ice. Paul sipped his, letting the ice cool it before he took a long pull. This hotel, a coral stone square around the blasted courtyard, had been General Curtis LeMay's headquarters during the war. Here LeMay had received the order to carry the bombs to Japan. They had called the island Manhattan, the proprietor, a bent half-Irish native man, had told him, because it is shaped, he said, like Manhattan Island turned upside down. Even now, he said, there are bombs. Paul had asked him what he meant. Atomic bombs? Unbroken bombs in the boonies, the old man had explained. And over there, he said, pointing down the long tiered hill toward the twilight-grayed Pacific—out there on Pig Island there are bombs. They drop them from planes at night. Bombing practice—from the air base in Guam. Can you see the explosions? Paul had wanted to know. Sometimes, the old man had said, like lightning in the dry season, except red, and you can hear the thunder.

The father broke off his pacing. The yellow liquid slopped in his glass. He leaned against the sink, then tacked to the table next to the other wicker armchair, picked up the magazine there—the overseas *Time*—and flopped its thin pages against his wrist. "I read this," he said, "and every story I could tell you. I could tell you every one and show you who they are."

"How long were you in the States?"

"I was in America six years. We lived in Virginia, the Old Dominion."

"In Richmond?"

"Yes."

"I went to school in Virginia." The priest ignored him.

"Then I was in Guam, where I was born—an American—then I was in Saipan, where I stayed two years. There I did the work of many men. They said I would be there eight years, but I did my work in two. Here I will work harder, faster."

"What is my brother doing?"

"Your brother is an infidel. He beats people up. He threatens them and takes their money."

"My brother?"

"Effen Hogan."

"Ephraim."

"He makes promises to people and then he robs them."

"Well, that sounds a little like him."

Paul pushed up from his chair. Out the window he could see stars, heavy clusters of them. "I want to go look for him."

"Not tonight. Please wait a little longer. I would like to stay and talk."

"I'll just drink all your liquor."

"It is for you. My gift."

"And the doughnuts."

"Yes. They are very good." He crossed the room and stood beside Paul's chair. "Let me read your palm," he said.

"I didn't think priests read palms."

"I do it just for fun; sometimes it is helpful. This is a changed time; now we use many ways to understand."

"All right."

The priest knelt over Paul's palm and pressed it open on the arm of the chair. His hair shone softly in the lamplight, and the cassock fell back from his smooth hairless arms. He brushed Paul's palm with his long, crooked finger as if sweeping away dust. Then he touched the finger to his tongue and brushed the palm gently with warm spit. The skin shone. He traced lines down from the fingers, up from the wrist. He was completely quiet for a moment; Paul could hear palm fronds ticking against the side of the building. Where is Helen? What have we invaded here?

The priest chuckled, then laughed out loud.

"What is it?"

The priest pumped his clenched fist twice in his groin and laughed, cackled, his eyes sparkling, his lips drawn back from large overlapping teeth.

"What?"

He pumped his hand once more and barked another laugh, stopped with his fist clenched before his narrow chest.

"Ah, teaser," Paul said, jerking his hand away, blood filling his face.

The priest sat farther back on his heels, his hands held like small shields in front of him. "I am only joking," he said, "just a seminary joke."

A happy priest.

"I'll have to see if I can find that in there myself," Paul said, his voice full of salt.

"Don't take it bad, I just like to joke. I thought you must be worried about things here. Don't let it upset you."

"Oh, I won't."

There was a knock at the door, birdlike. The priest scampered to his feet. Paul heard his brother's voice. " 'Sweetest love, I do not go for weariness of thee' "—some Recitation John Donne his brother had spoken when they were children. There was another knock, and the door flew open. His brother stood there in white clothes, grinning. His hair was slicked and pulled back from his face. The priest shrank away—Paul could see something in his retreat—and let out a small reptilian hiss.

"How goes it, Padre?" his brother said. "Got all the souls in order?"

"I must go," the priest said, suddenly bustling.

"What are you up to in here?" Effie said to the priest. He tapped his palm with one long finger. His palm was yellow as butter. "You trying to seduce my brother?"

"I gave him a ride to the hotel."

"Fast worker."

"I must go." He waved a hand at Paul, tightened his cincture, making his small belly bulge.

"Not through the door," Effie said.

"What do you mean?"

"Roaches, rats, scum—out the window."

"I am a man of God."

"God loves the flesh, Father, but he doesn't fuck it."

"*Bauguerro.*"

"Speak English, Padrone."

"Devil."

"Out the window, old scout."

"You are joking with me."

"I don't joke with men of God."

He winked at Paul. The action made his handsome face look demonic, Paul thought. There were yellow smudges under his eyes.

"No," the priest said. "I will go through the door."

"Have it your way."

Effie leapt across the room—as if he had coiled himself, Paul thought, some way he couldn't see—hoisted the priest in his arms, carried him to the window, and pushed him through. The priest screamed for Mother Mary.

Effie leaned out the window after him. "Don't come around here again," he said. "No sweets, no whiskey, no nothing, Padre—Buffalo Bill's defunct."

He turned back to the room.

Paul felt a thrill move in his body, felt blood rush. His mouth didn't taste of Scotch, it tasted, oddly, of pumpkin pie, something tart and sweet at the same time. He was dizzy.

Effie took him in his arms, squeezed him hard, and thrust him away from him. "I was wondering when you'd show up, little brother man." He looked around the room. Took a sip from the priest's glass. He grinned, showing his large even teeth. "This is the room where old Curtis LeMay gave the order to drop the bombs. In this very room thirty years ago he gave the word to his commander, who gave the word to Tibbets, who gave the word to No One, who gave the word to the Japanese." He sloshed the Scotch in his mouth. "Papa would love it; he would stand here and pontificate about the death of the soul; he would have wry sad comments to make that would lead us to the inevitable conclusion that Western civilization has wasted its substance, its mandate, on the pursuit of false gods. We would, because we are helpless before the truth, feel our hope and substance drain from our bodies, and we would then walk forth into the world and lie down in the grass and cry—you know what I mean."

Paul sat down. He was tired and dizzy. The air smelled of a sweet blossoming, of salt and worn-out things.

"You are crazy," he said.

"Not only that, I am vigorous."

"What are you doing here?"

"I have come to find the lost Japanese, who it turns out wasn't lost after all. The one they've got here anyway. However, it doesn't matter. There's richer quarry."

"Such as?"

Effie held a finger to his lips. "Don't ask," he said. "I'll show you."

"I don't want to go anywhere right now. I want to take a nap."

"You can take a nap later."

He let his brother lead him to his truck, a small gray Datsun, and he rode with him across the top of the island. The road was paved and in the headlights dwindled grayly ahead of them. On the left side was massed, piled growth, a jungle of the same ferny bushes that grew around the docks. On the right was an open plain, grassy and stippled with rock outcroppings. In the moonlight the rocks shone like skulls embedded in the ground and made Paul think of the trips with his father into the swamp woods near St. Lukes. Maybe the world was simply a place that repeated itself to you over and over like a song you were supposed to memorize, until you got the lesson right. His brother, pumping the wheel as if movement made the truck go faster, chattered beside him. Going overseas had made him talkative. He told stories about the island that Paul was sure he made up as he told them, stories of the old ghost people who lived under banyan and breadfruit trees, who would come out into the road in long white dresses—"The women, that is"—and call young girls into the jungle at night. "They take them back into the jungle," he said, "and they charm them and change them, make them into their servants, their faceless acolytes, and they keep them and never let them go—so the story is told. They rise up off the ground, or out of the ground, I'm not exactly sure, and they call out to lonely people and they destroy them."

He swiveled in the seat. "It's like the stories we grew up on, Paulie. They do the same thing here."

Here and there single palms stuck up out of the jungle, but the growth was otherwise steadily uniform. The bushes were too thick to see through; they had a faint licoricy odor. There was something appalling and tremendous about the sameness of them, a rankness that saw no reason to break itself up into variation, a darkness that was complete and at peace with itself. There were snails in the road the size of tennis balls. They made popping sounds, like acorns you walked on, as the tires ran over them. Then Paul saw a large black spider creeping along near the centerline ahead of them. He couldn't believe it; it looked like an oversized tarantula. His breath caught. "What is that?" he said.

"Coconut crab. They live in the boonies and are very good to eat. They call them coconut crabs because they feed on coconuts. Their pincers are so strong they can unhusk and split a coconut shell. Magnificent, eh?"

"They're terrifying."

"We're busy now, or otherwise we would stop to pick him up.

The belly, which is filled with bright-orange goo, like school paste, is delicious. You spoon it out and eat it with rice."

"Where is Mama?"

"Doing fancy dances in Guam."

"She's dancing?"

"Yes. She does the hootchy-kootchy in service clubs. It's quite wild. She takes her clothes off to rock music."

"Everything?"

"Right down to the skin. She shows it all: tits, pussy—the works."

"I'd like to see that."

"It's something."

"Why does she do it?"

"She supports a couple of families here on the money she makes. Mother missionary she is, in her Catholic nun's hat. But mostly I believe she does it because she likes it."

"That's where she is now?"

"She goes down on the mail boat, stays three days, and comes back. She got off the boat you got onto."

"How could I have missed her?"

"This is a place of ghosts and shadows," his brother said with ironic gravity. He laughed and punched Paul in the shoulder. "You are a sight, little brother man, you are a sight for sore mad eyes." The dashboard lights had turned his brother's face green. Effie's narrowed eyes gleamed.

Thinking of his mother, picturing her, in a blue light maybe, shedding her clothes for soldiers, frightened Paul, angered him, fascinated him. He felt his penis humbly stir.

"Where are we going?" he said.

"To look at the monument."

"What monument?"

"You'll see."

They were driving at high speed. The straining engine echoed off the wall of bushes. His brother drove in the center of the road. He slapped the outside door, as if it were the side of a horse.

"Where's Helen?"

"I don't want to talk about Helen."

"Is she here?"

"She's here. But I don't want to talk about it. It hurts too much to even think about it, much less talk. I am a crazy man, lovesick, an embarrassment to my friends, a trial to myself. 'Inside these breastbones,' " he said, tapping his chest, quoting Whitman, " 'I lie smutch'd and choked, / Beneath this face that appears so impassive hell's tides continually run.' " Paul joined him on the last phrase. During the year Effie was eighteen, he had quoted that line all day long. He was speaking it when he came downstairs, he said it as he cleaned the barn, as he drove the baler over the yellow fields, said it until Queen Mary Voss screamed at him to stop. Once, she chased him with an elm switch.

As he spoke it this time, he poked his long lips into the words, as if they were bits of seed he was expelling. Paul leaned his head out the window, caught the wind in his face. It smelled salty and cloistral, light.

Up ahead, the road curved and disappeared into bushes. Effie slowed the truck, and they turned left onto a dirt track that ran through the wild growth. In a few minutes the track ended at a wide expanse of concrete. The truck bumped out onto the open space, and Effie gunned it up to speed again.

"What's this?" Paul said.

"The first runway. They built four ten-thousand-foot runways, a scad of other, shorter ones. This was a city, a war city, once."

Now it was a field of concrete run with pea vines, encroachments of rank rounded bushes, islands of them that they soared around, nothing but jungle beyond, no buildings or towers. The tires hissed on the pavement. Effie said, "The local folks come out here hunting coconut crab. The place is so vast that sometimes a man who has lived on this island his whole life will get lost."

"Which man?"

"Ha ha. I could push you out the door, and you'd never find your way back."

"I found my way here. I ought to be able to find my way out of an airport."

They made turns, bumping over piles of brush, crossing runways, shooting down the length of them toward the high dark tangles, veering toward an opening that appeared like conjury among the ferny tiers. Paul was immediately lost. He looked up at the stars; they were a jumble, unrecognizable. It was like coming into a place you know from a direction you've never taken before: the alien familiarity, the thrill of discovery, terror that appears when the familiar becomes strange. Then he began to relax, he let himself go, as if he were riding on a train or a plane, and a small soft happiness began to rise in him like dough. He was happy to have found his brother.

They came around a long curve, shot down a straightaway; the runway widened into a roundabout, and they slowed at the bottom of it. Effie stopped the truck, turned the motor off. He sat looking out the windshield. There were a couple of coconut palms, not close together, a clutch of small waxy-leaved bushes. In the dim starlight it looked as if there were white flowers, like cotton bolls, in the bushes.

"Where are we?" Paul said.

"The bomb pits."

"I don't see anything."

"There's nothing to see. They're filled-in holes."

"What happened here?"

"This is where they loaded the bombs into the planes. They carried them from the storage house by underground railway to these shafts—I'll show you—and lifted them on hydraulic platforms into the bellies of the bombers. One day Fat Man. Another day Little Boy." Effie opened his door. "Come on."

Paul trailed him to the pits. Each was a rectangular concrete-rimmed hole, as long as a grave but wider, filled to the brim with earth. A bush—a plumeria, Effie said—was planted in one corner, a palm beside it. The white flowers he thought he saw were flowers after all, but they were waxy and petaled, they smelled sweeter than magnolia. Half hidden by the bush were two markers, one for each pit, stuccoed pedestals as high as his waist, with slanted tops to which were attached brass plaques. The plaques told brief stories: named the bombs, the planes, the members of the crew. Beyond the pits the bushes rose tall and black.

Effie said, "You have to work hard to imagine it, but you can."

"There's nothing here."

"It's odd, isn't it."

"Where're the buildings?"

"Gone mostly back to the woods."

Paul plucked a plumiera blossom, held it to his nose. They were standing by the Hiroshima pit, where the bomb had been pushed into the belly of the *Enola Gay*. Effie touched his shoulder. "Kneel here with me," he said.

"What for?"

"I want to do the ceremony."

Paul knelt down beside his brother. He could smell him, a rank animal smell, like the odor of bear.

"O God," his brother shouted, making Paul start. "O God." He looked at Effie: his eyes were closed, his face contorted into a grimace, his wide brow clenched. "God, here we are," he cried at the top of his voice. "We've come all this long way to kneel at this pit of destruction. We have seen your works and we have taken it on ourselves to destroy them. We believe it is with your approval. Thank you for these bombs, dear God, for the mighty show they put on for us. Thank you for upping the ante. Now, God," he said, his voice softening, becoming whispery in his throat, confidential, "now, sweet upper being, what about this woman down the road—what about her? She is a brier in my soul —no, not a brier, a wound, a suppurating hole. What of her, then, O Lordie? What are you going to do? Are you going to leave it up to me the way you left it up to Oppenheimer and the boys, let me come up with the explosive device that will rid us all of her noxious presence? What do you say?" He fell silent. Paul opened his eyes, started to speak, but Effie, still blind, held up his hand. Breeze rustled in the bushes; it rattled in the palm fronds above their heads and died. Paul looked back the way they had come: the runway was a wide, ghostly-bottomed corridor headed straight for darkness. Far off, so distant that it must be only a figment, he thought he could hear the surf.

Effie bent forward and touched his forehead to the ground. There were a few sprigs of stiff grass, but mostly the earth was bare, whitish with coral sand. He raised his body and leaned his head back so that his face was aimed straight up. "All right," he said, "I get it: no answer for the supplicant. So we are left here to our own means. I accept. But"—and he pointed at the sky, shaking his finger—"don't come around later complaining. Don't show up later with the mealy mouth, saying I went too far. You're on your own. You have to take what you get."

He sprang to his feet, so suddenly that Paul almost fell over. "All right," he cried, "all goddamn right." He whirled in a circle, stamped his feet.

Paul got slowly up. He had slept on the ship, but it wasn't enough. His sleep was troubled by dreams, dreams like cries, stabs from the darkness. In one he had returned home to find all the trees cut down around the house, the barns burned. He wondered if his father had traveled this far, if he waked his mother in the night to complain about his dead-man troubles.

Effie looked at him. He smiled, a slow, ironic, yet almost tender smile. There were times when Paul could see straight through his face to the boy he must have been. He wished he had known him then; he wished he were the elder brother. Effie was close; he touched his shoulder, leaned against him, and kissed him on the lips. Drawing back, he said, "Every moment of life is an attempt to come to life."

"Who is that?"

"How do you know it's somebody?"

"Because your voice changes when you quote."

"Robert Duncan, homoerotic mystic wandering genius." He shook his head. "Sometimes I think I quote poems only because I love the sound. The rhythms are a comfort to me, like a clock to a puppy."

Facsimile of the mother's heart, Paul thought, but he didn't say anything.

Effie threw his arms out. "I love it," he cried. "I love every bit of it—this fucking world where I can do anything I like."

He turned and sprinted to the truck. For a moment Paul stood there, next to the bomb graves. Maybe it's not genius I'm trying to save, he thought; maybe I only want to get a look at destruction. I would have looked back, he thought, plucking another flower, I would have looked back to see what the bomb did.

"Come on, buddy boy," his brother called.

. . .

They did not go straight back to the hotel. "I have one more stop to make," Effie said. He drove fast again, running close to the bushes; the tiny fronds grazed the side of the truck, making a snapping, whispering noise. They reached the main road, ran along it for a mile, then turned down a coral track that ran through fields planted in vegetables. Paul could smell tomatoes. The road was white and rocky. In the west the moon was a yellow flush against low hills, descending. One hill, a cliff edge, hung out over distant fields like the prow of a ship. It looked almost like a face, a massive head, black and permanent against the lighter sky. From off to the right, beyond high bushes, came the hum and throb of machinery. The sound was a heavy rhythm, chunk and hum, chunk and hum. That's the water pump, Effie told him. The well. We're riding into the heart of the island, which rests, as all these islands do, on a lake of fresh water, which rides in turn on the back of the sea. You mean we're afloat? Paul asked, not believing him. Not exactly. We're more like a hat jammed on the skull of a water brain. Is there a lake? Paul asked. No, only pools in the woods, seeps and muddy patches. Like the river swamp at home? Not exactly.

Off to the left, on the other side of the grooved vegetable fields, gray shapes rose. The agriculture compound, Effie said.

"Ah," Paul said, understanding.

Beyond the low gray buildings, off to the side, in a narrow patch before the woods raised themselves again along a low ridge, a light shone, a single bulb, like a hunting light on a stick. A two-rut track appeared; Effie turned down it, and they bounced through the field. The tomatoes were dark in the heavy bushes. The air stank of rotten fruit.

Effie laughed, a harsh croaking laugh. He had unloosed his hair; it hung in a narrow fan over his shoulders. In a high false voice he began to quote Stevens, his nasty poem about how glad he was to get out of Florida:

"To be free again, [ah, ah] to return to the violent mind
That is their mind, these men, and that will bind

Me round, carry me, [ah, ah] misty deck, carry me
To the cold, go on, high ship, go on, plunge on."

He smacked the dashboard, hummed, hawked, and spit out the
window. He said, "It's a combination of coarseness and fineness.
In this life there's a continual contention between those two—
those two or their equivalents. You know," he said earnestly, as if
Paul had disagreed with him, "the whole angel-devil business,
dichotomies, paradoxes, strike and retreat, light and dark, you
name it."

"Yeah," Paul said, "but then how do you get home from the
store?" Sometimes there were pictures in his mind so vivid that
they seemed to step out of his mind into the world around him.
Above the field, just above it, tall narrow white shadows loomed.
The chunk and hum of the water pump followed them.

The light belonged to a small house. They pulled up in the
yard and stopped. The house was a rectangular box made of plywood, with a tin roof. Moths the size of small birds flopped around
the light that spilled itself over the door and the grassless yard.
Garden tools were leaned against the front wall, on either side of
the door, rakes and hoes, a large shovel. Effie crouched in the seat,
both hands on the steering wheel.

"You know this, don't you?" he said.

"Yeah, I do."

"You can sit here or come; I don't care."

"Maybe I'll trail behind."

His heart beat harshly; his hands were sweating. He wanted to
see her, he wanted to see her coppery head lean out the door, he
wanted to hear her voice, he wanted to be under the influence of
the sound of her voice, its softened vowels, brisk consonants. His
father would take him around to the shacks of the black river
families; he would say, Listen carefully now, and you will hear the
language spoken on a beach in South Carolina in 1632. And he
would listen, bending his head to make out among the slow
murky roll of speech the words and phrases, the manner, of long-
ago times, the pictures and faces coming alive again from the dead
world. So it was with her, in richness and a deep reach.

"It's come to this," Effie said. His body rose, as if it were being lifted; he pressed his shoulder against the truck door and swung it open. He stood upright, shook himself. "I will walk right *through* the fire," he said. "I will reach in and grab what I want."

The front door opened. Just as in his dream, she stuck her head out. On her wide face, darker than life under the light, shadows riding under her eyes, was stiff anger. In her hands was a long bamboo pole, a spear, not a fishing pole. Paul leaned across the seat, pushed his head out the door. She saw him; a look of delight flashed, she started to speak, but then Effie leapt toward her. He ran across the small yard, caught the stick in his hands, lowered his shoulder against her body, and shoved her through the door, slamming it behind him.

There were shouts, there was banging.

Paul got out of the truck, crept around the side of the house to the window. Inside, his brother jumped up and down on the bed. He jumped so fiercely that the bed jumped. He was shouting, he was accusing her of not living up to what she should be. It was the usual heartbroken stuff, Paul thought, only at higher volume than usual. Helen stood in a corner, her arms crossed over her breasts. She wore a loose white dress gathered by small blue buttons all the way down. Her thick copper hair was pulled back under a green ribbon. He watched them: Effie screamed—pleading riding in the screams like branches in a river. Helen stood stiffly, leaning back into the corner; her face, what he could see from the side—the fine profile of straight nose, the long embellishment of her upper lip, the chin under the crest of jaw that looked always a little swollen—was stony. She spoke one word, dropping it in random punctuation into his brother's tirade: *No.*

He looked away a moment, to see if neighbors heard, but there were no neighbors, none but the water pump itself, half a mile away across the fields, speaking its chunk and hum into the night. The stars were a froth of white. The earth, the fields around him, shaped blackly at his back, smelled murky, dense with life. Testify, he thought; we have these awkward ways of telling our story, but somehow we have to stand up and speak. He turned back, to sounds of breaking. A plywood panel under the corner bucked, shivered, and tore loose, leaving a jagged hole of light. As he stepped to look through, bending down, the panel beside him burst loose and banged him in the shoulder. He ran around the house. The door was locked. "Effie," he yelled, "Helen. What are you doing?"

"Watch this," he heard his brother cry. "You won't let me live in your world, then you won't have a world to live in."

The house shuddered, something hit the window, shattering glass and mullion. He shook the doorknob, crying for them to let him in. "Aye, conversion," his brother yelled, even in his madness and frenzy an irony in his voice, and another panel, this one head high on the front of the house, cracked and sprung out, to dangle loosely from the studs. Paul stepped back then to watch; he could only wait for his moment. Blow by blow, the house came down. The panels split, cracked, they shuddered, as kicks, blows from furniture, shoves, split them from the frame. Soon he could see inside, where Helen, her arms still crossed over her breasts, stood in the middle of the single room watching Effie tear down every created thing. It was marvelous in its way, Paul thought, a wonderment. His brother didn't stop, he didn't slow down—whirling, kicking, popping with his forearm—until the walls were all down, until the house was an open-sided shed spilling the light of a single overhead bulb into the night of tropic fields and island. He did not then go directly after the roof, didn't reach above his head into the low eaves and begin to tear out the sheets of new tin, but instead leaned his shoulder, then his back, against a corner post and shoved, pressing it steadily until there was a small, then a larger, tearing sound over their heads and the two-by-four gave way, popping out to hang snagged like a bottom tooth in the air. The roof sighed down over their heads. It hung like a rakish cap.

All this while Helen said nothing, nor did she attempt to stop him. She continued to man her station in the center of the room, stolid as a statue, though her eyes never left her husband's face. Effie did not look at her as he worked, but he spoke to her steadily. "Genuine torment," he said, his voice conversational, as if he were ordering breakfast in the café at home, "that's what you are getting here. You are getting the impossibility of continuance. When there is no place further to go, you must either die or turn back. In each breath we make this choice, but the small parable of breath

is one we get used to. Occasionally we need a more pungent
stroke. This is yours, darling, this is yours." His hair had flown
over his face. Dark and wet, it covered his forehead, made a thatch
over his cold alien eyes, which Paul saw, as he crouched in the
yard gritting his teeth, held no emotion at all, only the cold fire
of distance. As Effie pushed against the opposite post, and the
roof, sagging and slightly canted toward the yard, began to sway
—it was then that Helen broke. She shivered, groaned, turned
slightly, her arms drifted loose, and she fell onto her side, moaning. Her eyes were closed, her face white. Her eyebrows, sooty
under the copper hair, shone. Her lips were pinched closed. Above
the up-fluttered hem of her dress, which Paul saw was a shift
fashioned from cotton sacks—Red Rose Rice, he read, in faded
pink letters across her breast—the scar gleamed, tallowy and
muddled. He wanted to touch it, he wanted to step in, and bend
all the way down to press his lips onto the blistered surface of it,
but there was no time for that queer homage, no time as his
brother shoved steadily against the back post, grunting a little,
speaking to himself now, in a language that sounded like the
language of tongues, of the mad churchmen from the country,
grinding the fullness of his slender strength against the yellow
post as above them the roof groaned and cried, releasing its voices
of heartwood and metal, speaking to them all in its own ancient
language, giving way.

   He dashed into the house, dragged her up by the shoulders,
and pulled her toward the door, crying out his brother's name,
crying for him in God's name to quit and come on. But he
wouldn't. Paul dragged her down the steps into the yard, and he
laid her in a patch of tall grass near the tomato rows. The grass
was sweetly fragrant. He knelt and touched her face; it was cold,
in the moonlight it whitely shone, like a marble face—she was
out, not dead, fainted only—and then he stood up and stepped
toward the house. The grass hid her like Moses in the bulrushes.
His brother strained at the post, his face blurred with sweat. The
roof seemed to lift slightly, to slide toward the darkness at the
back, and then the post gave way and he saw his brother, just
before the crashing beams and tin obscured him, leap away, a yell
in his mouth, and the last of the house came blustering down, the

roof turning slightly as it fell, hitting on the edge and collapsing back like a clam shell closing, crashing through the plywood and studs, coming to rest half off the floor, split along the beam as if it had been broken across a knee. From the other side of the ruin his brother shouted, Yes. Yes, by God, he shouted, yes goddamn yes. Paul saw him: thin in white clothes, his hair wild about his face, his arms uplifted like an actor's. Effie cried out in triumph.

Then, head upright, a man undefeated in battle, he strode toward him through the wreckage, not looking down as he lifted his knees as one might lift his knees to step through the surf, reached the two plank steps, and skipped down them into the yard.

"Where is she?" he said.

"She's in the grass."

"Ah."

He crossed the yard and stood over her. He looked at her for a long time. Breeze shuddered in the tops of the tomato bushes. The stars were tiny and sharp, like grains of dust. He raised his face. Sweat gleamed under his eyes. "Snowy earth," he said, "its whiteness drifts toward the white fires of space." He turned and looked at Paul. "I've never touched her," he said, "not in anger. What I hold against her is not physical."

His brother had never thought to explain himself to him before. For the first time in life—naive child—he wondered if his brother knew what he was doing, if there was any plan at all.

Effie hitched his pants with his wrists, began to whistle; he crossed the yard and got in the truck. Paul followed him. "Aren't we going to do anything about Helen?" he said.

Effie grinned. "This'll cover it for tonight."

When Paul still hesitated, he said, "Don't worry, buddy; there's nothing to worry about—you can't save the dead."

IV

BUT WHO was dead? Not Effie yet, not Helen, who had sat up in the tall grass as they drove away, certainly not his mother, who hailed him from the doorway of her pink plywood cottage as he came up the walk, which was lined with small heads of brain coral painted with faces. The house was tucked under breadfruit trees. The dark-green frog-foot leaves shambled and swayed above the roof, making a noise like rubber garments rustling, releasing splatters of sunlight that glanced off the new tin. Behind him, if he turned to look, beyond a bushy field, beyond the shell-strewn beach, beyond the lagoon shallows where tanks, stranded forever on the stone-footed bottom, rusted, the Pacific lay, a blue shining uptilted shelf, sharply rimmed by a sky piled with white monuments of cumulus, Pig Island set like a small square hat in the center of distance. He had seen it all in his week, walked it all, visited the three stores, the screen-door school, the district office, where the sheriff sat across the room from the mayor in a greasy shirt open to his navel, making deals for trinkets on the shortwave radio. He had lain out in the village baseball field watching the white detonations of the southern stars, he had toured the church, which Father Marco told him was constructed partially from the packing crates the atomic bombs came in, he had attended a samurai double feature in the roofless shell-smacked former firehouse that his friend Jacabo ran as a sideline to his family's number one business of vegetable farming, paying his quarter along with two dozen others to sit on handmade benches under the massed stars to watch black-and-white leather-clad warriors pummel each other as children scurried like roaches up and down the aisles and old native men exclaimed in Japanese. Chamorros they were called, these people, who were small and brown-skinned, maybe five hundred of them on this island that had once been owned entirely by the Japanese—before that the Germans and before that, for nearly four hundred years, the Spanish, who brought Catholicism and a hatred of the natural world and a taste for spices to the native peoples—which the Americans, in July of 1944, after heavy bombardment from the sea, had splashed ashore on Puntan Azoor (Blue Beach) to take away from them, take it away and blast to pieces the sugar mill and the fish-packing plant and the concrete office buildings and the paper houses and the gardens of bougainvillea and hibiscus and polished coral stone. His father would love it here, he thought, it would be for him a living

laboratory in which he could test his theories of the inevitable
diminishment of the Western spark, that fluttering rising light
that set worlds aflame and left them to burn and crumble back
into bitter ashes. The Americans had built an airfield and laid
down roads. They had thrown up Quonset warehouses that they
filled with supplies, with guns and buckets of peanut butter and
tractors and trumpets. From here they had bombed Iwo Jima and
Okinawa, here they had massed troops for the invasion of the
Japanese mainland, from here in darkness the B-29s had lifted off
the slick runways, teetering a little, fragile as damselflies for one
second in the trade wind, the heavy Allis-Chalmers engines clattering, then settling in to the pull and drone of flight as they
circled once over the northern fields waiting for the fighters to rise
like cicadas up to them before heading away north-northwest over
Saipan toward the cloudy seascape of Honshu Island.

He had seen his brother only once, but he had heard stories of
him. In the middle of the night Effie had come to his door and
called him out and driven him breakneck to Blue Beach, where
under a pared moon they had stripped their clothes and swum
naked in the warm clear waters of the lagoon. His brother had led
him a hundred yards out into the chest-high water, to a tank, a
creation turned the rusted color of rock, and had clambered with
him into the turret, where they sat in the corroded seats under the
gun, looking out at the milky beach as the slinky lagoon waves
trickled and slapped against the metal. Effie had not spoken a
word to him, though he had made firing noises. Afterward he led
him back to the truck and returned him to the hotel, his hard
wolfish face shining with salt, and let him off. Paul heard later,
the next day, from the proprietor of the grocery store at the
bottom of the hill, that his brother had that night flipped his
truck in the boonies, among the tangin-tangin bushes, as they
were called, rolled it, smashing the roof and knocking the bed
loose, destroying it.

"He laughed for that," the proprietor, Temelio, a short dark
man with eyebrows that looked oiled, father of twenty children,
said.

Paul misunderstood.

"Yes, he laughed for that. He passed down to the cockfight bar and bought some beer and sat at his table and he laughed for that."

At night, at the cockfight bar, his brother gambled at dice. There were stories of fights, of threats, of angry men pacing outside under the flame trees, working their anger into their fists as the laughter of his brother, like applause, sounded from the open windows. After midnight, with shotguns and pistols, his brother and a few of the young men hunted fruit bats in the papaya groves on the plateau. He could hear the guns firing, small sharp sounds that seemed close, then far off.

He had met them, some of these men and others, he had made the rounds, spoken to farmers in their fields of eggplant and bell pepper, to housewives musing in betel-nut dreams in the doorways of their plywood houses, to the schoolteachers and the few fishermen, to children. In the two bars he had met the sporting boys, limber ratty Cerone and his mentor, Fin Vert, who was tall and wore his long furry hair sleeked back from a high narrow forehead and, draped over his shoulder, in sun or rain, a wrinkled khaki raincoat. He had met the mayor, up for election again now, running against his officemate the sheriff; the two of them, Maze Manglona and Daniet Sablan, spent their days staring across the wide room at each other, watching each other, like fighters, each waiting for the other to make a move. When one would use the radio the other would begin to speak or sing loudly, chanting old Chamorro songs and Filipino popular ballads, calling loudly to friends passing on the road. Over the radio they made loud and pompous deals, with the air force (to bring the military back to Tinian), with the governor (for new municipal buildings, extra ration food, and typhoon shelters), with the owner of the Celex department store in Guam (for television sets and fiberglass fishing boats), with Japanese investors (for hotels and golf courses)—deals which when they related them later in the bar or outside the church, which the mayor on orders from Father Marco was banned from, took on the flesh and tone, the muscularity, of living beings, each raconteur snorting and guffawing with clear ridicule of the other, each accusing the other of crimes, both old and new, each watching sharply, with the fateful clarity of hunted animals, for the other to spring. They were both, in fact, so his friend

Jacabo told him, convicted felons: Daniet, the badge wearer, for collaboration with the Japanese (which since generally more of his fellow islanders had collaborated than not wasn't such a high crime) and Maze for running bolita numbers while he was a student at Wayne State University in Detroit (which also was not held against the perpetrator, since it occurred in America and was not directed against local folk), and many remembered the day in 1959 when Maze stepped off the airplane in Saipan and from the top of the gangway raised his manacled hands as if in triumph.

He had met the two of them—each rising to be the first to greet a visitor—and thought that the boldness in their movements masked something; as they loudly and falsely welcomed him he thought that they were men who wished above all else to subsume some great fear, to lose it so completely in the crowd of other lives and fears that its existence became a more and more distant rumor. He thought then that maybe his uncle, who practiced as a life's work the invigoration of the proposition that God's grace was boundless, might be stumped by these two, at least for the moment, since there had to be a large measure of subtlety in their method, of seamless guile, for them, one after the other pumping his hand—one blocky and pockmarked, the other small but lanky, almost wizened—to portray on whatever platform of venality the electorate's fancy of mayor, or sheriff.

But in that week he was lost, or he recognized that he was lost, not in his spirit maybe—there was hope there, and direction—but simply in the banal articles of his normal life, of brand names and language, of intent maybe, of community. The village, so Jacabo told him, was five thousand years old; it consisted of four lateral streets and the two paved roads crossing them on their way from the docks to the highlands and the old airfields, a scattered array of boxy houses, the three stores built of concrete block, the Japanese ruins, and among it all the gigantic debris, like the detritus of some grandiloquent and glamorous typhoon, the tracks and discards of American war power. At night he went out and stood in the road outside the hotel, looking down the long hill at the village, in which no lights burned, or only an occasional light flickered among the trees, like the lights on the other side of a mountain range, and listened to the low distant rumble of the bombs as they fell from 35,000 feet onto the tabletop of rock off the Pig Island cliffs, and saw the brief surge of light, like red heat lightning, and watched the sky snap back into blackness.

And not his mother—no, she wasn't dead yet. She waved her broom at him, laughing in a bright yellow head rag. She had arrived the night before on the supply boat—in his sleep he had heard the whistle; it changed in his dream to a silver river curving away through trees—and she would leave again tomorrow after her Sunday at home. The family she supported lived next door in a large sagging wooden house with a green canvas roof, in the center of a grassless yard in which chickens pecked at bits of debris and children in ripped shorts shouted and cried. In her face he saw his life. Saw himself in the wide-set eyes, the cleft chin, the thick shoulders. A gaiety took him, and he sprinted the last few steps and swept her into his arms, lifting her, joyous in the feeling of her light supple weight against him. She laughed out loud and kissed him on the ear and led him into the house, which was painted white entirely, and flushed with light from large windows in east and west, and nearly bare except for rice mats on the floor, a cotton pallet in the corner, and a severe table and chair pulled under the west window. On the walls she had pinned pictures torn from magazines, reproductions of Vermeer and Brueghel and Winslow Homer's painting of a black man sprawled alone in a lifeboat with sharks circling. He had never been sure if the black man saw the distant ship passing; he wondered about it as a child, wondered if he saw it and didn't care, or if, horribly, as he supposed Homer intended, it was passing by—his only melodramatic rescue—unnoticed. On the table was a brass crucifix on a stand and a little Christmas crèche complete with blue-robed Mary and her Joseph and the Baby Jesus in ceramic swaddling clothes in a wooden manger. What's that? he said in mock horror, pointing at the crèche, and she told him it was her new discovery, Catholicism; she said she loved the colors in the churches—"all that extruded gold"—and loved the extravagance of the liturgical claims. "Saints," she said. "Can you believe that?"

"Why not?" he said. "You believe Daddy talks to you in the night."

"That rascal. He thinks I'm crazy to have come out here. it's only his jealousy. They wouldn't let him in the war—too valuable at home, they said (he said), or fallen arches—and now he's jealous that I get to see all this ruin and history without him."

"If he's here, can't he see it?"

"He's a nut; he can't see anything. He doesn't know where he is if I don't tell him."

"Ah, my Maria, who reveals the truth of every situation."

"I am good at that, aren't I?"

She didn't ask him why he wasn't in school, didn't want, he supposed, to know. She took him out to the kitchen and fed him a lunch of pickled fish, breadfruit porridge, and green olives. The fish were tiny, no larger than minnows; their briny silver skin slaked off under his fingers. She scooped them with a strainer out of a heavy blue crock. The kitchen was an airy screened room behind the house, connected to it by a stone-flagged passageway. "It's like the negro houses at home," she said, "like the old times. My family here eats chitlins and tripe, something you never see anymore in north Florida. Sometimes I help the little girl wash them with the hose. We go out in the yard and clean them in a tub. The father, a scrawny little devil who spends all his spare time pitying himself, works at the slaughterhouse. He brings home innards by the bucketload."

"I like these pickled fish," Paul said.

"Eat all of it," she said. "Eat the head too. It's good."

But what, he wanted to know, of her job? Was it true she danced hootchy-kootchy at a serviceman's club in Guam?

Of course, she told him, and I am very good at it too.

But why? (Why does my mother do this?)

"My body," she said, "it's a small thing, but it's something I can give back. Sex has given me such a sweet ride, and these boys are so young, they're troubled and scared, some of them are going to Vietnam—I guess they are—some of them fly high in the planes that bomb people: I guess I want to save them a little, to knit up their lives for them a moment, a little. Here, let me show you."

"No," he said. "I don't want that."

"Oh, it's all right. It's uncanny—a mystery. You'll be amazed."

Then his mother, a women of forty-five with hair black as a storm petrel's wing and skin of silk, danced for him.

First, she disappeared into the house, pulling the door shut behind her. He could hear her moving about. Outside the window, which was propped open with a stick, chickens hung in the branches of a lemon tree, like party hats. He heard the snuffle and snort of a pig, a child's falsetto shout, from the room the crackle of rice straw. In the blue sky the puffed clouds looked like permanent fixtures. For a moment, for one second, in the dazzle of waiting, he thought he saw a life of restitution and then rest, a life lived on a sunny riverbank under the shade of sycamores. *I can never make it all right.* The words came to him sharply, like the stink of brine. No one—not his father—spoke them, but he heard them clearly. And then he saw—didn't see: felt—the doors ahead of him, doors of his life blow open, blow open and slam shut, one after the other rapidly, like machine-gun fire. From the one room of the house, he heard a tape start up—snatch of song—stop, whine, and start again: Dinah Washington singing "Red Sails in the Sunset," and then the door swung slowly open and his mother, Queen Mary Voss Hogan, stood in the opening wearing a blue women's air force uniform.

"My God, Mama," he said.

She pressed her finger to her lips. "Clap a little," she said, her amber eyes sparkling as if she'd been in there polishing them. "Just a little."

He pushed the heels of his numb hands together. She smiled, letting her white gap-fronted teeth shine; here was the smile that had thrilled him all his life, the smile of his first love, of hope and life and all the world's promise. She began to release the clothes from her body, first the buttoned blouse, then the skirt, which hissed stiffly down her thighs, swaying and sliding in an approximation of a stripper's moves and stark against the ordinariness of her clothes: the military outer garments, the white cotton underwear. Only her pale-blue transparent stockings, held up by a meager garter belt, contained any erotic extravagance. As she unclipped the tops and began to roll the filmy nylon down her legs, he raised his hand to stop her, but the gesture was feeble; she didn't notice, and there was no voice in his mouth. Very suddenly then and from nowhere he felt a baffling tenderness, like a caress or a giving way inside his body. He felt something in himself rise and meet her softly.

One stocking off, then the other—foot propped against the pink plywood wall—she reached behind and popped the garter belt. It snapped around her waist; she winced, grinned, and tossed it behind her. Now the song ended, there was the hiss of tape, and another song began, one he didn't recognize, a charged, quivering music, sung by a woman, or by a man singing like a woman, a song of such delicacy in its portrayal of loss and pity that for a moment he forgot her as he listened to it. She was nearly naked now, preening, stretching her body, the soft white undergarments furling; she reached behind her and unfastened the bra, turning as she did so that her back was to him, so that he could see her hands, which were the hands of a woman of forty-five, eroded around the knuckles, slightly veiny, each finger segment sharply delineated.

She caught the cups and whirled back around, dipping once and rising in the slow motion of one rising through water; she arched her back, straightened, and with a vivid motion, hands turned inward, she dragged—let fall—the plain garment from her breasts: they were pale, silky, descendant, slightly flushed at the tops; the nipples were the color of coffee—he saw them.

He felt the stirring in his groin, and the sorrow, and the cry of laughter that cracked like a blow in his chest, and he half rose to stop her, but she would not be stopped now, not by him; she danced, rising on the shudder of the music, strutted on the frail platform of the man-woman voice. Her thumbs hooked into the band of her panties, she rolled them down the smooth bowl of her belly, turned again so that in the—what seemed to him a dismemberment: that was the word that came to mind—the *clarification* of her flesh, he saw the soft hillocks of her ass, the dark separation. She stooped and swept the panties down her legs, rose and turned, dashed the cloth across her pelvis, pushed one leg forward opened, threw her arms over her head, and stood before him, statuesque plunder, the black feast in her groin matted and shining, his mother, entirely naked.

The tape spun, hissed, died.

"Ah," he croaked, "deliverance."

She grinned, whirled, and disappeared into the house. In a minute she came back out, wearing her red silk robe.

"They love it," she said. "All the little soldier boys go wild."

"I'll bet they do."

"Did you think it was sexy?"

"I don't think of you as sexy."

"Of course you do. Every little boy thinks of that. He just changes it into something else."

"Whatever I've changed it into, I don't recognize you anymore."

"Helen, that's all she is—your mother in red hair."

"Jesus."

"It's true."

"It's not true, but even if it was, you should bite your tongue before you say it."

"He's driven her crazy." She said this quietly, her voice lingering in her throat, as she stood before a lime-green cupboard, from which she drew a bottle of Japanese whiskey and poured two small drinks in water glasses.

"Maybe she will recover."

"Not as long as *he's* on earth." She tossed the whiskey off. "I told him this would happen."

"Telling doesn't help."

She pressed the rim of the glass to her mouth, ran it slowly around her lips. The flush of the dance was still in her face. "He has too much capacity," she said.

"You mean he's too fine for this world?"

"No," she said definitely. "He's just set at a speed that can't help but wreck him."

Then he felt the sadness again, the same old one, the gentle tearing inside him like a vine detaching from a wall, and an old sense of uselessness, of hopelessness, began to filter through his body so that, to dam it, to divert it from what he always thought of as the center of himself, his strongest place, he leapt to his feet

—he moved—lop-danced the two steps to her, and took her in his arms. "Oh, Mama," he said, "you are the most selfish, self-blinded woman I have ever met, but I love you like a crazy man."

Her arms fluttered about him; she pushed against his chest. "Dash away, child," she said. "I want to lie down now. I want to fantasize about sexual things and boys' bodies, and it's best that my son not be around."

She shooed him off her. "Go away, boy."

Into the bold blue gigantic Pacific day, trailing his brother, he went.

From the doorway of his Quonset, in his underwear, the mayor hailed him. It was his campaign speech he held rolled in his thick hand, the one he would give at the rally in a couple of weeks, or whenever anyone asked him, which he wanted Paul to read. The floor against the living room wall and four feet into the room was covered with shellacked coconut crabs fixed to plywood plaques, claws raised in attack. "Making souvenirs," Maze said, and motioned him to a chair. The speech was typed. He read it through as Maze sat across from him, his whole body thrust forward, as if he was about to be called away; Paul looked up to see him moving his lips as Paul read. Two children, a boy and a girl of about four, raced into the room and were suddenly dumb. "What are you going to do?" Maze said to them. "Go to Mama"—who poked her small head into the room and jerked it back out. The children stared and didn't move.

The speech was heavy, vicious, and oddly submissive. From a melancholy hope for fairness and equality at the beginning, it plunged into staccato promises: bags of golden glory for everyone. Maze portrayed himself as the servant of the people. A servant, so he said, who would rather die than betray those he served. "I will cut out my own heart," the speech said, "before I will let you down." He attacked his rival, who had been born on the island, as a foreigner and a troublemaker. "He will sell your children to the Japanese," the speech claimed flatly. "Kill him," the speech said.

"That last is a little strong," Maze said when Paul looked up from the final page.

"Why is it in English?"

"For my files. My papers. Got to think of history."

"It's strong."

"Tough, huh?"

"You get your points across."

"You think they'll go for it?" he said solemnly, leaning back in his flowered armchair.

"Sure."

Paul looked at the children, squatting near their father's chair. "Go to Mama," Maze said. "You go to Mama."

The children looked at him and did nothing.

"We talk to them in English," he said, smiling. "You want a drink? Vodka?" His wife poked her head into the room. "Come," she said to the children, making a wide gesture with her full arm. "Come Mama." The children popped up and sprinted out of the room. "We want them to be prepared," Maze said.

Paul got up, went over to the coconut crab display, and picked one up. Claws raised high, its purple armored body reared off the board. The claws could snap a child's hand off. "Looks okay," Paul said. "Is it hard to do?"

"Nah, I'll show you. Come on."

They went out through the back, through the kitchen, where his wife scolded the children in Chamorro as they sat at the table eating plates of rice and Spam. "Eat food," she said as they came through, Paul wasn't sure whether to him or to the children. He waved his hand slightly, declining.

They went out back into an open shed surrounded thickly by clumped banana trees. The long purple tears of the flowers hung down almost to the ground. Several live crabs trussed in rubber strips cut from inner tubes hung from the ceiling. "I caught these last night," Maze said, "your brother and me. We got drunk at the bomb pits." Oil gleamed in the pockmarks on his face. His movements were slow and awkward, lead foot stepping gingerly out, as if not long before his body had become unfamiliar to him. "Your brother is too hard to stop," he said. "I had to leave him."

"In the jungle?"

"On the road. Other hunters bring him in. He's too much for me."

"I don't doubt it."

Maze thumped one of the hanging crabs with his thumb. "Some of these are maybe too small." He shook his head.

"Is there a season?"

"No. They try that on Saipan, though, no good. Sure—people won't follow orders." The crabs made a soft clacking noise, like small teeth chattering.

Out of a shoebox on a table against the wall he took a large brown bottle and a syringe.

"Ah, I see."

"Yeah, it's simple. Formaldehyde."

He filled the syringe, laid it on the table, and took a crab down. Holding it hard against the streaked wood, he undid the stripping. Unleashed, the crab scurried uselessly backward, making a metal rushing sound on the wood with its pipy legs. Long banana claws rose from under the thorax, but Maze held them, two stalks clenched in his fist. He picked the crab up—its legs shrank in under the exposed belly—slipped the needle intimately between the shell plates behind the narrow head, and pressed down the plunger. Turning the crab, he shot preservative into the joints, like a man oiling hinges, one last long squirt into the soft beaded sack of the abdomen; the crab closed slowly, stiff petals collapsing toward the heart, one thin foreleg reaching out, then pulling fastidiously back, and was still.

"Simple," he said, placing the crab on the table. "You have to be careful not to give them too much—this stuff's expensive, and if you shoot too much it'll drip out later." He arranged the crab on a sawn plaque, raised its dead claws. "A little varnish and glue for the board, and you have authentic Chamorro handicraft. Ha ha." Paul brushed his fingers over the smooth back shell, streamlined as a jet. The claws were as long as his fingers. "You ought to do pretty well with these," he said.

"Not enough crabs," he answered, a small rueful expression gathering in his puffy face, "and the market's not good. But business is business. A businessman got to do business."

"I don't see why not."

Maze cocked his head. His clever eyes shone. "You don't think too much, huh?"

"I don't mind. You do what you can."

"Your brother tells me I am insane. He calls me a crook to my face." Maze laughed, a small clucking sound. "But your brother he will say anything. I like that, except when he tells Daniet Sablan to shoot me."

"Effie said that?"

"Your brother will say anything." He thumbed a tiny black wad out of his flat nose. "You like the speech, huh?"

"The speech is fine." He remembered the river in one of his dreams, the long silvery reach, the rush of pines, the mullet streaking upstream. Yes, in the dream he had reached his arms out, or he had tried to, to embrace—but he couldn't remember what.

The white dust on her legs fascinated him. She paced up and down the street outside the cockfight arena, which was a wooden ring under a large open shed beside the Picaro Bar, which itself was only a small purple frame house the owner had converted into a bar, placing a few card tables and rusty folding chairs in the living room and a wide board across the kitchen door that he and his billowy wife could pass beer and Japanese vodka across. In the same white dress, cinched now with a belt of woven pandanus, her fine head held high, not speaking to anyone, not acknowledging the roars from the shed or the passage of time, Helen paced through the afternoon as the trade wind pushed at the tangin-tangin and streamed in the flame tree over her head, tugging at the clusters of lurid blossom.

From the yard he could see down the hill to the ocean: blue as a blue ballroom beyond the rusty dock, the stacked reefers; soaring like a runway that rose with the flight, small clouds like cannon fire hanging in the south. She had moved—and she wouldn't let him in when Jacabo drove him out there, wouldn't speak to him —into the back room of the agriculture station; she slept on a pallet on the floor and bathed in the cattle tank behind the sheds. Everyone knew that she cried herself to sleep at night, everyone knew that she ran wildly through the tomato rows, everyone had heard her brokenhearted conversations on the shortwave radio, her shouts for mercy, her accusations, her pleas. This couldn't go on, everyone said, this must stop, someone must help this poor girl, someone must put an end to this torture, but no one did. Even the night, as everyone knew, when, after buying fish and pepper sauce and the last four potatoes sprouting in the wire-footed bin at Temelio's store, she had, like one tranced by a spell, spun in a slow descent to the floor, where she began to howl and slobber like a beast gone mad. No one stepped over her, no one ignored her, but no one came to her rescue either. She twitched and moaned, her hands clutching at nothing, until finally something seemed to give way and she lay exhausted on the floor, curled on her side, whimpering slightly. The old women in their mestizo dresses, handkerchiefs covering their hair, the men in their baggy-legged Japanese pedal pushers, bowed to her as she crawled to her feet, but they did not extend a hand to help her up. Temelio had placed her groceries in a creased sack, and this he slid diffidently across the counter—in acknowledgment or compassion, no one could say—and his wife, a tiny woman with a scrawl of aubergine face, mother of twenty, clucked in her throat, but in her eyes there was more fascination than horror. No one reached to hold the door she went out of.

The white dust was splashed on her long legs like water, as if she had been wading in a white pool, and her copper hair was wild, loose on her head, which, when she stooped to make her turn at the top of the street, she shook violently, as one would shake an animal, or a horror, off. He watched her, and he watched his brother too, from his seat in the men's outhouse, a high perch raised on coral slabs above double oil drums, which stank of recent and ancient shit only barely cut by the lime that he sprinkled from a bean can between his legs as he excreted what felt like knobs of fire—hot peppers from Jacabo's table last night—groaning. Through a warp in the door he could sight past his brother, who stood against the curve of the ring closest to him, and see her pacing, and it was as if his brother, dressed in pressed white clothes, his panther-colored hair coiled and tied back with a piece of parachute cord, leaning away from the hooligan commotion of the rooster fight taking place in front of him—which he had, as was his way, covered all bets on—held her by an invisible cord, a cord of such delicate strength that her every step, every shake of her head, every shudder that rippled in her shoulders, every breath, was at his volition, his pluck and caress.

He thought: Well, yes, now: this is when it will happen, while I am in this rank cave shitting fire, now is the moment when she will reach the end—recalling her in Florida as she strode up the walk with her sweaty bandanna looped in her hands like white handcuffs, back there in the early days—now is the moment when she will murder him.

But it was not to be. She did not whirl and charge after him, did not even turn her head—each time she spun on her heel under the throbbing flame tree, it was away from the arena—to look at him, or at any of them; and they, thirty men, drink-spurred, with money on the line, their harsh, premonitory cries ricocheting off the creosoted eaves, piercing the dry steady flight of the trade breeze, did not look at her; only here and there one, such as the tiny, mincing Cerone, off Fin's khaki shoulder, as a thief peering through a fence might, cast a quick covetous glance.

Then the door banged, and he heard his friend's voice. "What's the matter you, lahi—you fall in?"

There was a crackle of laughter, and Jacabo began to explain to those nearby how he had joked Paulo into eating a handful of the tiny explosive peppers his father grew for fina deni sauce. "You should see this one, primo. His face turned as red as the pepper itself. No finagaga, it is true. We thought fire would come from his mouth." He rapped on the door again. "Fire," he cried. "Is not this true—a face like fire?"

"It is the truth," Paul said.

The men outside laughed, the laughter coarse and celebratory, friendly, grateful for his acknowledgment of the taunts. "I will never eat peppers again," he said, complying.

The men hooted.

But he didn't take his eyes off Helen. Maybe his mother was right, that his fascination with her was only his way of carrying mother love into the world, but it was his father that she reminded him of, his father's last days at least, which he did not remember clearly except in tone and in a few random specifics, one incident especially: of his father on the dock at the lower pond, which was not a pond really but only a swollen diversion of the river, a hollow, that his grandfather had his workmen dig entrance and exit ditches to, remembered him on his knees leaning his face down to the black water, remembered his white shirt pulling out of his trousers so that a pale scoop of back flesh and the tops of his buttocks were exposed, remembered specifically the black tail of hair at the bottom of his spine, which in the twilight and in the unexpectedness of his father's gesture he thought was actually a tail, a small curled braid of sooty hair—sacral fawn tail it is called when a child is born with it—and he thought of this tail, which he had never noticed before—as he had not noticed Helen's scar —as an emblem of his father's secret life, of the secret life of fathers, a life that as his father pushed suddenly his whole face into the black mirror of water seemed to him suddenly and for the first time the greater life (greater than the day-filling extruded life of family obligation, worldly tasks) and a life, he realized—as if the thin tail and the gesture of kneeling, the soft rings of water enlarging, were proofs of it—that his father had failed, and that the failure in this hidden, uncelebrated, mysterious secret life was all. And so with Helen now, as in some leap between flickering sparks he thought she must be one who had, through guile or greed or through some terrible misapprehension of her needs or powers, come to maddeningly in a cage she was unable to tear her way out of—this place, this man, this arrangement of circum-stance and will—so that now it had become unendurable to her in its particulars, not only of job and place and marriage, but in everything, in the taste of the salt breeze in her mouth, in the pearls of candle wax littering the kitchen table, in the torn flesh of a tomato, in every thought, breath, in every heartbeat.

But she did not turn then, did not suddenly skid among them; she paced on, and she did not heed the cries of the men, or the mute crackle and flutter of the roosters as they tore each other's bodies. He came from the outhouse, bowing a little to the laugh-ter of the men, to his brother's back, and stood among them at ringside, where now Fin Vert held his black-and-yellow rooster high toward the four points of the compass, bowing to each direction. *Nort, nort,* he said at each station—it was the word one used to greet elders—his voice braying. The short curved sword of the rooster's steel fighting spur, attached by narrow wound strips of leather, caught the light. His opponent, José Contuma, a stout man with three widow's peaks and a red aloha shirt, waited for him to finish. He stood with one leg canted out, holding his bronze rooster against his hip. Every few moments he raised the rooster and blew softly in its face.

Helen did nothing as the two men knelt on opposite sides of a line scratched with a heel into the dirt, holding their roosters with both hands, pushing them forward and dragging their feet back through the dirt—as a child might play with a toy roadster—raising them on the forward upswing so that the birds, snapping out of their idiocy, for one second recognized each other, in hatred, and slashed with their spurs, nor did she make a sound when old Alphonzo Jak, the bar owner, regal in bare chest that gleamed like water-dipped rubber, gave the signal to let the birds go, which the men did, springing back as the roosters leapt high, spurs bared at each other's breasts, nor do anything when quickly, as is the case in knife fights, when there is no time or inclination to study the enemy, José Contuma's bronze fowl slashed with a single downward stroke the belly of Fin's black, striking as it leapt up and over, flipping the other on his back.

Fin's bird staggered upright with its purple guts shining on its breast like buttons. The fight was over then, the rooster could not live, but Fin waved Alphonzo off.

"Fight," he said, "fight on."

He picked the bird up and took its head in his mouth. Released, the wet head rose between his hands, the yellow beak closed. Again they knelt at the line, again they scratched forward and back, again they released the roosters, and again the birds lunged at each other. The bronze caught the black in the wing, near the joint, rising, flapping its weight forward so that they all could hear the short small snap of bone. The black fell, pushed up, and staggered away, reeling toward the ring fence, wing dragging. Fin intercepted it, grabbed it up. He snatched a bottle of vodka from Cerone's hand, took a large mouthful, and blew it into the rooster's face. Once more the bird came to life. José raised his hand no, but Fin, his khaki coat bunched on his shoulders, bared his teeth and cried, Yes, hoo-oo preem—fight.

"Fight what?" José laughed.

"Fight this champion," Fin answered.

Again he sucked the rooster's head into his mouth—it looked for a second as if he might suck the brains out of it—released it and blew his hot breath into its face, turned it and blew softly up its feathery ass. He stepped forward, with the bird held in front of him at his waist, knelt, and on the signal, given with a dismissive wave by Alphonzo Jak, thrust the bird forward against the oncoming body of the bronze.

Its beak, jerking reflexively down, pierced the bronze rooster's eye.

José, just folding his arms over his fat chest in triumph, roared outrage. Fin leapt to his feet. José's bird wobbled sideways; Fin kicked it aside. Then José leapt at Fin. They grappled in the center of the ring. For a moment they seemed to dance. Fin shoved his body close to José's, lifted him, turned him in his arms, and slammed him down onto his side. José came up quickly, but Fin caught him with a closed right hand in the temple. José's arms flew out, and he sprawled backward onto his ass. "Get up, baugerro," Fin said, his voice breathless and low. "Rise."

José pushed up on his hands and knees. He shook his head, passed a hand across his face. For one second Paul, staring at him from across the ring, saw a flare of panic in his eyes, and then he saw him, for one more, longer, moment, look hard and steadily at his rooster, which leaned like a paralyzed drunk against one of the wooden fence slats; it was a look of bafflement and tenderness, the look one might give to a scraped child, and then with a roar he thrust to his feet and swung. But his righteousness did not help; Fin caught him on the swing, ducked under the oaken blow, and cracked his chin with the crown of his head. José sighed sharply and slumped to his knees, blood streaming from his mouth.

This could have been the end but it was not, because just then his brother, shouting Fin's name, leapt into the ring. Paul's heart surged. He looked to see what Helen would do now, the madwoman pacing at the gate, but she did nothing. His brother grinned. His large teeth, which when he exposed them seemed too heavy for his mouth, shone. In his left hand was an open knife. "Come," he said, "come, cocksucker, to your fate."

Fin raised both hands, backing away. He pushed out a cracked laugh. "No, thank you, amigo, not with you."

Effie held the knife out to him. It was a long narrow melon knife. On the Panhandle it was called a pig sticker. "Here, you can have it. I will take it back from you and kill you."

"Aye. No, thank you, amigo."

"Then give me your coat."

"What do you say?"

"Give me your coat."

Fin looked up into the eaves, where wasps sizzled around their paper nests. His glance raked downward across Effie's chest. Effie smiled. "Your coat."

"This?"

"Yes."

Slowly Fin loosed the garment from his shoulders. He shot a glance at Cerone, who hung his head. Bunching the coat in both hands, he held it out to Effie. "You can have my coat," he said. Effie hooked it with the knife and held it up away from him.

"Thank you, sweetheart."

He balled the coat in his hand and, smiling, pressed it against his groin, slid it between his legs and along his ass. Someone in the crowd laughed. He pulled the coat out and threw it at Fin. The Chamorro caught it in both hands and dropped it. His eyes burned, and on his face was an expression of shock and disgust.

Effie laughed. "Thank you, pal," he said.

"All bets *off*," Alphonzo cried, stepping to the center of the ring. "Return all money. Free beer before the next bout."

The crowd seemed to sigh and collapse back into itself. Effie and Fin had not moved, but outside the ring a surge began as men broke for the bar. A few stepped over the fence into the ring; they pressed around Fin, joshing him, plucking him by the arm. The air smelled of the pale, sourdough fragrance of chicken guts, pepper sweat, and, faintly, of the stink of fresh shit. Effie closed the knife against his pants leg and slipped it smoothly into his pocket. Paul called to him, but he didn't respond. Effie looked at Helen.

She had stopped pacing. She stood in the center of the road, looking toward the cockpit.

She looked as if she were watching eagles mate, her eyes were so wild and wondering. I will swear, Paul thought, I will swear that she wants to murder him. He thought of a story his father told, about Benjamin Franklin in Paris, of the old man stepping out of his elegant hotel one morning into the shit stink and chestnut-blossom smell of the ancien régime, of Franklin turning to his companion to say, "This world, my friend, all this"— including with the sweep of his small freckled hand the gray stones, the streets—"is nothing more than a perfumed corpse." And then a picture came into his mind of convicts watering the courthouse lawn in St. Lukes, of himself and his father sitting on a bench under the great magnolia tree that shaded one side of the square, of his father speaking to him, earnestly—desperately, he thought now—of strange doings, of his mother, of his mother and other men—was that it? was it a fable he was telling?—of the fear in his soul, of his dream in which he waked at night holding in his arms the man his mother loved, of *the inconceivability of this,* as he put it; and then he saw that his father was crying, saw his pale broad face lifted undefended, crying tears like beads of glass, and he looked away at the convicts who stood in their spanking-white uniforms four abreast on the tussocky grass fanning streams from four hoses, and he saw the morning sunlight catch in the fans of water and make rainbows, and this seemed a miracle to him, the rainbows surging and fading, lighting again, a miracle of complicity, as if the sun and the grass and the streaming water were all somehow related in a secret and fabulous way, and his father's tears were a part of this and the strange story of betrayal, and he was too, a child in short pants drawing figures with a stick in the cinnamon dust. And he thought now, thinking this here on an island in the western Pacific as he watched his brother cross the rocky grass to Helen and take her brusquely into his arms and hold her strongly—as if he might between his arms compress her body into some new alchemy—and, just as abruptly, release her, and then walk away with her under the throbbing flame trees: I am not safe; I am only young.

V

THE VILLAGE creaked and groaned under the obligations of the election process. Old friendships broke apart, ancient jealousies flared, families split into murderous factions. In broad daylight, in front of Temelio's store, Ricky Flambo, Mother of Life party candidate for city council president, broke the jaw of old Consuela Sablan with a rock, picked up from the road and pitched with all his strength after she called him a whoremonger and a thief, accusations that stemmed, so Jacabo said, from his bachelor practice of importing young girls from Guam to keep house for him and his refusal to pay for a box of mangled war trinkets the sheriff's nephew had given him. The assault, for which he was promptly arrested and led, handcuffed to the tailgate of the sheriff's pickup, to the jail—which was actually the lounge in the district headquarters, a room of more pleasant appointments than any in Ricky's own house—was enough, so gossip went, to end Ricky's political career, though there were many who believed that Consuela Sablan cursed him only out of her frustration and unresolved grief over Ricky's refusal twenty years before to take her withered daughter off her hands. Jamey Oglona, Sea of Dreams party candidate for council, a Vietnam veteran, was observed out on the breakwater after midnight, high on marijuana, shouting warnings to his dead comrades. José Jam, an eighteen-year-old fifth-grade history teacher, candidate for council and darling of the Mother of Lifes, lost his nerve, or came to himself in some scarifying manner, and began to appear on his neighbor's back doorsteps, weeping and begging for rice pudding. Cary Montoya, council candidate, farmer, locked himself in his house and wouldn't speak to anyone. Davido Soap, of the Mother of Life party and the island's only Protestant, passed out leaflets announcing that the end of the world was at hand. And the mayor and the sheriff, from across their great bare desks, stared at each other.

Paul waded in the fever river. On weekends he met his mother on the beach, where they swam together and picknicked on a little bare patch under the turtle tree that she had swept clear of shells. Slowly, in her house, the island treasures began to accrue. She collected the shells, trochus and cat's-eye mainly but an occasional bleached whelk and sea scallop too, plants, a stuffed fruit bat as large as a rabbit, ammo casings, the joystick from a Japanese Zero, helmets, and bones, including two black-and-gray skulls, one complete and the other missing its jawbone but including a perfect bullet hole in the center of the forehead, like the third eye the Buddhists speak of. Still fascinated by uniforms, she wore through the village the various apparel of the women's armed services, nurses' uniforms and capes, the cap and blouse of the Los Angeles Parking and Meter Department, and to Mass one morning, much to the consternation of Father Marco, the puttees and trousers of the Japanese Overseas Army.

Lying on her back under a blue and silvery evening sky, she told him that she was dying. "I feel the wells of my body emptying," she said. "I understand now that old age is the husking of the seed, and it is irreversible."

You're not old, he told her, but she paid no attention.

"I know why your father visits me," she said. "I thought it was because he left this life so abruptly that he wasn't quite able to get all the way out of it, but that's not the reason. He comes to me because I am partially in his world, not the other way around."

"I think Daddy's just a figment in your mind."

She ignored him.

"I had hoped to join a convent. I wanted to wear one of those white gushing gowns and pray on my face, but I see now that there won't be enough time." Strings of grapevine hung from the branches of the turtle tree. They twisted in the breeze, touching each other. There was the smell of stagnant water, and the croaking of frogs came from the cistern nearby.

He said, "I would think you would be glad to be free."

She looked at him. Her opaque amber eyes were grave. "Don't let anybody kid you," she said. "More life is the only thing we want."

With her teeth she began to peel an orange, biting the rind and spitting it onto the ground beside her. He listened to the sound of her teeth tearing the fruit. Long bands of silvery light lay on the water, fading to gray and finally to blue in the distance. Pig Island, wearing its hat of cloud, steamed on the horizon.

. . .

His brother said, "Here they don't know the difference between dream and reality."

He had stepped out of the bushes and now walked beside him on the white road. His white clothes shone, his black hair gleamed as if it were polished. His pale face was untouched by sun. It's as if the sun goes around him, Paul thought. "They're not the only ones," he said.

"I know the difference," Effie said. "I just don't care."

"What have you done with Helen?" She had disappeared from the agricultural station, was not seen in the village.

"She's off uttering joyous leaves without a friend a lover near."

"Don't quote."

" 'Oh, but the difference to me.' "

"I don't want to hear that. Wordsworth doesn't know where she is."

"*Whitman* and Wordsworth—no, neither of them would recognize her." They walked along silently for a while. The road descended through steep bushes toward the water. An iridescent green bird, its forked tail flashing, veered and dropped away behind a large mango in Tedocio Bang's yard. From across the village came the *puttputtputt* of a tractor. "Where are you living now?" his brother said.

"With Jacabo."

"Soaking up the culture, eh."

"They're good people. I'm grateful." Some nights, simply because of the strangeness of this place, he went to bed stiff with fright. But no, not just the place—these events.

His brother took his hand, raised it to his lips, and kissed it. He let it go and pushed his arm around Paul's shoulders. "Don't you love how in this culture men can openly caress each other?" he said.

"Yeah."

Effie patted his back. "She has established in her mind that I am of the devil's party. My experiment is almost complete. She's ready now, I think, to do anything necessary to rid herself of me."

"I thought you were in love with her."

"Ah, love—that's work, that's endless obligation and effort, that's the willingness to do for someone else, to help them out. I like other conniptions. I want to see a peacock burst into flames. I want to hear screams. I want to eat flesh." He spit on the ground. "Urgency," he said, "that's the key; demand, necessity. The invasion, not the republic we establish. Art, life, all this, is simply an assault."

"Crappy platitudes. Posturing."

"What matter, sonny? I'm an American; by definition a crackpot."

"Human."

"As in humanity. As in humane. As in lit by the Spirit."

"Yes."

"But that's only one more way to *control* things. By extension a corollary to technology. The axis of life doesn't turn on that grease."

"Somebody ought to get down on their knees and pray for you."

"I welcome it."

As he claimed he would welcome anything, welcome all, his brother.

They reached the docks and walked along them past the emptied and rusty reefers toward the narrow concrete shelf that joined the long platform to the breakwater. In the angle of the far side, where the island lay in against the pilings, there was a patch of grass sloping down to the water. Half a dozen plywood skiffs, painted in pastel colors, were beached in the grass. A few had small outboard motors canted against their sides. The keels were bleached, frayed, as if the boats had been dragged over rock. Two boats, their bows tied to stakes, stood out a dozen feet from the beach, their motors cocked. An old man and a boy squatted on a broken slab, fishing with hand lines. The brothers approached them. "Hafa dai. Good evening," Effie said, bowing to touch his forehead to the old man's hand. He peered into the blue plastic bucket beside the man; it was half filled with red-and-silver fish. "Ichi ban, senort." The old man grinned. The boy, perhaps ten, sucked his teeth and jigged his line along in front of him. Effie made signs for purchase. The old man nodded his head, reached into the bucket, and drew out three palm-sized fish, which he wrapped in sheets of flimsy paper torn from a department store catalogue and handed to Effie. He refused the bill Effie offered him. "De nada, amigo, de nada." "Thank you," Effie said in English. Paul could see the colors of the fish through the paper. In the fading sky the moon was a small white china basin. "Good eat," the old man said.

Effie bowed again and they moved away, climbing up the short slope to the dock. They walked along the dock to the end. From there Paul could see across the crescent of lagoon to the beach where he and his mother picnicked Sundays. Beyond the bushline the silver roof of his mother's house was just visible among the breadfruit trees. The landward breeze smelled of sunny stone and oranges and, faintly, of rancid cooking oil. Effie unwrapped the fish, grasped a piling, and leaned out. The water around the dock was light green and opaque, deep enough for battleships. He tossed the fish, underhanded. They made three small plops. The water was still and then, coming from underneath, a brief churning stirred the surface. A shadowy gray fin rose and sank away. Small bits of bone, a patch of oil the size of a hand, wallowed in a momentary froth. Effie studied the spot where the fish had disappeared. He swung himself upright. "Isn't that nice," he said. "We think the war's been over for thirty years, and they're still down there waiting."

Paul realized he didn't know where his brother lived, where he slept at night.

The lights strung in the flame trees outside the cockfight bar were blue and white, the colors of the Mother of Life party. On the other side of the village, in front of Temelio's store, the Sea of Dreams had raised bamboo poles and strung the red and green lights of their own party's colors over the street. The long swags swayed in breeze, hanging so low that some of the older boys leapt to touch them, until one of Daniet's deputies had to threaten them with arrest. The deputy, a small fastidious man with bushy receding hair, had placed barricades at either end of the street, on Daniet's orders, restricting traffic, which, since there were only eight vehicles on the island, was not a hardship for most, though

Gondola Reyes, a farmer who lived with his wife and ten children in a fenced compound beside his fields of bell pepper and eggplant, whose son Juno had drowned last year while fishing off the Red Cliffs (where Japanese soldiers hid in caves during the invasion—you could still see the nostalgic graffiti, translated by Effie, they had chiseled with bayonets into the walls—and where the Americans, after Tokyo Bay, had pushed with bulldozers their stockpiles of supplies and matériel: deuce-and-a-halfs, howitzers, barrels of fuel, cans of peanut butter and cherries in heavy syrup, and cases of band instruments among the useless surplus; in the end pushing the bulldozers too), from the waters beneath which Constantine Goya, one of the sheriff's nephews, had retrieved his body, which lay across the corroded front seat—so he said—of a sunken jeep, as if he had pulled over for a nap, an occasion that, according to Jacabo, had twisted Gondola Reyes's mind so that the yellow barricade at the corner of Nagasaki Street and Hiroshima Road seemed an unendurable emblem of the terrifying detour his life had already taken—Juno, a sweet boy, was his eldest son—a detour he could not, in fact, bear, so that for a few minutes neighbors just getting up from dinner could hear his thin voice raised, hear the anger that converted hazily to pleading and then back to anger until it became a string of curses directed specifically and torrentially at Daniet Sablan and all members of his family, until it was abruptly stopped by the deputy's nervous blackjack, and Gondola Reyes, laid like his son across the seat of a jeep, was transported to the community jail, there to join his mortal enemy, the picaro Ricky Flambo, for the rest of the night.

The night was clear, salted with stars, but in the breeze was a touch of chill, or not of chill exactly, since at fifteen degrees north latitude there is no such thing as chill—except possibly on the morning after a typhoon, when volumes of rain and wind drawn up from the sea have transformed the world into chaos, and a memory, perhaps, of the original mornings when the earth was young, a springtime creation—a change of weather maybe, as of the slow approach of a distant typhoon, the small shift in pressure, the slight licking taste of the far Pacific reaches in the breeze, perceptions as delicate as intuition, felt first by the young mothers in the theater across the street from Temelio's as they pressed their backs against the cool grainy concrete of Japanese enterprise while they watched over the scattering of young children who on this night were the theater's only patrons; a mood almost, so that soon, even before the samurai western flickering on the screen made of boards was over, a couple of them had snatched up their children and, almost embarrassed but at the same time sure of themselves, carried them away home, where they tucked them in bed early, singing maybe a couple of verses of an old song over their small bodies, restless on the rice mats, and later, after preparing a few betel-nut chews (splitting the green nut, loading it with lime, wrapping it in a fresh pepper leaf), had left the house and, by now, for no reason they understood, lain down in the grass, which was grass—none of them knew this—originally grown on the island from seed imported from a former shogun's estate, lain down on their backs, the skirts of their soft cotton dresses fanned out from their legs, cooing softly, convinced that their bodies were being eaten by the night.

From the abundant vine above the back door Jacabo's mother had picked one of the long tubular squash—lime green and as big around as the barrel of a young banana tree—chopped it, placed it with a shoat's head in a pot over the open kitchen fire, and served it with fina deni and a crock of rice for supper. Jacabo's father, old Holderlin Boo, as Paul sucked pig's teeth, told them his favorite story, of Koro, the Green Sea King, who had been lifted up by the White-Faced Sea Mother onto the shores of the island, the first man and the first colonizer, who, with the wife the Sea Mother had given him, built a temple and a palace raised on piers he hewed with his hands out of the coral cliffs. The piers, conical columns capped by hemispheres of white coral stone, still existed—"I showed them to you," Jacabo reminded him—in a clearing among the tangin-tangin jungle between the village and the docks. "The priest," Jacabo said, before his father shushed him, "not the priest of this moment but the one before him, Father John D'Arc, tried to dig for relics among the ruins, but the Taotaomona struck him down with a sickness. . . ." Koro was a man of great strength and creative enterprise—"much taller than men of today," the old raconteur said. He invented, with the Sea Mother's help, the coconut and the breadfruit, and it was

he who came to understand the uses of the mango and the melon,
he who taught the sea birds to nest in the cliffs; and he was the
one who first fastened an outrigger blade to a canoe—which you
will not see today on this island because since Spanish times the
people are frightened of water—and he who began the great voy-
ages that took him far away to the country of the crazy men who
hew their coins out of rocks, and the men who sell their women
for treasure, and the men who eat other men for merinda. It was
after returning from one of these journeys that Koro realized that
in his absence his son had grown strong. Looking from the window of the palace one afternoon, he saw the boy playing with a
small white crab around the base of a coconut tree. As the father
watched, the crab darted down a hole at the bottom of the tree.
His son, Keme, angered by this, grasped the tree around the base
and tore it out of the earth to retrieve his pet crab. Koro was
frightened. My son has grown strong, he thought, soon he will
overpower me. Straightaway he ran out into the yard, grabbed his
son into his arms, and killed him.

"It is a mystery," the old man said, "why a father would do
this. It is the oldest story in our history. I think it must explain
why we are a small and weak people, why so many stronger people
have come to crush us."

"Maybe it's because they know we are powerful," Jacabo put
in, his black eyes sparkling. They were drinking vodka with dinner, from a bottle the old man drew periodically out of the chest
freezer behind him.

"No," his father said, "it is not because we are powerful; I
think it is so we will learn humility. It teaches us that life is
tragic, that it is beautiful and sad all at once."

They were on the back porch, a room screened from the street
by a lattice of pandanus fronds. A small kerosene lantern, though
it was not quite dark yet, burned huskily in the center of the
table. The old man dipped his fingertips in the fina deni and
licked them slowly, one by one. The nail of his index finger was
an inch long. It curved over the small joint like a claw. There was
a dent just above his right jawbone where, when he was a boy, a
barracuda had bitten him in the face. His skin, which at seventy
was as smooth and thick as the skin of a mango, was the color of

an old penny. He farmed by himself a small plot of land on the plateau, raising papaya and melons, and collected from his son the receipts from the movie house. His mother had been a German woman, who, when Jacabo told him the story, Paul realized was probably a camp follower of the garrison that controlled the island after it was ceded to Germany following the Spanish-American War. The woman, apparently after her marriage, a stout and righteous matriarch, had been murdered, so Jacabo said, by the Japanese. Before she was murdered, he said, she had been put into a prison on Saipan, where the famous American pilot and spy Amelia Earhart had for a time, before she died of dysentery and was buried at the edge of the Garapan dump, been her cellmate. Why, Paul had asked, would the Japanese kill someone who was from an allied country? Because she hated them, Jacabo told him, and because she spoke her hatred out loud. His father, so Jacabo said, a grown man with children, had been taken from the village and transported with the other men to Saipan, where he worked as a conscript building runways. At night, he said, his father would sneak out of the compound and slip through the boondocks to the prison, where, through a back window in the old warehouse —which is what it had been—he would pass bits of his measly supper in to his mother, who would pass them to Amelia Earhart and the other women. I would live in shame, Jacabo said, formally, touching the rim of his vodka glass as if it were a symbol of his fidelity, if I did not so honor my father and my mother.

Paul agreed that such devotion was probably a good thing. But the bitterness that groped at the body of grief he carried for his father was alive in him tonight, and he felt it. As he looked out the small window torn in the lattice—turning his face away from the family—he saw his mother pass in the street. She was dressed all in white—white gown, white shoes, on her dark head the white lace mantilla worn by the island women to Mass—and about her frolicked and pranced the children of the family she supported. There must have been a dozen of them, dressed too, he could see in the twilight, in their best clothes. Small bats, dipping and soaring like swallows, whirled above their heads, unnoticed. They were on their way to the rally, he thought, supporters, since he was sure his mother had taken adamant sides, of Maze Manglona. As he watched, his mother, without breaking her spangling stride, bent down and kissed the top of the head of the nearest child, a girl of perhaps eleven. A small sadness, the husk of an old pity, stirred in his heart. He had never known whom he was saddest for: for his mother, or for himself, or for all of them together, or for his father, who, for reasons of his own, had had to leave early. The game is over, his father had said, the history we are stumbling behind now is only the fly-bitten tail of a worn-out beast. But here they were nonetheless, alive, in the midst of struggle, on an island in the western Pacific, an island that, for one moment, had been the center of the world. He thought then that when he finished here, which he knew he would do soon, he would travel on west, toward the setting sun, until he came to a place where there was no more west. She did not see him, his mother, she did not turn her head from her charges, but he raised his hand to her anyway and waved. Whether it was a wave of goodbye or homage, or both, he was not sure.

There were times when his father's suicide seemed to him an honorable act of great courage, as if, come to the end of the age of adventuring, the explorer was undertaking the next, and noblest, journey. Like a kamikaze pilot, he lifted off the deck of his life and turned, with an idiot courage, toward the distant enemy. Reckless, wholly abandoned, surrendered to his overwhelming idea, he had flung the machine of his aging body into the heart of disaster. It was an act of such bravery, and such stupidity, that even now, eight years later, to think of it made Paul's skin crawl.

He lowered his hand. Darkness slipped like a thief into the yard. It climbed into the pepper trees, slid along the body of the old jeep Jacabo's father had salvaged from military scrap. Across the street, which was empty for the moment, breeze clacked in a bamboo thicket. Jacabo's mother began to clear away the dregs of dinner. In the large pot the unfleshed skull of the young pig gleamed.

From outside came a crackling sound. There was a high metallic whine, followed by a series of grainy thumps, and then a voice, ghostly but clear, said, *Buenos noches, amigas y amigos. This is Maze Manglona, your mayor, speaking.*

Paul and Jacabo looked at each other and laughed. "The rally has begun," Jacabo said.

The microphone cleared its throat, and again the mayor's voice filled the air. He began the speech he had showed Paul.

"Let's go," Jacabo said.

They bowed to the old man and to Jacabo's mother and left the house at a run.

The village was empty, the houses dark. From each yard a mongrel dog stepped forth to comment on their passage. Above their heads the air crackled and spit, the words of promise soaring. From far off to the right, down the narrow street leading to Temelio's, came the sound of singing, an old political song from the Philippines. "Daniet is having his say too," Jacabo said. For a moment they slowed to a walk to listen. The words of the song were indecipherable to Paul. "It's a song about struggle," Jacabo said, "about the triumph of the warrior." Paul thought of his brother, realized he had been thinking of Effie all evening. Money had been stolen from the cockfight bar; people said it was the American, Effie Hogan, who had done it, sneaking into the house while Alphonzo and his wife slept and taking the money, which Alphonzo kept under his pillow in a sack made of parachute silk. Alphonzo had waked before dawn with a terrible premonition. In a dream someone had come into his house and desecrated the statue of the Virgin. In the dream there were blood and feces on the family altar, a pair of lace panties hiding the Virgin's face. He had waked in a sweat, clucking like a chicken. In the blue light of dawn he thought he saw shapes moving. Stumbling from the bed, he ran to the kitchen, where, since they had opened the bar, the altar was kept. Everything was in place; the small white china clock he had bought in Hawaii ticked above the sink. Relieved, chaffing himself for his superstitions, shaking his head at the vividness of his dream, he returned to the bed. He slipped his hand under the pillow, as he did whenever he came into the bedroom, to check his fortune, and discovered it was gone. He ran into the street screaming. The priest had to be called. And the village nurse, Alicia Montez, who practiced both the old and the new medicine. I know who it was, Alphonzo had cried before the sedative she gave him snapped out his lights. It was the American picaro. It was Effie Hogan.

But his brother was not supposed to be on the island. Cerone, smirking over a beer at Temelio's, claimed he had seen him board the mail boat for Saipan. Chasing his woman, he said. But no one else had corroborated this story, though it was true that as far as Paul knew, neither his brother nor Helen had been seen on the island for several days. Paul had gone looking for her, driving with Jacabo in his jeep out to the compound, where the director, a florid Australian who hated his job and hated the tropics, told him she had gotten down off a tractor three days before, taken the commission truck—"Without permission, I might add," he added—and disappeared toward the old airfields. They drove out there to look. In daylight the runways were desolate abandoned places without much meaning, like ghost town streets. Runners of sea grape stretched snaky lengths across the gray concrete, and islands of tangin-tangin, squat and ferny, prospered in the breaks of pavement. In a few places the shattered walls of buildings, Quonsets and mortar bunkers, poked up out of the jungle. Above their heads sea birds cried.

At a crossroads, where a crumbled access road led to another set of flightways, near the corroded footings of a small building, a lime tree thrived, its branches creaking with fruit. Jacabo had stopped the truck so they could fill their shirts. Then they drove on to the bomb pits, where they found no one, though somebody had built a small campfire between the two markers. Maybe it was them, or one of them, Jacabo said. Maybe, Paul had answered. He imagined Effie and Helen out in the jungle, calling to each other, remembered his brother lying on the glider at Helen's farm, the careless grace of the way he had caught the knife with his book and tossed it aside. There was a Japanese poem his brother recited about a man's lover joining him in the bath. The poem described the doubling intimacy of the warm water and the warm embrace of the beloved. He couldn't remember it; it was a poem about death, though it didn't seem to be at first, it was so tender and celebratory. His brother told him that years ago, in his teens, in the year he discovered his vocation as a poet, he had lived for a summer on a beach on the Pacific coast in Mexico. He built a hut for himself out of fronds and grasses and lived in it, among the dunes in sight of the sea, alone, for three months. His only contact with the world of men had been with the storekeeper in the village four miles away, where he shopped for food. Even then the contact had been sporadic, because, so he said, he had taken many of his supplies from the winter homes of American tourists that he broke into. Unless you stay alone that long, he told him, you have no idea the places this world can take you to. It was the summer after their father's suicide, a summer in which his mother screamed all night long, cursing her dead husband and her life. Wildly, her hair in ruins, she appeared in their bedrooms and ordered them to join the army. Paul, who was ten, would have done this for her, to please her. His brother fled the house.

Effie said, telling him of his months on the beach, There is a wind, no, not a wind exactly, an odor, you can smell it if you sit still long enough, a circulation in the underfirmament that is not the breath of death but death itself. We wade in it, we sit down in it to eat our supper. It penetrates us, the world—everything. If you sit still long enough—maybe this is not true in everyone's life; I don't know—it will become so important to you that you don't want to leave it. You'll go out on the beach at night and lie down on your back in the sand and call to it. You'll beg for it to come to you. It is more beautiful than anything else on earth. It's what earth is about, and our journey is a journey toward love of it.

Paul had stared at him in disbelief. You're crazy, he said. That's what you call it, Effie answered, smiling his bird-song smile. Me, sometimes I envy the murderers.

The song, raised by fifty voices, streamed above them, it rose beyond the darkness at the turn of the street like the faint glow marking a town. From the other side of the village, ahead of them, the mayor's voice promised money and power.

"I am the one who can bring the air force back," he cried. "I am the friend of the military; they will return for me. We will all become rich; there will be plenty for everyone." His voice rose until it seemed to blend with the whine from the microphone. "What is it you lack?" he screamed. "You lack automobiles, you lack televisions, you lack linoleum tile. Your daughters, for lack of strong men to love, cluck like hens in their bedrooms. Your men are sad; they have only their small plots of vegetables to work, they are angry, they believe they are nothing, worthless, dust. I promise you," he cried, "I promise you on my heart, on the heads of my children—I will kill myself if I do not do this—I promise you that I will make you *somebody,* I will make you into the great people of the world, I will release you to your future, which is the future of money and material, of power, of milk in plastic cartons and car radios and lingerie."

There was a scattering of cheers, the unamplified voices of the crowd thin and insubstantial. The Milky Way drooped above their heads like a pulverized necklace. The breeze smelled of shellfish and seaweed; a good smell, Paul thought, and he turned his head to sniff it. They had stopped in the road. Jacabo stood beside him in the rich tropical darkness, his small head on his chest, listening. Paul started to continue up the hill, toward the road that ran along the school playing fields to the cockfight bar, but Jacabo raised his hand. "Momento," he said.

Then they heard another voice. It was the voice of Daniet Sablan, harsh, thin, and strident, rising on the wings of mechanical amplification above the town.

"I am the friend of the Japanese," he cried. "They are your friends. When I am the mayor they will build great hotels on Tinian. There will be golf courses and swimming pools, jobs for everyone."

"I thought he didn't admit he liked the Japanese," Paul whispered.

"It is a time for true colors."

They were next to an empty lot. A set of wide concrete steps led up from the street to a patch of weeds and rubble. Jacabo indicated they should sit down. They settled themselves side by side on the steps.

"Japanese cars are inexpensive," the sheriff cried, his thin voice howling. "*Qualiteeee.* They make beautiful televisions and radios. You already use their rice cookers, and you know how dependable they are. . . ." There was a brief pause, faint laughter, and then Daniet's voice: "But, Antonio, you mustn't stick your hand into the pot when it is plugged in. Ah, friends, my compadres, I have lived my whole life with you. I never ran off to America to steal and betray. I was not returned to my island in handcuffs. I am no criminal. . . ."

"He is stretching things here, isn't he?" Paul whispered.

"Pocito," said Jacabo.

"I go to church," Daniet shouted. "I love the Father, and the Father loves me—not like one I could speak of, who is not allowed through the door of our holy mother."

There was a single moment of silence. Then from the other side of the village, from the cockfight bar, the microphone whinnied. *Son of a puta,* Maze Manglona shouted, the words clear and distinct. *Japanese whore son.*

"I protect your homes and your property," Daniet shouted. "I am no man to steal from you in the dark."

Miser. Liar. Japanese testicle. The words were like cannon shots, fired into the huge clear night. Paul stood up. He looked into the sky. The frayed white seeds of the stars looked as if they were about to sprout.

"Antichrist," Daniet shouted.

Devil whore, Maze answered.

"Speck of shit under the feet of Jesus," Daniet yelled.

Withered dick, Maze answered.

"Murderer."

Child fucker.

Corollary shouts, cries, rose from the polar crowds. The microphones sang and screeched. A car horn bleated; wild barking came from the empty yards.

I will cut you into tiny pieces and feed you to my hogs, Maze shouted.

"Seducer of animals," Daniet answered.

The shouts of the crowds grew louder. They could hear individual voices, almost identifiable, words, growls. A woman shrieked a string of words that sounded like another language, the words clacking and jumping against each other, rising to a pure thrill of sound, a single operatic note. Then, at the top of the street, Paul saw the first white shirts of the Mother of Lifes. Scouts, a few men scurrying along under torches. Their fists were raised; wild shouts blew from their mouths. From the other direction, out of the ball of darkness at the corner where the ruined shell of the old Japanese sugar offices stood among bamboo, leftover walls that looked in the darkness like dinosaur flukes, headlights flashed, and new shouts were raised as the Sea of Dreams believers approached.

"Santa Maria," Jacabo said.

Paul grinned. He felt a surge of delight. "I guess it'll be the last man living wins," he said.

"It's crazy."

They retreated up the steps into the lot. Moving sideways, his eyes on the road, Paul felt his foot strike something metal. He picked it up. It was an American army helmet, a patch blown out of the crown. He put it on. Unlined, it came down over his eyes. He pushed it back and peered out into the darkness. Off to his right he saw the early standard bearers of the Sea of Dreams. One or two carried torches. Their pale-blue shirts were luminescent, flickering under the yellow light of kerosene.

The amplified cries and threats surged above them.

I will sink you in the sea, Maze cried. *I will use your testicles for fish bait.*

"Crabs will snap out the eyes of your children," Daniet responded. "Your wife will suck the devil's penis."

You eat the shit of Japanese lepers.

"American slave."

Now the crowd's shouts were as loud as the amplified curses. Devils, they screamed. Thieves.

"Somebody's going to get killed," Paul whispered.

"No," Jacabo said. "They are too afraid. They'll just shout at each other."

He was right. The two groups stopped in the road, fifty feet apart. The Sea of Dreams brandished their torches. The Mother of Lifes shook their fists, squawking threats. Paul knew some of the marchers, had met them in the cockfight bar or in the store. Among the Sea of Dreams he saw the white robes of the priest. Father Marco's face shone with sweat and a predatory delight. Up the hill, near the back of the crowd, he thought for a second that he saw his mother, a flash of white dress, but he couldn't be sure. He stepped forward to see better. And he did so, from off to his left, from among the tangin-tangin bushes at the edge of the lot, he saw a white stone fly. No one in the crowd saw it. The stone arced high and fell among the Sea of Dreams supporters, striking a woman on the shoulder. She screamed and fell to her knees. The crowd surged around her, there were shouts of rage, the torches trembled, dipped, three or four men leapt forward and ran at the Mother of Lifes, whose believers rushed to meet them. There was a striking, a clatter of feet; a torch rose from the crowd, tumbled end over end, spewing sparks, and fell among the crowd; there were cries of anguish, of anger, of terror.

Paul had not taken his eyes away from the spot where the stone was launched. The bushes were still, then they began to shake, and then he heard his brother's low laugh. The branches parted and Effie stepped out, slapping coral dust from his clothes. "Hello, boys," he said. He was dressed in black; a pale scarf was tied around his neck. "You bastard," Paul said.

Effie looked at him; his eyes were bright and distant, yellowish in the light of the torches. He gazed out over the melee. Villager struck villager; women screamed; at the bottom of the steps two boys struck at each other with lengths of rope. Effie grinned. "Their hearts sought release," he said under his breath, his voice soft.

"You ought to be locked up," Paul said. "Somebody should just put you someplace where you can't touch anybody. What's wrong with you?"

His brother slowly raised his hand and blessed the crowd. "Let them see what they are made of," he said. "Let each make the discovery in himself. Later," he added, his voice whispery, "they'll love the silence."

"You just destroy everything."

Effie stared at him. Paul saw the yellow absence in his eyes. "You're a fool, sport," Effie said, "if you think you can fix anything."

Then, from the back of the crowd, Paul saw a figure rise, a slender figure that wobbled slightly, as if balancing: a wax woman. It was Helen; she rose from the back of a jeep, held around the legs by Fin Vert. She had a gun in her hand, a black pistol. Effie didn't see her; he gazed out over the crowd, feasting.

Paul watched in amazement, in wonder, as she raised the gun; he saw the look of hatred on Fin Vert's face, saw the cool blank face of his sister-in-law, saw the gun lift as if she were drawing it up out of a well, saw the short snout level and come to rest, aimed at his brother. He cried out, he dived at his brother's waist, he heard the flat *blak* of the shot as they tumbled down the steps, felt the harsh grip of his brother's hand in the quick of his shoulder. He writhed, hit the pavement, crumpled stunned; and saw Effie, who had not lost his feet, rise partly, heard the hiss in his mouth, saw him move, the flow of his body like the quick animal flowing of a wild creature, saw, for an instant, his face in profile—the long straight nose, the thin bared lips, the high forehead, the slick backsweep of dark hair—and for that second he saw not his brother but a being wholly alien to him, a creature without place in his life, without place in any human life, and saw in this scrap of form the remarkable, charged, solid presence, saw the strangeness of the world, and as something deeper in himself than he knew before dismissed this being, his brother, let him go, with an ease that startled him, something else fell back, fell to its knees —if that could be—in awe maybe, in celebration perhaps, in wonderment no doubt, at the vividness, at the pure rising glut of being animated before him, which he did not raise his hand to stop, or even touch.

There was another shot, and a third, the red flash of wild firing, there were screams of terror, a shriven clamoring. The crowd broke apart, scattering, the heaped thrashing mass becoming suddenly individual, each fleeing for his life. He saw his brother running away, saw the rough black back, humped, slipping through the crowd; and he saw Helen bending, craning to catch a glimpse of him, saw her rise on her toes like someone looking over a wall, and then he saw her jump, lightly, like a child jumping—free of Fin's grasp—the gun waving wildly, saw her raise and level the gun and pull it back unsure . . . and then the crowd seemed to rise around her, not selecting her but plucking her up anyway; he saw her topple backward into the arms of Father Marco, who, his hair wild, caught her in surprise and swung her away from him and threw her to the ground.

From the top of the steps, on his knees, Jacabo looked at him. His face was wild with fright. He motioned to Paul—come, come.

Paul dashed up the steps and followed his friend through a slit in the bushes that opened out onto a wide path. The path, over-arched in spots by the tangin-tangin, ran parallel to the upper street, then sloped downward toward the docks. The voices of the candidates continued obliviously to bark insults into the micro-phones. The path passed close to someone's backyard; Paul could smell the heavy fragrance of plumeria; like gardenias, he thought. Among the bushes were shapes, shadowy piles of twisted metal, cairns maybe, the stacked bones maybe that Father Marco had said the Japanese came to pray to. A coconut palm reared up, its slender trunk like an exclamation, its round ragged head snapping in the breeze. Rats scurried away from their feet. Paul thought of his brother, who seemed distant from him now; he wondered, as one might wonder about a passing ship, where he was headed. He could play his mind back through the years, he could see his brother in red bathing trunks standing on the high diving board, directing the swimmers spotting the water beneath him as if they were an orchestra. He could see him leaning against the mantel at home as he recited a poem, his voice following the rise and fall of the lines like a swift. The memories were stones in a basket, found, polished, ornamental.

The path opened into a stubbly clearing, almost closed again at the far end, and debouched them onto the docks, among a small fortress of rusted reefers. They walked out into the open air and stopped. The breeze was fresh, the sky was glazed with stars. Out in the sea, which lapped and hissed at the pilings, beyond Pig Island, the red night sunset of the bombs glowed and faded. The rumbling of the explosions reached them. "Big action tonight," Jacabo said.

Paul wasn't sure whether it was the fight or the bombs he was talking about. They panted, like dogs, leaning over with their hands on their knees. Off to their right, down near the fishing boats, a lantern winked on. "Must be Daniet," Jacabo said, "mak-ing his escape."

"No," Paul said, sure that it was not. "It's Effie."

"His wife tried to shoot him."

"Yes, I saw."

He wasn't sure whether Jacabo saw Effie throw the rock. He didn't say anything about it.

"Let's go that way," he said, indicating the light.

"But not to trouble," Jacabo said.

They walked slowly toward the light. In the south, beyond the target island, orange light flared high, sank back redly, and died. The slow grave rumble of sound fled over them. Volcanoes must be something like that, Paul thought. They approached the lantern, the figure that moved in and out of its light. It was Effie. He looked up, stepped off into the darkness, and quickly returned, carrying a gas can.

"What are you doing?" Paul said.

Effie placed the can in the boat. "Help me with this," he said.

"What are you doing?" Paul said again.

"I'm fleeing, as they say—what the hell do you think?"

"Fleeing where?"

Effie nodded south.

"The island?"

"Time to find the Japanese."

"There's nothing over there. It's a desert island."

"There's enough for me."

He straightened up, grinned at Paul. " 'I know that I shall meet my fate.' " he said, " 'Somewhere among the stars above . . . Come on—help me here."

"That's Temelio's boat," Jacabo said.

"Honey," Effie said, "I don't care if it's the Virgin Mary's. It's time for me to move on."

He began to drag the boat toward the water. "Come on, boys."

Despite himself, despite the abrupt letting go he had only just realized—is that what it was?—he helped his brother drag the small boat into the water. Jacabo helped too, though Paul could tell his friend was angry.

"You know that island?" Effie said to Jacabo as he climbed over the gunwale.

"I went there once when I was a child."

"What's there? Anything to eat?"

"Plenty. It is the Garden of Eden. Plenty chickens, coconut crabs, even fruit bat. And melons and squash, all the fruits and vegetables that went wild after the Japanese left."

Effie knelt to fasten the fuel hose to the gas can. "What about this guy, this soldier?"

"He is there."

"It's really true?"

"Oh, yes. There were once many more. Now there is only one. Ichi Ban. Number One."

"Is he dangerous?"

"He runs and hides."

"I would expect that after thirty years of living the wrong decision he might be a little agitated."

"You two ought to get along fine," Paul said.

His brother looked at him. There were dark patches under his eyes. The bones in his bony face were more pronounced than ever, the cleft in his chin like a cut. "There's a bit more to play, bro," he said. "Only a bit, but it's there." He looked up at the weather. Clear sky ran on forever. Face raised, touching his long neck, he said, "It was selfishness. It wasn't nobility or courage. He was simply a man whose pride made him believe he was something he was not. He couldn't face the truth."

"I don't care," Paul said. "I love him anyway."

Effie looked at him from the sides of his eyes. "You do, don't you, sport? You can't help it, can you?"

"No, I can't."

Effie raised two bent fingers and pressed their knuckles lightly against Paul's lips. "It's your protection," he said. "—your helplessness. But it won't last forever."

"I know."

"Maybe," his brother said, "maybe you do."

Effie knelt and pumped up the fuel bulb. He snapped the cord of the small outboard. The motor coughed, caught, roared. Paul and Jacabo slid the thin boat out. Effie backed into deeper water. He stood in the stern, like a gondolier, his hand on the steering arm. "See you later, sport," he said.

"Don't expect me to come after you."

"I don't." He laughed. "I wouldn't dream of expecting that."

The shadows leaning out from the breakwater behind him seemed to stretch their arms forward and take him in. The motor flared, they heard the wallow of his turn, and then they saw him, still on his feet, moving through the shadows, the white pearls of his wake spilling behind him.

VI

LIKE A resurrection, it took three days for Paul to change his mind. In that time his sister-in-law, who had been briefly and so dramatically found, disappeared again. The sheriff had put her in jail in the plasterboard yellow lounge with the grieving Gondola Reyes and the picaro Ricky Flambo. There were no separate facilities for women. Though women had been arrested in the past, their punishment had been confinement in their homes—an impossibility in Helen's case, since her boss, the Australian, James Whitehead, refused to allow her back inside the agricultural compound. He had already begun the process, he said, of having her returned to the mainland, and he did not want to confuse things by letting her back into the station. The sheriff, embarrassed, and somewhat humbled after his night of curses, apologized to Helen for the state of affairs, but since he could not think of anything else to do, he put her in the jail and left her alone with the two men.

Helen, so she said, didn't mind. I don't care where you put me, she said, her bright hair wild about her face; nothing you can do means anything to me. As the door swung shut behind her she laughed. "It was like the laugh of a devil," Daniet said, wiping beads of sweat off his upper lip. He had charged her with attempted murder—though no one had been hit by her shots, several people had seen her fire them—a charge he did not mention to her. He was afraid, so Jacabo said, that if he told her she would kill him. "First I am cursed by that Santa Bitchee, and now this," Daniet said. "And since I don't sleep now, my wife won't even let me in the bed."

From his mother Paul learned the story of their first disappearance. She'd learned it from the island gossip, which she had always enjoyed, she said, more than real life. Like Uncle Maurice, she believed that it was in the wild speculations and claims on the fringe that the true life of people was lived. "He took her off the plane in Saipan," she told him. "She'd bought a ticket, and she was leaving. He came onto the plane and got her. He told the pilot that she had tuberculosis. He showed him a document; I don't know where he got it. They say she tried to fight at first— nobody but Effie would touch her—but then she just gave up and came along with him meek as a mouse."

They sat on a rice mat on Blue Beach, looking out to sea. Clouds, wispy as smoke, curled around the flattened heights of Pig Island in the distance. Paul wondered if they were smoke.

She said, "We come out to these places that are foreign to us but home to everybody else, and for some of us something in us lets go—as for others the same thing clenches—and we begin to say and do things we never would have at home. We see it in language when we begin to pick up the native words. Offended, it's easier, in Chamorro, to curse the offender. We make greater promises. We claim excellence and possibility." She patted her hair. "For someone like your brother, this is a fatal condition. He's over the brink anyway, and out here, where so much history and disaster have already taken place, out here where the skies don't scrutinize him, where he knows no one, where he can speak in a language that doesn't strike him as true, he can do what he likes, or what the murderous devil he thinks is his soul directs him to do. I understand it all," she said, "as I understand your father—though he claims, to this day, that I never understood him a bit—but there's nothing I can do. The world's not about mastery, or about rebellion against it. . . ."

She lowered her face to her updrawn knees. The kneecaps were scuffed, roughed a little by age, but her legs were slender, brown, and firm. For a second, not as a son, but as a man, Paul wanted to stroke them. He waited for her to go on, but she didn't.

"So what did they do?"

"What did who do?"

"Effie and Helen."

"He used to sing like a bird. Out of nowhere, an infant—he

had the stubbiest little legs, and the rosiest bottom. I was only eighteen years old when he was born, a child myself; I used to put him in a chair and look at him, I used to dress him up like a doll—"

"What did they do?"

"He took her to a hotel, and he kept her there. I think he gave her drugs. Then he chartered a plane—one of those little Piper Cubs—and brought her back to the island. I heard it—I heard the plane—but I didn't know who it was."

"Were you here?"

"I don't know, but I heard it."

"What did they do?"

"He kept her up at the airfield, at the monument for the atomic bombs—"

"Jacabo and I saw where their fire had been—"

"Yes. He kept her there. He couldn't let her go; he was afraid to let her go; I think he tied her up. . . ."

Her voice trailed away. She looked out toward the island. The ocean, smooth and clear inside the lagoon, was choppy and fretful beyond the reef. They could hear the grainy boom of surf against the coral barriers. There were tears in her eyes. She threw her head back and let it fall slowly forward. She wiped her eyes on her knees. "I walked out to the end of the island," she said. "The island stops, but the coral goes on for half a mile, like an apron, like some gross bride fallen across the surf. I walked out on the rocks—they're so sharp they'll cut through your shoes. I walked out to the end. There was nothing left there, just the rest of the Pacific. The sun was shining on the water. It looked as if the ocean was on fire. I sat down in a little cleft of rock; I wanted to see what kind of animals lived there, if there was any life. I found some limpets—I think that's what they are called—and some little curls of green weed, but there was nothing else. I didn't see the wave. It picked me up like someone had suddenly lifted me in a sheet and it threw me on the rocks. It tried to drag me out to sea. I screamed, I screamed for God to help me. I thought it would drown me. I hadn't called out to God since I was a little girl—who would think of it, among our kind, now, in America? —I screamed, *God help me!* and I held fast to the rocks. Then the wave was gone and I was lying on my back on a coral head, like a new-spanked baby in the sunlight."

He looked at her body. Except for a small raw place on her shoulder, there were no cuts he could see.

"Here," she said, "the rocks tore my side." In a crooked motion she reached across her body and pulled the strap of her swimsuit down, exposing her breast and her left side. A long purple bruise, streaked with cuts, ran from below her armpit to her waist. "I was in its mouth," she said, a note of regret in her voice. "It tasted me and spit me out."

With the tips of his fingers he touched the place.

"Oh."

"I'm sorry."

"It's all right. I like having it."

She drew her suit up, pouring her breast into the cloth as if it was a handful of grain.

He said, "What about the rest?"

"What?"

"Helen."

"She got away from him. She made her way through the jungle back to town, broke into the sheriff's office, and took a gun. Fin Vert helped her."

"I saw the gun."

"Yes."

She was silent again. The breeze rattled the flat spatulate leaves in the top of the turtle tree. Paul watched it step down the massed side as if the branches were a ladder. From the docks, someone fishing waved in their direction. Paul waved absently back.

"I'm sorry, Mama," he said.

His mother blew a single sharp breath, inhaled deeply. "I'm just glad I don't believe in anything," she said.

"You're lucky."

"It's funny how we are." She wiped her eyes again on her kneecaps. Her face was blotchy. "Our lives just drag us on no matter what. Sometimes I can't believe it. You know, it's possible to make mistakes that can't be corrected. You can go too far. The day comes when you add one more handful to what's already too much, and your life falls in on you. But what's odd—and this is what I mean—is that the life inside you, the spark of it, doesn't know that; it just keeps pressing through, gulping for the next breath. You see it, you see the murderer who's choked his wife, the foreman who's stolen the neighbor's money, and you'd think the outraged world would rise up and strike him down—or no, you think his insides would explode, that his own life would rise up and tear him apart, but that isn't what happens at all. In the interview he's sassy and defiant, he jokes about the prosecutor's hairdo, he blames some obscure event for the trouble he's in."

"Maybe there's more to it than that."

"Could there be? I don't think the answer's in the past. I think the surface has gotten so complex we don't look any deeper. Who knows anymore what goes on underneath? I don't think it even makes any difference."

"Why despair, though? Nobody's paying any attention anyway, so why despair?"

"You're as bad as Effie."

"And you sound like Daddy."

"There's no reason I shouldn't. I married him because I liked to hear him talk. I'd be an idiot not to think some of the talk didn't rub off on me."

Along the range of yellow beach, shells were heaped in piles and long undulant sea rows. He had shuffled through them looking for something unusual, but most were broken, pieces smashed and thrown up. Sometimes, down here at night, when the wind blew, and the surf skidded up the sand, sometimes, by himself, walking a little ways and then sitting down just above the waveline, sometimes in the darkness underneath the small bright stars, he would know, for a second, that the creation of the world, the great force and tumble of the world's making, was still going on, that he was not at the end of it, that the world wasn't a museum and life its explication but that the dice were still rolling, that the ocean out there pearling over the face of the outer reef was still clapping life out of itself, that the mix still burned and fumed. He would see himself, this small encased being, and for a second he could understand his own dilemma, the dilemma of one built into a shell of flesh that the world couldn't penetrate; he could feel the nonabsorbency of his flesh, and for an instant he could think that all of it, the bustle of the wind, the sound of leaves stroking other leaves, the taste of seaweed in his mouth, was only the brief small syllable that was built for the single purpose of breaking his heart. Anybody's heart.

He cupped sand, poured it slowly over his feet. He said, "What amazes *me* is that we are built for this world. Everything's familiar. I mean we get scared and we get surprised and we feel out of place sometimes, but that's not really anything; if the world were really strange, then trees would drive us crazy, a fish would be so alien it'd make us shriek, but that's not the way it is at all. We see deer tracks in the sand or a swag of spiderweb between two bushes, and we are startled by the beauty, by the wild flights the world makes, the way it breaks its back to entertain us, but it's not unfamiliar, not really strange. Actually, it's the hardest thing imaginable to think there's something larger than this, you know, some spirit of aggregation that we owe allegiance to, that we are trying—or supposed to be trying—to be like."

With his knuckles he rubbed the underside of her calf. The muscle was slack. "It's what gets me about all your ghost stuff," he said. "You want the world to be more than it is. It's so dangerous to hope for that. It's that kind of shit that gets us murdered."

"Sometimes I think you don't know what you are talking about."

"Well, sometimes I don't."

But he could talk on nonetheless. He had talked for years, one of the talkers, born into a family of talkers. You talk and you talk and then you write it down and it becomes a poem or a story or the history of something and you hand it on to other people and they read it and talk about it and you think you are describing the world but you are not. He didn't want to hear anything more. He looked at her, hunched over her knees, the black bathing suit wrinkled over her belly, her painted nails ticking at her shins, and she was the woman who bore him, the route by which he came through into the world, but that was all. His mind lurched away, fled. In the distance the narrow coral headland forming the limit of the bay seemed a finger plunging into the sea. The waves spewed over the far rocks. Beating them, he thought, trying to break through. Trying to make them give up.

He was the one who saw her disappear again. As he came across the schoolyard carrying a small basket of oranges, he saw her— the form, someone; he knew it was Helen—plunge through the back wall of the jail and disappear into the bushes. It was evening; in the west the sky massed redly. Sea birds clattered in the air above the wide field. Across the road the priest stood on a ladder, painting the front of the church. His brush led a patch of deep red over the old pink surface. The road, dull gray asphalt peppered with gravel, snaked away past the church and the district offices, slid by the mayor's house and the houses of his relatives, and plunged into the jungle. A little farther on it reappeared, running in a straight line up the long hill to the hotel and the plateau. He was thinking as he stepped onto the pavement that it could be a road leading anywhere; it had the amiability and meandrousness of American country roads; if he wanted, he thought, he could almost put out his thumb and catch a ride to Florida, or anywhere.

He glanced at the pale-green district building, set at an angle to the road, and as he did so he saw an arm poke through the back wall. The wall bulged a little, and then he saw her body slide through, saw her fall to her knees and push up, dusting her hands. She looked around, she smoothed her pale dress, she crossed in two strides the cleared space behind the building and disappeared into the bushes. He looked to see if the priest had noticed, but Father Marco was busy with his brush. He could hear voices from down at Temelio's, and there came a clatter of pots from the widow woman's house at the edge of the schoolyard. *Menan Zues,* a voice said clearly—but there was no one about. He wanted to call out, but he didn't, afraid to rouse the village. He crossed the road and walked quickly around the side of the building. The plywood had been forced out. He pulled the sheet away from the stud and looked in. Ricky Flambo and Gondola Reyes, sitting in flimsy armchairs, stared back at him. "What's up?" he said. They grinned at him foolishly. Their faces glistened with sweat. "It's okay here," Ricky said finally. He got up slowly, as if he were exhausted, crossed the room, and, without speaking to Paul, pulled the plywood back into place.

He wasn't sure where she would go, but he drifted down through the village, looking for her. He spoke to the people he saw in passing, nodding greeting. Pedro Gum sat on his front steps, eating olives out of a can. Under a large broken-crowned mango, Dano Clip leaned into the belly of his jeep, swearing in Chamorro. The air smelled of frying pork, of the sweet tang of sugarcane wine. The trades had begun their shift into the southwest; soon the rainy season would come. He stopped by Jacabo's house, but his friend's mother told him her son was up on the plateau, farming. She invited him to supper, but he told her he had something to do first and promised to come back later. He walked down to the docks, stopping for a moment at the generating plant to watch the dynamos work. Out back, a couple of kids filled a gallon soya bottle with kerosene from a large tank. He could hear the light chirp of their speech in the twilight. Up the hill, the lights came on at the cockfight bar. The boat had come the night before from Guam, bringing a flock of card and dice players. In early morning someone walking by the bar would see them sitting on the steps or lying in the yard under blankets of parachute silk provided by Alphonzo, sleeping off their losses. In the gray dawnlight they looked like corpses. Rudy Mantalna waved to him from the roof of the generating plant. Paul waved back and looked at him expectantly, afraid to ask if he had seen Helen, hoping that if he had he would say, but Rudy only asked him if he was going to Daniet's house to watch television. The sheriff had the island's only set, which showed, on the single channel, the same movies one could see at Jacabo's theater. Not tonight, he said, and continued on down the road past the ruins of Koro's house, where the first king had killed his son. Shadows leaned against the tumbled columns, dragging the night up from the weeds.

The docks were empty. He almost turned back but then thought of the boats. Maybe she had taken one. He walked down that way. He was about to descend the short slope to the marina, when he looked out toward the island and saw her. If it wasn't Helen it was someone, some thin patch of white in a small green boat. The boat was headed south, toward the island. It climbed the swollen sea, chugging slowly up the dark flanks of the long swells and disappearing down the other side, only to reappear again, climbing the next. She was too far away to shout at, only a scrap on the sea, incidental almost, almost a figment. He thought of the first western sailors, of Magellan's crew, of what they must have thought when they saw these green dark islands rising out of the sea. No matter what would happen here, no matter what was coming in the Philippines, the green lift of landfall must have seemed for a moment, after thousands of miles of salt sea, to be a paradise.

He thought of these things as the gray tiers of Pig Island rose before them. Thought of the events of the past weeks, of his brother and his brother's wife, of the long distance they had come. Off to the south, hardly a quarter of a mile away, the flat sea-washed table of rock, smaller than a ballroom, that the air force bombed, wallowed in the ocean. Splinters of rock, chunks the size of cars, hung off its sides and stood out in the lashy waves; they might have been knocked there by bombs, but he couldn't tell; and the top of the rock—it was too small to call an island—though seamed and wrenched, showed no craters or gaps, no gouges bombs might have blasted.

They had argued all the way across about what they would do. Jacabo hadn't wanted to come, but because he was his friend and the situation was dire he couldn't see any way to avoid it. His fear, Paul thought, made him fractious. He complained about the sea, complained about the island, complained about Americans in general, the Hogan family in particular. We aren't going to stay, he said, we must do what's necessary, but we won't stay. Like everyone, he was frightened of strangers. It is too unusual, he said. They had rice, guns—a .32 caliber revolver and a .410 shotgun, the stock of which was bound to the chamber with black electrical tape—pandanus sleeping mats, and water in a jug. Jacabo wore religious medals and a necklace made of ti seeds to ward off spirits. The men come here once in their lives; it's the rule, he said. I've already come here once; it's not right for me to return.

You'll be okay, Paul told him, but he didn't really pay attention to his friend. His eyes were on the island. It rose out of the blue sea like a smashed hat, canted flattened tiers lifting greenly to a low plateau. It was maybe five miles square, twenty-five thousand acres maybe, once a Japanese sugarcane farm. There were no beaches, only the gold-gray rubble of coral cliffs humping up out of the wave lick; the rocks were wild with birds. On the south side—the bombing side—above a small natural terrace, steps had been cut into the cliff. Easing into the small cove—which was actually more alcove than cove, only a shallow indentation in the rock wall—Jacabo, standing in the stern with cloudy brow, said, This is where they should be, but where are their boats? From above them the arms of rusted derricks hung over the cliff edge, naked and spindly. Effie probably sank them, Paul said, which was a joke but which he figured was also probably the truth.

"Storm took them," Jacabo said, "that's it."

"What storm?"

"Probably something special to this place. Storm will take our boat too."

It hurt him, Paul could see, to be there. Sure, this is it, Paul thought, looking at him, this is what we do: force others to our will, breaking love up into little pieces that we use to caulk our flimsy lives.

They made it ashore, lifting the boat out of the water and leaning it against the side of the cliff, and climbed the steep path, hauling themselves up along a rusted chain that had been strung with rings hammered into the wall. They were, in that moment, in that demilitarized zone between safety and danger when the last gaiety still flickers and the battle is still only a rumor; he could feel assurance begin to leak, feel the light flutter along the surfaces of his skin, feel the trickle in his body—as if his body were a sanctuary being not overrun but abandoned—and he gripped the shotgun, becoming as he climbed afraid of it all: brother and woman; Japanese soldier; the unknown battered island; the bombs; his own slight self.

They came over the cliff side to a scattering of goats: large flocks that clattered away through the trees. There was a narrow clearing that ran along the cliff edge, piles of metal rubble, and more derricks, some fallen on their sides, a gun emplacement complete with rusted howitzer, another gun swivel, and beyond a small deserted settlement, hugging the uprise, groves of low gray-leaved trees, split with grassy meadows in which large flowering hedges swayed in breeze, tumbles of white and yellow and red flowers. Beyond the meadows more cliffs rose softly white and shaggy with trailing flower vines, with bougainvillea and passionflower. A two-track road led away through the meadows and rose through a gully toward the plateau.

"What is this?" Paul said. "This is a garden."

"Nice, huh?"

"Look at all the fruit trees. And these goats. I never saw so many goats."

"Japanese time."

There was no tangin-tangin, only the wild natural growth, only the fruit trees and the canker tree—which was the name for the small twisted trees scattered like blackjack oaks through the woods —and banyan trees as large as houses, and a few clumps of coconut and betel-nut palm, seedy groves of lime and orange trees. All human sign was in ruins. They walked among broken buildings, all of concrete or native stone, built to last; they could see where there had once been narrow streets, now weedy, their stone pavements uprooted, came to terraces grown up in pepper trees, passed cisterns and small metal warehouses bruised with rust and bitten by decay. There were garden bushes—hibiscus, cotton trees, plumiera—that had overleapt their confinements and shot forth ragged replicas of themselves, which sagged against the eaten sides of buildings; tin cans; wood-handle plows and push cultivators; tin plates with holes in the bottoms. And here and there, regularly, among the ruins, were bomb craters, blast sockets of newly scarred stone. They looked like molds, Paul thought, where small suns had been forged. Or teeth marks. It's as if we can't get enough, he thought. Thirty years later and still bombing: there's one left, don't quit yet. A sense of devilment and disgust surged in him; it raced through the silence that was everywhere, a silence in which even the wind seemed to lose heart and die. There was no sign of his kin, or of any living Japanese.

"Let's go find them," Paul said.

"I know where Ichi is," Jacabo said. "But he won't be any help."

Bait, Paul thought: Effie will be nearby. He figured that even on this small island his brother could elude him. And he knew that he didn't know what he was doing anymore. He didn't know why he was pursuing his brother, except that he couldn't think of what else to do—leave? no—except push forward. The hesitancy, the doubt, must be a human condition: it was always there, and always you kept going, or someone did. Then there was something else, something he thought he felt—remembering stories from his childhood—something that was like the hopelessness of the old pioneers, the ones his uncle sometimes talked about, and he remembered his father, his arguments about the end of things, and it seemed, as they crossed the flowery meadow and began to climb the road toward the plateau, that there must have been a vast hopelessness in the men who trekked across the plains, not promise, as the history books said, but a sense in them of the ruin they were pushing ahead of them, the emptiness in their own souls that forced them onward. He thought of them digging graves in the sagebrush, which they patted smooth and left unmarked so Indians or animals wouldn't dig them up, and it seemed then for a second, as he and Jacabo stepped through weeds, their packs riding high on their shoulders, the sky like a tight blue cap above them, the world empty around them, the pale scattering birds whirling above the trees, that it was only desolation and some huge encephalitic need, the itch of future millionaires and smelly prophets and marauders, that drove them. It must have filled them up, he thought, it must have swelled on their backs like a goiter, this knowledge that they were bringing death into the wilderness; they must have known it all along. He tried to remember all the conqueror groups, as if to number them, as if to rifle through their luggage: the Romans rowing up the darkened Thames, the Hebrews careening around the Sinai, Cortés's tough Castilians fighting their way out of Tehuantepec, the U.S. cavalry charging up the Sand River. We're here to take, his father had said, his voice bleak as bones. We are here to subdue, and I cannot accept this anymore. And then, idiot hero, he had shouldered his sorrow, as if it were the pain of the world—fool! fool!—and walked out to meet his maker in the barn.

Where were they, these bastards? The plateau, flat as a dance floor, an interior grassy sea, ringed with trees and edged by a low rim of cliffs, leaned brightly away. It was like a pasture at home, a prairie; the grass was yellow and thick; here and there small gatherings of trees rose like the masts of ships sailing across the vastness. Where were they? He thought to call out, but he didn't. The silence would be disturbed soon enough. A string of goats trotted across the middle distance. A small herd lay in the shade of a few mango trees over near the cliffs. The road had twisted up the island tiers, rising through heavy woods that were strung with vines and huge empty spiderwebs. Jacabo was grim, his full mouth compressed to a short thin line. "Supper," he said wanly, pointing at the nearest goats. A couple of the animals had rumps painted red.

"What is that?" Paul asked.

"Ichi. It's his fun."

Paul thought of a soldier in a khaki uniform and peaked campaign hat, the long rifle, the ceremonial sword. "Why does he do that?"

"He does many things like that. Look over there."

High in a grove along the eastern edge were patches of glittering metal through the branches, like tinsel in Christmas trees. "What is it?"

"Ichi's ornaments."

"Ornaments?"

"He took pieces of war debris and shit and shined them and hung them in the trees."

"He did that?"

"Yes. On the other side of the island he used dye to paint the rocks."

"A message?"

"No—a pleasure. All different colors, like a rainbow, a whole field of rocks."

"I thought the imperial Japanese were cruel fighting men."

"Not Ichi."

"Then why is everyone afraid to come here?"

"The ghosts are too strong."

"Taotaomona, eh?"

"Yes, preem."

Then, from the distance, from among the small herd under the mango trees, a goat stood up and waved at them.

"Jesus Christ."

"That's Ichi."

The figure—a small man, he saw, dressed in goatskins—waved broadly, like a man on a stage, bent nearly double—he's laughing, Paul thought—straightened up, and trotted off, followed by the goats, into the trees.

"He's friendly," Paul said.

"Yes. If you catch him, he'll want you to stay."

"If you catch him?"

"He's like a girl," Jacabo said dipping his head to laugh. "You have to chase him, but then when you catch him he wants you never to go away."

Unlike the girl—woman—we are looking for on this island, Paul thought. Where are they? There had been no sign. They hadn't left a trail, no markers. Caught so deeply in the tangle of their obsession, they didn't notice others, didn't care who came after them, whether they were found or not. We'll have to wait, he thought, until the next explosion.

They continued across the prairie. As he walked through the thick shin-high grass—patted down in places where the goats had rested, cropped to the bone in others—the illusion that had come to him as he crossed the road to the jail—that this was America, that, like America, it could go on almost forever—came to him again. Pale-green butterflies fluttered off the grass, and there was a churning of insects—not cicadas, he thought, or crickets, but some droning bug like them—and the smell of the sun-tarnished grass was, if not the smell of his own country hay, its cousin, familiar enough. What is it, he thought, that we drag around with us, that in strange places makes us mournful and disaffected? He was only nineteen, but there was already so much in his life that it was too late to blame it, his life—it was too late, too much had happened, there was no way to sort it down to a slick article he could hold up, saying Here, this is it, it was this splinter that caused the debacle. He had known since he was ten that you could bet your life on a proposition that—*Sacré bleu,* as his uncle would say—might not carry you all the way. This place was a garden now—a flock of fork-tailed black birds lifting over the mango trees, orchids hanging from the white cliffs, sweet acid scent of fallen limes—but it had once been a farm, once a place of orderly rows and equipment and harvest time and the conversion of the natural world into sustenance. Then, as empire heaved against empire, it had been flung back, cut loose, tossed into the vat for remixing, left to itself. The goats multiplied and the flowers went wild and the ghosts stirred like an overture among the trees. It was only change, he thought, only the clank and rumble of the world refashioning itself, as it did every day, everywhere, forever. But now his brother, and his brother's wife, moved across this landscape. As he bent to pluck a stem of grass—just to taste it— he saw them, in his mind, as small whirling centers of passion and intellect, small denser gouts of matter streaking the world with their passage. What could you do but push on to the edge of the world and then keep going? You either fell or you flew. His father's suicide was not a feat but only the next thing, the end of a life's walk. It was a natural conclusion. For one second, with a brilliance like sunlight slapping water, he saw himself, this boy —almost man—walking across a tropic prairie: you are afraid to make any choice, he thought, that's why you are here; you are afraid to choose any way, or to believe that you are being led, to even look, because you are afraid that if you are in fact on a road —by choice or fate; whatever—it can only lead to the same place that your father was led to, to the dark reeking corner where he died.

It was as if someone had struck him. He saw himself as an old man living in a furnished room in a small city, boiling an egg, speaking poems to a sullen cat, sitting by the window watching children on the corner as they made up their lives. He could feel the creak in his bones, the small deliquescence of organs, the flicker of memory drifting like hay chaff through his mind. He would lie on the narrow bed in the dark, listening to the rattling cries of the city, obedient, surrendered, without hope or resolution. In the end was not peace, only exhaustion.

He stumbled; Jacabo caught him by the arm. "Oh," he said, his voice very small.

"You look spooked," his friend said.

"I am spooked."

"This island is too much for human beings. We better go. Let your brother come back when he wants to."

"No," he said. "I can't."

Jacabo laughed. "You need to be like me," he said. "Say yes, then do what you want."

They reached the other side of the prairie, where the cliffs—not even cliffs really: wooded humps—rose shallowly, wooded in guinea bushes and pines, and climbed to the low ridge. Beyond them, and on either side, a wide terrace stretched away to the lifted sea edge. On this side the heights were not steep; they made their way straight down the face, moving in and out among the trees where birds sang shrill and clattery songs and the sun splashed in the leaves. Lizards, colored like party favors, scurried in the undergrowth.

They came to a small clearing in which a large banyan tree spread its heavy propped limbs over bare ground. In the dark massed foliage, too thick to see through, shadows throve. Jacabo would not approach the tree. "It's their home," he said. "We have no business here." From his pack he took a handful of rice and poured it ceremonially on the ground. From his shirt he plucked a button and placed it on top of the heaped grains. His movements were solemn and filled with an authority Paul had not seen before. He didn't ask him why he did this. Jacabo knelt, leaned down until his forehead touched the ground, and spoke a few thick words that were different from any Chamorro Paul had heard. Then he straightened and crossed himself. He can still go all the way back, Paul thought; the road is still open.

Under the shadow of the tree no grass grew; there was a stillness beneath it, a stagnation. The air was dank, like the air of a long-unopened greenhouse.

"This way," Jacabo said, taking his arm, pushing him off through the trees. The Chamorro followed, walking slowly backward, half bowed to the tree. Thinking of the dark figure the tree made, of the investment and surrender of his friend's actions, absently pushing branches aside as he walked, he didn't see the bomb. Like a joke, like someone knelt in his path, it tripped him, and he fell sprawling. "Jacabo," he cried. His friend raised his hand, turned. Between them was the long torpedo shape. It was gray, the color of battleships, fat-nosed, a ring of yellow and black around the squared tail flukes. Jacabo reached out his hand to it. "Don't touch it," Paul whispered. He got carefully to his feet, his breath coming short in his chest. Maybe a vibration would set it off. It had fallen, splintering pines, and come to rest in a bed of wet leaves. There was no crater, no scar in the earth; it was as if —but for the broken branches—as if someone had angrily carried it there and left it.

They moved quietly around it, afraid. Near the nose in small black letters was printed U.S. AIR FORCE 10000 POUND ORDNANCE. There were small blocks of other numbers like serial numbers. Slanted up the flank in red paint, rubbed out by the weather, was a handwritten word he couldn't read. Around the scene was only the woods: twisted pines, canker trees, the rustling top of a coconut palm, fragrance of plumeria. "This is the other side of the island," he said, meaning: how did this get here? "Yes," Jacabo answered. Paul stretched out his hand and touched the hard body. The metal was cold, without charm. He drew his hand back. "Let's get out of here," he said. "Okay, preem." His mind hissed; he wanted to black out the world, blanken it, make it mute. His death was a thin mouth opening. A picture flashed in his mind of his brother hugging the neck of a donkey their father had bought them in Texas. Of his brother's naked body whitely falling. Of light, and of shapes moving in the light. Of a heart peeling like an onion. "Ah, God," he cried, and began to run. Senseless, he crashed through the woods. Branches whipped his face. He stumbled, caught himself, ran on. He broke free of the woods, onto the rocky open ground before the sea cliffs. He fell. A large lizard, bronze and green, spurted away from his hand. He rolled onto his back. Above his head the blue canopy bucked and whipped like a tent collapsing in wind.

Later they continued the search, but they found nothing.

"It's curious," Jacabo said. "There's no sign at all."

On the northern side they came on a grove of cedars a quarter mile across, growing to the edge of the cliff. They followed what seemed paths, but then he wasn't sure if they were paths; goat tracks maybe. Bleating could be heard everywhere. The trees were so dense that he almost stepped out of them into space. The Pacific, blue as lapis, rolled away, its surface chipped by wind. Off northward the green shelves of the big island smoked under sunset clouds. There was a patch of blood on the water under the cliffs. Goat, Jacabo said. They fall in and the sharks eat them. Gulls and terns dived at the water. Black, yellow-speckled lizards rattled in the rocks. Maybe we ought to camp, Paul said. That was fine with Jacabo. This side is best, he said. Away from the bombs. Do you think they'll come tonight? Jacabo had sent a message to the air force in Guam, which was regular procedure, requesting permission to visit the island. There had been no answer, but Paul, anxious, the reel drawing him, had wanted to go anyway. Now he said yes when Jacabo wanted to find shelter on this side of the island. They unrolled their sleeping mats in a tuck of rock between the cedars and the cliffs. A slab of broken coral would keep out bombs, at least rain. Dinner was melon with papaya. In the twilight—already starry, dark—winged shapes rustled in the trees, slipped into air wheeling silently: fruit bats, the great delicacy, boiled in a pot and eaten whole, skin, meat, guts, everything but bone. Jacabo wanted to shoot one, but Paul said no—no noise tonight. The dark came swiftly, unrolling like an awning from the east. The moon was brilliant, cold, cut in half. They talked awhile, fed the fire, lay on their backs listening to the trades whispering through the cedars, said good night.

A little later—from a dream that he thought was himself awake —his brother touched his face.

"Let's go," he said. "Come on, brother man."

It wasn't a dream—a rocky landscape, large dark shapes like cattle moving across a murky plain—but he had been asleep. His brother's hand was over his mouth. In the moon darkness he could see the white skin, the dark, trespassing eyes. "Come on," his brother said. "Hoist yourself."

It was what he had been waiting for. He got up and followed him, without waking Jacabo, into the darkness.

They climbed through the cliffs onto the plateau, winding up a trail that his brother seemed familiar with. Effie moved quickly, running low. Paul almost lost him several times, but each time he would find him waiting ahead, looking back. "Hurry," he whispered. "We don't want to be out here too long."

"Where are we—?" Paul started to say, but Effie shushed him. "Follow," he said. "Just follow."

They reached the prairie and skirted it, running along under the trees. In the moonlight he could see the breeze touch the grass, bending it, pressing it flat in places and letting it go. In the air above the prairie the bats, their bodies as large as cats, whirled silently. Paul said, "Where's Helen?"

Effie sighed. An alien discrete sound in the entangled darkness. "She's all over this place," he whispered. "There's nowhere she's not." He gave a low chuckle, the sound sinking back into his throat. "I'm trapped," he said. "She's going to kill me."

"Why don't you take the boat and go?"

"She sank the boat. Hers too. This is the end." He chuckled again, his voice wet and drifting. "Pretty dramatic, huh?"

Paul didn't say anything.

Effie ducked away, veering off through trees. Paul stopped. His brother had disappeared. He moved forward slowly, into dense blackness, feeling with his hand. "Where are you?"

"Right here. By the bush."

"What bush?"

Effie touched his hand. "Here."

He squatted next to a slick bush that Paul as he groped found was full of small round berries. "Where are we?"

"In the vestibule of Kyoro's place."

"Kyoro?"

"That's his name."

"You're buddies?"

"Colleagues."

Around them, as if conjured from rock, shapes stirred. Frightened, imagining ghosts, Helen wild with a gun, Paul

lurched backward. "Don't worry," Effie said. "It's just the goats."
The animals rose from grassy beds; there was a small one bleating;
he felt their bodies brush against his legs. "It's just the does and
the kids," Effie said. "Actually they're glad to see you."

A small dry muzzle poked Paul's hand. He stroked a dark nappy
head. "Hello, little goat," he whispered.

"This way."

A dark shape, rock or roof, blacker than the darkness, projected
toward them. It was, Paul saw as they reached it, a canopy, made
of skins and wood, something like an umbrella, that hung over a
small stone-floored passageway. Inside it, at the cliff wall, a rift
opened, angling narrowly away through the rock. Barely wider
than his shoulders, it switched back at least twice—his fingers
stubbed on rock—and opened onto a small meadow, meadow and
garden, moon-soaked and fragrant with honeysuckle. At the back
of the meadow, near the lift of the cliffs, was a small house, a hut
really, made of wood with a roof of coconut thatch. Before the
house, on a straw mat, a small man sat tending a fire.

Effie approached him. The man rose, creaking up angularly, as
if he were maimed, or old. They spoke Japanese and bowed, slowly
and formally. Wind chimes, fashioned from bits of metal and
glass, from scraps of shell and bone, tinkled in the lime trees
beside the house. The small man grinned at Effie and looked
toward Paul. Effie motioned him close. He murmured to the man.
The man grinned and bowed elastically. Paul bowed back.

"This is Kyoro," Effie said, "a gentleman of the old school."

"How do you do?" Paul said.

The old man's face was small and ruddy. He had a long thin
mouth, dimpled cheeks, and his faded hair was swept up in a loose
coil on the top of his head. His hand, which, after he bowed,
tentatively, knuckles up, groped lightly in the air between them,
was kinked with arthritis. He listed slightly to one side. In the
firelight Paul saw that the area around the house was filled with
objects: bits of weaving, carved wood, shells strung in long chains
that were coiled like snakes. The air was filled with the random
clattering and tinkle of the chimes.

"Mr. Kyoro is a soldier?"

Effie laughed. "Well, he was. That was over a long time ago."

He spoke a few words in Japanese to the old man. They both laughed. The old man's laugh was high-pitched but soft; a little like the cry of a woodcock, Paul thought.

There was tea, served in wooden bowls, and conversation by the fire, which Effie translated, clumsily carpentering together whole sentences out of the old man's Hokkaido dialect. A farmer, from the western provinces, the old man had entered the army, so he said, a foolish and naive young man, compliant but so awkward and slow to learn the intricate ceremonies of army discipline that he had become a burden to his superiors and to his comrades. He knew nothing of the world. Each place, each experience, had the magic of a peddler's wares, baffled and amazed him. Each carried the shock—so Effie said he said—of stepping from the fragrant steam of a bath into snow: the sudden constriction of blood, his mind whirling, speed. He could show, if they liked, the scars on his back the world had given him. The past was a mystery, the future impossible. He lived here, in a well of time.

Then there was a series of ceremonial maneuvers, dance steps they looked like, that Effie and the old man performed, much later, after the moon had drifted behind the cliffs, and there were a few ritual shouts—which Effie shushed—a few grunts and clacks, and a long chanted song, or sung chant, of many verses, each of which was punctuated by formal stamps of both feet, that Effie and Kyoro sang in unison, their bodies rocking, flame-lit and flickering, their faces lifted like the faces of dogs to the sky, tears shining along the rims of their closed eyes.

Paul lay on his back on a mat of woven grass. Framed by the cliffs and the trees, the sky was a picture of sky above him. Long streaks of cloud rushed through the stars westward. They seemed to erase and redraw the firmament, leaving uncollected fragments here and there, releasing the full body of a constellation, of hunter and bull, the weeping sisters. As he listened to the gutturals, the coarse imperatives of the chant, felt in his body the vibrations as their feet pounded the grassy ground, he began to see, as if dark gentlemen were stepping forward, the deep spaces between the stars. Now the clouds cleared a patch and the stars kindled again, and the emptiness between them took on shape and mass, like the openings of tunnels that as darkness comes on seem to reach forth into the world. What is it to die? he thought. It's nothing. But he couldn't erase his grief. It swelled and boomed, it made him dizzy. He placed his hands flat on the grass and pressed. He wanted to sink his body in the earth. He saw the indifference of the world, he could taste it, like a sourness in the grass, and he knew that it wasn't there to prove anything to him, not to lift him up, not for instruction, not for solace, not a gift, not a claim, not a performance, not a proof, not a vessel, not . . . not . . .

Now and then his brother would break free of the dance and kneel beside him, his face glistening with sweat, and speak to him. I'm speaking poems to him, he would say. I told him the words of two Bashō haiku that he had been trying to remember for thirty years. He doesn't like our poems; he thinks they are too ornate and afraid of the world. He thinks we have dressed the world up in funeral clothes—typical farmer—rouged and painted it and let it go. It's amazing. . . . And then he would spring to his feet and whirl back, not briskly but with a ceremonious slow motion, as if the blood in him had begun to slow down, careen into the dance, into the arch and bend of the old man's body, a body that seemed to Paul at first to be searching: peering, hands cupped around the bony face, to see into the darkness, or *seeing* into darkness—but this was only at first; it seemed, later—though he didn't reckon the night's passing—that the dance was an act of acceptance, of surrender, an accomplishment of integration, as one moves through water, for a moment becoming water or of the water; and it seemed to him, for a time, that the trees, the dark globes, swayed in the incantation of purpose, harmonious and perfected, without wit or reason, which was completely unnecessary, and the clouds streaking the star-baited sky—moonless now—and the wind itself, seemed to drift like a ruined relative among the shadows, accompanying, as reflection or mimicry, the slow bob and weave of the dance. But this was only a figment, and in fact only collateral, and a forgery, because through none of it, through none of the winged and stately movements, did he forget the approach of what his brother had fashioned for himself, this gun in the hand of the woman he had married, these planes flying so high that they made no sound anyone on earth could hear until the earth exploded.

Now his brother was beside him again, kneeling; he could feel
the heat radiating from his body. His hand touched Paul's wrist
and the hand was hard and hot and it touched him, caressing his
wrist, drawing him, as if he had drifted away, back into the circle
of dancing. It's purely, he said, his voice hoarse—all location,
place, gone out of it—it's nakedly incantation. Now he says he
doesn't even remember being a soldier, though he won't believe
me when I tell him the war is over—What of the bombs? he says.
He doesn't remember Nippon—except when he dances. He
doesn't remember America, doesn't know who is trying to destroy
him. He thinks the bombs, this island, the trade winds, the bats,
even the Chamorros who show up here, are all conjury; he thinks
his dance and the prayers—the songs, that's what it is—sustain
them; he thinks what he does, his living here, is necessary, that
it's one of the piers holding up the world. . . .

"But what about the planes—aren't they coming tonight?"

"You guys should have sent a message—stopped 'em. You're
the ones living in the real world; that's your job."

"We did, but I don't know if it worked."

Effie grinned. His face was hollow, the teeth like white paint.
"Don't worry. There's a back door to the house that leads into a
cave. If it gets bad you can go in there."

"If it gets bad? How are you going to know before it kills you
if it's gotten bad?"

"Hell, sport, you could ask me that about my whole life. How
would I know?"

He plunged away, springing on his long thin legs back into the
dance.

What you do, Paul thought, is you take your life and you make
it race. You just drive it as hard as it will go. What you see in the
blur of passage is what is. The world was a wind, a mad dance, all
that crap. He said, out loud, My name is Paul Hogan. I was born
on a farm near St. Lukes, Florida, U.S. of A. I am nineteen years
old. It is October 2, 1974. I am on Isla Babwi, Northern Mariana
Islands, United Nations Trust Territory of the Pacific. My
brother, who is about to die, is dancing with a Japanese soldier. I
am neither savior nor abettor. I am a witness. I am a witness. . . .

He saw her, saw the white shift, saw her slip from between the rocks on the far side of the meadow. She ran a few steps, crouching low, and knelt in the grass. He could see the white mask of her face, but not her features. Her hectic hair was dark. He sat up. The men thudded on in their dance. They stooped low, shoulders angling downward, like gross birds slipping toward the rocks. He raised his hand. As he did so there was a huge flash of light: not red as he had expected, but yellow, almost white. There was a sharp crack, as if the air had turned solid and snapped, then no sound at all, and he was lifted and tossed against the side of the hut.

He waked to silence and to empires of light. Flashes, great bolts and structures of light, roved across the sky. They were yellow and red, purple-tinged green. He pressed his fingers to his ears; he couldn't hear anything. The meadow was empty, the fire scattered. There was a smell of ammonia in the air, and a smell like the smell of gasoline. He got to his feet and groped around the cleared yard. His whole body ached. The wind chimes were scattered on the ground. There was a blockage, a cry in him that stuck. Everyone was gone. He remembered the cave, stumbled into the hut. It was too dark; he felt his way along the rough board walls. Pots, metal shapes, pieces of carved wood, which felt to his fingers as if they were covered with blood, fell as he touched them. He called his brother's name. A small hand brushed his leg, groping from behind a straw screen leaned against the back wall. It was Kyoro. Paul knelt down. The little man held the screen aside. "Where's Effie?" Paul asked. It was like speaking underwater. The old man shook his head. They made signs to each other. Paul peered past his head into the cave. It was black in there. "Where is my brother?" he cried. The man made a wave motion away from his body. "What?" Light surged through the hut and died, surged again; the ground shivered. It can't penetrate me, he thought, unless it breaks me. The shock wave pressed against his back. He could feel it thrust and grope at his body. It's like a giant rapist, he thought. He pushed himself up. The man had retreated into the cave, but he came back. His head, an arm, poked past the screen. He pointed outside, waved him away. Paul understood. He turned to go, but then he looked back at the little man. In the illumination, which was vivid and undiluted,

like some outrageous false dawn in a dream, and seemed both to
clarify and to transform the interior of the small hut, he saw—
before it vanished—the man's face, this Kyoro the abandoned
soldier. It was the hopelessly defeated, self-pitying face of a beggar
man. The face of a man who might speak his misery to trees. A
face of such empty, tedious sadness—of sadness beyond regret—a
face left with nothing but the mission to hold back the light, that
he recognized it. It was the most familiar face of all; he had known
it all his life. He stretched his hand out to touch it, crying the
name, but it was gone.

The cell rang with light, with the stabbing darkness. He got
to his feet and stumbled out of the hut. The bombs fell, at a
distance now, spurting light. The emptiness of the meadow, the
scattering of objects, the broken fire, danced in his eyes. He
wanted to loot, steal, carry things off to a dark hidden place. He
wanted to praise the world. He crossed the meadow, scrabbled
through the switchback rift, felt his way through the scattered
bleating goats—a kid, pinto, plunged at the black rock face—he
careened through the stubby trees, and fell out, still on his feet,
into the prairie. It was empty. He turned only once, thinking of
Jacabo, said a slight prayer for him; he knew where he was going,
knew what was going to happen: he headed across the grassy plain,
toward the western rim, toward the ruins and the confused derricks and the blast rock. The rolls of light, the carnival smoke, lit
his way.

He could only run. Not walk, because if he walked he might
think, he might turn back. Free of the cliffs, of the sheltering
woods, sprinting through the small ruined town where broken
doorways propped up sheets of darkness, where the broken implements and heaps of rusted cans, the slabs of broken roof and wall
associated with shadows, where above his head, and above the
island, the explosions roved like giant red and yellow wings,
beating at the night, sinking back in a rush to reveal the same old
derelict stars, the same sprawled space, he peered ahead, into the
smash of light, where he could see them, scrambling one ahead of
the other, along the sea cliff edge toward the target rock. He
raised his hands, crying, "It's all right, it's all right," but they
didn't hear, they didn't turn back; he couldn't hear himself. His

brother ran crouching, Helen twenty yards behind him, leaping
like a goat over boulders and coral heads that in the pulsing light
seemed just risen from the sea, black, suddenly bronze and sickly
green, wet, slimy, drenched with remnants of sea life, so disor-
derly that they could be emblems of the world before creation,
random. He was close now, running hard. His brother reached
the slightly risen rim, stopped, and turned. Helen stood upright
and walked toward him.

"Wait," Paul cried. "Wait." He could see his brother's face,
the long high-browed face, white, he could see him, see the slender body, erect, shoulders back, a negligence in the tilt of his
hips, the arrogant, lazy hands turning slowly, rising.

She walked toward him, the gun uplifted, stately and mad.
Effie's mouth moved; he grinned. She stopped. The gun didn't
waver while they looked at each other. His brother made a single
small gesture, dismissive, or a slight surrender maybe, turned,
and leapt from the cliff. Paul cried out then; the scream vibrated
in the bones of his head. He ran to the cliff edge and grabbed
Helen in his arms. The gun clattered down the rock face. There
was no sign of Effie, then he saw him swimming strongly toward
the target rock. Paul leaned out. She touched his shoulder. He
glanced at her, "Don't," her mouth said softly. "Don't." He
wasn't going to jump. He watched his brother swim, saw the dark
head rise and fall in the gray swells. An explosion off beyond the
rock blistered the water, raking small waves across the surface.
Paul pulled her down. They lay on their stomachs, watching him.
Effie disappeared, he was gone, then he was there again, approach-
ing the rock. The black table rose above him. He hoisted himself
up, scrambled up the side, and walked out to the center of the
rock. For a moment they were between blasts. The sky was filled
with stars. The dark shape of his brother stood on the rock,
looking out to sea. His hands were in his pockets; he looked like
a man waiting for a bus, or a lover. There was a white explosion
that blew fire into their faces. When they opened their eyes the
rock was empty.

VII

FROM A small balcony five flights up he watched the rainy night take over the city. In the street below, workmen repaired a broken water main. They passed, in yellow slickers, in and out of the light. He could smell the river. In the distance he could see the red and yellow fog lights along the embankment. In a moment he would go down in the elevator for dinner. The night was cold. He thought of the old Romans wallowing up the ancient river in their clumsy boats. The marsh this once was, the swamp, the bosky plain. A wilderness where men painted themselves purple and climbed into the trees to await civilization. *I have never understood anyone's dream.*

ABOUT THE AUTHOR

CHARLIE SMITH was born in Moultrie, Georgia, in
1947. He attended schools and colleges in Georgia, New
Hampshire, North Carolina, and Iowa. From 1968 to 1970
he worked as a schoolteacher and government adviser in the
Mariana Islands. He has made his living as a newspaper writer
and editor, a businessman, a farmer, a laborer, and, for two
years, as part-time assistant to the painter Myron Stout. Over
the past twenty years he has traveled or lived in Micronesia,
Great Britain, Greece, Italy, Turkey, Mexico, the Caribbean,
Venezuela, Cape Cod, Arizona, North Carolina, and Georgia.
He currently lives in New York City. His books of fiction
include the novels *Canaan, Shine Hawk,* and *The Lives of the
Dead.* He has published two books of poems, *Red Roads,* selected for the National Poetry Series in 1987, and *Indistin-*
guishable from the Darkness. In 1984, he received the Aga Khan
Prize from *The Paris Review* for his novella "Crystal River."